ONE
OF US
IS NEXT

BOOKS BY KAREN M. McMANUS

One of Us Is Lying

Two Can Keep a Secret

One of Us Is Next

ONE
OF US
IS NEXT

KAREN M. McMANUS

DELACORTE
PRESS

For Mom and Dad

Text copyright © 2020 by Karen M. McManus, LLC
Jacket photograph (second girl) © 2020 by Nabi Tang/Stocksy; all other photographs used under license from Shutterstock.com

Visit us on the Web! GetUnderlined.com

Educators and librarians, for a variety of teaching tools, visit us at RHTeachersLibrarians.com

Library of Congress Cataloging-in-Publication Data
Names: McManus, Karen M., author.
Title: One of us is next / Karen M. McManus.
Description: First edition. | New York : Delacorte Press, [2020] | Summary: "A year after the Bayview four were cleared of Simon Kelleher's death, a new mystery has cropped up—a game with dangerous consequences that's targeting students at Bayview again. And if the creator isn't found soon, dangerous could prove deadly"— Provided by publisher.
Identifiers: LCCN 2019004154 | ISBN 978-0-525-70796-7 (hc) | ISBN 978-0-525-70797-4 (glb) | ISBN 978-0-525-70798-1 (ebook) | ISBN 978-0-593-17547-7 (intl. tr. pbk.)
Subjects: | CYAC: Mystery and detective stories. | Gossip—Fiction. | High schools—Fiction. | Schools—Fiction.
Classification: LCC PZ7.1.M4637 Or 2020 | DDC [Fic]—dc23

The text of this book is set in 11.75-point Adobe Garamond.
Interior design by Ken Crossland

Printed in the United States of America
10 9 8 7 6 5 4 3 2 1
First Edition

+   Edit

Favorites

(MR) Maeve Rojas
Bayview High junior, Bronwyn's sister   ⓘ

(KM) Knox Myers
Bayview High junior, Until Proven   ⓘ

(PL) Phoebe Lawton
Bayview High junior, Café Contigo   ⓘ

(BR) Bronwyn Rojas
One of the original Bayview Four, Maeve's sister   ⓘ

(NM) Nate Macauley
One of the original Bayview Four   ⓘ

(AP) Addy Prentiss
One of the original Bayview Four, Café Contigo   ⓘ

(CC) Cooper Clay
One of the original Bayview Four   ⓘ

(LS) Luis Santos
Cooper's best friend, Café Contigo   ⓘ

(EL) Emma Lawton
Bayview High senior, Phoebe's sister   ⓘ

(OL) Owen Lawton
Phoebe's brother   ⓘ

(AP) Ashton Prentiss
Addy's sister   ⓘ

(KM) Kiersten Myers
Knox's sister   ⓘ

(EK) Eli Kleinfelter
Lawyer, Until Proven   ⓘ

(JC) Jules Crandall
Bayview High junior, Phoebe's best friend   ⓘ

(BW) Brandon Weber
Bayview High junior, quarterback   ⓘ

(SM) Sean Murdock
Bayview High junior, baseball player   ⓘ

PART ONE

REPORTER (standing at the edge of a winding street with a large white stucco building behind her): Good morning. This is Liz Rosen with Channel Seven News, reporting live from Bayview High, where students are reeling from the loss of one of their classmates yesterday. It's the second tragic teenage death in the past eighteen months for this small town, and the mood outside the school is one of shocked déjà vu.

(Cut to two girls, one wiping tears, the other stone-faced.)

CRYING GIRL: It's just . . . it's just really sad. Like, sometimes it feels as though Bayview is cursed, you know? First Simon, and now this.

STOIC GIRL: This isn't anything like what happened with Simon.

REPORTER (angling her microphone toward the crying girl): Were you and the deceased student close?

CRYING GIRL: Not like, *close* close. Or at all close. I mean, I'm just a freshman.

REPORTER (turning toward the other girl): And how about you?

STOIC GIRL: I don't think we're supposed to be talking to you.

Ten Weeks Earlier

**Reddit, Vengeance Is Mine subforum
Thread started by Bayview2020**

Hey.
Is this the same group Simon Kelleher used to
post with?—Bayview2020

Greetings.
One and the same.—Darkestmind

Why'd you move? And why are there hardly
any posts?—Bayview2020

Too many gawkers and reporters on the
old site.

5

And we have new security measures. Lesson
learned from our friend Simon.
Who I'm guessing you know, based on your
user name?—Darkestmind

Everyone knows Simon. Well. Knew him.
It's not like we were friends, though.
—Bayview2020

Okay. So what brings you here?—Darkestmind

I don't know. Just stumbled across it.
—Bayview2020

Bullshit. This is a forum dedicated to revenge,
and it's not easy to find.
You're here for a reason.
What is it? Or should I say who?—Darkestmind

Who.
Somebody did something horrible.
It wrecked my life and so many others.
Meanwhile NOTHING happened to them.
And I can't do anything about it.—Bayview2020

Same, same.
We have a lot in common.
It sucks when the person who ruined your life
gets to walk around like always.

As if what they did doesn't matter.
I beg to disagree with your conclusion,
though.
There's always something you can do.
—Darkestmind

CHAPTER ONE

Maeve
Monday, February 17

My sister thinks I'm a slacker. She's not coming right out and saying it—or texting it, technically—but it's heavily implied:

Did you check out that list of colleges I sent?

Winter of your junior year isn't too early to start looking. It's actually kind of late.

We could visit some places when I'm home for Ashton's bachelorette party if you want.

You should apply somewhere totally out of your comfort zone, too. What about the University of Hawaii?

I look up from the texts flashing across my phone to meet Knox Myers's questioning gaze. "Bronwyn thinks I should go to college at the University of Hawaii," I report, and he almost chokes on his mouthful of empanada.

"She does realize that's on an island, right?" he asks, reaching for a glass of ice water and draining half of it in one gulp. The empanadas at Café Contigo are legendary in Bayview but they're a lot to take if you're not used to spicy food. Knox, who moved here from Kansas in middle school and still counts mushroom-soup-based casseroles among his favorite meals, most definitely is not. "Has she already forgotten that you're vehemently anti-beach?"

"I'm not anti-beach," I protest. "I'm just not a proponent of sand. Or too much sun. Or undertow. Or sea creatures." Knox's eyebrows climb higher with every sentence. "Look, you're the one who made me watch *Monsters of the Deep,*" I remind him. "My ocean phobia is mostly your fault." Knox was my first-ever boyfriend last summer, both of us too inexperienced to realize we weren't actually attracted to one another. We spent most of our relationship watching the Science Channel, which should have clued us in quicker that we were better off as friends.

"You've convinced me," Knox says drily. "This is the school for you. I look forward to reading what will undoubtedly be a heartfelt application essay when it's due." He leans forward and raises his voice for emphasis. "Next year."

I sigh, drumming my fingers on the brightly tiled table. Café Contigo is an Argentinean café with deep blue walls and a tin ceiling, the air a fragrant mix of sweet and savory scents. It's less than a mile from my house and became my favorite place to do homework once Bronwyn left for Yale and my room was suddenly much too quiet. I like the friendly bustle of the café and the fact that nobody minds if I spend three hours here and only order coffee. "Bronwyn thinks I'm behind schedule," I tell Knox.

"Yeah, well, Bronwyn practically had her Yale application ready in preschool, didn't she?" he says. "We have plenty of time." Knox is like me—a seventeen-year-old junior at Bayview High, older than most of our classmates. In his case, it's because he was small for his age in kindergarten and his parents held him back. In mine, it's because I was in and out of hospitals with leukemia for half my childhood.

"I guess." I reach over to grab Knox's empty plate and stack it on top of mine but knock over the saltshaker instead, sending white crystals scattering across the table. Almost without thinking, I take a pinch between two fingers and throw it over my shoulder. Warding off bad luck, like Ita taught me. My grandmother has dozens of superstitions: some Colombian, and some she's picked up after living in the United States for thirty years. I used to follow them all when I was little, especially when I was sick. *If I wear the beaded bracelet Ita gave me, this test won't hurt. If I avoid all the cracks in the floor, my white cell count will be normal. If I eat twelve grapes at midnight on New Year's Eve, I won't die this year.*

"Anyway, it's not the end of the world if you don't go to college right away," Knox says. He slouches in his chair, pushing a shock of brown hair off his forehead. Knox is so lean and angular that even after stuffing himself with all of his empanadas and half of mine, he still looks hungry. Every time he's at our house, one or both of my parents try to feed him. "Lots of people don't." His glance flicks around the restaurant before landing on Addy Prentiss pushing through the kitchen doors with a tray balanced in one hand.

I watch Addy wind her way through Café Contigo, dropping

off plates of food with practiced ease. Over Thanksgiving, when the true crime show *Mikhail Powers Investigates* aired its special report "The Bayview Four: Where Are They Now," Addy agreed to be interviewed for the first time ever. Probably because she could tell that the producers were gearing up to present her as the slacker of the group—my sister made it to Yale, Cooper had a splashy scholarship to Cal State Fullerton, even Nate was taking a few community college classes—and she wasn't having it. No "Bayview's Former Beauty Queen Peaks in High School" headline for Adelaide Prentiss.

"If you know what you want to do when you graduate, great," she'd said, perched on a stool in Café Contigo with the day's specials written in brightly colored chalk on the blackboard behind her. "If you don't, why pay a fortune for a degree you might never use? There's nothing wrong with not having your entire life mapped out when you're eighteen."

Or seventeen. I eye my phone warily, waiting for another barrage of Bronwyn texts. I love my sister, but her perfectionism is a hard act to follow.

The evening crowd is starting to arrive, filling the last of the tables as someone turns all the wall-mounted big-screen televisions to Cal State Fullerton's baseball season opener. Addy pauses when her tray is almost empty and scans the room, smiling when she catches my eye. She makes her way to our corner table and places a small plate of alfajores between Knox and me. The dulce de leche sandwich cookies are a Café Contigo specialty, and they're the only thing Addy has learned to make during her nine months working here.

Knox and I both reach for them at the same time. "You

guys want anything else?" Addy asks, tucking a lock of silvery pink hair behind her ear. She's tried a few different colors over the past year, but nothing that isn't pink or purple lasts for very long. "You should get your order in now if you do. Everyone's taking a break once Cooper starts pitching in"—she glances at the clock on the wall—"five minutes or so."

I shake my head as Knox stands, brushing crumbs from the front of his favorite gray sweatshirt. "I'm good, but I have to hit the restroom," he says. "Can you save my seat, Maeve?"

"You got it," I say, sliding my bag onto his chair.

Addy half turns, then almost drops her tray. "Oh my God! There he is!"

Every screen in the restaurant fills with the same image: Cooper Clay walking to the mound to warm up for his first college baseball game. I just saw Cooper over Christmas, not even two months ago, but he looks bigger than I remember. As square-jawed and handsome as ever, but with a steely glint in his eyes that I've never seen before. Then again, until right this second, I've always watched Cooper pitch from a distance.

I can't hear the announcers over the chatter in the café, but I can guess what they're saying: Cooper's debut is the talk of college baseball right now, big enough that a local cable sports show is covering the whole game. Part of the buzz is due to lingering Bayview Four notoriety, and the fact that he's one of the few openly gay players in baseball, but it's also because he's been tearing up spring training. Sports analysts are taking bets on whether he'll jump to the majors before he's finished a single college season.

"Our superstar is finally going to meet his destiny," Addy

says fondly as Cooper adjusts his cap on screen. "I need to do one last check on my tables, then I'll join you guys." She starts moving through the restaurant with her tray tucked under her arm and her order pad in hand, but the attention of the room has already shifted from food to baseball.

My eyes linger on the television, even though the scene has switched from Cooper to an interview with the other team's coach. *If Cooper wins, this year will turn out fine.* I try to push the thought out of my head as soon as it pops in, because I won't be able to enjoy the game if I turn it into yet another bet against fate.

A chair scrapes noisily beside me, and a familiar black leather jacket brushes against my arm. "What's up, Maeve?" Nate Macauley asks, settling into his chair. His eyes rove across the sodium-spattered tabletop. "Uh-oh. Salt massacre. We're doomed, aren't we?"

"Ha and ha," I say, but my lips twitch. Nate's become like a brother to me since he and Bronwyn started dating almost a year ago, so I suppose teasing comes with the territory. Even now, when they're "on a break" for the third time since Bronwyn left for college. After spending last summer angsting over whether a three-thousand-mile long-distance relationship could work, my sister and her boyfriend have settled into a pattern of being inseparable, arguing, breaking up, and getting back together that, oddly, seems to work for both of them.

Nate just grins, and we lapse into a comfortable silence. It's easy hanging out with him, and Addy, and the rest of Bronwyn's friends. *Our friends,* she always says, but it's not really true. They were hers first, and they wouldn't be mine without her.

My phone buzzes as if on cue, and I look down to another text from Bronwyn. *Has the game started?*

Soon, I type. *Cooper's warming up.*

I wish it were on ESPN so I could watch!!! Pacific Coast Sports Network does not, sadly, air in New Haven, Connecticut. Or anyplace outside a three-hour radius of San Diego. And they don't live-stream online, either.

I'm recording it for you, I remind her.

I know, but it's not the same.

Sorry :(

I swallow the last of my cookie, watching the gray dots linger on my phone screen for so long that I'm positive I know what's coming next. Bronwyn is a lightning-fast texter. She never hesitates unless she's about to say something she thinks she shouldn't, and there's currently only one topic on her self-imposed Do Not Raise list.

Sure enough: *Is Nate there?*

My sister may not live one room away from me anymore, but that doesn't mean I can't still give her a hard time. *Who?* I text back, then glance at Nate. "Bronwyn says hi," I tell him.

His dark-blue eyes flash, but his expression remains impassive. "Hi back."

I get it, I guess. No matter how much you care about someone, things change when they used to be around all the time and then suddenly, they're not. I feel it too, in a different way. But Nate and I don't have the sort of dynamic where we talk

15

about our feelings—neither of us has that with anyone, really, except for Bronwyn—so I just make a face at him. "Repression is unhealthy, you know."

Before Nate can reply, there's a sudden flurry of activity around us: Knox returns, Addy pulls a chair over to our table, and a plate of tortilla chips covered with shredded steak, melted cheese, and chimichurri—Café Contigo's version of nachos—materializes in front of me.

I look up in the direction they came from to meet a pair of deep-brown eyes. "Game snacks," Luis Santos says, transferring the towel he used to hold the plate from his hand to his shoulder. Luis is Cooper's best friend from Bayview High, the catcher to Cooper's pitcher on the baseball team until they both graduated last year. His parents own Café Contigo, and he works here part-time while taking classes at City College. Ever since I made this corner table my second home, I see more of Luis than I did when we went to school together.

Knox lunges for the nachos like he didn't just polish off two servings of empanadas and a plate of cookies five minutes ago. "Careful, it's hot," Luis warns, lowering himself into the chair across from me. I immediately think, *Yeah you are*, because I have an embarrassing weakness for good-looking jocks that brings out my inner twelve-year-old. You'd think I would have learned after my one-sided crush on a basketball player landed me a humiliating post on Simon Kelleher's About That gossip blog freshman year, but no.

I'm not really hungry, but I extract a chip from the bottom of the pile anyway. "Thanks, Luis," I say, sucking the salt from one corner.

Nate smirks. "What were you saying about repression, Maeve?"

My face heats, and I can't think of a better response than to stuff the entire chip into my mouth and chew aggressively in Nate's general direction. Sometimes I don't know what my sister sees in him.

Damn it. My sister. I glance at my phone with a stab of guilt at the string of sad-face emojis from Bronwyn. *Just kidding. Nate looks miserable,* I reassure her. He doesn't, because nobody wears the *don't give a crap* mask as effortlessly as Nate Macauley, but I'm sure he is.

Phoebe Lawton, another Café Contigo waitress and a junior in our class, hands around glasses of water before taking a seat at the far edge of the table just as the first batter from the opposing team saunters up to home plate. The camera zooms in on Cooper's face as he brings up his glove and narrows his eyes. "Come on, Coop," Luis murmurs, his left hand curling instinctively like it's in a catcher's mitt. "Play ball."

Two hours later, the entire café is filled with an excited buzz after Cooper's near-flawless performance: eight strikeouts, one walk, one hit, and no runs through seven innings. The Cal State Fullerton Titans are winning by three, but nobody in Bayview cares all that much now that a relief pitcher has taken over for Cooper.

"I'm so happy for him," Addy beams. "He deserves this so much after . . . you know." Her smile falters. "After everything."

Everything. It's too small a word to cover what happened

when Simon Kelleher decided to stage his own death almost eighteen months ago, and frame my sister, Cooper, Addy, and Nate for his murder. The *Mikhail Powers Investigates* Thanksgiving special rehashed it all in excruciating detail, from Simon's plot to trap everyone in detention together to the secrets he arranged to leak on About That to make it seem like the other four had reasons for wanting him dead.

I watched the special with Bronwyn while she was home on break. It brought me right back to the year before, when the story became a national obsession and news vans crowded our driveway every day. The entire country learned that Bronwyn stole tests to get an A in chemistry, that Nate sold drugs while on probation *for* selling drugs, and that Addy cheated on her boyfriend, Jake—who turned out to be such a controlling trash fire that he agreed to be Simon's accomplice. And Cooper was falsely accused of using steroids, then outed before he was ready to come out to his family and friends.

All of which was a nightmare, but not nearly as bad as being suspected of murder.

The investigation unfolded almost exactly the way Simon planned—except for the part where Bronwyn, Cooper, Addy, and Nate banded together instead of turning on one another. It's hard to imagine what this night would look like if they hadn't. I doubt Cooper would've almost pitched a no-hitter in his first college game, or that Bronwyn would have made it to Yale. Nate would probably be in jail. And Addy—I don't like to think about where Addy would be. Mostly because I'm afraid she wouldn't be here at all.

I shiver, and Luis catches my eye. He raises his glass with the determined look of a guy who's not about to let his best friend's triumph turn sour. "Yeah, well, here's to karma. And to Coop, for kicking ass in his first college game."

"To Cooper," everyone echoes.

"We have to plan a road trip to see him!" Addy exclaims. She reaches across the table and taps Nate's arm as he starts gazing around the room like he's calculating how soon he can leave. "That includes you. Don't try to get out of it."

"The whole baseball team will want to go," Luis says. Nate grimaces in a resigned sort of way, because Addy is a force of nature when she's determined to make him socialize.

Phoebe, who shifted closer to Knox and me as the game wore on and other people left, reaches out to pour herself a glass of water. "Bayview is so different without Simon, but it also . . . *isn't*. You know?" she murmurs, so quietly that only Knox and I can hear. "It's not like people got any nicer once the shock wore off. We just don't have About That to keep tabs on who's being horrible from one week to the next."

"Not from lack of effort," Knox mutters.

About That copycats were everywhere for a while after Simon died. Most of them fizzled out within days, although one site, Simon Says, stayed up nearly a month last fall before the school got involved and shut it down. But nobody took it seriously, because the site's creator—one of those quiet kids hardly anyone knows—never posted a single piece of gossip that everyone hadn't already heard.

That was the thing about Simon Kelleher: he knew secrets

most people couldn't even have guessed. He was patient, willing to wait until he could wring the maximum amount of drama and pain from any given situation. And he was good at hiding how much he hated everyone at Bayview High; the only place he let it out was on the revenge forum I'd found when I was looking for clues to his death. Reading Simon's posts back then made me sick to my stomach. It still chills me, sometimes, to think how little any of us understood what it meant to go up against a mind like Simon's.

Everything could have turned out so differently.

"Hey." Knox nudges me back to the present, and I blink until his face comes into focus. It's still just the three of us locked into our side conversation; I don't think last year's seniors ever let themselves dwell on Simon for too long. "Don't look so serious. The past is past, right?"

"Right," I say, then twist in my seat as a loud groan goes up from the Café Contigo crowd. It takes a minute for me to understand what's going on, and when I do, my heart sinks: Cooper's replacement loaded the bases in the bottom of the ninth inning, got pulled, and the new pitcher just gave up a grand slam. All of a sudden, Cal State's three-run lead has turned into a walk-off, one-run loss. The other team mobs the hitter at home base, piling on top of him until they collapse in a joyful heap. Cooper, despite pitching like a dream, didn't get his win.

"Nooooo," Luis moans, burying his head in his hands. He sounds like he's in physical pain. "That is *bullshit*."

Phoebe winces. "Ooh, tough luck. Not Cooper's fault, though."

My eyes find the only person at the table I can always count on for an unfiltered reaction: Nate. He looks from my tense face to the salt still scattered across our table and shakes his head like he knows the superstitious bet I made with myself. I can read the gesture as plainly as if he spoke: *It doesn't mean anything, Maeve. It's just a game.*

I'm sure he's right. But still. I really wish Cooper had won.

CHAPTER TWO

Phoebe
Tuesday, February 18

The logical part of my brain knows my mother isn't playing with dolls. But it's early, I'm tired, and I'm not wearing my contacts yet. So instead of squinting harder, I lean against the kitchen counter and ask, "What's with the dolls?"

"They're wedding cake toppers," Mom says, yanking one away from my twelve-year-old brother, Owen, and handing it to me. I look down to see a white-clad bride with her legs wrapped around the groom's waist. Some underappreciated artist has managed to pack a lot of lust into their tiny plastic faces.

"Classy," I say. I should have guessed it was wedding-related. Last week the kitchen table was covered with stationery samples, and before that it was do-it-yourself floral centerpieces.

"That's the only one like that," she says with a hint of defensiveness. "I suppose you have to account for all kinds of tastes. Could you put it in the box?" She juts her chin toward a cardboard box half-full of foam peanuts on the counter.

I drop the happy couple inside and pull a glass from the cabinet next to our sink, filling it from the tap and finishing the whole thing in two long, greedy gulps. "Cake toppers, huh?" I ask. "Do people still use those?"

"They're just samples from Golden Rings," Mom says. Ever since she joined the local wedding planners' organization, boxes full of stuff like this show up at our apartment every couple of weeks. Mom takes pictures, makes notes of what she likes, and then packs it back up to send along to the next wedding planner in the group. "Some of them are cute, though." She holds up one of a bride and groom waltzing in silhouette. "What do you think?"

There's an open box of Eggo waffles on the counter. I pull out the last two and pop them into the toaster. "I think plastic people on top of a cake isn't really Ashton and Eli's style. Aren't they trying to keep things simple?"

"Sometimes you don't know what you want until you see it," Mom says brightly. "Part of my job is opening their eyes to what's out there."

Poor Ashton. Addy's older sister has been a dream neighbor ever since we moved into the apartment across from them last summer—giving takeout recommendations, showing us which washing machines never eat your quarters, and sharing concert tickets from her job as a graphic designer with the California Center for the Arts. She had no idea what she was getting into when she agreed to help Mom launch a side business in wedding planning by coordinating "a few details" of her upcoming wedding to Eli Kleinfelter.

Mom's gone a little overboard. She wants to make a good impression, especially since Eli is something of a local celebrity. He's the lawyer who defended Nate Macauley when Nate was framed for killing Simon Kelleher, and now he's always being interviewed about some big case or another. The press loves the fact that he's marrying the sister of one of the Bayview Four, so they reference his upcoming wedding a lot. That means free publicity for Mom, including a mention in the *San Diego Tribune* and an in-depth profile last December in the *Bayview Blade*. Which has turned into a total gossip rag since covering the Simon story, so of course they took the most dramatic angle possible: "After Heartbreaking Loss, Area Widow Launches a Business Based on Joy."

We all could've done without *that* reminder.

Still, Mom has put more energy into this wedding than just about anything else over the past few years, so I should be grateful for Ashton and Eli's endless patience.

"Your waffles are burning," Owen says placidly, stuffing a forkful of syrup-soaked squares into his mouth.

"Shit!" I yank my Eggos out with a whimper of pain as my fingers graze hot metal. "Mom, can we please buy a new toaster? This one has gotten completely useless. It goes from zero to scalding in thirty seconds."

Mom's eyebrows come together with the worried look she always gets when any of us talks about spending money. "I noticed that. But we should probably try cleaning it before we replace it. There must be ten years' worth of bread crumbs built up in there."

"I'll do it," Owen volunteers, pushing his glasses up on his nose. "And if that doesn't work, I'll take it apart. I bet I can fix it."

I smile absently at him. "No doubt, brainiac. I should've thought of that first."

"I don't want you playing around with anything electrical, Owen," Mom objects.

He looks affronted. "It wouldn't be *playing*."

A door clicks as my older sister, Emma, leaves our bedroom and heads for the kitchen. That's something I'll never get used to about apartment living—how being on a single floor makes you acutely aware of where everyone is, all the time. There's nowhere to hide. Nothing like our old house, where not only did we all have our own bedrooms, but we had a family room, an office that eventually turned into a game room for Owen, and Dad's basement workroom.

Plus, we had Dad.

My throat tightens as Emma runs her eyes over the piles of formally clad plastic people on our kitchen table. "Do people still use cake toppers?"

"Your sister asked the exact same thing," Mom says. She's always doing that—pointing out threads of similarity between Emma and me, as though acknowledging them will somehow knit us back into the tight sisterly unit we were as kids.

Emma makes a *hmm* noise, and I stay focused on my waffle as she steps closer. "Could you move?" she asks politely. "I need the blender."

I shift to one side as Owen picks up a cake topper featuring a bride with dark red hair. "This one looks like you, Emma," he says.

All of us Lawton kids are some version of redhead—Emma's hair is a deep auburn, mine is a coppery bronze, and Owen's strawberry blond—but it was our father who really stood out in a crowd, with hair so orange that his high school nickname was Cheeto. One time when we were at the Bayview Mall food court, Dad went to the bathroom and came back to see an older couple surreptitiously checking out my dark-haired, olive-skinned mother and her three pale, redheaded kids. Dad plopped down next to Mom and put an arm around her shoulders, flashing a grin at the couple. "See, *now* we make sense," he said.

And now, three years after he died? We don't.

If I had to pinpoint Emma's least favorite part of the day . . . I'd be hard-pressed, because there doesn't seem to be a lot that Emma enjoys lately. But having to pick my friend Jules up on the way to school easily ranks in the top three.

"Oh my God," Jules says breathlessly when she climbs into the backseat of our ten-year-old Corolla, shoving her backpack ahead of her. I turn in my seat, and she whips off her sunglasses to fasten me with a death stare. "Phoebe. I cannot *stand* you."

"What? Why?" I ask, confused. I shift in my seat, smoothing my skirt when it rides up on my thighs. After years of trial and error I've finally found the wardrobe that works best for my body type: a short, flouncy skirt, preferably in a bold pattern; a brightly colored V-neck or scoop-neck top; and some kind of stack-heeled bootie.

"Seat belt, please," Emma says.

Jules clips her belt, still glaring at me. "You know why."

"I seriously do not," I protest. Emma pulls away from the curb in front of Jules's modest split-level house, which is just one street away from where we used to live. Our old neighborhood isn't Bayview's wealthiest by a long shot, but the young couple Mom sold our house to was still thrilled to get a starter home here.

Jules's green eyes, striking against her brown skin and dark hair, pop for dramatic effect. "Nate Macauley was at Café Contigo last night and you didn't text me!"

"Oh well . . ." I turn up the radio so my mumbled response will get lost in Taylor Swift's latest. Jules has always had a thing for Nate—she's a total sucker for the dark, handsome bad-boy type—but she never considered him boyfriend material until Bronwyn Rojas did. Now she circles like a vulture every time they break up. Which has caused divided loyalties since I started working at Café Contigo and became friendly with Addy, who, obviously, is firmly on Team Bronwyn.

"And he *never* goes out," Jules moans. "That was such a missed opportunity. Major friend failure, Phoebe Jeebies. Not cool." She pulls out a tube of wine-colored lip gloss and leans forward so she can see herself in the rearview mirror as she applies a fresh coat. "How did he seem? Do you think he's over Bronwyn?"

27

"I mean. It's hard to tell," I say. "He didn't really talk to anyone except Maeve and Addy. Mostly Addy."

Jules smacks her lips together, an expression of mild panic crossing her face. "Oh my God. Do you think *they're* together now?"

"No. Definitely not. They're friends. Not everyone finds him irresistible, Jules."

Jules drops the lip gloss back into her bag and leans her head against the window with a sigh. "Says you. He's so hot, I could die."

Emma pauses at a red light and rubs her eyes, then reaches for the volume button on the radio. "I need to turn this down," she says. "My head is pounding."

"Are you getting sick?" I ask.

"Just tired. My tutoring session with Sean Murdock went too long last night."

"No surprise there," I mutter. If you're searching for signs of intelligent life in the Bayview High junior class, Sean Murdock isn't where you'll find it. But his parents have money, and they'll happily throw it at Emma for the chance that either her work ethic or her grades might rub off on Sean.

"I should hire you, Emma," Jules says. "Chemistry is going to be a nightmare this semester unless I get some help. Or pull a Bronwyn Rojas and steal the tests."

"Bronwyn made up that class," I remind her, and Jules kicks my seat.

"Don't defend her," she says sulkily. "She's ruining my love life."

"If you're serious about tutoring, I have a slot free this weekend," Emma says.

"Chemistry on the *weekend*?" Jules sounds scandalized. "No thank you."

"Okay, then." My sister exhales a light sigh, like she shouldn't have expected anything different. "Not serious."

Emma's only a year older than Jules and me, but most of the time she seems more Ashton Prentiss's age than ours. Emma doesn't act seventeen; she acts like she's in her midtwenties and stressing her way through graduate school instead of senior AP classes. Even now, when her college applications are all in and she's just waiting to hear back, she can't relax.

We drive the rest of the way in silence, until my phone chimes when Emma pulls into the parking lot. I look down to a text. *Bleachers?*

I shouldn't. But even as my brain reminds me that I've already gotten two late warnings this month, my fingers type *OK*. I put my phone in my pocket and have the passenger door halfway open before Emma's even shifted into Park. She raises her eyebrows as I climb out.

"I have to go to the football field real quick," I say, hiking my backpack over my shoulder and resting my hand on the car door.

"What for? You don't want to be late again," Emma says, narrowing her light brown eyes at me. They're exactly like Dad's, and—along with the reddish hair—the only trait she and I share. Emma is tall and thin, I'm short and curvy. Her hair is stick-straight and doesn't quite reach her shoulders, mine

29

is long and curly. She freckles in the sun, and I tan. We're both February-pale now, though, and I can feel my cheeks redden as I look down at the ground.

"It's, um, for homework," I mumble.

Jules grins as she climbs out of the car. "Is that what we're calling it now?"

I turn on my heel and beat a hasty retreat, but I can still feel the weight of Emma's disapproval settling over my shoulders like a cloak. Emma has always been the serious one, but when we were younger it didn't matter. We were so close that we used to have entire conversations without talking. Mom would joke that we must be telepaths, but it wasn't that. We just knew one another so well that we could read every expression as clearly as a word.

We were close with Owen too, despite the age difference. Dad used to call us the Three Amigos, and every childhood photo shows us posed exactly the same way: Emma and me on either side of Owen, our arms around one another, grinning widely. We look inseparable, and I thought we were. It never occurred to me that Dad was the glue keeping us together.

The pulling apart was so subtle that I didn't notice it right away. Emma withdrew first, burying herself in schoolwork. "It's her way of grieving," Mom said, so I let her be, even though *my* way of grieving would have been to do it together. I compensated by throwing myself into every social activity I could find—especially once boys started getting interested in me— while Owen retreated into the comforting fantasy world of video games. Before I'd realized it, those had become our lanes, and we stayed in them. Our card last Christmas featured the three of us standing beside the tree, arranged by height, hands clasped in front of us with stiff smiles. Dad would've been so disappointed by that picture.

And by me shortly after we took it, for what happened at Jules's Christmas party. It's one thing to treat your older sister like a polite stranger, and quite another thing to . . . do what I did. I used to feel a wistful kind of loneliness when I thought about Emma, but now I just feel guilt. And relief that she can't read my feelings on my face anymore.

"Hey!" I'm so caught up in my thoughts that I would've walked right into a pole under the bleachers if a hand hadn't reached out and stopped me. Then it pulls me forward so quickly that my phone slides out of my pocket and makes a faint bouncing noise on the grass.

"Shit," I say, but Brandon Weber's lips are pressed against mine before I can get anything else out. I shimmy my shoulders until my backpack joins my phone on the ground. Brandon tugs at the hem of my shirt, and since this is one hundred percent what I came for, I help him along by untucking it.

Brandon's hands move up and across my bare skin, pushing aside the lace of my bra, and he groans against my mouth. "God, you're so sexy."

He is, too. Brandon quarterbacks the football team, and the *Bayview Blade* likes to call him "the next Cooper Clay" because he's good enough that colleges are already starting to scout him. I don't think that's an accurate comparison, though. For one thing, Cooper has next-level talent, and for another, he's a sweetheart. Brandon, on the other hand, is basically an asshole.

The boy can kiss, though. All the tension flows out of me as he pushes me against the pole behind us, replaced with a heady spark of anticipation. I wrap one arm around his neck, trying to pull him down to my height, while my other hand teases at the waistband of his jeans. Then my foot sends something skidding across the ground, and the sound of my text tone distracts me.

"My phone," I say, pulling away. "We're going to smash it if I don't pick it up."

"I'll buy you a new one," Brandon says, his tongue in my ear. Which I don't like—*why* do guys think that's hot?—so I shove at him until he lets go. His front pocket dings loudly, and I smirk at the bulge there as I retrieve my phone.

"Is that a text, or are you just happy to see me?" I say, brushing off my screen. Then I glance down and catch my breath. "Ugh, are you kidding me? This again?"

"What?" Brandon asks, pulling out his own phone.

"Unknown number, and guess what it says?" I put on an affected voice. "*Still missing About That? I know I am. Let's play a new game.* I can't believe somebody would pull this crap after Principal Gupta's warning."

Brandon's eyes flick over his screen. "I got the same thing. You see the link?"

"Yeah. Don't click it! It's probably a virus or—"

"Too late," Brandon laughs. He squints at his phone while I take him in: over six feet tall with dirty-blond hair, blue-green eyes, and the kind of full lips a girl would kill for. He's so pretty, he looks like he could fly off with a harp any second. And nobody knows it more than he does. "Jesus, this is a freaking book," he complains.

"Let me see." I grab his phone, because no way am I following that link with mine. I angle the screen away from the sun until I can see it clearly. I'm looking at a website with a bad replica of the About That logo, and a big block of text beneath it. *"Pay attention, Bayview High. I'm only going to explain the rules once,"* I read. *"Here's how we play Truth or Dare. I'll send a prompt to one person only—and you can't tell ANYONE if it's you. Don't spoil the element of surprise. It makes me cranky, and I'm not nearly as nice when I'm cranky. You get 24 hours to text your choice back. Pick Truth, and I'll reveal one of your secrets. Pick Dare, and I'll give you a challenge. Either way, we'll have a little fun and relieve the monotony of our tedious existence."*

Brandon runs a hand through his thick, tawny hair. "Speak for yourself, loser."

"Come on, Bayview, you know you've missed this." I scowl when I finish. "Do you think this went to everyone at school? People better not say anything if they want to keep their phones." Last fall, after Principal Gupta shut down the latest Simon copycat, she told us she was instituting a zero-tolerance policy: if she saw even a hint of another About That, she'd ban phones at school permanently. And expel anyone caught trying to bring one in.

We've all been model citizens since then, at least when it comes to online gossip. Nobody can imagine getting through a school day—never mind *years*—without their phones.

"No one cares. It's old news," Brandon says dismissively.

He pockets his phone and wraps an arm around my waist, pulling me close. "So where were we?"

I'm still holding my own phone, pressed against his chest now, and it chimes in my hand before I can answer. When I pull my head back to look at the screen, there's another message from an unknown contact. But this time, there's no simultaneous text tone from Brandon's pocket.

Phoebe Lawton, you're up first! Text back your choice: Should I reveal a Truth, or will you take a Dare?

CHAPTER THREE

Knox
Wednesday, February 19

I scan the half-off clothing rack next to me with a feeling of existential dread. I hate department stores. They're too bright, too loud, and too crammed full of junk that nobody needs. Whenever I'm forced to spend time in one I start thinking about how consumer culture is just one long, expensive, planet-killing distraction from the fact that we're all going to die eventually.

Then I suck down the last of my six-dollar iced coffee, because I'm nothing if not a willing participant in the charade.

"That'll be forty-two sixty, hon," the woman behind the counter says when it's my turn. I'm picking up a new wallet for my mother, and I hope I got it right. Even with her detailed written instructions, it still looks like twelve other black wallets. I spent too long debating between them, and now I'm running late for work.

It probably doesn't matter, since Eli Kleinfelter doesn't pay me or, most days, even notice I'm there. Still, I pick up my pace after leaving the Bayview Mall, following a sidewalk behind the building until it narrows to nothing but asphalt. Then, after a quick glance over my shoulder to make sure no one's watching, I approach the flimsy chain-link fence surrounding an empty construction site.

There's supposed to be a new parking garage going into the hillside behind the mall, but the company building it went bankrupt after they'd started. A bunch of construction companies are bidding to take over, including my dad's. Until then, the site is cutting off what used to be a path between the mall and Bayview Center. Now you have to walk all the way around the building and down a main road, which takes ten times as long.

Unless you do what I'm about to do.

I duck under a giant gap in the fence and skirt around a half-dozen orange-and-white barrels until I'm overlooking a partially constructed garage and what was supposed to become its roof. The whole thing is covered with thick plastic tarp, except for a wooden landing with a set of metal stairs along one side, leading to part of the hill that hasn't been dug into yet.

I don't know who at Bayview High first had the bright idea to jump the five-foot drop onto the landing, but now it's a well-known shortcut from the mall to downtown. Which, to be clear, my dad would *kill* me for taking. But he's not here and even if he were, he pays less attention to me than Eli does. So I brace myself against one of the construction barrels and look down.

There's just one problem.

It's not that I'm afraid of heights. It's more that I have a preference for firm ground. When I played Peter Pan at drama camp last summer, I got so freaked out about getting flown around on a pulley that they had to lower me to barely two feet off the stage. "You're not flying, Knox," the production manager grumbled every time I swung past him. "You're skimming at best."

All right. I'm afraid of heights. But I'm trying to get over it. I stare down at the wooden planks below me. They look twenty feet away. Did someone lower the roof?

"It's a great day for someone to die. Just not me," I mutter like I'm Dax Reaper, the most ruthless bounty hunter in *Bounty Wars.* Because the only way I can make this nervous hovering even more pathetic is to quote a video game character.

I can't do it. Not a real jump, anyway. I sit at the edge, squeeze my eyes shut, and push off so that I slither down the last few feet like a cowardly snake. I land awkwardly, wincing on impact and stumbling across the uneven wooden planks. Athletic, I am not.

I manage to regain my balance and limp toward the stairs. The lightweight metal clangs loudly with every step as I make my way down. I heave a sigh of relief once I hit solid ground and follow what's left of the hillside path to the bottom fence. People used to climb over it until somebody broke the lock. I slip through the gate and into the tree grove at the edge of Bayview Center. The number 11 bus to downtown San Diego is idling at the depot in front of Town Hall, and I jog across the street to the still-open doors.

Made it with a minute to spare. I might get to Until Proven on time after all. I pay my fare, sink into one of the last empty seats, and pull my phone out of my pocket.

There's a loud sniff beside me. "Those things are practically part of your hand nowadays, aren't they? My grandson won't put his down. I suggested he leave it behind the last time I took him out to eat, and you would have thought I'd threatened him with bodily harm."

I look up to a pair of watery blue eyes behind bifocals. Of course. It never fails: any time I'm out in public and there's an old woman nearby, she starts up a conversation with me. Maeve calls it the Nice Young Man Factor. "You have one of those faces," she says. "They can tell you won't be rude."

I call it the Knox Myers Curse: irresistible to octogenarians, invisible to girls my own age. During the Cal State Fullerton season opener at Café Contigo, Phoebe Lawton literally tripped over me to get to Brandon Weber when he sauntered in at the end of the night.

I should keep scrolling and pretend I didn't hear, like Brandon would. *What Would Brandon Do* is a terrible life mantra, since he's a soul-sucking waste of space who skates through life on good hair, symmetrical features, and the ability to throw a perfect spiral—but he also gets whatever he wants and is probably never trapped in awkward geriatric bus conversations.

So, yeah. Selective hearing loss for the next fifteen minutes would be the way to go. Instead, I find myself saying, "There's a word for that. Nomophobia. Fear of being without your phone."

"Is that right?" she asks, and now I've done it. The floodgates are open. By the time we reach downtown I know all about her six grandkids and her hip replacement surgery. It's not until I get off the bus a block from Eli's office that I can go back to what I was doing on my phone in the first place—checking to see if there's another text from whoever sent the Truth or Dare rules yesterday.

I should pretend I never saw it. Everyone at Bayview High should. But we don't. After what happened with Simon, it's baked into our collective DNA to be morbidly fascinated with this stuff. Last night, while a bunch of us were supposed to be running lines for the spring play, we kept getting sidetracked by trying to guess who the unknown texter might be.

The whole thing was probably a joke, though. It's four o'clock when I push through the doors of Until Proven's office building—well past the twenty-four-hour deadline for whoever's supposed to be playing the game to respond—and the latest Simon wannabe has gone silent.

I pass the coffee shop in the lobby and take an elevator to the third floor. Until Proven is at the far end of a narrow corridor, next to one of those hair replacement clinics that fills the entire hall with a rank chemical smell. A balding guy comes out of its door, his forehead unevenly dotted with wispy tufts of hair. He lowers his eyes and slinks past me like I just caught him buying porn.

When I crack open Until Proven's door, I'm immediately hit with the buzzing sound of too many people crammed into too small a space, all of them talking at once.

"How many convictions?"

"Twelve that we know of, but there's gotta be more."

"Did anybody call Channel Seven back?"

"Eighteen months, then released, then right back in."

"Knox!" Sandeep Ghai, a Harvard Law grad who started working for Eli last fall, barrels toward me from behind an armful of red folders stacked up to his nose. "Just the man I was looking for. I need forty employer kits compiled and sent out today. Sample kit's on top along with all the addresses. Can you get these out for the five o'clock mail run?"

"Forty?" I raise my eyebrows as I take the stack from him. Until Proven doesn't only defend people who Eli and the other lawyers think are wrongfully accused; it also helps them find jobs after getting out of jail. So every once in a while, I mail out folders full of résumés and a cover letter about why hiring *exonerees,* as Eli calls them, is good for business. But we're usually lucky if one local company a week is interested. "Why so many?"

"Publicity from the D'Agostino case," Sandeep says, like that explains everything. When I still look confused, he adds, "Everyone turns into a concerned corporate citizen when there's a chance for free PR."

I should've guessed. Eli's been all over the news after proving that a bunch of people convicted on drug charges had actually been blackmailed and framed by a San Diego police sergeant, Carl D'Agostino, and two of his subordinates. They're all in jail awaiting trial, and Until Proven is working on getting the phony convictions reversed.

The last time Eli got this much press was for the Simon Kelleher case. Back then, Eli was the lead story on every news show after getting Nate Macauley out of jail. My dad's company hired Nate a couple of weeks later. He still works there, and now they're paying for him to take college classes.

After Bronwyn Rojas left for Yale and Until Proven started looking for another high school intern, I figured Maeve would take it. She's tight with Eli, plus she was a big part of why Simon's plan unraveled in the first place. Nobody would've looked at Simon as anything except a victim if Maeve hadn't tracked down his secret online persona.

But Maeve didn't want the job. "That's Bronwyn's thing. Not mine," she'd said, in that voice she uses when she wants to end a conversation.

So I applied. Partly because it's interesting, but also because I wasn't exactly fighting off other job opportunities. My father, who tells anybody who'll listen that Nate Macauley is "one helluva kid," never bothered asking if I wanted to work at Myers Construction.

To be fair: I suck at anything tool-related. I once wound up in the emergency room after hammering my thumb to a pulp when hanging a picture. But still. He could've asked.

"Five o'clock," Sandeep repeats, cocking finger guns at me as he backs away toward his desk. "I can count on you, right?"

"I got it," I say, looking around for some empty space. My gaze lands on Eli, who's the only person at Until Proven who gets an entire desk to himself. It's stacked so high with folders that when he hunches forward while talking on the phone, all you can see is his mad scientist hair. By some miracle, the table behind him is empty.

41

I head that way, hoping that maybe I'll get a chance to talk with him. Eli fascinates me, not only because he's ridiculously good at his job but because he's this guy you probably wouldn't look at twice if you passed him in the street. Yet he's so confident and, I don't know, *magnetic* or something. Now that I've worked with him for a few months, it doesn't surprise me that he has a gorgeous fiancée, or that he manages to get people who are involved in criminal cases to spill all kinds of things they probably shouldn't. I want him to teach me his ways.

Plus, it would be great if he learned my name.

I haven't even made it halfway across the room, though, before Sandeep yells out, "Eli! We need you in Winterfell."

Eli rolls his chair back and peers around the folders. "In what?"

"Winterfell," Sandeep says expectantly.

When Eli still looks blank, I clear my throat. "It's the small conference room," I say. "Remember? Sandeep gave them names so we could tell them apart. The other one is, um, King's Landing." Sandeep, like me, is a huge *Game of Thrones* fan, so he named the rooms after two locations in the story. But Eli's never read the books or seen an episode of the TV show, and the whole thing confuses the hell out of him.

"Oh. Right. Thank you." Eli nods distractedly at me, then turns back to Sandeep. "What was wrong with just saying 'the small conference room'?"

"We need you in Winterfell," Sandeep repeats, his voice edging into impatience. Eli stands with a sigh, and I get a wry smile as he passes. Progress.

I spread my files across the empty conference table, lay my phone beside them, and start assembling employer packets. As soon as I do my phone starts buzzing with a string of texts from, of course, my sisters. I have four of them, all older than me, all with *K* names: Kiersten, Katie, Kelsey, and Kara. We're like the Kardashians, except without any money.

My sisters will start a group conversation about anything. Birthdays, TV shows, current boyfriends or girlfriends, exes. Me, frequently. It's a nightmare when they all start caring about my love life or my future at once. *Knox, what happened with Maeve? She was so nice! Knox, who are you taking to prom? Knox, are you thinking about colleges yet? Next year will be here before you know it!*

But this time, they're talking about Katie's surprise engagement on Valentine's Day. She'll be the first Myers to get married, so there's a *lot* to discuss.

They go quiet eventually, and I'm halfway through the packets when another text comes in. I glance down, expecting to see one of my sisters' names—probably Kiersten, because she has to have the last word on everything—but it's a private number.

Tsk, no response from our first player. That means you forfeit. I expected better from you, Phoebe Lawton. No fun at all. Now I get to reveal one of your secrets in true About That style.

Crap. I guess this is really happening. Though, how bad could it be? Simon never bothered featuring Phoebe on About That, because she's an open book. She hooks up a lot, but she doesn't cheat on people or break them up. And she's one of those girls who flits easily between Bayview High social groups, like the invisible boundaries that keep most of us apart don't apply to her. I'm pretty sure there's nothing anyone could say about Phoebe that we don't already know.

Gray dots linger for a while. The anonymous texter is trying to build suspense, and even though I know I shouldn't take the bait, my pulse speeds up. Then I kind of hate myself for it, and I'm about to put my phone facedown on the table when a text finally appears.

Phoebe slept with her sister Emma's boyfriend.

Hold up. What?

I look around the Until Proven office like I'm expecting some kind of group reaction. Sometimes I forget I'm the only high school student here. Everybody ignores me, since they have shit to deal with that actually matters, so I look back at my phone. It's gone dark, and I press the Home button to reactivate the screen.

Phoebe slept with her sister Emma's boyfriend.

This can't be real. First off, does Emma Lawton even have a boyfriend? She's one of the quietest, least social girls in the senior class. As far as I can tell, she's in an intimate relationship with her homework and that's it. Plus, Phoebe wouldn't do that to her sister. Right? I mean, I don't know her well, but there are rules. My sisters would draw blood over something like that.

More texts appear, one right after the other.

What's that, Bayview? You didn't know?

Shame. You're behind on your gossip.

Here's a little advice for the next time we play:

Always take the Dare.

CHAPTER FOUR

Maeve
Thursday, February 20

I should know the protocol for checking in with someone who just got their deepest, darkest secret leaked to the entire school. I'm kind of rusty, though. It's been a while.

I was at Café Contigo yesterday doing homework when the texts about Phoebe came through. As soon as she took a break from serving tables and checked her phone, I knew the gossip was true. The look on her face was exactly the same as Bronwyn's eighteen months ago, when the About This copycat site that Jake Riordan kept up after Simon died revealed she'd cheated in chemistry. Not just horror, but guilt.

Emma came barreling through the café door soon after, red-faced and shaking. I almost didn't recognize her. "Is this true? Is that why you've been acting so weird?" she choked out, holding up her phone. Phoebe was at the cash register counter next to Luis's father, taking her apron off. I'm pretty sure she was about to play sick and get out of there. She froze, eyes round, and didn't answer. Emma kept coming until she was inches away from Phoebe's face, and for a second I was afraid she might slap her. "Was it while we were *dating*?"

"After," Phoebe said, so quickly and emphatically that I was sure that was true, too. Then Mr. Santos sprang into action, putting an arm around both Phoebe and Emma and shepherding them into the kitchen. That was the last I saw of either of them for the night.

I thought Mr. Santos had been quick enough to keep their fight private until I noticed two sophomores from the Bayview High baseball team approaching the counter. "Takeout for Reynolds," one of them said to the waiter, who was suddenly covering the entire room plus the cash register. The other boy never looked up from his phone. By the time I got home and checked in with Knox, he'd already heard everything.

"Guess the latest Bayview gossipmonger knows their dirt," he said.

Last night, I kept wondering if I should text Phoebe: *You okay?* But the thing is, even though I've always liked her, we're not friends. We're *friendly*, mostly because I spend way too much time where she works, and because she's one of those extroverted people who talks to everyone. She gave me her number once, "just so you'll have it," but I've never used it before, and it felt like a weird time to start. Like I was curious instead of concerned. Now, heading downstairs for breakfast, I still don't know if that was the right call.

Mom's sitting at the table when I enter the kitchen, frowning at her laptop. When Bronwyn was here we used to always eat breakfast at the kitchen island, but something about sitting next to her empty stool makes me lose my appetite. Mom would never say it, because Bronwyn being at Yale is a lifelong dream for both of them, but I think she feels the same way.

She looks up and flashes me a bright smile. "Guess what I got?" Then her eyes narrow as I pull a box of Froot Loops from the cabinet next to the sink. "I don't remember buying those."

"You didn't," I say. I fill a bowl to the brim with rainbow-hued loops, then grab a carton of milk from the refrigerator and take a seat beside her. My dad comes into the kitchen, straightening his tie, and Mom shoots him the evil eye.

"Really, Javier? I thought we agreed on healthy breakfast foods."

He only looks guilty for a second. "They're fortified, though. With essential vitamins and minerals. It says so right on the box." He grabs a few from my bowl before I add milk and pops them into his mouth.

Mom rolls her eyes. "You're as bad as she is. Don't come crying to me when your teeth rot."

Dad swallows his cereal and kisses her cheek, then the top of my head. "I promise to endure all cavities with the appropriate level of stoicism," he says. My father moved to the States from Colombia when he was ten, so he doesn't have an accent, exactly, but there's a rhythm to the way he speaks that's a little bit formal and a little bit musical. It's one of my favorite things about him. Well, that and our mutual appreciation of refined sugar, which is something Mom and Bronwyn don't share. "Don't wait on me for dinner, okay? We've got that board meeting today. I'm sure it'll go late."

"All right, enabler," Mom says affectionately. He grabs his keys from a hook on the wall and heads out the door.

I swallow a giant mouthful of already-soggy Froot Loops and gesture toward her laptop. "So what'd you get?"

She blinks at the shift in conversation, then beams. "Oh! You'll love this. *Into the Woods* tickets, for when Bronwyn is back next week. It's playing at the Civic. You can see how Bayview High stacks up against the professionals. That's the play the drama club is doing this spring, right?"

I eat another spoonful of cereal before answering. I need a second to muster the appropriate level of enthusiasm. "Right. Fantastic! That'll be so fun."

Too much. I overdid it. Mom frowns. "You don't want to go?"

"No, I totally do," I lie.

She's unconvinced. "What's wrong? I thought you loved musical theater!"

My mom. You have to give her credit for how tirelessly she champions every single one of my passing interests. *Maeve did a play once. Ergo, Maeve loves all plays!* I was in the school play last year and it was—fine. But I didn't try out this year. It felt like one of those things that I'd done once and could now safely put on the shelf of experiences that don't need to be repeated. *Yep, tried it, it was all right but not for me.* Which is where I put most things.

"I do," I say. "But hasn't Bronwyn already seen *Into the Woods*?"

Mom's forehead creases. "She has? When?"

I chase the last of the Froot Loops with my spoon and take my time swallowing them. "Over Christmas, I thought? With, um . . . Nate."

Ugh. Bad lie. Nate wouldn't be caught dead at a musical.

Mom's frown deepens. She doesn't dislike Nate, exactly, but she doesn't make a secret of the fact that she thinks he and Bronwyn come from, as she puts it, "different worlds." Plus, she keeps insisting that Bronwyn is too young to be in a serious relationship. When I remind her that she met Dad in college, she says, "When we were *juniors*," like she'd matured a decade by then. "Well, let me try to catch her and check," Mom says, reaching for her phone. "I have thirty minutes to return them."

I smack my forehead. "You know what? Never mind. They didn't see *Into the Woods*. They saw *The Fast and the Furious* part twelve, or whatever. You know. Same thing, pretty much." Mom looks confused, then exasperated as I tip my bowl to loudly guzzle the pink milk.

"Maeve, stop that. You're not six anymore." She turns back to her laptop, brow furrowed. "Oh, for God's sake, I just *checked* my email. How can there be so many already?"

I put down my bowl and grab a napkin, because all of a sudden my nose is running. I wipe it without thinking much more than *It's kind of early for allergies,* but when I lower my hand—oh.

Oh my God.

I get up without a word, the napkin clutched in my fist, and go to our first-floor bathroom. I can feel wetness continuing to gather beneath my nose, and even before I look in the mirror I know what I'll see. Pale face, tense mouth, dazed eyes—and a tiny river of bright red blood dripping from each nostril.

The dread hits so hard and so fast that it feels as if someone's Tasered me: there's a moment of cold shock and then I'm a trembling, twitching mess, shaking so hard that I can barely keep the napkin pressed to my nose. Red seeps into its cheery pattern as my heart bangs against my rib cage, the frantic beat echoing in my ears. My eyes in the mirror won't stop blinking, keeping perfect time to the two-word sentence rattling through my brain.

It's back. It's back. It's back.

Every time my leukemia has ever returned, it's started with a nosebleed.

I imagine walking into the kitchen and showing the bloody napkin to my mother, and all the air leaves my lungs. I can't watch her face do that *thing* again—that thing where she's like a time-lapse movie, aging twenty years in twenty seconds. She'll call my dad, and when he comes back to the house, all his cheeriness from this morning will be gone. He'll be wearing that expression that I hate more than anything, because I know the internal prayer that accompanies it. I heard him once after I'd nearly died when I was eight, the words in Spanish barely a whisper as he sat with his head bowed next to my hospital bed. "Por favor, Dios, llévame a mi en su lugar. Yo por ella. Por favor." Even though I was barely conscious, I thought, *No, God, don't listen,* because I reject any prayer that has my dad asking to take my place.

If I show my mother this napkin, we'll have to climb back

on the testing carousel. They'll start with the least invasive and least painful, but eventually you have to do them all. Then we'll sit in Dr. Gutierrez's office, staring at his thin, worried face while he weighs the pros and cons of equally horrible treatment options and reminds us that *every time it comes back, it's harder to treat and we must adjust accordingly.* And finally we'll pick our poison, followed by months of losing weight, losing hair, losing energy, losing time. Losing hope.

I told myself the last time, when I was thirteen, that I would never do it again.

My nose has stopped bleeding. I examine the napkin with my best effort at clinical detachment. There's not that much blood, really. Maybe it's just dry air; it's February, after all. Sometimes a nosebleed is just a nosebleed, and there's no need to send people into a frenzy about it. My pulse slows as I press my lips together and inhale deeply, hearing nothing but air. I drop the napkin into the toilet and flush quickly so I don't have to watch thin threads of my blood fan into the water. Then I pull a Kleenex from the box on top of the toilet and wet it, wiping away the last traces of red.

"It's fine," I tell my reflection, gripping the sides of the sink. "Everything is fine."

Bayview High's new gossip game sent two texts this morning: an alert that the next player would be contacted soon, and a reminder link to the rules post. Now everyone is reading the new About That website en masse at lunch, absently shoving food into their mouths with their eyes glued to their phones. I can't help but think that Simon would be *loving* this.

And if I'm being perfectly honest—I don't mind the distraction right now.

"I'm still mostly surprised that Emma had a boyfriend," Knox says, glancing at the table where Phoebe is sitting with her friend Jules Crandall and a bunch of other junior girls. Emma is nowhere in sight, but then again, she never is. I'm pretty sure she eats lunch outside with the only friend I've ever seen her with, a quiet girl named Gillian. "Do you think he goes here?"

I grab one of the fries we're sharing and swirl it in ketchup before popping it into my mouth. "I've never seen her with anyone."

Lucy Chen, who'd been deep in another conversation at our table, swings around in her chair. "Are you guys talking about Phoebe and Emma?" she asks, fixing us with a judgmental stare. Because Lucy Chen is *that* girl: the one who complains about whatever you're doing while trying to horn in on it. She's also this year's literal drama queen, since she has the lead in *Into the Woods* opposite Knox. "Everybody needs to just ignore that game."

Her boyfriend, Chase Russo, blinks at her. "Luce, *that game* is all you've been talking about for the past ten minutes."

"About how *dangerous* it is," Lucy says self-righteously. "Bayview High is a high-risk population when it comes to this kind of thing."

I suppress a sigh. This is what happens when you're bad at

making friends: you end up with ones you don't particularly like. Most of the time I'm grateful for the easy camaraderie of the drama club group, because they keep me company even when Knox isn't around. Other times I wonder what school, and life, would be like if I made more of an effort. If I ever actively chose somebody instead of just letting myself get pulled into whatever orbit will have me.

My eyes stray toward Phoebe, who's chewing with her eyes straight ahead. Today must be rough, but she's here, facing it head-on. She reminds me of Bronwyn that way. Phoebe is wearing one of her usual bright dresses, her bronze curls tumbling around her shoulders and her makeup perfect. No fading into the background for her.

I wish I'd texted her last night after all.

"Anyway, I'm sure we all know who's behind this," Lucy adds, jerking her head toward a corner table where Matthias Schroeder is eating alone, his face barely visible behind a thick book. "Matthias should've been expelled after Simon Says. Principal Gupta's zero-tolerance policy came too late."

"Really? You think Matthias did this? But Simon Says was so tame," I say. I can't bring myself to dislike Matthias, even though my name was all over his short-lived copycat blog last fall. Matthias moved here freshman year, right around the time I started coming to school more, and he never really fit in anywhere. I'd watch him sidle past groups that either mocked or ignored him, and I knew that could easily have been me without Bronwyn.

Chase grins. "That guy had the worst gossip ever." He puts

on a breathless voice. "*Maeve Rojas and Knox Myers broke up!* Like, yeah, dude. Everybody already knows and nobody cares. Most drama-free breakup ever. Try again."

"Still," Lucy sniffs. "I don't trust him. He has that same disgruntled-loner vibe that Simon had."

"Simon didn't have—" I start, but I'm interrupted by a booming voice behind us calling out, "What's up, Phoebe?" We all turn, and Knox lets out a muted "Ugh," when we see Sean Murdock leaning back in his chair, his thick torso twisted in the direction of Phoebe's table. Sean is Brandon Weber's most assholish friend, which is really saying something. He used to call me Dead Girl Walking freshman year, and I'm pretty sure he still doesn't know my actual name.

Phoebe doesn't answer, and Sean pushes his chair away from the table with a loud scraping noise. "I didn't know you and Emma were so close," he calls over the chattering buzz of the cafeteria. "If you're looking for a new guy to share, I volunteer my services." His friends start snickering, and Sean raises his voice another notch. "You can take turns. Or double-team me. I'm good either way."

Monica Hill, one of the junior girls who's always hanging around with Sean and Brandon, gasps loudly and slaps Sean on his arm, but more like she's trying to egg him on than stop him. As for Brandon, he's laughing harder than anyone else at his table. "In your dreams, bro," he says, not even glancing in Phoebe's direction.

"Don't get greedy just cause you're hitting that," Sean says. "There's plenty of Lawton love to go around. Right, Phoebe?

Twice as nice. Sharing is caring." He's cackling now. "Listen to me, Bran. I'm a poet and I know it."

It's too quiet, suddenly. The kind of silence that only happens when everyone in a room is focused on the same thing. Phoebe is looking at the ground, her cheeks pale and her mouth pressed into a tight line. I'm half on my feet with the overwhelming need to do *something,* although I have no clue what, when Phoebe raises her head and looks directly at Sean.

"Thanks but no thanks," she says in a loud, clear voice. "If I wanted to be bored and disappointed, I'd just watch you play baseball." Then she takes a large, deliberate bite from a bright green apple.

The hum in the room erupts into full-on hoots and catcalls as Chase says, "*Damn,* girl." Sean's face turns an ugly red, but before he can say anything one of the lunch workers steps out from the kitchen. It's Robert, who's built like a linebacker and is the only person at Bayview High with a louder voice than Sean. He cups his hands around his mouth like a megaphone as I sink back into my seat.

"Everyone gonna settle down in here, or you need me to get a teacher?" he calls.

The noise volume cuts in half instantly, but that only makes it easier to hear Sean's parting words as he turns back toward his table. "Spoken like the slut you are, Lawton."

Robert doesn't hesitate. "Principal's office, Murdock."

"What?" Sean protests, spreading his hands wide. "She started it! She came on to me and insulted me all at once. That's a violation of the school bullying policy."

Resentment surges through my veins. Why am I keeping quiet, exactly? What on earth do I have to lose? "Liar," I call out, startling Knox so much that he actually jumps. "You provoked her and everyone knows it."

Sean snorts over the murmur of agreement in the room. "Nobody asked you, Cancer Girl."

The words make my stomach plunge, but I roll my eyes like it's an outdated insult. "Ooh, burn," I snap.

Robert folds his tattooed arms and takes a few steps forward. Rumor has it that he used to work in a prison kitchen, which is pretty solid job training for what he does now. In fact, it's probably why he was hired. Principal Gupta learned at least a few things from last year. "Principal's office, Murdock," he growls. "You can go on your own, or I can take you. I promise you will not like it."

This time, I can't hear whatever Sean mutters under his breath as he gets to his feet. He shoots Phoebe a death glare as he passes her table, and she gives it right back. But once he's gone, her face just sort of—crumples.

"Someone's getting detention," Chase calls in a singsong voice. "Try not to die, Murdock." I suck in a breath, and he grimaces apologetically. "Too soon?"

The bell rings, and we start getting our things together. A few tables over, Jules takes Phoebe's tray and whispers something in her ear. Phoebe nods and loops her backpack over one shoulder. She heads for the door, pausing beside our table to let a knot of sophomore girls push through the narrow space between chairs. They all look back at her and burst into muted laughter.

I touch Phoebe's arm. "Are you all right?" I ask. She looks up, but before she can answer I spot Lucy approaching from her other side.

"You shouldn't have to put up with that, Phoebe," Lucy says, and for a second I almost like her. Then she gets that self-righteous look on her face again. "Maybe we should tell Principal Gupta what's going on. I'm beginning to think this school would be better off if nobody had a phone in the first—"

Phoebe whips around in her direction, eyes blazing. Lucy gasps and stumbles backward, because she's overdramatic like that. Although Phoebe *does* look poised for an attack, and when she speaks, her voice is ice cold.

"Don't. You. *Dare.*"

CHAPTER FIVE

Phoebe
Thursday, February 20

"Bizarre," I say to Owen.

He leans forward on his stool at the kitchen island, scrunching his face in concentration. "Can you use it in a sentence?"

"Um . . ." I hesitate, and he lets out a small sigh.

"There's one the back of the index card."

"Oh. Right." I flip the card I'm holding and read, *"The bizarre movie was so strange that we left the theater in stunned silence."*

"Bizarre," Owen says. *"B-A-Z-A-A-R."* Then he grins expectantly, like he's waiting for the same thumbs-up I've given for a dozen words straight.

I blink at him, flash card in hand. There aren't a lot of things that could distract me from the past twenty-four hours, but Owen getting tripped up while practicing for his middle school spelling bee is one of them. He's usually at high school level with that kind of stuff. "No," I tell him. "You spelled the wrong word."

"What?" He blinks, adjusting his glasses. "I spelled the word you gave me."

"*B-A-Z-A-A-R* is, like, a marketplace. The word for *strange* is spelled *B-I-Z-A-R-R-E.*"

"Can I see?" Owen asks, holding his hand out for the flash card. I don't usually help him with anything school-related, but guilt over being such a horrible sister to Emma prompted me to offer when I got home. He was so pleasantly surprised that now I feel even worse. I know Owen wants more attention from Emma and me; it's obvious from how much hovering he does. My brother is nosy by nature and gets worse when we have friends over. He wanders into my room constantly when Jules is around, and he trails Emma to her tutoring sessions at the library sometimes. We both get annoyed with him, even though I know—and I'm sure Emma does, too—that he just wants to be part of things.

It would be so easy to invite him in, but we don't. We stay in our lanes.

"Of course!" Fresh guilt makes my voice overly sweet, and Owen darts me a confused look as he takes the card.

We're alone in the apartment, with Mom at her office manager job and Emma—not here. I've barely seen her since Mr. Santos pulled us into the Café Contigo kitchen and suggested we go home and talk. Emma agreed, but as soon as we left the

59

restaurant she took off for her friend Gillian's house and spent the night there instead. She wouldn't answer any of my texts and avoided me at school.

Which was kind of a relief, except for the part where it's only postponing the inevitable.

"Huh. I always thought it was the other way around." Owen drops the flash card onto the counter and blows a raspberry. "That's embarrassing."

I resist the urge to ruffle his hair. He's not a little kid anymore, although he still acts like one. Sometimes I feel like Owen froze in time after Dad died, perpetually nine years old no matter how much taller he gets. Owen is smarter than either Emma or me—he tests at near-genius levels, and he keeps our old laptop running and synced with everyone's phones in ways that mystify the rest of us. But he's so emotionally young that Mom has never had him skip a grade, even though he could easily do the work.

Before I can reply a key turns in our front door lock, and my heart starts to pound. It's too early for Mom to be home, which means Emma is finally making her appearance.

My sister comes through the door with her backpack slung over one shoulder and a duffel bag on the other. She's dressed in a pale-blue oxford shirt and jeans, her hair pulled back with a navy headband. Her lips are thin and chapped. She stops short when she sees me and lets both bags drop to the ground.

"Hey," I say. My voice comes out like a squeak, then disappears.

"Hi, Emma!" Owen says cheerfully. "You won't believe how bad I just messed up a spelling word." He waits expectantly, but when all she can manage is a strained smile, he adds, "You know the word *bizarre*? Like when something is really strange?"

"I do," Emma says, her eyes on me.

"I spelled it *B-A-Z-A-A-R*. Like the shopping place."

"Oh well, that's understandable," Emma says. She looks like she's making a massive effort to speak normally. "Are you going to try again?"

"Nah, I got it now," Owen says, sliding off his stool. "I'm gonna play *Bounty Wars* for a while." Neither Emma nor I reply as he shuffles down the hallway to his bedroom. As soon as the door closes with a soft click, Emma folds her arms and turns to me.

"Why?" she asks quietly.

My mouth is desert-dry. I grab for the half-full glass of warm Fanta that Owen left on the counter and drink the whole thing down before answering. "I'm sorry."

Emma's face tightens, and I can see her throat move when she swallows. "That's not a reason."

"I know. But I am. Sorry, I mean. I never meant . . . it's just, there was this party at Jules's house the night before Christmas Eve, and Derek—" She flinches when I say the name, but I keep going. "Um, it turns out that he knows Jules's cousin. They went to band camp together. They both play saxophone." I'm babbling now, and Emma just stares at me with an increasingly pinched expression. "I went to the party to hang out with Jules, and he was . . . there."

"He was there," Emma repeats in a dull monotone. "So that's your reason? Proximity?"

I open my mouth, then close it. I don't have a good answer. Not for her, and not for myself. I've been trying to figure it out for almost two months.

Because I was drunk. Sure, but that's just an excuse. Alcohol doesn't make me do stuff I wouldn't otherwise do. It just gives me a push to do things I would've done anyway.

Because you were broken up. Yeah, for three whole weeks. Emma met Derek at Model UN over the summer, and they dated for five months before he ended things. I don't know why. She never told me, just like she never talked about their dates. But I saw firsthand, in our uncomfortably close quarters, how much time she always spent getting ready. They might eventually have gotten back together if Derek and I hadn't smashed that possibility to bits.

Because I liked him. Ugh. That's the cherry on top of my bad-decision sundae. I didn't even, much.

Because I wanted to hurt you. Not consciously, but . . . sometimes I wonder if I'm edging toward an uncomfortable truth with this one. I've been trying to get Emma's attention ever since Dad died, but most of the time she just looks right through me. Maybe some twisted corner of my brain wanted to *force* her to notice me. In which case: mission accomplished.

Her eyes bore into mine. "He was my first, you know," she says. "My *only.*"

I didn't know, because she never told me. But I'd guessed as much, and I know that Derek holding that place in her life makes all of this even worse. I feel a sharp stab of regret as I say, "I'm sorry, Emma. Truly. I'd do anything to make it up to you.

And I swear to God, I didn't tell anyone, not even Jules. Derek must have—"

"Stop saying his name!" Emma's shriek is so piercing that it startles me into silence. "I don't want to hear it. I hate him, and I hate you, and I never want to talk to either one of you again as long as I live!"

Tears start spilling down her cheeks, and for a second I can't breathe. Emma almost never cries; the last time was at Dad's funeral. "Emma, can we please—"

"I mean it, Phoebe! Leave me alone!" She stalks past me into our bedroom, slamming the door so hard that it rattles on its hinges. Owen's door swings slowly open, but before he can pop his head out and start asking questions, I grab my keys and get the hell out of our apartment.

My eyes are starting to swim, and I have to blink a few times before the person waving at me in the hallway comes into focus. "Hi," Addy Prentiss calls. "I was just going to check if your mom's home—" She pauses when she gets closer, her pixie features scrunching in concern. "Are you all right?"

"Fine. Allergies," I say, wiping my eyes. Addy looks unconvinced, so I talk faster. "My mom is still at work, but she should be back in an hour or so. Do you need something before then? I could call her."

"Oh, there's no rush," Addy says. "I'm planning Ashton's bachelorette party and I wanted to run some restaurant ideas by her. I'll just text her."

She smiles, and the knot in my chest loosens a little. Addy gives me hope, because even though her life fell apart when

Simon's blog revealed her worst mistake, she put things back together—better than before. She's stronger, happier, and much closer to her sister. Addy is the queen of second chances, and right now I really need the reminder that those exist.

"What kind of places are you thinking?" I ask.

"Something low-key." Addy makes a wry face. "I'm not sure I should even use the term *bachelorette party*. That conjures a certain image, doesn't it? It's just a girls' night out, really. Someplace where I can get in."

I have a sudden impulse to invite Addy to come with me, even though I have no idea where I'm going. I was just looking for an escape hatch. But before I can come up with a good reason to hang out, she glances back at her door and says, "I'd better go. I need to order stuff for Ashton's wedding favors. Maid of honor duties are never done."

"What kind of favors?"

"Candied almonds in bags. Super original, right? But Ash and Eli both love them."

"Do you want help putting them together?" I ask. "I've become kind of an expert on wedding favors now that my mom's constantly testing them out."

Addy beams. "That would be amazing! I'll let you know when I have them." She turns back to her apartment with a little wave. "Enjoy wherever you're headed. It's beautiful out."

"I will." I stuff my keys into my pocket, the boost in mood I got from talking to Addy fading as quickly as it came. Emma's words keep looping through my brain as I take the elevator down to the lobby: *I hate him, and I hate you, and I never want to talk to either one of you again as long as I live.* Addy and Ashton might not have gotten along before last year, but I'll bet they never had *that* conversation.

When the doors spring open, I cross fake-marble floors and push through the heavy glass door into bright sunshine. I didn't grab my sunglasses when I left, so I have to shade my eyes as I walk to the park across the street. It's small, the length of a street block, and popular with hip young Bayview parents because of the toddler-sized climbing gym and nearby Whole Foods. I pass through the arched entrance, skirting around two little boys playing catch, and head for the relative quiet of a shaded corner with an empty bench.

I pull my phone from my pocket with a sinking feeling. I got dozens of texts today, but other than confirming that none were from Emma, I couldn't stand to look at them. I wish, for about the hundredth time today, that I'd realized this particular Simon copycat was the real thing.

I ignore the texts from people I don't know well, and zero in on a few from Jules:

You could have told me, you know.

I don't judge.

I mean, that was shady but we all make mistakes.

My stomach drops. Jules was great today, a shield between me and the rest of school. But I knew she was hurt that she found out about Derek at the same time as the rest of Bayview High. We usually tell each other everything, but I couldn't bring myself to tell her this.

Jules's last text to me reads, *Monica's giving me a ride home.*

You need one? I wish I'd read that before walking the two miles from school to my apartment. Except . . . Monica? Since when do she and Jules hang out? I picture Monica's gleefully phony outrage toward Sean during lunch and have a feeling that it started as soon as she saw the chance to dig up more dirt.

The next text is from a number I don't recognize and don't have programmed into Contacts. *Hi, it's Maeve. Just checking in. You okay?* Maeve's never texted me before. It's nice that she bothered, I guess, and that she stood up to Sean at lunch today, but I don't really know what to say back. I'm not okay, but there's nothing that Maeve—with her perfect parents, her perfect sister, and an ex-boyfriend who's now her best friend because even the people she dumps don't get mad at her—can do about it.

Brandon: *Come by? Parents are out ;)*

My face flames and my temper spikes. "I can't *believe* you," I growl at my screen. Except I can, because I've always known that Brandon cares less about me than he would about a new pair of football cleats. Laughing at me during lunch is totally in character, and I should have known better than to hook up with him in the first place.

Unlike Emma, I've had a lot of boyfriends. And while I haven't slept with all of them, I did whenever it felt right. Sex always felt like a positive part of my life until last December, when I slipped into Jules's laundry room with Derek. Then I ran straight from him to Brandon, despite all the gigantic red flags that should've warned me away. Maybe after I'd screwed up so badly with Derek, I didn't think I deserved any better.

But I do. One mistake shouldn't condemn anyone to a future filled with Brandon Webers. I delete Brandon's message, then his number from my phone. That gives me a half second of satisfaction until I see the next text.

Unknown: *Well that was fun, wasn't it? Who's up for . . .*

I can't see anything else in the preview. I debate deleting this one, too, without reading any further, but there's no point. If this twisted little game is talking about me, I'll hear about it eventually. So I click.

Well, that was fun, wasn't it? Who's up for another round? Then there's, like, fifty responding texts from Bayview students begging for more. Assholes. I scroll through them until I get to the last one from Unknown:

The next player will be contacted soon. Tick-tock.

And then I remember why About That was so popular for so long. Because even though I hate Unknown, and it freaks me out that they revealed a secret I thought would never get out, and the idea of another Simon Kelleher prowling around Bayview High is straight-up nauseating—I can't help being curious.

What's going to happen now?

CHAPTER SIX

Knox
Saturday, February 22

I'm about to kill my sister.

"Sorry, Kiersten, but you're in my way." With a flick of my thumb on the controller, Kiersten's *Bounty Wars* avatar crumples to the ground, blood gushing from her neck. My sister blinks, fruitlessly presses a few buttons, and turns to me with an incredulous scowl.

"Did you just *slit my throat*?" She glares at the television screen as Dax Reaper steps over her lifeless body. "I thought we were working together!" Our geriatric golden retriever, Fritz, who'd been half-asleep at Kiersten's feet, lifts his head and lets out a wheezy snort.

"We were," I say, taking one hand off my controller to scratch between Fritz's ears. "But you outlived your usefulness."

Dax agrees with me on-screen. "It's a good day for someone

to die," he growls, sheathing his knife and flexing his muscles. "Just not me."

Kiersten makes a face. "This game is vile. And I'm starving." She's sitting next to me on our basement sofa and shifts closer to nudge my knee with hers. Kiersten lives an hour away and doesn't usually spend her Saturdays with us, but her girlfriend is teaching in Japan for six weeks and she's at loose ends. "Come on, pause your ridiculously buff alter ego and get some lunch with me."

"You mean my doppelgänger," I say. "The resemblance is uncanny." I put down my controller and flex one arm, then instantly wish I hadn't. What's the opposite of *ridiculously buff*? Pathetically spindly? Kiersten and I look the most alike of any of our siblings, down to our spiky short hair, but she has much better muscle tone from rowing crew on the weekends. Usually, I try not to call attention to that fact.

Kiersten ignores my sorry excuse for a joke. "What are you in the mood to eat?" She holds up her hand before I can speak. "Please don't say fast food. I'm ancient, remember? I need a glass of wine and some vegetables." Kiersten is thirty, the oldest of my four sisters. They were all born one right after the other, and then my parents thought they were done until I showed up a decade later. My sisters treated me like a living doll for years, carrying me around so much that I didn't bother learning to walk until I was almost two.

"Wing Zone," I say instantly. It's a Bayview institution, famous for its extra-hot wings and a giant inflatable chicken on the roof. Now that Bayview's getting trendy, new people are starting to grumble that the chicken is tacky and "doesn't fit the town aesthetic." Direct quote from a letter to the editor in last week's *Bayview Blade*. So the Wing Zone owners are doubling down; on Valentine's Day, they strung a garland of blinking red neon hearts around its neck that still hasn't come off. That's some professional-level petty, and I'm all for it.

"Wing Zone?" Kiersten frowns as we head for the basement stairs, Fritz padding behind us. "Didn't I just specifically request vegetables?"

"They have celery sticks."

"Those don't count. They're ninety-nine percent water."

"And coleslaw."

"One hundred percent mayonnaise."

"The lemon-pepper wings have . . . citrus?"

"Here's a life lesson for you, Knox. Fake fruit flavoring is not, and never will be, a vegetable." Kiersten looks back at me as she opens the basement door, and I give her the kind of hopeful, ingratiating smile that works on absolutely nobody except my sisters. "Ugh, fine," she groans. "But you owe me."

"Sure," I say. She's never going to collect, though. That's the upside of having sisters who think they're your mom.

Our basement opens into the kitchen, and when we get upstairs my dad's sitting at the table, hunched over some paperwork. He looks a lot more like Dax Reaper than I do. Now that he owns his own company Dad doesn't necessarily *have* to do hands-on construction work, but he still does, which makes him the most in-shape guy in his fifties I know. He glances up, and his eyes flick past me—the boring kid who still lives at home—and twinkle at Kiersten.

"Didn't know you were still here," he says. Fritz, who's always liked my alpha male father better than anybody, leans adoringly against his chair.

She sighs. "Knox roped me into video game hell."

Dad frowns, because he thinks video games are a waste of time. As opposed to actual sportsball games, which he'd love for me to play. But he just waves the folder he's holding at me and says, "I'll leave this for you to take to work on Monday."

"What is it?" I ask.

"Letter of intent. We're gonna hire a couple of the D'Agostino exonerees," he says. "I got a packet in the mail the other day from Until Proven."

Great, except he didn't get it in the mail. I brought it home and put it on his desk. With a *note*. Which, I guess, he never even noticed.

Kiersten beams. "Fantastic, Dad! Way to set an example for local businesses."

My father and Kiersten are a strangely amicable pair. He's this conservative, macho, old-school guy who somehow gets along better with my bleeding-heart lesbian sister than he does with anyone else. Maybe because they're both athletic, take-charge, self-starter types. "Well, it's worked out well so far," Dad says, pushing the folder to one corner of the table. "Nate's a good worker. And you know, he got A's in both the classes we covered last semester. Kid's a lot brighter than he gets credit for."

I mean, he gets plenty of credit in this house. But okay.

"It's so great that you're doing that for him," Kiersten says, and the genuine warmth in her tone makes me feel like a prick. I don't have anything against Nate, but I can't shake the feeling that he's the son my father *wishes* he had. I grab my sweatshirt from the chair where I dropped it earlier, pulling it on as Kiersten adds, "Want to come to lunch, Dad? We're getting wings." She only grimaces a little on the last word.

"No thanks. I need to get back to work and finish up our proposal for the mall parking garage. It's been sitting empty for much too long and frankly, it's both an eyesore and a hazard." He frowns and turns back to me. "One of my guys said he heard a rumor that kids have been cutting through the site. You seen anything like that, Knox?"

"What? No. Definitely not!" I practically yell it, way too loudly and emphatically. God, my father makes me nervous. His frown deepens, and Kiersten tugs on my arm.

"All right, we're off. See you later!" We're through the front door and halfway down the driveway before she speaks again. "Work on your poker face, Knox," she mutters, pulling a set of keys out of her bag and aiming them at her silver Civic. "And stop taking shortcuts through abandoned construction sites."

It's a sunny but cool Saturday. I pull the hood of my sweatshirt up as I slide into the passenger seat. "It was just a couple times."

"Still," Kiersten says, climbing in beside me. "It's my duty as your significantly older sibling to remind you how Not Safe that is. Consider yourself warned." She turns the motor, and we both wince as music blasts through the car at top volume. I always forget how loudly Kiersten plays her radio when she drives alone. "Sorry," she says, turning it down. She glances into the rearview mirror and starts to back out of our driveway. "So, I barely got to talk to you during that creepy bounty hunter game. It's still bullshit that you killed me, by the way. Not over it. But what's new with you? How's the job, how's the play, how's school?"

"It's all good. Well, pretty good."

She taps the blinker and prepares to turn out of our road. "Why only pretty good?"

I'm not sure where to start. But I don't have to, because Kiersten's phone rings. "Hang on," she says, her foot still on the brake as she roots through her bag. "It's Katie," she says, handing me the phone. "Put her on speaker, would you?" I do, and Kiersten calls, "Hey, Katie. I'm in the car with Knox. What's up?"

My second-oldest sister's voice, tinny from the speaker, starts ranting about something that's pink but was supposed to be peach. Or maybe it's the other way around. "Katie, stop," Kiersten says, inching onto the main road that will take us to Bayview Center. "I can't even understand you. Is this about . . . flowers? Okay, Bridezilla, let's take it down a few notches."

I tune them out, unlocking my own phone with a prickle of anticipation. Like everybody else at Bayview High this weekend, I've been waiting for a text from Unknown. But there's been nothing. I'm guessing whoever their target was decided to take the Dare, and now I don't know what to expect. It's new territory. Simon never bothered with that kind of gamesmanship.

Is it wrong that I'm kind of . . . I don't know, *interested*? I shouldn't be, after what happened to Phoebe. Not to mention last year's months-long shit show. But there's a video game quality to all this that has me weirdly hooked. Like, I could just

73

block texts from Unknown and be done with it, but I don't. Hardly anyone at Bayview High has, as far as I can tell. What did Lucy Chen call us at lunch the other day? *A high-risk population.* Conditioned to respond to the right kind of prompt like overstimulated lab rats.

Or lemmings. That was Simon's preferred term.

A text from Maeve pops up while I'm scrolling. *Hey, a bunch of us are getting together Friday when Bronwyn's in town. You in?*

Maybe, I reply. *Is it spring break?*

No, she's just here for the weekend. Ashton's bachelorette party. Also, we're seeing Into the Woods. She adds the grimacing emoji, and I send three of them back. I'm already sick of that play, and we're still weeks away from performing it. My singing range is microscopic, but I ended up with a lead role anyway because I'm one of the only guys in drama club. Now my throat hurts constantly from all the straining, plus rehearsals are messing with my Until Proven work schedule.

It's weird, and kind of uncomfortable, to realize you might've started outgrowing a thing that used to almost be your whole life. Especially if you're not sure what else to do with yourself. It's not like I'm tearing it up at school, or work. My biggest contribution at Until Proven so far is seconding Sandeep's suggestions for the conference room names. But I like it there. I'd intern more hours if I had the time.

We're in downtown Bayview before Katie finally hangs up. Kiersten shoots me an apologetic glance as she pulls into a parking lot across the street from Wing Zone. "Sorry we got interrupted by a quote, floral emergency, unquote. Which is not a thing. Who've you been texting while I was ignoring you?"

"Maeve," I say. The battery on my phone is almost dead, so I shut it off and put it back into my pocket.

"Ah, Maeve." Kiersten sighs nostalgically. "The one that got away." She pulls into a spot and cuts the engine. "From me, I mean. I was shipping you two hard. I had your couple name picked out and everything. Did I ever tell you that? It was Knaeve." I groan as I open my door. "But you seem fine. *Are* you fine? Do you want to talk about it?"

She always asks that, and I never accept. "Of course I'm fine. We broke up a long time ago."

We exit the car and head for an opening in the parking lot gate. "I know, I know," Kiersten says. "I just don't understand *why.* You guys were perfect for each other!"

It's times like these that, as great as my sisters are, I kind of wish I had an older brother. Or a close guy friend who liked girls. Maeve and I weren't perfect, but that's not a conversation I know how to open up with Kiersten. I don't know how to open it up with anyone. "We're better as friends," I say.

"Well, I think it's great that . . . Huh." Kiersten stops so suddenly that I almost bump into her. "What's with the crowd? Is it always this busy on a Saturday?"

We're within sight of the restaurant, and she's right—the sidewalk is packed. "No, never," I say, and a guy in front of me turns at my voice. For a second, I don't recognize him, because I've never seen him outside of school. But there's no mistaking Matthias Schroeder, even out of context. He looks like a scarecrow: tall and thin with baggy clothes, wispy blond hair, and strangely dark eyes. I find myself peering at them too closely, wondering if they're real or contact lenses. "Hi, Knox," he says tonelessly. "It's the chicken."

"Huh?" I ask. Is he speaking in code? Am I supposed to reply *The crow flies at midnight* or something? Kiersten waits expectantly, like I'm about to introduce her, but I don't know what to say. *This is Matthias. He got suspended for copycatting Simon Kelleher last fall. We've never spoken before. Awkward, right?*

Matthias points upward with one long, pale finger. I follow his gaze to Wing Zone's roof, and then I can't believe I didn't notice it sooner. The inflatable chicken's red heart necklace is finally gone—and so is its head. Well, it's probably still there, but somebody's stuck what looks like the head of the Bayview Wildcat mascot costume onto its neck. Now the whole thing has turned into some kind of freaky oversized cat-chicken, and I can't look away. I snort but choke back a full-on laugh when I catch Kiersten's exasperated expression.

"Oh, for God's sake," she mutters. "Why would someone do that?"

"Yuppie revenge?" I ask, but then immediately reject the idea. The kind of people who complain about an inflatable chicken lowering their real estate values aren't going to be any happier about this.

"You don't get it?" Matthias asks. He looks hard at me, and God, that kid is weird. I can practically hear Maeve saying *He's just lonely,* which might be true, but it's *also* true that he's weird. Sometimes things are related, is my point.

My stomach growls. It knows we're in close proximity to wings and it's not happy about the delay. "Get what?" I ask impatiently.

"Always take the Dare, right?" Matthias says. He gives me this stiff little salute and turns on his heel, slipping through the crowd.

Kiersten looks mystified. "What's his deal?"

"Beats me," I say distractedly, pulling out my phone to turn it back on. There are two texts waiting from Unknown:

DARE: Put the Bayview Wildcat mascot's head onto the Wing Zone chicken.

STATUS: Achieved by Sean Murdock. Congratulations, Sean. Nice work.

The second text comes with a photo of the Wildcat-slash-chicken. Up close, like it was taken by somebody standing right next to it. Everything around it is dark, which makes me think the head-swapping happened last night, but attention didn't reach critical mass till the Wing Zone lunchtime crowd appeared.

More texts start piling up, from Bayview High kids responding to Unknown.

Nailed it!!!

Bahahaha I can't stop laughing

Epic af Sean

Lmaooooooo

Disappointment claws at my gut. As soon as I moved to Bayview in seventh grade, Sean—along with Brandon Weber— made my life hell with hilarious games like *How Many of Knox's Books Can We Fit into One Toilet?* Even now, Sean likes to ask me how my "fag hag" sister is doing, because he's a Neander-thal who doesn't know what his crap insults mean. If there's anyone at Bayview I would've liked to see taken down a peg by this game, it's him. But all this is going to do is swell Sean's meathead even bigger.

There are no consequences for guys like him and Brandon. Ever.

"Your phone is going nuts," Kiersten says. "What are your friends talking about?"

I turn it off and shove it into my pocket, wishing I could shut down all my useless rage that easily. "It's just a stupid group text getting out of control," I say. "They're not my friends."

And neither is Unknown. Which I should've known from the start, obviously, but now I *really* know it.

CHAPTER SEVEN

Maeve
Thursday, February 27

I can't stop grinning at Bronwyn. "It's so weird that you're here."

"I was here less than two months ago," she reminds me.

"You look different," I say, even though she doesn't. I mean, the side braid is a cute style I haven't seen before, but other than that she hasn't changed a bit. She's even wearing her favorite ancient cashmere sweater, so old that she has to roll up its sleeves to hide how frayed the cuffs are. It's the rest of the world that seems brighter when she's around, I guess. Even the chalk-scrawled specials on Café Contigo's blackboard wall look extra vibrant. "You need to come home for grad school, okay? This distance thing isn't working for me."

"Me either," Bronwyn sighs. "Turns out I'm a California girl at heart. Who knew?" She dunks a spoon into her latte to redistribute the foam in a thin layer. "But you might not even be here then if you go to school in Hawaii."

"Bronwyn, come on. We both know I'm not going to the University of Hawaii," I say, chasing my last bite of alfajore with a sip of water. My voice is light, casual. The kind of tone that says *I won't go there because I'm not an island person* and not *I won't go there because I had another nosebleed this morning.* It was minor, though. Stopped within a few minutes. I don't have any joint pain, fever, or weird bruises, so it's fine.

Everything's fine.

Bronwyn puts down her spoon and folds her hands, giving me one of her serious looks. "If you could be anywhere in five years, doing anything at all, what would you pick?"

Nope. We are absolutely not discussing this. If I start talking five years in the future with my sister, all my careful compart-mentalizing will vanish and I'll crack open like an egg. Spoiling her visit, her semester, and a million other things. "You can't analyze my future right now," I say, grabbing another cookie. "It's bad luck."

"What?" Bronwyn's brow creases. "Why?"

I point to the clock on the wall, which has been reading ten o'clock since the batteries died a week ago. "Because that's broken. Time is literally standing still."

"Oh my God, Maeve." Bronwyn rolls her eyes. "That's not even an actual superstition. That's just something you and Ita made up. She says hi, by the way." Now that Bronwyn lives in Connecticut, she gets to see our grandparents regularly. Our grandfather, Ito, is still a visiting lecturer at Yale. "Also that you're perfect and her favorite."

80

"She did not say that."

"It was implied. It's *always* implied. Sunday dinners with Ito and Ita are basically Maeve Appreciation Night." Bronwyn sips her coffee, suddenly looking pensive. "So . . . if today is already bad luck, does that mean we can talk about me and Nate maybe being broken up for good this time?"

"Bronwyn. What is *with* you guys?" I shake my head as her mouth droops. "Why can't you figure this out? Your entire relationship started from talking on the phone, for crying out loud! Just do that for like, three months at a time and you'll be fine."

"I don't know," she says unhappily. She takes off her glasses and rubs her eyes. I brought her here straight from the airport, and she's obviously a little jet-lagged after her cross-country flight. She's missing some classes to be here, which Dad isn't wild about, but Mom can't resist bringing Bronwyn home for an extra day when she visits. "We're just never in sync anymore," she says. "When I'm feeling good about things, he's feeling like he's *holding me back*." She puts up finger quotes with a grimace. "When he starts talking about what we should do over spring break, I wonder if I made a mistake not signing up for that volunteer trip I was interested in. Then I think about him living in that house with all those roommates, and girls in and out all the time, and I get so jealous that it makes me irrational. Which is *not* like me."

"No, it's not," I agree. "Plus, you live in a dorm, so. Same thing."

"I know," she sighs. "It's just so much harder than I thought it would be. Everything I do or say feels wrong with him."

I don't bother asking if she still loves Nate. I know she does. "You're overthinking it," I tell her, and she snorts out a laugh.

"Oh, you *think*? That'd be a first." Her phone vibrates on the table, and she makes a face at it. "Is it four already? Evan's outside."

"What? Evan *Neiman*?" My voice ticks up on the last name. "What's he doing here?"

"Giving me a ride to Yumiko's," Bronwyn says, draining the last of her latte. "She's having a bunch of people from our old Mathlete team over to watch something Avengers-related. Don't ask me what. You know I don't care." She stuffs her phone in her bag and peers into its depths. "Ugh, did I forget my prescription sunglasses? I'm so bad at keeping track of those. I hardly ever need them in Connecticut."

"Why is Evan taking you? Isn't he at Caltech?"

Bronwyn is still rooting around in her bag. "Yeah, but he and Yumiko hang out sometimes. And he was at Yale last month for a Debate Club Smackdown, so . . . aha! Here they are." I clear my throat loudly and she finally glances up, her bright blue glasses case in one hand. "Why are you looking at me like that?"

"*Evan?*"

She shifts in her chair. "It's not a big deal."

"You getting a ride from your ex, after you just finished angsting about how you can't make things work with your *other* ex, is not a big deal?" I fold my arms. For someone so smart, my sister can be ridiculously naïve. "Come on. I spent half my life in a cancer ward and even I know that's a bad idea."

"Evan and I are just friends who happened to date a long time ago. Like you and Knox."

"No, it's not at all like me and Knox. That was mutual. You dumped Evan for Nate and Evan moped about it for the rest of senior year. He wrote *poetry*. Have you forgotten 'Kilns of Despair'? Because I have not. And now he's driving two and a half hours on a Thursday to watch *Iron Man* with you?"

"I don't think it's *Iron Man*," Bronwyn says doubtfully.

"Focus, Bronwyn. That's not the point. Evan is carrying a torch, and everybody knows it except you." I brandish the saltshaker at her like it's covered in flames, but I end up spilling it, and then I have to do the whole over-the-shoulder ritual. Bronwyn takes advantage of my distraction to get to her feet and corral me in a one-armed hug. She's starting to look worried, but her ride is outside, and I can practically see the wheels turning in her head as she calculates the awkwardness quotient of backing out now. Too high.

"I have to go. See you at home," she says. "I'll be back before dinner." She loops her messenger bag over one shoulder and heads for the door.

"Make good choices," I call after her.

I glance around the café as the door shuts behind her. Phoebe is working today, her brow knitted in concentration as she jots down an order from two beanie-wearing hipsters. Ever since Sean Murdock's infuriating Wing Zone triumph, people have been acting like Bayview High Truth or Dare is a hilarious new game. A text went out yesterday from Unknown—*The next player has been contacted. Tick-tock*—and now everyone is taking bets on who it is and what they'll choose. Given how the first two rounds have gone, odds favor the Dare.

It's like everyone at Bayview High has forgotten that Simon was a real person who ended up suffering more than anyone from the way he used gossip as a weapon. But all you have to do is look at Phoebe's sad eyes and hollow cheeks to know there's nothing funny about any of this.

I pull my laptop out of my bag and open the new About That website, where Sean's Wing Zone chicken photo is prominently displayed. There's a comment section below, and when people aren't congratulating Sean, they're speculating about the identity of Unknown.

It's Janae Vargas, guys. Finishing what Simon started. I don't buy that one for a second. Simon's former best friend couldn't get out of Bayview fast enough when she graduated. She goes to college in Seattle now, and I don't think she's been back once.

Madman Matthias Schroeder, obvs.

Simon himself. He's not dead, he just wanted us to think he is.

I open another browser tab and type AnarchiSK—Simon's old user name—into the search bar. I used to Google that name all the time, back when I was trying to figure out who might have it in for Simon. There are thousands of results, mostly from old news articles, so I narrow the search to the past twenty-four hours. One link remains, to a Reddit subforum with the words *Vengeance Is Mine* in the URL.

The skin on the back of my neck starts to prickle. Simon used to post his revenge rants on a forum called Vengeance Is

Mine, but that was on 4chan. I should know; I spent hours reading through them before I sent a link to the *Mikhail Powers Investigates* show. Mikhail ran a spotlight series on Simon's death, and as soon as he covered the revenge forum it got overrun with fake posts and rubberneckers. Eventually, the whole thing shut down.

At least, that's what I thought. In the half second before I click the link, the words *He's not dead, he just wanted us to think he is* don't seem as far-fetched as they should.

But the page is nearly blank except for a handful of posts:

My teacher needs to btfo or I will kill him for real.—Jellyfish

I almost pounded his face in today lol. —Jellyfish

Well now you can't kill him. What did AnarchiSK always tell us? "Don't be so obvious."—Darkestmind

Fuck that guy. He got caught.—Jellyfish

The café door opens and Luis steps inside, wearing a faded San Diego City College T-shirt and a backward baseball cap over his dark hair. He spots me and does one of those chin-jut things he and Cooper are always doing—jock-speak for *Yeah, I see you, but I'm too cool to actually wave.* Then, to my surprise, he shifts course and heads my way, dropping into Bronwyn's recently vacated seat. "What's up, Maeve?"

My white blood cell count, probably. God, I'm fun.

"Not much," I say, pushing my laptop to one side. "You coming from class?"

"Yup. Accounting." Luis makes a wry face. "Not my favorite. But we can't spend every day in the kitchen. Unfortunately." Luis is getting a hospitality degree so he can run his own restaurant one day, which is the kind of thing I never would have guessed when he was a big man on campus at Bayview.

"You just missed Bronwyn," I say, because I assume that's why he stopped at my table. The two of them aren't close, exactly, but they hang out occasionally because of Cooper. "She's at Yumiko's if you . . ." And then I trail off, because the Venn diagram of Luis's and Bronwyn's social overlap starts and ends with Cooper. I'm pretty sure Luis isn't planning to attend the Bayview Mathlete movie night.

"Cool." Luis flashes a smile and stretches his legs out under the table. I'm so used to Knox sitting with me that Luis's presence is a little disconcerting. He takes up more space, both physically and . . . confidence-wise, I guess. Knox always looks as though he's not sure he's supposed to be wherever he is. Luis sprawls out like he owns the place. Well, in this particular case his parents do, so maybe that's part of it. But still. There's an ease to him that, I think, comes from being athletic and popular his entire life. Luis has spent years at the center of one team or another. He's always belonged. "I had a question for you, actually."

I can feel my face getting red, and cup my chin in both hands to hide it. I wish I weren't constantly attracted to the kind of guys who either ignore me or treat me like their little sister, but here we are. I have no defense against the cute jock demographic. "Oh?"

"Do you live here now?" he asks.

I blink, not sure if I'm disappointed or caught off guard. Probably both. "What?"

"You're in this restaurant more than I am, and I get paid for it."

His dark eyes twinkle, and my stomach drops. Oh God. Does he think I'm here for *him*? I mean, yes, catching sight of Luis in one of those well-fitting T-shirts he always wears is typically a highlight of my day, but I didn't think I was being obvious about it.

I narrow my eyes at him and aim for a detached tone. "Your customer appreciation skills need work."

Luis grins. "It's not that. I'm just wondering if you're familiar with this thing called *outside*? It has sun and fresh air, or so I've heard."

"Pure rumor and speculation," I say. "Doesn't exist. Besides, I'm doing my part for the Bayview economy. Supporting local business." Then I drink the rest of my water to force myself to shut up. This is the longest conversation I've ever had alone with Luis, and I'm working so hard at playing it cool that I barely know what I'm saying.

"That would be a better argument if you ever got anything besides coffee," Luis points out, and I laugh in spite of myself.

"I see those accounting classes are paying off," I say. He laughs too, and I finally relax enough that my face returns to a normal temperature. "Do you think you'll take over from your parents someday? Run Café Contigo, I mean?"

"Probably not," Luis says. "This is their place, you know? I want something of my own. Plus I'm more interested in the fine dining scene. Pa thinks I'm full of it, though." He mimics his dad's deep tone. "Tienes el ego por las nubes, Luis."

I smile. Luis's ego *is* in the clouds, but at least he knows it. "He must be happy you're interested in the family business, though."

"I think so," Luis says. "Especially since Manny can't make toast without burning it." Luis's older brother, the one named after their dad, has always been more into cars than kitchens. But he's been working at the restaurant since he got laid off from an auto repair shop. "He's helping out tomorrow night and Pa is all, *Please don't touch anything. Just wash dishes.*" Luis takes his cap off, runs a hand through his hair, and puts it back on. "You'll be here, right? I think Cooper might make it after all."

"He will?" I ask, genuinely happy. All of Bronwyn's and Addy's friends are getting together at Café Contigo before Ashton's bachelorette party tomorrow night, but last I'd heard Cooper's schedule was still up in the air.

"Yup. We're a big enough crowd now that Pa's giving us the back room." Luis glances at a door frame in the rear of the restaurant, where hanging beads separate a small private dining area. "Hope it doesn't get too busy once people hear Cooper's gonna be around. The actual table only fits, like, ten." He starts counting on his fingers. "You, me, Coop, Kris, Addy, Bronwyn, Nate, Keely . . . who else? Is your boyfriend coming?"

"My what? You mean Knox?" I blink when Luis nods. "He's not my boyfriend. We broke up ages ago."

"Really?" Luis's eyebrows shoot up. God, when you graduate you just fall right out of the gossip loop, apparently. "But he's always here with you."

"Yeah, we're still friends. We're not going out anymore, though."

"Huh," Luis says. His eyes flick over me, and my cheeks heat again. "Interesting."

"Luis!" Mr. Santos pokes his head out of the kitchen. He's much shorter and rounder than any of his sons, even the pre-teen ones. They all get their height from their mom. "Are you working or flirting today?"

I duck my head and pull my laptop back in front of me, hoping that I look busy instead of deflated. I was having such a good time talking to Luis that I almost forgot: this is standard operating procedure for him. He's great at turning on the charm, which is why half of Café Contigo's customer base is made up of girls between the ages of fourteen and twenty.

Luis shrugs as he gets to his feet. "I'm multitasking, Pa."

Mr. Santos's eyes shift toward me, his eyebrows pulled together in exaggerated concern. "Is he bothering you, mija? Say the word and I'll throw him out."

I force a smile. "He's just doing his job."

Luis pauses at the edge of the table, shooting me a look I can't decipher. "You want anything? Coffee or . . . coffee?"

"I'm good, thanks," I say. My smile is more of a grimace now, so I let it drop.

"I'll bring you some cookies," he says over his shoulder as he heads for the kitchen.

Phoebe's passing by just then, and she pauses, lowering her empty tray to watch Luis's retreating back. "Why did that sound dirty?" she asks wonderingly. She kicks at my foot and lowers her voice. "He's so cute. You should make that happen."

"In my dreams," I mutter, returning my eyes to my computer screen. Then I let out a startled yelp of pain when Phoebe kicks me again. Harder. "Ow! What was that for?"

"For being dense," she says, dropping into the chair across from me. "He's into you."

"Are you kidding?" I gesture toward the kitchen door as though Luis were standing there, even though he's not. "I mean, look at him."

"Look at *you*," Phoebe says. "Please don't tell me you're one of those pretty girls who insists she's not pretty. That's tired. You're hot, own it. And you like him, right? You should let him know instead of getting all weird and frowny when he flirts with you."

"I'm not weird and frowny!" I protest. Phoebe just tilts her head, slowly twisting a coppery curl around one finger until I add, "Most of the time. Besides, Luis flirts with everyone. It doesn't mean anything."

Phoebe shrugs. "That's not my impression. And I'm pretty good at reading guys." It's a simple statement of fact, but as soon as she says it the whole mess about her and Emma's boyfriend pops into my head, and I can't keep my eyes from widening reflexively. Phoebe bites her lip and looks away. "Although I realize I have zero credibility in that department at the moment, so I'll let you get back to—whatever," she says, pushing her chair away from the table.

My hand is on her wrist before I realize what I'm doing. "No, wait. Don't go. I'm sorry," I say quickly. "I didn't mean to act judgey but . . . apparently I'm weird and frowny in lots of situations." She almost smiles, so I feel brave enough to add, "Look, I know what all this must be like for you. I went through it with Bronwyn last year, so . . . I'm a good listener if you ever want to talk sometime. Or even, you know, just hang out and set our phones on fire."

I'm relieved when Phoebe laughs. I don't have a lot of practice reaching out to people who haven't sought me out first, and I half expected her to edge away and never talk to me again. "I might take you up on that," she says. Then her face falls, and she plucks at a stray thread on her apron. "Emma's so mad at me. I keep trying to apologize, but she won't listen."

"I'm sorry," I say. "Maybe you just need to give her a little more time." Phoebe nods gloomily, and I add, "I hope she's not mad at *just* you. I mean, you weren't the only person involved. Her ex was, too."

Phoebe makes a face. "I don't know if they've even talked since she found out. I don't dare ask." She cups her chin in one hand and gazes thoughtfully at the brightly colored mosaic tiles mounted on the wall next to us. "I wish I knew how the whole thing got out in the first place. I mean, obviously Derek must've told someone, because I sure as hell didn't. But he lives in Laguna. He doesn't know anybody here."

"How'd you run into him, then? After he and Emma broke up, I mean."

"Christmas party at Jules's house," Phoebe says. I raise my eyebrows, and she adds, "But Jules doesn't know him. Derek was there with her cousin. I don't think they even met that night."

"Okay," I say, filing that nugget of information away for future reference. If there's one thing last year taught me, it's to be wary of coincidences. "Well, here's something that might interest you. Hang on a sec." My laptop screen has gone dark, so I hit a key to bring the Reddit forum back. "I was Googling some stuff related to Simon and last year, and . . ." I refresh the page so it'll display any newer posts, then trail off in confusion. The short thread I was just looking at has disappeared, and there's nothing left on my screen except the forum heading. "Wait. What happened?"

"What?" Phoebe asks, moving her chair so she can peer at my laptop. "Vengeance Is Mine? Why does that sound familiar?"

"It's the name of the revenge forum Simon Kelleher used to post on last year, except this one's in a different location." I frown, tapping a finger on my chin. "So weird. I was going to show you a thread that mentioned Simon, but it's gone."

"Did you try refreshing?" Phoebe leans across from me to hit the arrow button next to the search bar.

"Yeah, that's what made it disappear in the first place. It was—"

"Is that it?" Phoebe interrupts when three new posts pop up.

"No," I say, scanning the short lines. "Those are new."

True, Jellyfish. He did get caught.
But his inspiration lives on in Bayview.
And he'd fucking love the game I'm playing
right now.—Darkestmind.

CHAPTER EIGHT

Phoebe
Friday, February 28

I send the texts to Jules rapid fire on Friday afternoon, one after the other.

You've been busy huh?
Feel like doing something tonight?
I have to work but only till 8.
Want to meet me there?

Then I sit on the edge of my bed, gazing around the room I share with Emma. It's smaller than the bedroom I had to myself in our old house, and crammed with twice as much stuff. Mom got a worker's comp settlement from Dad's company when he died, and while she never talked about how much it was, I thought it was *enough*. Enough that she wouldn't have to go back to work unless she wanted to, and we could stay where we were.

Now Mom works at an office manager job she hates,

and we live here. When we moved last summer, she told us that downsizing to an apartment was about convenience, not money. But nobody except Owen believed her.

I get up and wander to Emma's side of the room, which is pristine compared to mine. Her bed is neatly made, every wrinkle smoothed away from the scalloped white coverlet. There's nothing on her desk except the laptop we share, a coffee mug filled with colored pencils, and a notebook with a Monet print on the cover. I have a sudden urge to open the notebook and scrawl a message in the most apologetic color I can find. Pale pink, maybe. *Emma, I miss you. I've been missing you for years. Just tell me how to make this up to you and I'll do it.*

Emma is at the library, and even though we're barely speaking the emptiness of our room almost tempts me to knock on Owen's door and offer to play *Bounty Wars.* I'm saved by the chime of my phone and glance down in surprise to a return text from Jules. She's been cool toward me ever since the Derek reveal, and I wasn't expecting a quick response.

Is that thing tonight? With Cooper Clay and everybody?

Yeah, around 6. It'll be packed, though You probably want to avoid that scene and just come at 8 when I get off.

The pre–Ashton's bachelorette party get-together at Café Contigo started spiraling out of control once people heard Cooper might be there. Dozens of Bayview students who don't even know him are saying they're going now, and I'm not sure the Santoses are ready for that kind of crowd.

Will Nate be there?

I sigh as I text back, *Probably.* Guess I'll be seeing her a lot earlier than eight o'clock.

My phone rings, startling me. *Jules wants to FaceTime.* I hit Accept and her face fills the screen, grinning expectantly. "Heyyy," she says, sounding like her usual self. "Do you have time for a wardrobe consult?"

"Of course."

"Which of these says, *I'm way more fun than your ex* and *I live right here?* This . . ." Jules holds up a plunging sequined tank top and waves it for a few seconds, then drops it and picks up a black ruffled halter. "Or this?"

Ugh. I don't want to encourage Jules in her Nate Macauley obsession. Even if Bronwyn weren't still in the picture, I'm pretty sure he and Jules would be a terrible pairing. Jules likes to be joined at the hip with whoever she dates, and I don't think that's Nate's style at all. "They're both gorgeous," I say. Jules pouts, so that's obviously the wrong answer. "But if I had to choose, the black." It's a little less revealing, anyway.

"All right, the black it is," she says breezily. "I'm going to watch some makeup videos and try to nail a smoky eye. See you tonight!" She waves and disconnects.

I toss my phone onto my rumpled comforter—it's balled up in the middle of my bed because I'm such a restless sleeper, especially lately—and grab an elastic from my end table. I pull my hair into a ponytail as I stand and cross to the bedroom door. When I yank it open, Owen almost tumbles inside.

"Owen!" I pull my ponytail tighter and narrow my eyes at him. "Were you eavesdropping?" Rhetorical question; he totally was. The longer my cold war with Emma goes on, the worse of a snoop Owen becomes. As though he knows something isn't right, and he's trying to figure out what it is.

"No," Owen says unconvincingly. "I was just . . ." A loud knock sounds on the front door, and he gets a total *saved by the bell* look on his face. "Going to tell you that someone's at the door."

"*Sure* you were," I say, and then I frown when the knock sounds again. "Weird. I didn't hear the intercom." I'm assuming it's some kind of delivery, but normally we have to buzz people through the front door before they can come upstairs. "Did you?"

"No," Owen says. "Are you going to answer it?"

"Let me see who it is." I cross the living room and press one eye against the peephole. The face on the other side is distorted, but still irritatingly familiar. "Ugh. You have got to be kidding me."

Owen hovers beside me. "Who is it?"

"Go to your room, okay?" He doesn't move, and I give him a gentle shove. "Just for a few minutes, and then I'll come play *Bounty Wars* with you."

Owen grins. "All right!" He scoots away, and I wait to hear the click of his bedroom door before undoing the deadbolt.

The door swings open to reveal Brandon Weber in the hallway, a lazy smirk on his face. "Took you long enough," he says, stepping inside and shutting the door behind him.

I cross my arms tightly over my chest, suddenly all too aware of the fact that I took my bra off when I got home from school. "What are you doing here? Who let you into the building?"

"Some grandma was coming out when I got here." Of course. That's how the world works when you're Brandon Weber; doors just open up whenever you want them to. He looms over me, way too close, and I step back as he asks, "How come you're not answering my texts?"

"Are you for real?" I scan his pretty, pouty face for a hint of comprehension, but there's nothing. "You *laughed* at me, Brandon. Sean was being a total creep, and you joined right in."

"Oh come on. It was a joke. Can't you take a joke?" He moves closer again, putting one hand on my waist. His fingers dig into my thin T-shirt, and his lips curl into a smug smile. "I thought you liked to have fun."

I push him away, anger buzzing through my veins. I've been the bad guy all week: the one who betrayed her sister and deserves whatever she gets in return. It's almost a relief to be mad at someone besides myself for a change. "Don't touch me," I snap. "We're done."

"You don't mean that." He's still smiling, clueless as ever. He thinks this is a game, one where he makes all the rules and I'm lucky just to get a chance at playing. "I miss you. Wanna see how much?" He tries to move my hand toward his crotch, and I yank it back.

"Knock it off. I'm not interested."

His face darkens as he pulls me toward him again, harder than before. "Don't be a tease."

For the first time since he arrived, I feel a spark of apprehension. I've always liked how strong Brandon is, but right now—I don't. I'm still angry, though, and use that adrenaline to wrench out of his grasp. "Really? Let me see if I have this straight. If I do what you want, I'm a slut. If I don't do what you want, I'm a tease. What *I* want doesn't count, but you're the big man at Bayview no matter what. Does that about sum it up?"

Brandon snorts. "What are you, some kind of feminazi now?"

I bite back another angry retort. There's no point. "Just leave, Brandon."

Instead, he lunges forward and mashes his lips against mine, sending a wave of horrified shock through my entire body. My hands are up in an instant and I press against his chest with all my strength, but his arms snake around my waist, anchoring me in place. I twist my head and almost spit to get the taste of him out of my mouth. "Stop it! I said no!" My voice comes out as a low hiss because somehow, even though my heart is about to pound out of my chest, I'm still worried about scaring Owen.

Brandon doesn't listen. His hands and his mouth are everywhere, and I don't know how to make him stop. I've never felt so small, in every possible way.

He forces another kiss on me, moving his body just enough that I can get an arm free. I keep my lips pressed tightly together against his probing tongue, reaching up to grab a fistful of his hair. I pull his head backward, then let go and slap him as hard as I can across the face. He lets out a surprised grunt of pain and loosens his grip. I twist away and shove him with enough force to make him stumble backward. "Get *out*!" This time I scream, the words scraping raw and rough across my dry throat.

Brandon stares at me, slack-jawed with shock, my handprint seared red across his pale cheek. His mouth twists and I take a step back, poised to run I don't even know where, when Owen's door bursts open. "Phoebe?" He pokes his head around the door frame, eyes wide. "What's going on?"

"Nothing," I say, trying to keep my voice steady. "Brandon was just leaving."

Brandon barks out a bitter laugh, his eyes flicking from me to Owen. "What's up, little man?" he says, his mouth twisted in a sneer. "Nothing to see here. Just your sister being a whore. But I guess your family knows all about that, right? Especially Emma." I inhale sharply and clench my fist, my sore palm stinging with an almost overwhelming urge to hit him again. Brandon's eyes gleam, his parting shot landed. He opens the door and lifts one hand in a jaunty wave. "See you around, Phoebe." Then he shoves his hands into his pockets and backs down the hallway, his eyes never leaving my face.

I slam the door shut and click the deadbolt. After that I can't seem to move, my hand frozen on the lock. "Phoebe?" Owen asks, his voice small.

My forehead presses against the closed door. I can't. I can*not* have this conversation with my little brother. "Go back to your room."

"Are you—"

"Go back to your room, Owen. *Please.*" I hear footsteps and a soft click. I wait another beat until I let the tears fall.

None of this would be happening if Dad were here. I know it, down to my core, that I'd be a better, smarter, stronger person if he hadn't died. I remember that day like it was yesterday: me and Emma both home sick with the flu, curled on opposite sides of the couch in our old house, covered in blankets. Mom was in the kitchen getting us Popsicles when her phone rang. I heard her harried *Hello*—we were starting to wear her out at that point—and then she went silent. "Is it serious?" she finally asked, in a voice I'd never heard before.

She appeared in the doorway a few minutes later, clutching her phone in one hand and a half-melted Popsicle in the other. "I have to leave you for a little while," she said in that same robotic tone. Purple liquid dripped down one arm. "There's been an accident."

A horrible, impossible, nightmare of a freak accident. My dad used to work as a supervisor at a granite manufacturing plant in Eastland, directing workers as they maneuvered giant slabs of stone to be cut into countertops. A forklift carrying one jammed at exactly the wrong moment—and that was all the detail I ever wanted to know. Nothing else mattered, anyway, except the fact that he was gone.

"I miss you," I say against the door. My eyes are squeezed shut, my cheeks wet, my breathing ragged. "I miss you, I miss you, I miss you." The words are a drumbeat in my head, still steady after three years. I don't think they'll ever go away. "I miss you."

It's a relief to be at work that night, surrounded by people. And I do mean surrounded: I've never seen Café Contigo so crowded. Not only is every table full, but Mr. Santos brought out all the extra chairs that are usually stored in the basement and it's still not enough. People are standing in groups against either side of the wall, shuffling back and forth as I weave through them with a drink-laden tray for Addy and her friends.

I push through the beaded curtain that separates the back room from the main restaurant. There's only one large table here, more than half-filled with familiar faces: Addy, Maeve, Bronwyn, Luis, and Cooper. A handsome, dark-haired boy gets up from beside Cooper as I approach the table and stretches his hand toward my tray with a questioning look. "Can I help?" he asks. "Will it mess you up if I start taking these off?"

I smile at him. I've never met Cooper's boyfriend, Kris, but I recognize him from press photos, and I like him instantly. He must have waited tables himself at some point, if he knows the importance of a balanced tray. "From the middle is great," I say.

The room is supposed to be private, but as Kris and I pass drinks around, people keep trickling in and craning their necks at Cooper. Most of them duck right back out, but a group of girls linger beside the entry, whispering to one another behind their hands until they dissolve into near-hysterical giggles.

"Sorry this is so weird," Cooper murmurs as I hand him a glass of Coke. I haven't seen Cooper in person since he graduated last year, and I can't fault the entryway girls for being starstruck. His hair is longer and attractively tousled, he's very tan, and he fills out his white Cal Fullerton T-shirt impossibly well. Looking straight at him is a little like staring into the sun.

"Well, you're Bayview's favorite boy," Kris says, settling himself back down beside Cooper. Cooper takes his hand, but his expression is preoccupied and a little tense.

"*Now,* maybe," he says. "We'll see how long it lasts."

I don't blame him for not trusting all the adoration. I remember how some people treated him when they learned he was gay—not just kids at Bayview High, but adults who should've known better. Cooper's been keeping most of the asshole comments at bay since spring training by being almost perfect every time he pitches. The pressure must be unbelievable. Eventually he's going to have to lose, because nobody can win forever. What happens then?

The boldest girl in the group of gigglers approaches Cooper. "Can I have your autograph?" She hands him a Sharpie, then puts one foot on the bottom rung of Cooper's chair and turns so her thigh, bare beneath a short skirt, is angled in front of him. "Right there."

"Um." Cooper looks completely flummoxed as Addy stifles a laugh. "Could I just . . . sign a napkin or something?" he asks.

I'm in and out of the room as it fills up, bringing more drinks and snacks that seem to disappear as soon as I put them down. "How's everyone doing back there?" Addy asks when I'm on my fifth trip from the kitchen.

"Great, except Manny's dropped, like, three orders of empanadas so far," I say, setting a plate between her and Bronwyn. "Here's the lone survivor. Enjoy."

Maeve is seated on Bronwyn's other side, wearing a scoop-neck black T-shirt that's more fitted than what she usually goes for, and really flattering. It has a cute design that looks like a bouquet of flowers at first but is actually a bunch of cartoony little monsters. I can't stop checking it out. Neither can Luis, although I'm pretty sure our reasons are different.

But Maeve doesn't notice either of us, because she keeps

staring at the entryway. I follow her gaze as the beads part once again and Nate Macauley walks through. The only empty chair remaining is all the way at the other end of the table, until Maeve jumps up. "You look like you could use some help, Phoebe," she says, moving quickly to my side. I don't, but I let her grab a random assortment of silverware off the table anyway.

Nate sits in Maeve's vacated chair, brushing his knuckles against Bronwyn's arm. When she turns, her entire face lights up. "Hi," she says, at the same time Nate goes, "Hey," and then he says, "You look—" while Bronwyn says, "I was hoping—" They stop and smile at one another, and all I can think is that Jules has no shot whatsoever. Nate leans closer to Bronwyn to say something in her ear, and she turns her entire body toward him when she laughs in response. She brushes at his jacket like there's something on it, which is the oldest trick in the book. It totally works when he catches hold of her hand and wow, that did not take long at all. I'm about to turn away and give them some privacy when another voice rings out.

"Whew, it is *packed* in here!" A nerdy-hipster-looking boy in an ice-blue polo shirt stands beside the beads, fanning himself as he glances around the room. It's Evan Neiman, Bronwyn's ex-boyfriend, who as far as I know wasn't invited to this little get-together. Evan spots the last empty chair and drags it as close to Bronwyn as he can manage. "Hey, you," he says, leaning across the table with a moony grin. "I made it."

Bronwyn freezes like a deer in headlights, eyes wide behind her glasses. "Evan? What are you doing here?" she asks. All the animation leaves Nate's face as he drops her hand and tips his chair backward. Bronwyn licks her lips. "Why aren't you in Pasadena?"

"I couldn't miss the chance to see you again before you leave," Evan says.

Nate returns his chair to the floor with a bang. "Again?" he asks, with a pointed look toward Bronwyn. He doesn't look mad, exactly, but he does look hurt. Bronwyn's eyes dart between him and Evan, who keeps beaming like there's no tension in the room whatsoever. I can't tell if he's clueless or diabolical. "Besides, you left your sunglasses in my car," Evan adds, holding up a bright blue rectangle like a trophy.

Maeve is standing beside me, frantically wiping a napkin across a clean knife. "Oh no, oh no, oh no," she mutters.

I tug the knife from her hand. "They do that in the kitchen, you know."

"Please take me there," she whispers. "I can't watch."

I give her my tray and we move toward the door, but pause when a hand whisks the beads to one side and a girl enters. I don't recognize Jules at first; she's really rocking whatever smoky eye tutorial she watched. Her dark hair is flat-ironed and she's wearing the sequined tank top with a pair of skintight jeans and high-heeled sandals. Objectively, I have to admit that her boobs look amazing in that shirt. "Hey, Ju—" I start, but she puts her finger to her lips.

She crosses a few feet to the table. Nate has pushed his chair away like he's about to get up, but Jules stops him with a hand on his shoulder. Before he can move, she straddles him so that she's sitting on his lap, her chest pressed against his, and then she grabs his face between both of her hands and kisses him. Hard and deep, for what feels like ages although it can't be more than a few seconds. I hope. A light flashes at the other end of the room, and I catch sight of Monica holding up her phone as she leans through the beaded curtain.

Nobody reacts until Jules gets up as quickly as she sat down, flipping her hair and turning toward the exit. Then Nate slowly wipes a layer of Jules's lip gloss from his mouth with a bemused expression. Cooper looks worried, and Addy looks furious. Bronwyn looks like she's about to cry. And Evan Neiman is grinning like he just won the lottery.

I let out a yelp of pain as Maeve drops the serving tray she was holding onto my foot. Jules catches my eye, and before she slips through the beads she gives me an exaggerated, triumphant wink.

Always take the Dare, she mouths at me.

Friday, March 6

REPORTER: Good evening, this is Liz Rosen with Channel Seven News, bringing you an update on our top news story: the untimely death of yet another student at Bayview High. I'm here with Sona Gupta, principal of Bayview High, for the administration's reaction.

PRINCIPAL GUPTA: A point of clarification, if I may. This particular tragedy did not happen *at* Bayview High. On the school grounds, that is.

REPORTER: I don't believe I said that it did?

PRINCIPAL GUPTA: It seemed implied. We are, of course, devastated at the loss of a cherished member of our tight-knit community, and committed to supporting our students in their time of need. We have many resources available to help them process their shock and grief.

REPORTER: Bayview High is a school that became infamous nationwide for its corrosive culture of gossip. Are you concerned that—

PRINCIPAL GUPTA: Excuse me. We're veering onto a topic that's unrelated to the subject at hand, not to mention quite unnecessary. Bayview High is a different school today than it was eighteen months ago. Our zero-tolerance policy toward gossip and bullying has proven highly effective. We were even profiled in *Education Today Magazine* last summer.

REPORTER: I'm not familiar with that.

PRINCIPAL GUPTA: It's very highly regarded.

CHAPTER NINE

Knox
Monday, March 2

It's a reflex to check my phone, even at work. But there's nothing new from Unknown on Monday. The last texts were from Friday night:

DARE: Kiss a member of the Bayview Four.

STATUS: Achieved by Jules Crandall. Congratulations, Jules. Nice work. Accompanied by a picture of Jules on Nate's lap, kissing him as though her life depended on staying attached to his face.

The next player will be contacted soon. Tick-tock.

I'm kind of glad I had rehearsal and couldn't make it to Café Contigo on Friday. Maeve said the night went downhill fast after Jules interrupted dinner. Plus, the whole restaurant turned into such a mob scene that they ran out of food and Cooper had to leave through the back entrance.

"In this particular instance, the contributing cause is false confession," Sandeep says beside me. We're sharing a desk today at Until Proven, and he's been on the phone nonstop since I arrived. He holds a pen in one hand, tapping it rhythmically on the desk while he talks. "So I don't see that it applies. What? No. Homicide-related." He waits a few beats, pen tapping. "I can't confirm that yet. I'll call you back when I can. All right." He hangs up. Until Proven still has desk phones—big, clunky things with actual cords plugged into the wall. "Knox, can you order some pizza?" Sandeep asks, rolling his shoulders. "I'm starving."

"Sure." I pick up my iPhone, because I don't even know how to work the desk ones, then put it back down when Eli materializes in front of us. He looks different, but I can't figure out why until Sandeep speaks up.

"You cut your hair," he says. Eli shrugs as Sandeep leans back in his chair and spins in a semicircle, his fingers steepling beneath his chin. "What's up? You *never* cut your hair."

"I assure you that I do," Eli says, pushing his glasses up on his nose. He looks a lot less like Einstein now. "Do you have the Henson file?"

"Is this a wedding thing?" Sandeep asks. "Did Ashton make you?"

Eli rubs his temple like he's trying to draw out some patience. "Ashton and I don't *make* one another do anything. Do you have the Henson file or not?"

"Um." Sandeep starts sifting through the piles on his desk. "Probably. It's here somewhere. What do you need?"

"The name of the convicting DA."

"I have it," I say, and they both turn toward me. "Not the file, but the name. I made a spreadsheet. Hang on." I pull up Google Docs and tilt my laptop toward Eli. "It has all the basic background information on the D'Agostino convictions. Names, dates, addresses, lawyers, things like that. I noticed you keep asking for that stuff, so . . ." I trail off as a crease appears on Eli's forehead. Was I not supposed to do this, maybe? It's all publicly available information, so I didn't think I was doing anything wrong by putting it into one document.

Eli's gaze roves across my screen. "This is great. Can you share it with me, please?"

"Um, yeah. Of course," I say.

He meets my eyes. "What's your name, again?"

"Knox. Knox Myers." I smile a little too widely, happy to be noticed for once.

"Thanks, Knox," Eli says sincerely. "You just saved me a lot of time."

"Eli!" Somebody yells from across the room. "Judge Balewa on line one for you!" Eli takes off without another word as Sandeep punches me lightly in the arm.

"Look at you, getting praise from the big man! Nice job, kid," he says. "Don't let it go to your head, though. I still want that pizza. And could you sort the mail?"

I order a few extra-large pizzas for the office, then grab a stack of envelopes from a tray next to the front door and bring them back to my chair. Some of it's registered and I'm not supposed to open that, so I put those aside for Sandeep. A lot of it's bills, and those go into another pile. Then I sort through what's left. Mostly, it's requests for Until Proven to take on a particular case. It's surprising how many people write letters instead of emailing, but I guess they're hoping to stand out. Until Proven gets way more pleas for help than it could ever handle, even if it tripled its staff.

I pick up a letter-sized envelope with Eli's name scrawled across the front. I tear it open and there's a single sheet of paper inside. I pull it out and read the few short sentences:

You messed with the wrong people, shithead.

I'm going to fuck you like you fucked us.

And I'll enjoy watching you die.

I recoil like somebody punched me. "Sandeep!" I croak. He looks up from his laptop with a quizzical expression, and I shove the paper toward him. "Look at this!"

Sandeep takes the letter and reads. He doesn't look nearly as shocked as I expected. "Oh yeah. We get these sometimes. I'll log it in the death threats file."

"The *what?*" I can't keep the horror out of my voice. "There's a whole *file?*"

"Death threats come in during every big case," he says matter-of-factly. "Disgruntled assholes blowing off steam, for the most part, but we need to document everything." He scans the sheet of paper again before folding it and putting it back into the envelope. "At least this one doesn't contain hate speech. Eli gets a lot of anti-Jewish rhetoric. Those go in a special file."

"Jesus," I say weakly. My pulse is racing uncomfortably fast. I knew Until Proven lawyers had to deal with a lot of crap, but I never imagined anything like this.

Sandeep pats my shoulder. "Sorry, Knox. I don't mean to be

blasé. I know these are disconcerting, especially the first time you see one. It's par for the course in this line of work, though, and we have procedures in place to deal with it." His brow knits in concern as he takes in my clammy, probably ghost-pale face. "Are you feeling unsafe? Do you want to go home?"

"No. I'm not worried about me." I swallow, watching Eli through a conference room window as he gestures animatedly. "But Eli—"

"Is used to it," Sandeep says gently. "He chose this line of work, and he's not afraid of people like this." Disgust settles over his features as he tosses the envelope onto the desk in front of us. "They're cowards, really. Hiding behind a screen to threaten and intimidate, instead of doing something meaningful to improve their situation."

I glance at my phone, full of gloating texts from Unknown. "Yeah. I know what you mean."

I'd planned on going straight home after work, but when five o'clock rolls around I'm still rattled and out of sorts. *Where are you?* I text Maeve as I walk toward the elevator, holding my breath to avoid the pungent aroma of the men's hair club.

She answers right away. *Café Contigo.*

Want some company?

Always.

There's a bus sitting in traffic a few yards ahead of me, and I jog to make it to the stop as it pulls up. My phone is still in my hand as I board, and it buzzes when I sit next to an old woman with tight gray curls. She beams at me as I dig out my earphones and plug them into my phone, giving her a polite smile before I stuff the buds into my ears. Not today, Florence.

Imagine Dragons blasts while I read a text from Kiersten. *Download this. New messaging app for family chats.* I follow the link for something called ChatApp. The icon is a text bubble surrounded by a lock.

Never heard of it, I text back. *What's wrong with the ten apps I already have?*

Kiersten sends a shrug emoji. *Idk. Kelsey wants it. Syncs easier with her laptop or something.* Our middle sister is a technology dinosaur who prefers messaging via computer instead of phone. *Better privacy, too.*

Oh good. Wouldn't want Katie's top-secret wedding details to leak.

Ha. Ha. Did Wing Zone fix the chicken yet?

Yes, it's fully a chicken once more. With a leprechaun hat in anticipation of St. Patrick's Day. Kiersten replies with six laughing emojis and a couple of shamrocks.

I finish downloading the new app, and once I sign up I see four invitations waiting for me, from Kiersten, Katie, Kelsey, and Kara. I'm not ready for the sisterly deluge, though, and exit the app without accepting any of them. It's practically my stop anyway, so I get up and make my way to the doors, hanging on to a pole for balance as we lurch toward the sidewalk.

Café Contigo is just a block away from the bus stop. When I get inside Maeve is at her usual corner table, a cup of coffee in front of her and her phone in one hand. I pull out my earbuds and take the seat across from her. "What's up?"

She lays her phone down on the table. It vibrates twice. "Not much. How was work?"

I don't want to get into the death threats just yet. I'd rather not think about them. I gesture to her phone, which vibrates again. "Do you need to get that?"

"No. It's just Bronwyn, sending pictures from some play she's watching. The set's really great, apparently."

"Is she into that kind of thing?"

"She thinks I am. Because I did a play once." Maeve shakes her head in amused exasperation. "She and my mom are exactly alike. Any time I show the slightest interest in something, they hope it's my new life's passion."

A waiter comes by, a tall, thin college student named Ahmed, and I order a Sprite. I wait until he walks away to ask, "How's Bronwyn doing after that whole mess on Friday? Did she and Nate break up again?"

"I'm not sure you can break up when you never officially got back together," Maeve says, resting her chin in her hand with a sigh. "Bronwyn's not talking about it. Well, she talked about it *at length* on Saturday, but now that she's back at Yale she's totally clammed up about Nate. I swear to God, that place short-circuits all her emotions or something." She takes a sip of coffee and makes a wry face. "She thinks Nate was into it. The kiss from Jules, I mean. Which wasn't my read on the situation at all, but Bronwyn won't listen."

"Did you tell her it was part of a game?"

"I tried." Maeve bites her lip. "I didn't want to go into too much detail, because she'd freak if she knew there was even a slight connection to Simon. And she was already so upset about Nate. That stupid picture Monica took was all over social media this weekend. Which reminds me . . . I've been meaning to show you something." Maeve swipes at her phone a few times, then holds it out to me. "I found this the other day. You remember that revenge forum Simon used to post on?" I nod. "Well, this is a new version, except now the posts disappear after a few hours."

"What?" My eyebrows shoot up as I take her phone. "How do you know that?"

"I found it when I was searching Simon's old user name last week. There was a post a while back that mentioned Bayview, and something about a game." She drums her fingers restlessly on the table. "I can't remember exactly what it said. I wish I'd taken a screenshot, but I didn't know then that the posts disappear."

I scan the handful of posts on the page. Somebody named Jellyfish is seriously pissed off at his teacher. "Okay, so . . . you think what, exactly? That this Jellyfish person is running the Truth or Dare game?"

"Not him specifically," Maeve says. "That guy seems to have a one-track mind. But maybe that other poster is involved. It's weird, don't you think? That the texting game starts by referencing Simon, and then this revenge forum pops up and does the same thing?"

"I guess," I say uncertainly. Seems kind of tenuous, but then again, Maeve knows a lot more about tracking vengeful gossips than I do.

"I should set up a monitoring service or something. Like PingMe," she says thoughtfully. At my puzzled expression, she adds, "A tool that notifies you when a website updates. It's faster than a Google Alert. Then I could keep track of these disappearing conversations."

Her eyes get a faraway look. Even though I think she's getting way too obsessed over a random Internet post, I can tell she won't listen if I tell her so. Instead, I hand back her phone without comment. When she takes it, her sleeve pulls up on her arm, exposing an angry-looking purple bruise. "Ouch, how'd you get that?" I ask.

"What?" Maeve follows my eyes, and I hear her breath catch. She pales and goes so still that she looks like a statue. Then she pushes her sleeve down as far as it can go, until the bruise is completely covered. "I don't know. Just—banged something, I guess."

"You guess?" Her eyes are on the floor, and unease stirs in my gut. "When?"

"I don't remember," she says.

I run my tongue over dry lips. "Maeve, did . . . did somebody do that to you?"

Maeve's head snaps up, and she lets out a startled, humorless laugh. "*What?* Oh my God, Knox, no. I promise, nothing like that happened." She looks me straight in the eye, and I relax a little. If there's one thing I've learned about Maeve, it's that she's incapable of maintaining eye contact when telling even the whitest of lies. You should never, for example, ask what she thinks of your new haircut if you're not fully prepared to handle the truth. I learned that the hard way when I decided to go a little shorter last week.

"Okay, so . . ." I pause, because now I can't remember

what we were talking about, and Maeve's gaze wanders over my shoulder. She waves, and I turn around to see a thin boy with strawberry-blond hair and glasses hovering a few feet away from us.

"Hi, Owen," Maeve calls. "Phoebe's not working today."

"I know. I'm picking up takeout."

Maeve lowers her voice as Owen approaches the counter. "That's Phoebe's little brother. He comes here a lot after school, even when he's not getting food. Just to hang out and talk with Phoebe or Mr. Santos when they're not busy. I think he's kind of lonely."

Somehow, this whole texting game mess turned Maeve and Phoebe into friends, which is the only silver lining so far. Maeve's been kind of lost since Bronwyn graduated, and Phoebe could use somebody on her side. Slut-shamey crap about her is still flying around school, and her friend Jules eats lunch with Monica Hill's clique now. I guess Jules found her own silver lining: social climbing via Truth or Dare success.

Mr. Santos appears from the back and hands Owen a large brown paper bag, then waves away the bill Owen tries to give him. "No, mijo, put that away," he says. "Your money's no good here. How is school? Phoebe tells me you have a big spelling bee coming up."

Owen starts talking a mile a minute, but I'm not really paying attention because I'm still thinking about the relieved look on his face when he put the money away. My mom was an insurance adjuster on Mr. Lawton's worker's comp settlement after he died. I remember her telling my dad, when she didn't know I was listening, that she thought the company's payout for the accident was a lot less than it should have been. *I don't think Melissa Lawton realizes how quickly that money will go when nothing's coming in,* she'd said.

When Owen finally turns away from the counter, he has a big smile on his face. *He needed that,* I think. Some kind of dad figure, or a big brother, maybe. I get it. I know what it's like to grow up surrounded by older sisters who might be great but can't tell you how you're supposed to function as a guy in the twenty-first century. When Owen passes by our table I find myself saying, "Hey, do you like *Bounty Wars?*"

Owen pauses and gestures to his T-shirt with his free hand. "Um, *yeah.*"

"Me too. I'm Knox, by the way. I go to school with Phoebe." Maeve nods and smiles, like she's confirming my trustworthiness. "Who's your avatar?" I ask.

Owen looks a little cautious, but answers me readily enough. "Dax Reaper."

"Mine too. What level are you on?"

"Fifteen."

"Damn, really? I can't get past twelve."

Owen's entire face lights up. "It's all about weapon choice," he says earnestly, and then bam, he's off. The two of us talk *Bounty Wars* strategy until I notice the bag he's holding is starting to soak through with grease from whatever's inside. "You should probably get that home, huh?" I say. "People must be waiting for dinner."

"I guess." Owen shifts from one foot to the other. "Are you and Phoebe friends?"

Good question. Not exactly, although now that Phoebe is

spending more time with Maeve at school she is also, by default, spending more time with me. In the snake pit that Bayview High has turned into lately, that's probably close enough. "Yeah, sure."

"You should come over and play *Bounty Wars* with us sometime. I'll tell Phoebe to invite you. See ya." Owen waves as he turns away. Maeve, who'd been scrolling through her phone the whole time, nudges my knee with hers.

"That was really nice," she says.

"Stop calling me that," I grumble, and she smiles.

A tall kid with shaggy brown hair comes through the door, holding it open for Owen to slip out under his arm. He scans the room, his eyes flicking past me and Maeve without much interest and pausing on a waitress arranging condiment baskets in the back. He looks like he's only a year or two older than I am, but there's something a little too intense about his gaze. Mr. Santos, counting receipts at the register, glances up and seems to notice it too. "Good evening," he calls.

The guy crosses half the dining room with his eyes still on the waitress's back. She turns, displaying a middle-aged face that doesn't match her bouncy ponytail. Intense Guy shifts his attention to Mr. Santos. "Yo, Phoebe here?" His voice is too loud for the small space.

Mr. Santos leans on the counter, arms folded. "I can help you with whatever you need, son," he says. No *mijo* for this kid.

"I'm looking for Phoebe. She works here, right?" Mr. Santos doesn't answer right away, and the guy's jaw gets tense. He shoves his hands into the pockets of his green hunting jacket.

"You understand English or what, señor?" he asks in a mocking Spanish accent.

Maeve sucks in a sharp breath between her teeth, but Mr. Santos's pleasant expression doesn't change. "I understand you perfectly."

"Then answer my question," the kid says.

"If you have a food order, I am happy to take it," Mr. Santos says in the same even tone.

"Look, old man—" The kid strides forward, then stops short when Luis and Manny emerge from the kitchen one after the other. Luis pulls a towel from his shoulder and snaps it hard between his hands, making every muscle in his arms stand out. It's probably the wrong time to wish I had another guy's moves, but damn, Luis is smooth. Somehow, he manages to come across like Captain America while wearing a grease-spattered T-shirt and a bandana.

Maeve notices, too. She's practically fanning herself across the table.

Manny's not as athletic as his brother, but he's big and burly and plenty intimidating when he crosses his arms and scowls. Like he's doing now. "They need you in the kitchen, Pa," he says, his eyes locked on Intense Guy. "We'll take over out here for a while."

Intense Guy might be an ass, but he's not stupid. He turns right around and leaves.

Maeve's eyes linger on the counter until Luis goes back into the kitchen, and then she turns toward me. "What the hell was that about?" she says. Her phone vibrates again, and she makes a frustrated sound in her throat. "God, Bronwyn, give it a rest. I don't care about set design nearly as much as you think I do." She picks up her phone and angles it so she can see the screen clearly, then pales. "Oh no."

"What?" I ask.

She holds her phone toward me, amber eyes wide. *Maeve Rojas, you're up next! Text back your choice: Should I reveal a Truth, or will you take a Dare?*

CHAPTER TEN

Maeve
Tuesday, March 3

If I text you a Truth or Dare prompt, you have 24 hours to make a choice.

I'm at Café Contigo with a full cup of coffee that's gone ice cold because I keep rereading the About That post with the Truth or Dare rules. It's three fifteen on Tuesday, which means I have a little less than three hours before the "deadline." Not that I care. I'm not doing it, obviously. I was in the middle of the whole Simon mess, and I refuse to take part in anything that makes light of what happened. It was a tragedy, not a joke, and it's sick that someone is trying to spin it into a fun game. I won't be Unknown's pawn, and they can do whatever they want in return because I don't have anything to hide.

Plus, in the grand scheme of things: who cares about Unknown.

I toggle away from About That to Key Contacts in my list of phone numbers. There are five: my parents, Bronwyn, Knox, and my oncologist. I press my fingertips against the large purple bruise on my forearm and can almost hear Dr. Gutierrez's voice: *Early treatment is absolutely critical. It's why you're still here.*

I dial his number before I can think too much about it. A woman picks up almost instantly. "Ramon Gutierrez's office."

"Hi. I have a question about, um, diagnostics."

"Are you a patient of Dr. Gutierrez?"

"Yes. I was wondering if . . ." I scrunch down in my seat and lower my voice. "Theoretically, if I wanted to get some tests run to . . . sort of check my remission status, is that the kind of thing that I could do without my parents being involved? If I'm not eighteen."

There's a moment of silence on the other end. "Could you tell me your name and your date of birth, please?"

I grip the phone more tightly in my suddenly sweaty palm. "Can you answer my question first?"

"Parental consent is required for treatment of minors, but if you could—"

I hang up. That's what I figured. I turn my arm so I can't see the bruise anymore. Last night I found one on my upper thigh, too. Just looking at them fills me with dread.

A shadow falls across my table, and I look up to see Luis standing there. "I'm staging an intervention," he says.

I blink, confused. Luis is entirely out of context in my mental space right now, and I have to forcibly shove away thoughts of cancer wards and anonymous texting before I can focus on him. Even then, I'm not sure I heard right. "What?"

"Remember that outdoors you don't believe in? I'm going to prove you wrong. Let's go." He gestures toward the door, then folds his arms. After the scene with Mr. Santos and the rude kid yesterday, I kind of can't stop looking at them. Maybe Luis could do that towel snap another two or three or twenty times.

He waits for a response, then sighs. "Conversations usually involve more than one person, Maeve."

I manage to unfreeze my tongue. "Go where?"

"Outside," Luis says patiently. As though he's speaking to a small and not particularly smart child.

"Don't you have to work?"

"Not till five."

My phone sits on the table in front of me, mocking me with its silence. Maybe if I call again, I'll get a different person and a different answer. "I don't know . . ."

"Come on. What do you have to lose?"

Luis gives one of his megawatt smiles, and what do you know, I'm on my feet. Like I said: I have no defense against his particular demographic. "What did you have in mind, in this alleged outdoors?"

"I'll show you," Luis says, holding open the door. I look left and right when we hit the sidewalk, wondering which way we're going to walk, but Luis pauses at a parking meter and starts unchaining a bicycle leaning against it.

"Um. Is that yours?" I ask.

"No. I pick locks on random bikes for fun," Luis says, detaching the chain and looping it beneath the bike's seat. He flashes me a grin when he's finished. "Of course it's mine. We're about a mile from where I want to take you."

"Okay, but—" I gesture at the empty space around us. "I don't have a bike. I drove here."

"You can ride with me." He straddles the bike so he's standing in front of the seat, hands on the outer edge of the bars to hold the frame steady. "Hop on."

"Hop—where?" He just looks at me, expectant. "You mean the *handlebars*?"

"Yeah. Didn't you do that when you were a kid?" Luis asks. Like he's not talking to somebody who spent most of their childhood in and out of hospitals. It's sort of refreshing, especially now, but the fact remains that I don't even know how to ride a bike the normal way.

"We're not kids," I hedge. "I won't fit."

"Sure you will. I do this all the time with my brothers, and they're bigger than you are."

"With Manny?" I ask, unable to keep a straight face at the mental image.

Luis laughs, too. "I meant the younger ones, but sure. I could haul Manny's ass if I had to." I keep hesitating, unable to picture how any of this is supposed to work, and his confident smile fades a little. "Or we could just walk somewhere."

"No, this is great," I say, because Luis with a disappointed face is just too weird. People who never get told no are *so bad* at hearing it. Anyway, how hard can it be, right? The saying *It's as easy as riding a bike* must exist for a reason. "I'll just . . . hop on." I gaze uneasily at the handlebars, which don't strike me as having any seatlike properties, and decide there's no way I can bluff my way through this. "How do I do that, exactly?"

Luis slips into coaching mode without missing a beat. "Face away from me and step over the front wheel, with one leg on either side," he instructs. It's a little awkward, but I do it. "Put your hands behind you and grab hold of the handlebars. Brace yourself, like this." His hands, warm and rough, close briefly over mine. "Now push down to lift yourself up and—yeah!" He laughs, startled, when I rise in one fluid motion to perch on the handlebars. Even I'm not sure how I did that. "You got it. Pro skills."

It's not the most comfortable thing I've ever done, and it feels more than a little precarious. Especially when Luis starts pedaling. "Oh my God, we're going to die," I gasp involuntarily, squeezing my eyes shut. But then Luis's chin is on my shoulder as a cool breeze hits my face and honestly, there are much worse ways to go.

He's a fast and assured cyclist, navigating a nonstop route to the bike path behind Bayview Center. The path is wide and almost empty, but every once in a while a speck appears ahead of us and then, before I know it, Luis has passed whoever it is. When he finally slows and says "Hang on tight, we're about to stop," I see a wrought-iron gate and a wooden sign beside it that reads BAYVIEW ARBORETUM.

My descent is a lot less graceful, but Luis doesn't seem to notice as he chains the bike to a post. "This okay?" he asks, pulling a water bottle from the bike's holder and drinking half of it in a few gulps. "I thought we could walk around for a while."

"It's perfect. I don't come here often enough."

We start down a smooth gravel path lined with cherry blossom trees that are just starting to bloom. "I love it here," Luis says, shading his eyes against the afternoon sun. "It's so peaceful. I come here whenever I need to think."

I sneak a glance at him, all bronzed skin and broad shoulders and that quick, easy smile. I never imagined that Luis was the sort of person who would go somewhere because he wanted a quiet place to think. "What do you think about?"

"Oh, you know," Luis says seriously. "Deep, profound things about humanity and the state of the universe. I have those kind of thoughts all the time." I tilt my head at him, eyebrows raised in a *go on* gesture, and he meets my eyes with a grin. "I'm not having any right now, though. Give me a minute."

I smile back. It's impossible not to. "How about when you're not pondering existential crises? What sort of ordinary things do you worry about?"

"Staying on top of everything," he says instantly. "Like, I have a full load of classes this semester plus extra practicum because I'm trying to graduate early. I work twenty to thirty hours a week at Contigo, depending on how much my parents need me. And I still play baseball every once in a while. Just pickup games with guys from school, nothing like the schedule I was on when I played at Bayview with Cooper, but we're trying to get a league together. Oh, and I help out with my brothers' Little League team sometimes. It's all good, but it's a lot. Sometimes I forget where I'm supposed to be, you know?"

I don't know. When Luis was at Bayview, I thought all he

did was play sports and go to parties. "I had no idea how much you have going on," I say.

He glances toward me as we approach a rose garden. It's early in the season and most buds are just starting to open, but a few show-offs are in full bloom. "Is that a polite way of saying you thought I was a dumb jock?"

"Of course not!" I stare at the roses so I don't have to meet his eyes, because I totally did. I always thought Luis was a nice enough guy by Bayview athlete standards—especially when he stood by Cooper when the rest of Cooper's friends turned on him their senior year—but not much else.

Except gorgeous, obviously. He's always been that. Now he's tossing out all these hidden depths and making himself even more appealing, which is frankly a little unfair. It's not like my crush needs more encouragement. "I just didn't realize you had your life figured out already," I tell him. "I'm impressed."

"I don't, really. I just do stuff I like and see how it goes."

"You make it sound so easy." I can't keep the wistful tone out of my voice.

"What about you?" Luis asks. "What do you spend your time thinking about?"

Lately? You. "The philosophical underpinnings of Western civilization. Obviously."

"Obviously. That goes without saying. What else?"

Dying. I catch myself before it slips out. *Try to keep the conversation a little less morbid, Maeve. Whether something horrifying is going to be texted to hundreds of my classmates in, oh, about two point five hours.* God. It hits me, all of a sudden, that Luis has been nothing but straightforward with me, and I can't manage to tell him a single true thing. I'm too wrapped up in self-doubt and secrets.

"It's not a trick question," Luis says, and I realize that I've been silent all the way through the rose garden. We're in a mini-meadow of wildflowers—all bright colors and tangled greens—and I still haven't told him what I spend my time thinking about. "You can say anything. Music, cat memes, Harry Potter, empanadas." He shoots me a grin. "Me."

My stomach does a flip that I try to ignore. "You caught me. I was just wondering how many flowers it would take to spell your name out in rose petals across the lawn."

"Fifteen," Luis says instantly, then gives me a look of wide-eyed innocence when I snort. "What? It's a very common oc-currence. The gardeners won't even let me come here during peak season."

My lips twitch. "Tienes el ego por las nubes, Luis," I say, and he smiles.

His hand brushes against mine, so quickly that I can't tell if it's on purpose or by accident. Then he says, "You know, I almost asked you out last year." My entire body goes hot, and I'm positive I heard him wrong until he adds, "Coop didn't want me to, though."

My pulse starts fluttering wildly. "Cooper?" I blurt out. What the hell? My love life, or lack thereof, is none of Cooper's damn business. "Why?"

Luis laughs a little. "He was being protective. Not a fan of my track record with girls when we were in school. And he didn't think I was serious about making a change." We're halfway past the wildflowers, and Luis glances at me sideways. "I was, though."

My breathing gets shallow. What does that mean? I could ask, I guess. It's a perfectly valid question, especially since he's the one who brought it up. Or I could say what's running through my head right now, which is *I wish you'd followed through. Want to try again?* Instead, I find myself forcing out a laugh and saying, "Oh well, you know Cooper. He always has to be everyone's dad, doesn't he? Father knows best."

Luis shoves his hands into his pockets. "Yeah," he says, his voice low and threaded with what almost sounds like disappointment. "I guess he does."

Bronwyn used to tell me, when we were younger, that I had crushes on unattainable boys because they were safe. "You like the dream, not the reality," she'd say. "So you can keep your distance." And I'd roll my eyes at her, because it's not like she'd ever had a boyfriend back then either. But maybe she had a point, because all I can bring myself to say is, "Well, thanks for the intervention. You were right. I needed it."

"Any time," Luis says, sounding like his usual carefree self. It hits me with dull certainty that if there was any chance for something to happen between us, I just let it pass.

After dinner, I'm restless and anxious. There are now three items on my list of Things I Can't Stand to Think About: nosebleeds and bruises, the Truth or Dare prompt that's hitting its deadline in fifteen minutes, and the fact that I'm an utter emotional coward. If I don't do something that at least *feels* productive, I'm going to crawl right out of my skin. So I take out my laptop and perch on my window seat, then plug my earbuds into my phone and call Knox.

"Is there a reason you're using voice technology?" he asks by way of greeting. "This is such a disconcerting mode of communication. It's weird trying to keep a conversation rolling without nonverbal cues or spell check."

"Nice speaking with you too, Knox," I say drily. "Sorry, but I'm on my laptop and I need my hands free. You can let the conversation lapse at any point." I type a bunch of search terms into Google and add, "Have you ever wondered how somebody can block their number from showing up in a text?"

"Is that a rhetorical question or are you going to tell me?"

"I'm looking it up right now." I wait a few beats until my screen fills. "There are three ways, according to wikiHow."

"Are you sure wikiHow is the authority on this subject?"

"It's a starting point." I clear my throat. To be honest, it's embarrassing to remember how eighteen months ago, I was hacking into Simon's About That control panel to grab evidence the police had missed, and now? I'm Googling wikiHow entries. I wish I understood mobile technology half as well as computer and network systems. "So, this says you can use a messaging website, an app, or an email address."

"Okay. And this is helpful why?"

"It's foundational knowledge. The more important question is, how do you trace a number from an anonymous message?" I frown at my screen. "Ugh, the top Google result is from three years ago. That's not a good sign."

Knox is quiet for a while as I read, and then he says, "Maeve, if you're worried about Unknown then maybe you should just text back *Dare*. Those are harmless."

"Jules kissing Nate wasn't *harmless*."

"True," Knox concedes. "But it could have been in different circumstances. If Nate and Bronwyn were solid, she might've been annoyed at Jules planting one on her boyfriend, but she would've gotten over it. She wouldn't have been mad at *him* for it, anyway. Or Jules could've picked someone else and made it into more of a friendly thing. Like a kiss on the cheek." His voice turns musing. "Or maybe that would have been considered cheating the game."

A window pops onto my screen, and I pause. It's a PingMe alert: *The website you are monitoring has been updated.* I've been getting these constantly for Vengeance Is Mine, on both my phone and my laptop, and I'm starting to regret setting it up. There's nothing useful, just lots of creepy venting. At least Jellyfish seems to have calmed down lately. Still, I open a new browser tab anyway and type in the familiar URL.

This time, there's a string of posts by someone named Darkestmind—and as soon as I see the name, I recognize it as the person who piqued my interest in the first place. The one who mentioned Simon, and Bayview.

"Knox," I say eagerly. "Darkestmind is posting again."

"Huh? Who's doing what?"

"On the revenge forum," I say, and hear Knox sigh through the phone.

"Are you still stalking that place?"

"Shh. I'm reading." I scan the short string of posts:

Cheers to all of us who are GETTING SHIT DONE this week.

And by us, I mean Bayview2020 and me.

Tip for the uninitiated: don't screw with us.

"He's talking about Bayview again," I report. "Or more specifically, someone who has Bayview in their user name. I'll bet it's someone who goes to school with us."

"Or—now, this is just a thought, but hear me out—maybe it's a weird Simon fanboy who uses the name *because* they're a weird Simon fanboy. Which we know, because they're hanging out on a weird Simon fanboy subforum," Knox says.

I take a screenshot of the posts before hitting Refresh. "Are you being sarcastic?" I ask mildly. I'm not surprised Knox isn't taking me seriously; Bronwyn didn't either until my research made national news on *Mikhail Powers Investigates*.

"Very."

When the page reloads, I yell so loudly and triumphantly that Knox lets out a muted "ow" on the other end of the line. "AHA! I knew it!" I say, my chest thumping with excitement. "There's a new post from Darkestmind and listen to what it says: *I've always wanted to out-Simon Simon and damn it, I think I have. More to come soon. Tick-tock.* Tick-freaking-tock, Knox! That's exactly what Unknown says when they're getting ready to send another Truth or Dare prompt. It's the same person!"

"Okay. That is admittedly interesting," Knox says. "Could be a coincidence, though."

"No way. There are no coincidences when it comes to this sort of thing. He mentioned Simon, too, so there's that whole gossip-as-a-weapon connection. This is our guy."

"Great. So now what? How do you find out who Darkest-mind actually is?"

Some of my excitement ebbs away. "Well. That's Phase Two, obviously, and I will get to that . . . later."

Knox's voice fades, like he's holding his phone at a distance. "Okay, yeah, sorry. I'll be right there." He returns at normal volume. "I have to go. I'm at work."

"You are?" I ask, surprised. "Don't you have play rehearsal tonight?"

"Yeah, but there's a ton going on at Until Proven and my understudy could use the practice, so I skipped." Knox says it like it's no big deal, but I can't remember him ever missing a rehearsal before. "Listen, Maeve, it's almost six, so—if you're gonna text back *Dare*, now would be the time."

"No way. I told you, I'm not playing their game." Even as I say it, though, I swallow hard and look at the clock on my laptop. Five fifty-nine.

I can't tell if Knox's answering sigh is frustrated or resigned. "Fine. But don't say I didn't warn you."

CHAPTER ELEVEN

Phoebe
Tuesday, March 3

Emma, the queen of punctuality, is late.

I've been standing at her locker for five minutes after last bell, and there's no sign of her. We're supposed to go to Owen's spelling bee together—presenting a united front so Mom can stay clueless about the fact that we're not speaking—but I'm starting to get the uneasy feeling that my sister has ditched me.

Two more minutes, I decide. Then I'll call it, and walk.

I shift a few feet to my right to scan the hallway bulletin board while I wait. BE THE KIND OF PERSON WHO MAKES EVERY-BODY FEEL LIKE SOMEBODY, a rainbow-lettered poster tells me, except someone's crossed out SOMEBODY and written SHIT under it.

Oh, Bayview High. You are nothing if not consistent.

A shoulder bumps mine, and I half turn. "Sorry!" Monica

Hill says breezily. She's in her basketball cheerleading uniform, her platinum hair pulled back with a purple-and-white ribbon. "Checking out your ad? It's so nice that you and Emma are going into business together."

"We're not," I say curtly. I have no idea what she's talking about, but it doesn't matter. Monica is tight with Sean and Brandon, so her fake-friendly act doesn't fool me. Besides, she's been trying to steal my best friend for weeks. And succeeding, I guess, considering Jules told her about the Dare instead of me.

Monica's lips curl into a small smile. "Your flyer says different." She reaches across me and taps a familiar pale-blue sheet of paper that says *Emma Lawton Tutoring* across the top. My sister puts them up all over school, with her phone number and a list of subjects: mathematics, chemistry/biology, Spanish. But this particular ad says more than that, in a Sharpie scrawl beneath Emma's neat printing:

Threesomes (special offer with Phoebe Lawton)
Contact us on Instagram!

I swallow against the lump in my throat as I stare silently at my Instagram handle written across the bottom of the page. Payback from Brandon, I guess, for me throwing him out of the apartment last week. That asshole.

There's no way I'm giving Monica the satisfaction of a reaction, though. Whatever I do or say right now is going straight back to Brandon. "Don't you have a game to go to?" I ask. Then a hand reaches over my shoulder, catching the blue sheet by one corner and yanking it off the bulletin board.

I turn to see Emma in her usual headband and oxford shirt, her face a smooth mask as she crumples the ad in one palm.

"Excuse me," she says to a smirking Monica. "You're trash. I mean, you're blocking the trash." Emma reaches around Monica to toss the paper ball into a recycling bin, then tilts her head toward me, still perfectly calm. "Sorry I was late. I had a few questions for Mr. Bose after history. Ready to leave?"

"Ready."

I follow her long strides down the hallway, almost running to keep up. My mind is churning as we go. Does this mean Emma forgives me? Or at least doesn't hate me anymore? "Thanks for that," I say, my voice low as we push through the doors leading to the parking lot.

Emma slides me a sideways glance that's not friendly, exactly, but it's not angry, either. "Some people take things too far," she says. "There are limits. There *have* to be limits."

The auditorium at Granger Middle School is exactly like I remember: stuffy, overly bright, and smelling like musty fabric and pencil shavings. The front half of the room is filled with folding chairs, and I spot Mom waving energetically from the third row as soon as Emma and I enter. A heavy curtain is pulled across the stage, and a middle-aged woman in a baggy cardigan and knee-length skirt steps through it. "We'll be starting in just a few minutes," she calls, but nobody pays attention. Mom keeps waving until we're practically on top of her, then pulls her bag and her coat from the two seats beside her, shifting her knees to one side so we can get past her and take our seats.

"Perfect timing," she says. My mother looks pretty today,

her dark hair spilling around an autumn-toned scarf that makes her olive skin glow. The sight of it cheers me up, because it reminds me of what my mother was like when I went to Granger Middle School—always the best-dressed parent at every school event. Mom has a lot of natural style, but she hasn't made much of an effort since Dad died. Working on Ashton and Eli's wedding has definitely been good for her state of mind. She plucks lightly at Emma's sleeve and adds, "I could use your help with a couple of wedding tasks."

Emma and Mom put their heads together, and I surreptitiously take out my phone. Emma actually talked to me on the ride over, and I didn't want to spoil our fragile truce by checking Instagram. But I need to know how much shit I'm getting.

Notifications flood my screen as soon as I pull up my account. So, a lot.

My last post was a work selfie that got twenty comments. Now it has more than a hundred. I read the first one—*yes hi sign me up for threesomes 101 please*—and immediately click away.

"Welcome, families, to Granger Middle School's annual spelling bee!" My heart is already thudding against my rib cage, and the loud voice booming through a microphone ratchets it up another notch. It's the same woman who spoke before, standing behind a lectern on one corner of the auditorium stage. Ten kids, Owen included, are arranged in a line beside her. "Let me introduce the scholars who will be dazzling you with their spelling prowess today. First up is our only sixth-grader in the contest, Owen Lawton!"

I clap loudly until the principal moves on to the next kid, then return my attention to my phone. It's like I just yanked off a bandage, and now I can't help but poke the wound beneath. I set my Instagram account to private, which I obviously should have done a week ago, and scroll to my message requests. They're full of guys I don't know begging me to "tutor" them. One of them just puts a phone number. Does that ever work? Has any girl in the history of the world texted a stranger because he slid his digits into her DMs? I'm about to hit Decline All and erase them from my account forever when a name at the bottom of the screen catches my eye.

Derekculpepper01 Hi, it's Derek. I was

That's all I can see without opening the message. Ugh, what does Emma's ex want? We haven't spoken since the night in Jules's laundry room. We never exchanged numbers, obviously, or he wouldn't be going through Instagram now. If he's going to apologize for telling someone about us, I don't care. Too late.

I eye Decline All again, but my curiosity gets the better of me. *Hi, it's Derek. I was hoping we could talk sometime. Can you text me?* With a phone number.

Well, that raises more questions than it answers.

I cup my hand around my phone so it blocks the screen from Emma's line of sight and navigate to Derek's profile. He has literally *no* selfies. His entire Instagram feed is pictures of food or his dog. Who does that? It's not as if he's terrible-looking. Just sort of unmemorable.

Emma coughs lightly, and I sneak another look at her. I would rather chop my own arm off and beat myself senseless with it than talk to Derek Culpepper again, and I'm pretty sure Emma feels the same way. That leaves Derek as the only person in our twisted triangle who's interested in reopening the channels of communication, and nobody cares about him.

"And now let's begin with our first word of the day, for Owen Lawton. Owen, can you spell *bizarre* for us, please?"

I look up just in time to catch Owen's eye as he grins and gives me what he thinks is a stealthy thumbs-up. I put my phone away and try to smile back.

A couple of hours later, Mom is at a Golden Rings wedding planner meeting and Emma and I are in our room. I'm stretched out on my bed with a textbook on my lap, and Emma is at her desk with headphones on, her head bobbing silently to whatever music she's playing. We're not being social, exactly, but everything feels less tense than it has for a while.

A knock sounds on our door, and Owen pokes his head in. "Hey," I say, sitting up. "Congratulations again, brainiac."

"Thanks," Owen says modestly as Emma pulls her headphones off. "It wasn't really a contest, though. Nobody else at that school can spell."

"Alex Chen made a solid showing," Emma points out.

Owen looks unconvinced. "You'd think an eighth-grader would know how to spell *parallel,* though." He perches on the edge of my bed and angles toward me. "Phoebe, I forgot to tell you." His glasses are a mess of smudges, so I pull them off and wipe the lenses with the hem of my T-shirt. His eyes look unfinished without them. "You have to invite your friend over. Knox something?"

"I have to—what?" I blink in surprise as I hand his glasses

back. He settles them unevenly on his nose. "How do you know Knox?"

"I met him at Café Contigo. He plays *Bounty Wars*," Owen says, like that's all the explanation I should require.

Emma wrinkles her brow at me. "You and Knox Myers are friends?"

"We're friend-adjacent," I say.

She nods approvingly. "He seems like a good guy."

"He is," I say, and turn back to Owen. "Why do you want me to invite Knox over?"

"So we can play *Bounty Wars*. We talked about it at Café Contigo," Owen explains, and now all of this is starting to make sense. My brother misreads social cues a *lot*. Knox was probably being nice, asking about Owen's favorite game while he waited for our food to be ready. I don't know Knox well, but he seems that type: the sort of boy parents love because he's friendly to kids and old people. Polite, clean-cut, and completely nonthreatening.

It confused me when I realized he and Maeve were going out a while back, because they made such an odd couple. She's the subtle kind of pretty that slides under the radar, but once you start noticing her you wonder how you missed it. Maybe it's the eyes; I've never seen that dark-honey color on anyone else. Or the way she sort of glides around Bayview High like she's just passing through and doesn't worry about the same kind of stuff the rest of us do. No wonder Luis Santos can't take his eyes off her. *Them* I can see together. They match.

It's a shallow way to look at things, but that doesn't make it less true.

Knox has potential, though. Add a few pounds, get a better haircut, amp up the confidence, and—wham. Knox Myers could be a heartbreaker, someday. Just not yet.

Owen is still looking at me expectantly. "Knox and I aren't really the kind of friends who go to each other's houses," I tell him.

His lower lip juts out in a pout. "Why not? You let *Brandon* come over."

My chest constricts at the memory of Brandon's slimy tongue trying to invade my mouth. "That's not—"

"Brandon *Weber*?" Owen and I both jump as Emma's voice spikes an octave. "That creep was in our apartment? Why?" I don't answer, and her expression gradually morphs from horrified to thunderous. "Oh my God. Is *that* who you've been hooking up with lately?"

"Can we not do this right now?" I say, with a pointed glance toward Owen.

But Emma's face has gone red and splotchy, which is always a bad sign. She yanks her headphones from around her neck and stands up, stalking toward me like she's about to shove me across my bed and into the wall. I almost flinch before she stops a foot away, hands on her hips. "Jesus Christ, Phoebe. You are *such* an idiot. Brandon Weber is a piece of shit who doesn't care about anyone except himself. You know that, right?"

I gape at her, hurt and confused. I thought we were finally getting past the Derek situation, and now she's mad at me about Brandon? Did she . . . Oh God. Oh please no. "Were you involved with Brandon too?" I burst out.

Emma's mouth drops open. "Are you for real? I would

never. Can you honestly think—no, of course you can't. That's the problem, isn't it? You don't think. You just *do*. Whatever you want." She goes back to her desk, piling her notebook on top of our laptop and hugging them both to her chest. "I'm going to the library. I can't get anything done in this shithole."

She leaves, slamming the door behind her, and Owen stares after her. "Are you guys ever gonna stop being mad at each other?" he asks.

I let my shoulders slump, too tired to pretend I don't know what he's talking about. "Eventually. Probably."

Owen kicks his legs back and forth so his sneakers scuff against the floor. "Everything's ruined, isn't it?" he asks, his voice so low it's barely audible. "Our whole family. We have been since Dad died."

"Owen, no!" I wrap an arm around his thin shoulders and pull him toward me, but he's so stiff that he just leans uncomfortably against my side. Everything in me aches as it hits me, all of a sudden, how long it's been since I hugged my brother. Or my sister. "Of course we're not ruined. We're fine. Emma and I are just going through a rough patch."

Even as the words leave my mouth, I know they're too little, too late. I should've been comforting Owen for the past three years, not just the past three minutes.

Owen disentangles himself from my arm and gets to his feet. "I'm not a little kid anymore, Phoebe. I know when you're lying." He opens the door and slips through, shutting it more quietly than Emma did, but just as emphatically.

I flop down on my bed and stare at the clock on my wall.

144

How is it only seven o'clock? This day has been going on forever.

A text tone chimes from somewhere in the depths of my tangled comforter. I don't have the energy to sit up, so I just root around with one hand until I find my phone and drag it a few inches from my face.

Unknown: Tsk, no response from our latest player.

That means you forfeit, Maeve Rojas.

Now I get to reveal one of your secrets in true About That style.

My eyes go wide. Maeve didn't tell me she'd been picked, even though we've been hanging out at school lately. That girl is either seriously reserved or has avoidance issues. Maybe both.

Still, there's nothing to worry about. Maeve isn't full of embarrassing secrets, like me. Unknown will probably just rehash that old story about her puking in some basketball player's basement when she was a freshman. Or maybe it'll be about her crush on Luis, although that's so glaringly obvious that it doesn't really qualify as a secret. Either way, I wish the text would come through so I can stop obsessing over this stupid game.

And then it does.

Unknown's latest piece of gossip fills my screen. I blink five or six times, but I still can't believe what I'm seeing. No. No way. Oh no. Oh *hell no.*

The *omg what?!?* messages start pouring in, so fast I can't keep up with them. I bolt upright and scramble to press Maeve's number, but she doesn't pick up. I'm not surprised. Right now, there's another call she'd better be making.

CHAPTER TWELVE

Knox
Tuesday, March 3

The guy in King's Landing is sweating up a storm. Twitching, rocking, constantly rubbing one hand over his jaw while he talks with Sandeep in the closed conference room. "It's weird how guilty innocent people can look, sometimes," I say to Bethany Okonjo, a law student who's one of Until Proven's paralegals.

We're stationed at a desk outside the conference room, collating news coverage about the D'Agostino case. Bethany shrugs and reaches into a drawer for more staples. "And vice versa, right?" she says. "Guilty people can look innocent as hell. Take our friend here." She holds up a long feature article about Sergeant Carl D'Agostino, accompanied by a picture of him wearing his cop uniform and a big grin. His arm is around a college-aged kid who's holding a plaque. "Funny how they use *this,* and not his mug shot," she adds, tossing her braids over one shoulder. "None of the people he framed got that kind of kid-glove treatment when they were arrested."

I glance at the caption under the photo. *The week before his arrest, Sergeant Carl D'Agostino commended San Diego State University students for excellence in community peer mentoring.* "I never really thought about it that way," I say, scanning the first few paragraphs of the article. "But you're right. This is all about what a great guy he was until—*whoops,* major scandal. Like he just accidentally stumbled into framing seventeen people."

I add the article to my pile and glance at the clock on the wall next to the conference room. It's almost seven at night. I've never stayed this late, but I'm starting to think I'm the only person at Until Proven who leaves on time. The office is still buzzing, every desk full and littered with empty pizza boxes and Coke cans. Bethany picks up her discarded crust and nibbles on the edge. "They gave that classmate of yours the same treatment. Jake Riordan, remember him?" Like I could forget. *"Star athlete involved in Simon Kelleher case,"* Bethany says in her newscaster voice. "Oh, you mean *involved* like how he tried to kill his girlfriend? That kind of *involved?*"

"That was bullshit," I agree.

Bethany snorts. "The justice system works very differently when you're white, male, rich, and good-looking." She nudges the last piece of pizza toward me. "Good to know, I guess, if you ever decide to turn to a life of crime."

I pick up the slice, but it's so cold and congealed that I can't bring myself to take a bite. "I'm only two of those things."

"Don't sell yourself short, kid."

Eli passes by, holding a phone with a familiar case that he waves at me. "Knox. This is yours, right? You left it in the copy room. Also, Maeve is calling." He looks at my screen. "Was calling. You just missed her."

I thought my phone had been strangely quiet. "Sorry about that," I say, taking it from him. I register a surprising number of texts before I lay it on my desk like a busy professional who doesn't have time for Bayview High gossip. Eli finally knows my name and has started giving me more interesting stuff to do. I don't want to blow it by acting like a phone-obsessed teenager in front of him. Even though I am. "Do you need anything?"

Eli runs a hand through his newly shorn hair. "I need you to go home. There are child labor laws, or so Sandeep keeps telling me, and we're probably violating them. Especially since we're not paying you. Anyway, call Maeve back and then get out of here, all right? Everything else can wait until tomorrow." He glances at Bethany, who's still stapling news articles. "Bethany, can you sit down with me and review next week's court schedule?"

"Yeah, sure." She gazes around the crowded office. "Should we go in Winterfell?"

Eli rolls his eyes. He's never going to get used to those names. "Fine."

They leave, and I eye my phone warily. I really do hate making calls, but maybe Maeve's on her laptop again and can't text. I press her name, and she picks up before it's even rung once.

"Oh thank God." Her voice is low, breathless. "I was afraid you wouldn't call me back."

The sweaty guy is pacing circles around Sandeep in the conference room, distracting me. "Why wouldn't I? I'm only kidding about being allergic to phone calls. Mostly." The line goes so silent that I think we've been disconnected. "Maeve? You there?"

"I . . . yeah. Um, what are you up to?"

"Still at work, but I'm gonna leave soon."

"Okay. Right. Have you . . ." She trails off, and I think I hear an audible gulp. "Have you been checking your phone?"

"No. I left it in the copy room for, like, an hour. What's up?" I look at the wall clock again, and it hits me. "Shit. Your Truth or Dare text came, didn't it? What did it say? Are you all right?"

"Oh God." Maeve's voice thickens. "I'm sorry, Knox. I am so, so sorry."

"What? Maeve, you're starting to freak me out." I pause, alarm snaking through my gut as her breath hitches. "Are you *crying*?"

"Um . . ." She definitely is. "So, I think . . . okay. I'm going to read you the text from Unknown because, um, I don't want you to have to read all the comments to get to it. Because they're stupid and pointless like always." Maeve draws in a shaky breath. "But before I do—I need you to know I didn't say that, okay? Not *exactly* that. I wouldn't. I've been racking my brains and I can only come up with a single conversation that's even a little bit pertinent but I swear to God, it was a *lot* more nuanced than that. And it was with Bronwyn, who would never breathe a word, so I honestly don't know how this even happened."

"Maeve, seriously. What's going on? Who do I need to fight?"

"Don't." She groans the word. "I, okay. This is what it said. *Maeve Rojas,* um . . ." I hear a deep breath, and then the rest of the words come out in a rush. *"Maeve Rojas dumped Knox Myers because he can't get it up."*

What. The. Fuck.

I listen to Maeve's ragged breathing for a minute. Or maybe that's mine. When she tentatively asks, "Knox? Are you—" I disconnect. The phone drops out of my hand, bouncing lightly on the desk, and I let it stay facedown while I press my fists to my forehead.

What the *fuck.* My heart's pounding out of my chest. No. No way. The entire school did not just read about the most humiliating moment of my life. Which was *private.* And supposed to stay that way forever.

Maeve and I—God. It was stupid. We talked about it for months, *losing our virginity,* like it was some project we had to finish before we could graduate high school. That should've been a clue, that we were so practical about it. But we thought we wanted to, and then my parents went out of town for their anniversary, so there it was: opportunity.

I was so nervous, though. I did a couple shots of my dad's vodka before Maeve came over, because I thought that'd calm me down, but all it did was make me dizzy and a little nauseated. And then we were kissing and it just . . . wasn't working. Any of it. I could tell she wasn't into it either, but we'd, like, *committed.* I didn't know how the hell I could just tap out all of a sudden. Especially since guys are supposed to be born ready.

It was a massive relief when Maeve pulled away and asked if we could take a break for a minute. Then she buttoned her shirt back up and said, "Do you ever feel like maybe we're trying too hard to be something we're not?"

I was grateful to her then. For getting it. For not making a big deal. For being as non-awkward as possible, both then and later, so I could pretend it hadn't happened. I'd almost convinced myself that it didn't. Until now.

Because she *told* people. More people than Bronwyn, I'm sure, because Bronwyn's not the type to spread gossip.

It doesn't even matter who it was. Damage done.

I turn my phone over. There are new messages from Maeve that I ignore, opening the giant group text from Unknown instead. *I don't want you to have to read all the comments to get to it,* Maeve had said. *Because they're stupid and pointless like always.*

And prolific. There must be a hundred of them.

Sorry about the soft serve, man.

I know a great pharmacy in Canada where you can bulk order Viagra.

Maybe it's because she's not a dude.

Jesus. How the hell am I supposed to show up at school tomorrow? Or ever? Or get up on a stage next month to perform *Into the Woods,* singing in front of everybody? Bayview High is ruthless. One incident is all it takes to define you for the rest of your life, and I just found mine. At our twentieth reunion, Brandon Weber and Sean Murdock will still be laughing about this.

"Knox?" I jump at Eli's voice. He and Bethany are approaching my desk, laptops in hand. "I thought you were going home." I scrape a hand across my face and he peers at me more closely, frowning. "You all right? You look sick all of a sudden."

"Headache," I croak. "No big deal. I'm just gonna—yeah. I'm gonna go." I grab my phone and get unsteadily to my feet as Eli watches with an increasingly furrowed brow. He sets down his laptop on the corner of the desk.

"Let me give you a ride. You're really pale."

I hesitate. What's a worse place to be while dick jokes pile up on my phone: in a car with my boss, or on a bus next to some grandmother I'll never see again? It's no contest. "No, I'm good," I force out. "Totally fine. See you tomorrow." I'm almost at the door when I feel a tug on my arm. I half turn, my temper spiking too fast to hold it in. "I said I'm *fine*!"

"I know," Bethany says. "But you probably still want this." She presses the strap of my backpack into my hand.

"Right. Sorry." I feel a surge of guilt, avoiding her eyes as I shoulder my backpack. I'm still pissed off, but none of this is Bethany's fault. I wait until I'm in the elevator, doors safely shut behind me, to find a better target.

Texts from Maeve are at the top of my message list:

I'm so sorry.

I never meant to hurt you.

Can we talk?

There's a lot I want to say, but I settle for short and to the point.

Go to hell, Maeve.

CHAPTER THIRTEEN

Maeve
Wednesday, March 4

The first person to greet me at school Wednesday morning is Sean Murdock, and he does it by grabbing the front of his pants. "Climb on any time you want a real man," he leers, thrusting his hips while Brandon Weber cackles behind him. "Satisfaction guaranteed."

My face burns with the kind of combined horror and shame I haven't felt since Simon Kelleher wrote a scathing blog post about me freshman year. This time, though, I can't slink into the shadows to get away from it all. For one thing, my sister's not around to fight for me. And for another, I'm not the only one affected.

"First off, gross," I say loudly. "Second, that stupid game is *lying*. Nothing like that ever happened." I spin my combination and yank the door to my locker so hard that I lose my grip and slam it into my neighbor's. "You're an idiot if you believe everything you read. Well, you're an idiot regardless. But either way, it's not true."

That's my story, and come hell or high water, I will stick with it.

"Sure, Maeve," Sean smirks. This is a sucky time to find out he knows my name after all. His eyes travel up and down my body, making my skin crawl. "Offer still stands."

Brandon laughs again. "Literally," he says. He puts his hand up for a high five, but Sean just looks confused.

Laughter echoes in the hall, and Sean brightens as he turns in its direction. There's a group of people clustered around the bay where Knox's locker is. "Looks like your boyfriend's here," Sean says. "Well, *ex*-boyfriend. Can't blame you for that. Hope he likes his present." My heart sinks as he and Brandon saunter down the hall toward the growing crowd. I grab a random assortment of books that probably aren't even what I need for class, stuff them into my backpack, and slam my locker door closed.

I'm halfway to Knox's locker when someone grabs hold of my arm. "I wouldn't," Phoebe says, pulling me to a stop. Her curly hair is in a high ponytail that swings when she turns her head to look behind us. "You being anywhere near him right now is only going to make things worse." She doesn't sound mean, just matter-of-fact, but the words still sting.

"What's going on?"

"Limp noodles glued to his locker. In a—shape. You can probably guess." She shrugs in what she clearly wants to be a breezy manner, but the tense lines of her mouth don't match.

154

"Could've been worse. At least noodles are easy to get off." Her jaw twitches. "I mean, clean."

I slump against the locker beside me. "Oh God. They're such assholes. And it's not even true." I raise my voice. "I *never* said that." I dart a glance at Phoebe, testing out the lie on somebody with significantly more brain cells than Sean.

"It doesn't matter," she says, in that same breezy-yet-bitter voice. "People will believe what they want anyway."

I grimace in frustration. "The worst thing is, I was actually making progress in figuring out who's doing this. Not fast enough, though."

Phoebe blinks. "Say what?"

I catch her up on the latest revenge forum posts from Darkestmind. "I'll bet that last one was about me," I say, holding out my phone so Phoebe can see the screenshot I took. *More to come soon. Tick-tock.*

She sucks her lower lip in between her teeth. "Hmm. Maybe? Still doesn't give you any idea who's talking, though."

"Not yet," I say. "But you'd be surprised. People who think they're being stealthy and anonymous give themselves away all the time." Simon certainly did.

"Can I give you some advice?" Phoebe asks. I nod as she leans against the locker beside me, her face serious. "I was thinking about this stupid game all last night, and how it has everybody dancing like puppets on a string. Whoever's behind Truth or Dare is on a massive power trip. And the thing is, we're *giving* them that power. By caring. Reacting. Spending all our time worrying about who's next and what's true. We're feeding the beast and I, for one, am done. I blocked Unknown last night, and I think you should too. Back away from the revenge forum. Stop handing those anonymous weirdos the attention they want so much. If everyone ignored them, they'd stop."

"But everyone *won't* ignore them," I protest. "This is Bayview High we're talking about. The gossip capital of North America."

Phoebe gives a little toss of her head. "Well, we have to start somewhere, don't we? I'm officially opting out of this mess."

"Sounds great in theory," I say. "I don't disagree. But that's not going to help Knox at this particular point in time."

"People are making way too big a deal of this," Phoebe says. She edges a little closer and lowers her voice. "It's not uncommon, you know. Especially during a first time. Was there alcohol involved, by any chance?"

I resist the urge to bash my head against the locker, but just barely. "Please don't." Then, because I'm desperate to understand what happened and Knox isn't speaking to me, I add in a whisper, "I don't know how anyone could have found out. I only told Bronwyn and she would never say anything."

"Are you sure?" Phoebe arches a skeptical brow, and I guess I can't blame her for asking. She doesn't exactly have an iron-clad bond of sisterly trust with Emma.

"Positive. Maybe Knox told somebody. He has a lot more friends than I do."

Phoebe shakes her head emphatically. "No way. A guy would never."

My throat aches. "He hates me now."

The bell rings, and Phoebe pats my arm. "Look, this sucks and of course he's upset. But you didn't actually do anything so terrible. The fact is, girls talk about this kind of stuff. *People* talk about this kind of stuff. He knows that. Just give him some time."

"Yeah," I mumble, and then my heart jumps into my throat as I spy Knox's familiar gray sweatshirt headed our way. His backpack is slung over one shoulder, his head down. When he gets close enough for me to see his face, he looks so miserable that I can't keep quiet. "Hi, Knox," I call, my voice wavering on his name.

His mouth twitches downward, so I know he heard me. But he walks past us without saying a word.

Phoebe pats my arm again, harder. "More time than that."

The rest of the day doesn't get any better. Flaccid penis pictures start showing up everywhere: on lockers, classroom doors, bathroom walls, even at the kitchen lunch line. Former prison worker Robert tears one down while I grab a soggy turkey sandwich that I have no intention of eating. "What fresh hell are these monsters up to now?" he mutters, with an expression that's equal parts mystified and apprehensive.

It's pushed every other worrying thought from my head. The nosebleeds and bruises can wait. Unknown's identity—I don't care anymore. Phoebe was right: whoever it is isn't worth all the time and attention I've been giving them. I need to focus my energy on fixing this mess with Knox. I mean, I have a measly five people in my Key Contacts, and he's the only one who's not related to me or getting paid to keep me from dying. I can't let this ruin our friendship.

After the last bell, I head for an *Into the Woods* rehearsal, hoping for one last chance to talk with him. I make my way slowly down the aisle of the auditorium, simultaneously scanning the small crowd and counting how many lights are blazing above the stage. *If it's an even number, Knox will forgive me today. Ten, eleven, twelve . . . thirteen.*

Damn it. Doubly unlucky.

Knox is nowhere in sight, and it doesn't look as though rehearsal has started yet. There are only two people onstage, and when I get closer I see that one of them is Mrs. Kaplan, the drama teacher, and the other is a sullen-looking Eddie Blalock.

"But I don't know the part," Eddie says. He's a sophomore, small and thin with dark hair that he gels into stiff points.

"You're the *understudy*." Mrs. Kaplan plants her hands on her hips. "You were supposed to have been learning the role of Jack for the past two months."

"Yeah, but." Eddie scratches the back of his head. "I didn't."

Mrs. Kaplan heaves a bone-weary sigh. "You had one job, Eddie."

Lucy Chen is perched on the edge of a chair in the front row, leaning forward with both her arms and legs crossed. She looks like an angry human pretzel.

"What's going on?" I ask.

She presses her lips together so tightly that they almost disappear. "Knox quit," she says, her eyes fixed on Eddie like a bird of prey. "In related news, Eddie sucks." I inhale a shocked breath, and Lucy seems to register who she's speaking to for the first time. "So, thanks a lot for ruining the play and everything."

My temper flares. I'll blame myself all day long, but I draw the line at Lucy doing the same. "This isn't my fault. It's that horrible game—"

"Do you mean the horrible game that *I* said we should report two weeks ago?" Lucy lifts her chin. "If anyone had listened to me, it probably would've been shut down by now and none of this would have happened."

God, I hate when Lucy's right. "Maybe we should tell someone now," I say, my eyes straying to Mrs. Kaplan.

"Oh no you don't," Lucy snaps. "She has enough to worry about. Besides, everyone knows how to win this game by now. Just take the Dare. You'd have to be out of your mind to do anything else."

Phoebe's words in the hallway come back to me then. *Whoever's behind Truth or Dare must be on a massive power trip. And the thing is, we're* giving *them that power.* "Or we could all jointly block this creep's number and stop playing altogether," I say. Then I pull out my phone so, finally, I can do exactly that.

"Mija, you've been here through dinnertime and haven't eaten a thing. Are you all right?"

I look up from my laptop at Mr. Santos's voice, startled when I see a baseball cap jammed over his unruly curls. He only wears that when he's leaving Café Contigo for the night, and he's usually the last one here. Then I realize how empty the restaurant is.

"I'm fine. Just not hungry." I was too anxious to sit at a dinner table with my parents tonight, so I told them I was meeting Knox here. That was a big fat lie, unfortunately. I can't even get him to text me back. And I'm way too stressed to eat. I've just been staring blankly at the history paper I'm supposed to be writing for . . . hours, apparently.

Mr. Santos makes a *tsk* noise. "I don't believe that. I think we just haven't found the right food to tempt you. Maybe you need a good old-fashioned Colombian recipe. What's your favorite?" He shudders a little. "Please don't say salchipapas."

I manage a laugh. Bronwyn refused to eat hot dogs when we were kids, so we've never had the traditional Colombian dish of them cut up and mixed with French fries. "Definitely not. We're more of an ajiaco family."

"Excellent choice. I'll make it for you."

"Mr. Santos, no!" I lunge for his sleeve as he turns for the kitchen. "I mean, that's so nice of you, but ajiaco takes hours. And you're closing."

"I'll make a fast-food version, Argentinean-style. It'll take fifteen minutes."

Oh God. I can't believe I'm such a sad puppy that this impossibly kind man thinks he has to work overtime to make me dinner. At least I'm in long sleeves so he can't see that I'm covered in bruises, too. "I'm honestly fine, Mr. Santos. It's really not—"

"I'll make it," calls a voice behind us. Luis is leaning against the half-open kitchen door, a grease-spattered gray T-shirt stretched tight across his shoulders. It's ridiculous how good it looks on him. "Go home, Pa. I'll close up." He crosses halfway to the dining room and holds up his right hand. I'm not sure what he's doing until Mr. Santos reaches into his pocket and tosses Luis a set of keys.

"Works for me," Mr. Santos says, and turns back to me with a gentle smile. "Don't look so guilty, mija. He needs the practice."

He waves amiably and shuffles out the door. I let him disappear around the corner of the building before I stand and stuff my laptop into my bag with an apologetic look at Luis. "Listen, just go home. If he asks, I'll tell him you fed me. I'm not even hungry." My empty stomach chooses that exact moment to rumble loudly. Luis raises his eyebrows as I fold my arms tightly over my rib cage. My stomach growls again anyway. "At all."

"Come on." A half smile teases the corners of his mouth. "It's not like you're not going to help." He turns and disappears into the back of the restaurant, leaving me no choice but to follow.

I've only ever glimpsed the kitchen from the dining room before, bright and chaotic and bursting with noise. Now it's so still and silent that Luis's voice echoes when he gestures to the row of appliances behind a long, well-worn metal table. "Here's where the magic happens."

I put my hands on my hips and look around the kitchen with what I hope is professional interest. "Very impressive."

"Hang on a sec. I need to get out of this shirt, it's a disaster." Luis goes behind a tall, freestanding rack of metal shelves and grabs something white out of a duffel bag. Before I can fully register what he's doing, he's pulled his T-shirt over his head and put on a clean one. I get a flash of shoulder muscles and then he's done, stuffing the old shirt into his bag and replacing it on the shelf.

I wish I'd known that was about to happen so I could've paid better attention.

Luis crosses to an industrial-sized refrigerator and pulls open the door. "Let's see . . . oh yeah, we're all set. We have chicken and potatoes already prepped for tomorrow. Not the right kind of potato, but it'll do. No corn, but I can make that quick." He starts pulling ingredients out and laying them across the counter, then selects a knife from a rack on the wall and hands it to me. "Can you chop some scallions?"

"Sure." I take the knife gingerly. It's the smallest one in the rack, but I've never handled anything quite so deadly-looking.

"There's a cutting board below the counter."

There are several. I shuffle through them, wondering if plastic or wood is better, but since Luis didn't specify I end up just grabbing the one on top. I lay the scallions across it and turn them a few different ways, trying to figure out the best angle for cutting. By the time I'm halfway through the bunch, Luis looks like he's been in the kitchen for hours. Pots are steaming, garlic is sautéing, and the chicken and potatoes are chopped into small, neat pieces. Luis puts down his knife, wipes the back of his hand across his forehead, then glances my way and grins.

"Take your time with that."

I laugh for the first time all day. "I'm the worst prep assistant ever."

"You haven't seen Manny in here." Luis adjusts a knob on a burner, and I speed up the rest of my chopping so I can finish and watch him work. He moves around the kitchen like he does on a baseball diamond: fluid and confident, as though he's

162

thinking ten steps ahead and knows exactly where he needs to be at all times. It's the sexiest thing I've ever seen.

He reaches for a pair of tongs and glances my way, catching me staring. Busted. My cheeks flame as his crease in a smile. "What's going on with you today?" he asks. "You were hunched over your computer for hours out there."

"I . . ." I hesitate. There's no way I can tell him the whole story. "I had a bad day. Knox and I had a fight. And, um, I think it's my fault. Scratch that. I *know* it's my fault."

I watch his reaction carefully, because Luis still has friends at Bayview High. It's possible he knows exactly what I'm talking about. Though, if he does, he hides it well. "Did you tell him that?" he asks.

"I tried. He's not talking to me right now."

Luis takes my cutting board full of scallions and dumps them into a bubbling pot. It smells amazing. I'm not sure how it's going to be stew in ten minutes, but I won't question his methods. "That sucks. You have to give people a chance to apologize."

"It's not his fault," I say. "He's just hurt. Stuff got out that shouldn't have, and now everyone is gossiping and it's a giant mess."

Luis grimaces. "Man, I do *not* miss that school. It's fucking toxic there."

"I feel like I'm the one who's toxic." The words slip out of me before I think, and as soon as I say them my eyes start stinging. Damn it. I take the cutting board to the sink and rinse it so I can keep my head down.

Luis leans against the counter. "You're not toxic. I don't

know what happened, but I do know that. Look, everybody does stuff they shouldn't. I was an ass at Bayview a lot of the time. Then that whole situation with Jake and Addy and Cooper started getting bad, and things changed." He's cleaning the station in front of him now, as quickly as he did the prep work. "I used to talk to Pa about what was happening at school and he'd say, 'Who do you want to be? The guy who goes along or the guy who stands up? This is the time to decide.'"

I put the cutting board away. "It was great, the way you stood up for Cooper."

"*Nate* stood up for Cooper," Luis corrects. A muscle in his jaw twitches. "All I did was not pile on. And I should've stood up for Addy way before that. I wasn't a badass like you, helping those guys from the start. But you can't change the past, you know? All you can do is try harder next time. So don't give up on yourself just yet."

At this moment, I've never wanted to do anything as much as I want to grab his face and kiss every inch of it. Which should make me feel guilty after what happened today with Knox but instead makes me edge closer to Luis. I'm suddenly beyond tired of never doing what I want or saying what I feel.

I mean, I could be dead in six months. What's the point in holding back?

Luis moves toward the stove and turns the burner down. He picks up a timer from the counter and twists it slightly. "This needs five minutes to simmer." He goes back to his station, wiping his hands on a towel, and I make up my mind. I move toward him until the space between us is nearly closed and put my hand on his arm. If nothing else, I've been wanting

164

to do that for ages. My pulse starts thrumming as I ask, "What should we do for the next five minutes, then?"

Luis goes still, and for one horrifying second I think he's going to burst out laughing. If he does, I won't have to worry about cancer because I'll die on the spot. Then his mouth curves in a slow smile. He glances down beneath lashes that are so long and thick, they almost look tangled. His hands circle my waist. "I don't know. You have any ideas?"

"A few." I bring one hand to the back of his neck and lean into him, sliding my fingers into his hair. It's softer than I expected, and his skin is warm from the stove and the bright lights above us. I pause to catch my breath because it's almost too much, the way every nerve in my body is buzzing with sensation when nothing's even happened yet.

Then Luis kisses me, his lips a gentle press of heat against my mouth. Soft and almost sweet, until I wind my arms around his neck and pull him closer. He kisses me harder, picking me up in one smooth motion and putting me on the counter behind us. There's no place for my legs to go except . . . around his waist. The softest groan escapes him as he slides his lips along my jawline and down to my neck. My hands find their way under the hem of his T-shirt, and every scattered thought that was still bouncing around in my brain dissolves when I feel his muscles contract beneath my fingertips. We keep kissing until I lose all sense of time and place, and the only thing I want is *more*.

A sudden noise brings me back to myself. Someone's whistling off-key, and heavy footsteps are coming our way. I pull away from Luis, face burning when I realize how far up his shirt my hands have gotten, and the intentional way I've twisted the fabric. I was seconds away from yanking it over his head.

Luis's eyes look drugged until he registers the noise. Then he frowns and disentangles from me, moving toward the door. "What the hell?" he mutters. I hop off the counter, weak-kneed, and try to smooth my hair. A second later Manny bursts into the kitchen, still whistling.

"What up, L?" He holds out his hand for a fist bump that turns into a shoulder punch when Luis doesn't respond. "Why are you still cooking?"

"I'm making something for Maeve," Luis says. His voice isn't nearly as friendly as it usually is when he talks to his brother. "What are you doing here?"

"Oh hey, Maeve." Manny catches sight of me and waves. "I forgot my gym bag, and it's got my wallet in it. Damn, that smells good. Did you make extra?"

Luis stares, arms folded, as Manny crosses over to the bubbling pot on the stove and peers inside. "Dude," Luis says. "Read the room."

"What?" Manny asks, giving the ajiaco a stir. The timer goes off just then, making me jump. "Is it done?"

"I should go," I say abruptly. My cheeks are still burning, my head spinning. I can't believe I just threw myself at Luis after everything that's happened in the past twenty-four hours. I mean, I *can,* but still. I'm both a walking cliché and a terrible friend. "Thanks for everything, Luis, but I'm still not hungry and I should probably just . . . go."

Manny glances between Luis and me and seems to finally catch on. "Oh hey, no. Stick around. I'm just gonna grab my wallet and head out," he says, but I'm already through the kitchen door. I pull my laptop bag off the chair where I left it without breaking stride, and head for the exit. I'm probably both a jerk and a wimp for leaving, but it's too much to process all at once; embarrassment and guilt on top of the sort of intense physical attraction I wasn't sure I was even capable of until just now. At least I finally know what all the fuss is about.

What all the fuss is about. Oh my God.

The memory hits right as I push through the front door. I'd said that to Bronwyn, when I was telling her about my disastrous night with Knox. "I wasn't disappointed," I told her. "Just relieved. The whole time we were kissing, I didn't feel anything. All I could think was *I don't understand what all the fuss is about.*"

I'd said it *here*. At my usual table, in public. Where anyone could have heard.

I'm an idiot.

CHAPTER FOURTEEN

Phoebe
Thursday, March 5

Today is shaping up to be a better-than-average day.

For one thing, Emma is sick. It's not like I'm happy about her being locked in the bathroom puking her guts out, but breakfast is a lot less tense without her glaring at me. Plus, now I have the car and can offer Jules a ride. I've been walking to and from school lately to give Emma space, which means Jules has been either taking the bus or getting a ride from Monica. And I miss her.

The second reason today sucks less is this: for the first time in weeks, I feel like the Truth or Dare game isn't hanging over my head. I know it's still out there, but not having to worry about it buzzing across my phone is a huge relief. I never realized that out of sight, out of mind could be so powerful. When

I get dressed I reach for my favorite skirt, which I haven't worn for a while because it's also my shortest skirt, and the familiar swish of fabric around my legs makes me feel more like myself than I have for a while.

"You look nice, honey," Mom says when I enter the kitchen area. She does too—she's wearing one of her old sweater dresses paired with chunky jewelry and boots, and I smile when I grab the car keys from their peg beside the door. Mom and I aren't as similar personality-wise as she and Emma are, but we both use fashion to express ourselves more than anyone else in our family does. If I'm reading Mom's outfit correctly, she's feeling more like her old self, too. Which makes a third reason to feel good about today.

When I pick up Jules, she grins at the sight of me in the driver's seat. "What happened to Miss Stick Up Her Ass?"

I feel a stab of defensiveness for Emma, but I don't want to argue with Jules when I've barely seen her all week. "Stomach virus," I say.

Jules laughs as she slides into the front seat instead of the back. "Too bad, so sad. I could get used to this." She flips the radio until it lands on a Beyoncé song, then fastens her seat belt as I pull away from the curb. We sing along for a few verses, and I'm starting to relax into the familiar rhythm of her company until she says, "So, I heard about a thing."

"What thing?"

"Coach Ruffalo bought a bunch of tickets for one of Cooper Clay's games at Fullerton. He's giving them out to anyone at Bayview who wants them. Including recent grads." She smacks her lips together like she's about to devour her favorite dessert when I don't reply. "We should go. I bet you anything Nate will be there."

"Probably, but . . ." This time I can't hold my tongue. "Don't you think it's maybe time to give that up?"

Her voice gets cool. "Give *what* up?"

"It's just—Nate knows you're interested, right? You kissed him. He's a pretty straightforward person, from what I've seen. If he wanted to follow up, I think he would've by now." She doesn't answer, which I hope means she's considering the point, so I press on. "The thing is, I saw Nate and Bronwyn talking at Café Contigo before you showed up that night and . . . I think the two of them are the real deal. I don't think it matters that she's three thousand miles away. She's still the one he wants. She'll probably *always* be the one he wants."

"Great," Jules says flatly. "Thanks for the support."

"I *am* being supportive," I protest. "You're amazing and you deserve somebody who knows it. Not a guy who's in love with someone else."

Jules flips the sun visor down and peers into its mirror, running a finger under each eye to catch microscopic mascara flecks. "Whatever. Maybe I should go for Brandon now that he's available."

My stomach lurches as I turn in to the Bayview High parking lot. "Jules. No." I didn't tell her about Brandon assaulting me at my apartment, but she has to know he's the one who put up the sex tutor ad. And she *definitely* saw him crack up when Sean made fun of me. I can't believe she'd joke about hooking up with him after that. Or, even worse—not joke.

"Slow down, Phoebe Jeebies, or you're going to hit that guy." Jules narrows her eyes at the tall, skinny boy who passes in front of the car. "Oh, never mind, it's Matthias Schroeder. Go ahead and mow that freak down." She tucks a strand of pin-straight hair behind her ear; she's been using a flat iron ever since the night she kissed Nate. "Such a weirdo. He looks like he beats off to erotic *Star Wars* fanfic, don't you think?"

I press my brakes, a vein in my temple starting to throb. Jules is punchy today, her teasing skirting the edge of mean in a way it doesn't usually. I roll down my window and call, "Sorry, Matthias!" He looks startled and darts away. "I try not to think about him, period," I mutter as I navigate into a parking space.

We get out of the car and head for the back entrance. I drop my keys into my bag as Jules checks her phone. "I thought we'd have another text from Unknown by now," she says.

I freeze. "What?"

"You know. *The next player has been contacted. Tick-tock.*"

She grins, and the last of my patience runs out. "I wouldn't know, because I'm not playing," I snap, yanking the door open. "That stopped being a *super fun game* as soon as it made Emma hate me, and it's only gone downhill from there. But you do you, I guess."

"You need to chill," Jules says as I stomp into the hallway. I don't bother telling her to find another ride home. I'm sure she was planning on it anyway.

School is almost over before I run into Knox in person, but I've seen the taunts left for him all day. Limp dick pictures are *everywhere.* The noodles are gone from his locker, but when I pass by it on the way to health class—which is the only class he and I have together—a giant pill bottle with *VIAGRA* scrawled across the front is duct-taped there instead.

I slow as I approach, feeling a tug in my chest as I watch Knox yank the bottle off and stuff it into his locker. Health class is going to be *horrible* for him. We're covering the male reproductive system, which is bad enough on a normal day, but torture on one like this. Especially since Brandon and Sean are both in the class. Impulsively, I walk over and tap Knox on the shoulder. He flinches and turns, and looks relieved when he sees it's only me.

"Hi," I say. "Wanna skip?"

His brow furrows. "Huh?"

"Do you want to skip last period?" I dig into my bag and pull out my keys, spinning them on one finger. "I have a car today."

Knox looks utterly confused. "What do . . . how does that even work?"

"We leave school instead of going to class, and go some-place fun instead," I say, enunciating each word slowly. "It's not rocket science, Knox."

His eyes dart around the hallway, like we just committed a felony and the authorities are closing in. "Won't we get in trouble?" he asks.

I shrug. "It's not a big deal if you aren't chronic about it. Your parents get a robocall, and you tell them you went to the nurse's office, but it was really busy and she never checked you in." I spin the keys faster. "Or, you could just go to health class."

At this point, I'm kind of hoping he says no. It starts to hit me, as everyone who passes us stares, that I'm going to bring all kinds of shit down on myself by being seen with him today. But then Knox slams his locker door closed and says, "The hell with it. Let's go."

No backing out now.

I keep my eyes straight ahead as we walk down the hall, willing myself not to run for the exit. There's a hushed, urgent voice in my head that sounds a lot like the narrator in a wildlife show I used to watch with my dad: *Rapid movement will only draw attention from the hungry pack.* Behind us, I hear Brandon hoot about something, but we're too far away for it to be us. I think. Still, I'm relieved when we push through the doors of the back stairwell.

"Welcome to your life of crime," I say to Knox as we exit the building into a light sprinkling of rain. His eyes widen, and I roll mine. "It's not an *actual* crime, Knox. Have you seriously never skipped a class before?"

"No," he admits as we descend the stairs. "I've gotten the perfect attendance award for two years running." He grimaces. "I have no idea why I just told you that. Pretend I didn't." There's a faint clanging noise ahead of us, and we both pause as someone jumps over the back fence behind the parking lot. I recognize Matthias Schroeder's tall frame and pale-blue hoodie just before he lopes into the woods behind school. Looks like we're not the only ones skipping health class. It's a nightmare for nerdy guys everywhere.

When we reach the car, Knox pulls on the handle like he's expecting it to be open, but our Corolla's power locks failed years ago. I unlock my door, climb into the driver's seat, and reach over to let him in. "So, where are we going?" he asks.

I hadn't really thought that far ahead. I start the engine and turn on the windshield wipers against what's now a steady rain. "Well, it's not very nice out, so we can forget about the beach or a park," I say, navigating for the exit. "We could drive to San Diego if you want. There's this coffee shop I like that has live music some afternoons. The only thing is—" I'm so busy talking that I don't notice I'm about to pull into the main road while a car is passing, and I have to slam the brakes to avoid it. Knox and I both lurch forward against our seat belts, hard. "I don't drive all that much, and I'm kind of bad in traffic. And rain. So we could go to Epoch Coffee in the mall instead."

"Epoch Coffee is good," Knox says, massaging his shoulder.

We lapse into silence, and I feel a lightning-quick flash of rage for us both. It's bullshit that I'm getting shamed for having sex, and Knox is getting shamed for *not* having it. Meanwhile nobody's attacking Derek or Maeve, even though they did the exact same things we did. Or didn't do. People like to think they're open-minded, but if you toss a tired gender stereotype in their path they'll run with it every time. I don't understand why the world insists on stuffing kids into boxes we never asked for, and then gets mad when we won't stay there.

If I start ranting about that, though, I'll never stop. And I'm pretty sure Knox needs a different kind of distraction right now. So I talk all the way to the Bayview Mall about whatever comes to mind: TV shows, music, my job, my brother. "He wants you to come over," I tell Knox as we pull into the mall parking lot. It's full on such a rainy day, but I get lucky when a Jeep pulls out from a front-row spot right when I'm cruising past. "Apparently you made quite an impression."

"*Bounty Wars* fans are a tight-knit bunch," Knox says. I take the Jeep's spot and cut the engine, frowning at the downpour outside my window. We're as close as we can get to the mall entrance, but we're still going to get soaked before we make it inside. Knox unclips his seat belt and reaches for his backpack, then straightens and looks at me full-on for the first time since we got into the car. His brown eyes have nice gold flecks in them, which I file away in my *Knox Is Going to Be Hot One Day* mental folder. "Thanks for doing this."

"No problem." I open my door and duck my head against the rain, but it only hits me for a few seconds before Knox is suddenly at my side, holding an umbrella over both our heads. I grin up at him. "Wow, you're prepared."

He smiles back, and I'm glad I rescued him from the fiery pits of health class hell. "Former Boy Scout," he says as we head for the entrance. "If we need to build a fire later, I can do that too."

Once we get to Epoch Coffee, we snag a prime corner table. Knox offers to get our drinks, and I pull out my phone while I wait for him to get back. I haven't been on Instagram since deleting all the gross comments last week, and I check it now to see if going private has kept the trolls away. It has, for the most part, although I have a bunch of new message requests. Most are from guys I don't know, except one.

Derekculpepper01 Hey, I don't mean

I frown at my screen and click the full message. *Hey, I don't mean to be a pain in your ass or anything, but I'd really like to talk to you. Can you text me? Or call if you'd rather.*

"No, dickhead, I can't," I say out loud as Knox returns to the table.

He freezes halfway to handing me my drink. "What?"

"Not you," I say, accepting the iced coffee. "Thank you." I hesitate before explaining further, but then I figure, what the hell. Nothing distracts you from your own problems like hearing about somebody else's. "So, you know that whole Truth or Dare drama with me and my sister, right? Well, the ex-boyfriend in question keeps messaging me and I don't know why. I don't care, either, but it's annoying. *He's* annoying."

"Social media sucks," Knox says. He's dumped a small mountain of sugar packets onto the table and grabs three, tearing them open together. His shoulders hunch as he stirs them into whatever he's drinking. "I haven't been on since—a while. I can't deal."

"Good," I say. "Stay away. I hope you've blocked Unknown's number, too."

"I have," Knox says grimly. He's starting to look miserable again, so I quickly change the subject, and for the next hour we talk about everything *but* the texting game. Every once in a while, I wonder if I should bring up Maeve, but—no. Too soon.

When Knox glances at his phone and announces that he has to leave for work, I'm surprised at how fast the time went by. I have to leave too; I'm supposed to be helping Addy and Maeve put together Ashton's wedding favors this afternoon.

I use a stray napkin to wipe the iced coffee condensation rings from our table and pick up my almost-empty drink. "Do you want a ride?" I ask, following Knox out of Epoch Coffee and into the main mall thoroughfare.

"Well, it's in San Diego." Knox looks nervous, like he's remembering every near-fender-bender from the ride over. To be fair, there were a lot for a mile-and-a-half drive. "That's pretty far out of your way." We reach the mall exit and push through the doors. It's still overcast, but the rain has stopped. "I'll just take the bus." He glances at his watch. "There's one leaving in ten minutes. If I cut through the construction site behind the mall, I can make it."

"Okay, well—" A familiar giggle stops me, and I turn to see Jules crossing the parking lot with Monica Hill. They're walking at an angle, toward the side of the mall instead of the front door. When they're a few feet away from us, Jules notices me and stops short. She grabs onto Monica's arm to make her stop, too.

"Heyyy," Jules says, with about half her usual enthusiasm. "What are you doing here?" Her eyes flick toward Knox and widen. Monica suppresses a laugh and whispers something in Jules's ear.

I can feel my cheeks turning beet red. I *hate* that I'm embarrassed to be seen with Knox in front of Jules and Monica, especially after we had such a good time hanging out. But I am. "Just getting coffee," I say.

"So are we," Jules says, even though they're obviously not headed for Epoch Coffee. "Too bad we missed you."

"Yeah, too bad," Monica echoes. They keep standing there,

so clearly waiting for me to leave that I want to stay just to annoy them. Except Knox is hovering awkwardly beside me, making everything a hundred times worse. God, what if they think this is a date? And why do I even care?

Ugh. The hell with them.

"Well, bye," I say to no one in particular, and stalk off to my car. When I get inside, though, I don't turn it on right away. Instead, I rest my head on the steering wheel and let myself cry for a good fifteen minutes about losing a friend I've had since elementary school. It's just one more thing in a long line of casualties from the Truth or Dare game, but still. It sucks.

Then I drive home in a haze, making turns on autopilot until the loud blare of sirens makes me jump. My heart starts to pound, because I know I haven't been paying attention, and I probably violated ten different traffic rules. But as I slow down, the flashing lights appear in front of me instead of in my rear-view mirror. I pull to the side of the road as two police cars, followed by a fire engine, roar past me in the direction of the Bayview Mall.

CHAPTER FIFTEEN

Maeve
Thursday, March 5

"I don't see what the problem is," Addy says, popping a candy-covered almond into her mouth.

We're both on the couch in Ashton's apartment, and Phoebe is sitting cross-legged on the floor in front of the coffee table. The three of us are putting candy into little netted bags, tying them with blue ribbon, and lining them up in rows on the table. They're favors for Ashton and Eli's wedding, which all of a sudden is less than a month away.

I pick up a ribbon and position it around a filled bag. "Everything," I say.

Addy takes her time chewing and swallowing. "Everything," she repeats. "Because you made out with a hot guy who cooked you dinner?" She shakes her head and reaches for another almond. She's eaten almost as many as she's bundled. "You have some serious first-world problems, girl."

She doesn't know the half of what my problems are, but that's not her fault. I'm the one who's been keeping secrets. "I practically *mauled* him," I correct. "And then I ran out on him." Every time I think about last night, I cringe. Luis probably does, too. I avoided Café Contigo today but still secretly hoped he'd get in touch. He didn't.

"Just talk to him," Addy says.

Phoebe heaves a dramatic sigh. "*Thank you.* I keep trying to tell her that."

I don't answer, and Addy taps me lightly on the arm. "It's not a weakness to let someone know you like them, you know," she says.

I do know. I've been telling myself that for weeks, trying to change. But I still can't bring myself to do it. "Then why does it feel like it?" I ask, almost to myself.

Addy laughs. "Because rejection sucks. I'm not saying Luis is going to reject you," she adds hastily when my head snaps up.

"He super is not," Phoebe murmurs, her brow knitted in concentration as she ties a careful bow.

"I mean in general," Addy continues. "We're all afraid of putting ourselves out there and not getting anything in return. The thing is, though, nobody looks back on their life thinking, 'Damn, I wish I'd been less honest with the people I care about.'"

Before I can answer I hear the sound of a key turning in a lock, followed by the squeal of hinges and the click of heels.

Ashton pokes her head around the small vestibule that leads into the apartment's open-concept living-dining area, loaded down with bags and a stack of mail. "Hi," she calls. She crosses the room and drops the envelopes onto the edge of the coffee table, beaming when she catches sight of the wedding favors. "Oh, thank you so much for doing this! They look amazing. I got pad Thai from Sweet Basil. Did you guys eat, or do you want some?"

"We ate," Addy says. She ties another bow, sets the netted candies down, and starts thumbing through the mail.

"All right," Ashton says, returning to the kitchen area. She sets her bags on the counter, then comes back and perches on the arm of the sofa. "Addy, are you around Saturday night? Eli's cousin Daniel is coming into town and I was thinking we could all go out to dinner." Addy looks up at her blankly, and Ashton adds, "Remember? I told you about him. He's going to be a groomsman in the wedding, and he's transferring to UCSD next fall. He's studying molecular biology." Ashton nudges Addy's foot with hers and smiles. "He saw that picture of you and me at Mom's last week on Eli's Instagram, and now he *really* wants to meet you."

Addy wrinkles her nose. "Molecular biology? I don't know. I might be busy."

"I think you'd like him. He's very nice. And funny." Ashton swipes her phone a few times before holding it out to Addy. "This is Daniel."

Phoebe rises and peers at Ashton's phone. I lean closer to Addy so I can see, too, and can't help the admiring *ooh* that comes out when I catch sight of Daniel's picture. That is one seriously cute molecular biologist. "He looks like the lost Hemsworth brother," I say.

Phoebe tilts her head for a better view. "Is that a filter, or are his eyes actually that blue?"

"No filter," Ashton says.

"All right, then." Addy nods so quickly, I'm afraid her neck might snap. "Saturday it is."

Ashton takes her phone back and gets to her feet, looking pleased. "Great, I'll have Eli make reservations someplace fun. I'm going to change clothes and inhale my dinner, then I'll help you finish the wedding favors." She disappears into her bedroom, and Phoebe settles herself back on the ground, reaching for another netted bag. Addy rips into a large, thick envelope with a pleased *aha* noise.

"What's that?" I ask.

Addy tucks a strand of pink hair behind her ear. "It's from this school called Colegio San Silvestre in Peru," she says.

I feel a sudden stab of panic. *No, you can't leave me too.* "Are you going there?"

She laughs. "No. Well, not as a student. It's an elementary school. But there's this summer program where the kids learn English, and they hire counselors from other countries. I was thinking of applying. You don't have to speak Spanish because you're supposed to have all your conversations in English so the kids can practice. I've been looking into teaching programs around here for next year, and I thought it would be good experience. Plus, I'd get to travel. I've never even left the country before." She flips slowly through the glossy pages of a brochure.

"Ashton says I can keep living with her and Eli however long I want, but at some point I have to figure out what's next. And I am *not* moving back in with my mom."

Addy's mother is the definition of a party mom. The last time I saw her, right before Addy moved in with Ashton, she offered me a glass of wine while her twenty-something Tinder date checked out my ass. She hasn't been all that involved in wedding planning, except to text Addy pictures of every potential mother-of-the-bride dress she tries on.

"Sounds great," I say, peering at the brochure over Addy's shoulder. "Can I see?"

Addy hands it to me with a smile. "You should look into it, too. You don't have to be a high school graduate to apply. We'd have fun."

She's right, we would. I can't think of anything I'd like better than a summer with Addy in South America, actually. But I can barely plan for next week, with all the crap going on with my life. Who knows what kind of shape I'll be in by the time applications are due? Still, the brochure draws me in with beautiful pictures of the school and the kids, and I'm flipping through with increasing interest when Ashton comes running out of her room.

She's barefoot, and her blouse is untucked as though she'd paused halfway through getting changed. "I just got a text from Eli," she says breathlessly, her eyes roving over the coffee table. "Where's the remote?"

"I think I'm sitting on it." Addy twists and reaches to pull it out from behind a cushion. She blinks, surprised, when Ashton snatches it from her hand. "Jeez, Ash, what's the rush?"

Ashton perches beside her on the arm of the sofa and aims the remote at the television. "There's been an accident," she says. The screen springs to life, and Ashton clicks away from the E! Network. "I think they're covering it on Channel Seven—yeah. Here it is."

A stone-faced news anchor sits behind a shiny, semicircular desk, the words *Breaking News* scrolling in all caps behind him. "Reporter Liz Rosen joins us now at the scene," he says, aiming an intense stare directly into the camera. "Liz, what can you tell us?"

"Ugh. *Her.*" Addy frowns as a dark-haired woman in a blue blazer fills the screen. Liz Rosen practically stalked Addy, Bronwyn, Cooper, and Nate last year while they were being investigated for Simon's death. Then Addy's brow furrows as she leans forward, craning her neck for a better look. "Is she at the mall?"

"Thank you, Tom," Liz says. "We're continuing to bring you the latest from Bayview, where tragedy has occurred at an abandoned construction site. The story is still developing, but what we know so far is that a group of local teens were in a blocked-off area when one boy fell through the roof of a partially constructed building. Another boy was also injured, although it's not yet clear how. And we just got word, from one of the officers here, that the young man who fell through the roof has been confirmed dead."

My hand flies to my mouth as I take in the familiar scene over Liz's shoulder. "Oh my God," Addy says. A half-dozen sugared almonds slip through her fingers and onto the floor.

Phoebe gasps and scrambles to her feet. "Knox," she breathes. "He cut through there."

"I know," I say, my eyes glued to the television. "He's always saying how mad his dad would be if he knew. And no wonder. It really *was* dangerous."

"No," Phoebe says urgently. "I mean he cut through there *today.* On his way to work, right before I came here."

Oh my God. *Knox.*

My entire heart seizes as a yellow banner reading TEEN DIES IN CONSTRUCTION SITE ACCIDENT appears at the bottom of the screen. Helpless, flailing panic rushes through me, and I fumble under piles of netting on the coffee table for my phone. "It can't be him," I say. My voice shakes, and I force more conviction into it. If it sounds true, maybe it will *be* true. "He's fine. I'm going to call him right now."

Liz continues to talk. "There are still a lot of unknowns. Police say they have yet to notify the next of kin, so they have not released the name of the deceased. It's also not clear what type of injuries the second teen has sustained. However, we understand that they are not life-threatening, and that the young man has been transported to Bayview Memorial Hospital for treatment."

My call to Knox goes straight to voice mail, and just like that, I start sobbing uncontrollably. "He—he's not answering," I manage to choke out as Addy puts an arm around my shoulders and pulls me close.

"Let me call Eli," Ashton says. "Hang on. I left my phone in my room."

My head is buried in Addy's shoulder as the desk anchor's deep voice turns mournful. "Of course, the town of Bayview is no stranger to tragedy, Liz."

"Turn it off," Addy says tightly.

"I can't . . . I can't find . . ." Phoebe sounds like she's in tears, too. "I think Ashton took the remote with her."

"That's absolutely true, Tom," Liz Rosen says. "The town is still recovering from the shocking death of Bayview High student Simon Kelleher eighteen months ago, which made national headlines. It remains to be seen how this story develops, but we'll continue to monitor and provide updates as they happen."

I clutch Addy's arm like a life preserver, my stomach twisted with fear and sick regret. If anything happened to Knox, and I never got the chance to make up with him . . .

"He's okay. Knox is okay!" Ashton's voice fills me with such intense relief that I can finally look up. "But he's the one in the hospital. Eli doesn't know what happened yet. I'll take you there right now."

Addy keeps her arm around me as we stand. I feel as unsteady as a newborn fawn; none of my limbs are working properly as I lurch toward the door. "Does Eli know who died?" I manage to get out.

Ashton nods, her pretty face somber. "Yeah. It was a boy named Brandon Weber. Did you know him?"

There's a loud thud from near the door. Phoebe, who'd been gathering all our backpacks and bags from where we'd left them, goes rigid with shock and they fall from her hands.

Two hours later, we finally get to see Knox.

Only family was allowed to visit at first, and his parents and sisters had to go in shifts. Information has been coming in spurts, and we're not sure how much is true. But a few things are starting to repeat consistently, both on the news and in the texts flying across our phones.

One: Brandon died trying to take a shortcut through the construction site.

Two: Sean, Jules, and Monica were all with him at the time.

Three: Knox has a concussion but is otherwise fine.

Four: Sean Murdock saved Knox's life by knocking him to the ground when he tried to rush after Brandon.

"Sean Murdock." Phoebe keeps repeating the name like she's never heard it before. She's sitting with her knees drawn up to her chest, her arms wrapped tightly around her legs. Her eyes are glazed, her cheeks pale. She looks almost catatonic, and I don't think the news about Brandon has sunk in yet. It hasn't for me, either. "You're telling me Sean Murdock saved Knox's life." She says it like you'd say, *You're telling me dogs can now talk and drive cars.*

Addy wrinkles her brow. "Sounds familiar, but I don't remember him."

"He's—" I almost finish with *a total asshole* but stop myself in the nick of time. Whatever else happened, Sean lost his best friend today. And might have saved Knox's life, although I'm having as hard a time as Phoebe is wrapping my brain around that one. "He was Brandon's friend. He and Knox are . . . not close."

Knox's sister Kiersten emerges from the hospital corridor, followed by two of his other sisters. Kiersten's eyes search the waiting area until they land on me. "Maeve, we're going to meet up with my parents in the cafeteria for a while. Knox is getting tired, but he's still okay to see people. Do you and your friends want to say hello?" She smiles so kindly that I'm positive she has no clue about the texting game, or what's been going on between me and Knox over the past couple of days. "He's right around the corner in room 307."

I jump to my feet, pulling Phoebe and Addy with me. "Yes, please. How is he?"

"He'll be fine," Kiersten says reassuringly. "They're keeping him overnight for observation, but everything looks good." Then her resolutely cheerful expression slips a little. "Well, almost everything. Prepare yourself. Poor kid's face is a little rough." She squeezes my arm as we pass by her.

Hospitals make me anxious, and I need to take a second to steel myself at the door to Knox's room. This section of Bayview Memorial doesn't look anything like the cancer ward, which is a lot more modern and high-tech, but the antiseptic smell and harsh fluorescent lighting are the same. I absorb the details of the room—the outdated pastel paint job, the framed print of a sad-looking vase full of sunflowers, the ceiling-mounted television in one corner, the thin curtain separating an empty bed from Knox's—before my eyes settle on him. Then I gasp.

"I know," Knox says through puffy lips. "I've looked better."

He's in regular clothes with only a small bandage on one side of his head, but his face is almost unrecognizable. One eye is blackened and half-closed, his nose is red and swollen, and the entire right side of his face is a giant bruise. I drop into the chair beside his bed and try to grab hold of his hand, but he tucks it beneath the threadbare blanket before I can.

I can't tell if it's coincidental timing or purposeful avoidance, and I remind myself it doesn't matter. At least he's okay. "What happened?" I ask, at the same time Phoebe says, "Sean did this?" She drags a chair from the corner of the room and drops into it beside me.

"Not so many questions at once," Addy says. "When I had a concussion, that kind of thing gave me an instant headache." She's still standing, her eyes on the television screen in the corner. "Hang on. They're about to interview Sean Murdock." She leans over me to pick up the remote on Knox's bedside table and points it toward the television to turn up the volume.

"Fantastic," Knox says flatly as we all look up.

Liz Rosen from Channel Seven is holding a microphone out to Sean, who's standing with his hands clasped like he's about to pray. They're in front of someone's house, the twilight sky a deep blue behind them. The words LIVE UPDATE: LOCAL TEEN RECALLS FATAL ACCIDENT flash along the bottom of the screen as Liz says, "Thank you for taking the time to speak with us, Sean, after such a traumatic day. Can you tell us in your own words what happened?"

Sean towers over Liz. He hunches his shoulders like he's trying to make himself look smaller and says, "It's all kind of a blur, but I'll try. A bunch of us were at the mall, and then we wanted to go downtown. We were trying to save a little time, and—God, that sounds so stupid now, doesn't it? Like, we should've just walked the regular way. But we'd cut through the site before. Lots of kids do it; we didn't think anything of it. Anyway, Bran was joking around like always, and then he jumped, and then . . ." Sean ducks his head and puts a hand to his temple, obscuring his face. "Then all of a sudden he wasn't there." Phoebe makes a strangled little noise beside me, and I reach for her hand. Unlike Knox, she lets me take it.

Brandon is dead.

Brandon Weber is dead.

Brandon.

Weber.

Is. Dead.

I can repeat the words a dozen times in my head, a dozen different ways, and it still doesn't seem real.

"It must have been a terrible shock," Liz says.

Sean nods, his head still down. I can't tell if he's crying or not. "It was," he says.

"Did you understand immediately what had happened?"

"We couldn't really see into the . . . under the roof. But we knew it was bad when he fell through."

"And what happened with the second boy? The one who's injured?"

"That kid—he was in shock, I think. He ran straight for the edge after Brandon, and all I could think was that he was gonna fall through, too. I panicked. I did the only thing I could think of to stop him in his tracks." Sean finally looks up, his mouth twisted in a regretful grimace. "I punched him. I think I ended up hurting him kinda bad, and I'm sorry about that. But at least he stopped, you know? At least he's safe."

"Bullshit," Knox says quietly.

We all turn toward him. "Is that not what happened?" I ask.

Knox touches the bandage at his temple and winces. "I . . . don't actually remember," he says haltingly. "Everything's a blur from the time I left Phoebe until I woke up with somebody

190

shining a light in my face. But I can't imagine myself chasing after Brandon when he just *fell through a roof*. I mean, I've been around construction sites my whole life, you know? That's not the kind of thing I'd ever do."

"Maybe you weren't thinking straight," Addy says. "I wouldn't be."

Knox still looks skeptical. "Maybe. Or maybe Sean is lying."

Addy blinks. "Why would he do that?"

Knox shakes his head, his face tensing as though the movement hurts. "I have no idea."

PART TWO

Sunday, March 15

REPORTER: Good evening, this is Liz Rosen with Channel Seven News. I'm live in the studio with special guest Lance Weber, whose sixteen-year-old son, Brandon, died tragically at the abandoned construction site behind the Bayview Mall just ten days ago. Mr. Weber, my heartfelt condolences for your loss.

LANCE WEBER: Thank you. My wife and I are beyond devastated.

REPORTER: You're here tonight, you told our producers, because you want answers.

LANCE WEBER: That's right. I've been a businessman for more than half my life, Liz, and in business the bottom line is accountability. Yet I can't get any of the entities involved in this horrible tragedy—the construction company, the mall, even town officials—to step forward and provide details about what I am sure are multiple instances of negligence that contributed to my son's death.

REPORTER: Are you saying that you believe one of those organizations—or perhaps all of them—are at fault?

LANCE WEBER: I'm saying that something like this doesn't just *happen*, Liz. There's always a responsible party.

One Day Later

Reddit, Vengeance Is Mine subforum
Thread started by Darkestmind

Where the hell are you Bayview2020?
ANSWER. MY. CHATS.
Don't you dare fucking ghost me.—Darkestmind

This isn't a joke.
I know where to find you.
And I'm not afraid to let this whole thing go up
in flames.
I'll do it just so I can watch you burn, too.
—Darkestmind

CHAPTER SIXTEEN

Phoebe
Monday, March 16

"I really appreciate the ride," Knox says.

Emma buckles her seat belt and shifts the car into reverse. "No problem."

It's been a week and a half since Brandon died, and nothing in Bayview feels quite the same. On the plus side, Knox and I have been hanging out more, enough that Emma and I drive him home from school sometimes. On the far, *far* worse side, Jules and Sean are a couple all of a sudden. I thought I was hallucinating the first time I saw them making out in the hallway. "The trauma brought us together," I heard her tell another girl in English class. Her eyes had the glazed devotion of a cult member. "We *need* each other."

From what I've heard around school, it looks as though the Truth or Dare game ended with the Knox/Maeve bombshell—

which makes me wonder if the whole point of the game was to mess with her. After all, she's the one who turned the tide against Simon last year. Maybe one of his acolytes decided to get his revenge. If so, job well done, because she and Knox are still barely speaking and it's making her miserable. Which sucks, but at least nobody at Bayview is talking about that stupid game anymore.

Another possibility, I guess, is that Brandon was behind the game all along and used it to help his friends win popularity points while messing with people he didn't like. But since the game kicked off with an ugly secret about me while Brandon and I were hooking up, I can't think about that for too long without wanting to throw up.

Meanwhile, Sean's started up a weird little bromance with Knox. He's suddenly calling Knox "my man" and yelling at anyone who tries to make a limp dick joke. Which is confusing for people, since he's the one who started them in the first place. Knox still can't remember what happened at the construction site the day Brandon died.

And Brandon—Brandon is buried and gone.

His funeral was last weekend, the first one I'd gone to since my father's. I'd never felt such a confusing mash-up of emotions—shock and disbelief and sadness, but also some anger still. It's strange, mourning someone who'd been legitimately horrible to you. When the priest eulogized Brandon, I felt like he was talking about a boy I'd never met. I wish I had, because *that* guy sounded great.

So much potential, wasted.

"Am I taking you to Until Proven, Knox?" Emma asks.

She's back to being calmly polite toward me, and hasn't mentioned Derek once since Brandon's funeral. Maybe his death shocked her out of her anger, or maybe it's just that I finally have a friend she likes. She doesn't even mind giving Knox the occasional lift to San Diego.

"No, I'm not working," Knox says. I glance at him in the rearview mirror, cataloging the state of his bruises like I do every day. The ring around his eye is still purple, but his cheek and jaw have calmed down to a yellowish color. If he wore makeup, he could totally cover it up with the right foundation. "Just home, thanks."

"You should come over," I say impulsively. "Play that *Bounty Wars* game Owen keeps asking about." My brother has been subdued lately, picking up on the sad vibe running through our house since Brandon died. A video game session with someone new would be the perfect way to cheer him up.

"Yeah, sure," Knox says. Then he frowns and leans forward. "Does the car feel kind of—lopsided to you guys?"

"Always," I say. "It's ancient."

"I was just thinking the same thing," Emma says. "Something's not right." She turns in to the parking garage beneath our building and pulls into our assigned spot. I grab my bag as she climbs out and steps backward to look at the driver's-side front tire.

"It's going flat," she groans as I get out.

Knox crouches down and examines the tire. "Looks like you picked up a nail," he says.

I pull out my phone, only to see the power drained to

nothing. "Emma, can you text Mom to call Triple A?" I ask. "I'm out of battery."

My sister shakes her head. "I lost my phone, remember?"

Emma lost her phone almost a week ago. Mom had a fit and said she couldn't afford a new one and Emma would have to pay for it out of her tutoring money. So far, Emma hasn't replaced it, which is unfathomable to me. I can't go an hour without my phone, let alone a week. But Emma acts like she doesn't even miss it.

"Do you have a spare tire?" Knox asks. "I can change it."

"Really?" I ask, surprised.

Knox flushes as he opens the trunk. "Don't look so shocked. I'm not completely useless."

"I didn't mean that," I say quickly, moving beside him to give his arm a reassuring pat. "I've just never met anybody who knows how to change a tire before. I thought it was a lost skill." Which is true, but also: if I'd been asked to guess Knox's car repair abilities on a scale of one to ten, I would've said zero. He doesn't need to know that, though.

"My dad wouldn't let me and my sisters take driver's ed until we learned. It took me a month but whatever." He pulls on a latch in the trunk I didn't even know was there and slides away part of the floor to reveal a tire beneath. "Oh wow, it's even regular size. Old cars are the best."

Knox changes the tire, so slowly and painstakingly that I debate sneaking upstairs to charge my phone so I can call Mom and plead for an assist from AAA, but eventually he finishes. "You still need a new tire, but this will get you to a repair shop," Knox says. It's kind of cute how nonchalant he's trying to sound when he's obviously proud of himself.

"Thanks so much," Emma says with genuine warmth in her voice. "You're the best."

"It's the least I can do," Knox says as we walk to the elevator. "You guys have been carting me all over town."

"Well, you're injured," I say, pressing the Up button.

"Nah, I'm fine now. Doctors gave me a clean bill of health at my last checkup," Knox says, leaning against the wall while we wait. His bruises look worse under the harsh fluorescent light of the garage. "Anyway, according to my dad it serves me right."

Emma gasps as the doors open and we step inside. *"What?"*

Knox instantly looks regretful. "That came out wrong. Those aren't his exact words or anything. He's just mad that I tried to cut through the construction site."

I frown. "He should be glad you're alive. Mr. Weber would trade places with him in a heartbeat." Brandon's father has been on every major San Diego news channel recently, threatening to sue the mall, the bankrupt construction company that started the parking garage, and the entire town of Bayview. "Did you catch him with Liz Rosen last night?"

"Yeah. He was really ranting," Knox says. The elevator stops on our floor and we all step into the hallway, which smells faintly of caramel and vanilla. Addy must be making cookies again. "I guess you can't blame him, though. I mean, that construction site *is* a hazard. My dad's been saying so for months. Plus Brandon's an only child, so it's like their whole family is gone all of a sudden. You know?"

"I know," I say with a pang of sadness.

Emma's been quiet since we got off the elevator. When we get into the apartment she mutters a muted "Gotta study" and heads for our bedroom, shutting the door behind her.

Knox holds up his hands, streaked black from tire grease. "Where can I wash these?"

I lead him to the kitchen sink and turn on the faucet, pouring dish detergent into his outstretched palms. "I like your place," he says, gazing at the large windows and exposed brick.

"It's all right," I say grudgingly. And it is—for a hip young couple with no kids. I'll bet Knox wouldn't find it so charming if he tried to squeeze his entire family inside, though. "Do you want something to drink? I'm getting a ginger ale. Owen won't be home for another ten minutes or so."

"Yeah, that's great. Thanks." Knox dries his hands on a dish towel and perches on one of our kitchen island stools while I grab a couple of glasses. It occurs to me, suddenly, that Knox is the only guy from Bayview High who's ever been in this apartment besides Brandon. I don't invite a lot of people over, especially not boys. And of course, I hadn't invited Brandon.

But he came anyway.

"You okay?" Knox asks, and I realize I've been frozen in place holding two glasses for I have no idea how long. I give myself a little shake and put them on the island.

"Yeah, sorry. I just—zone out sometimes lately. You know?"

"I know," Knox says as I pull a bottle of ginger ale out of the refrigerator. "Last night there were blueprints all over our kitchen table and I almost had a heart attack when I realized they were from the parking garage site. My dad's been helping investigators piece things together. They're trying to understand why the roof collapsed on Brandon and nobody else. People have been taking that shortcut for months."

I pour us both a half glass of ginger ale, letting it fizz to the top and then recede before I pour some more. "Well, Brandon is—he *was*—a lot bigger than most kids at school."

"Yeah, but the landing should've been engineered to bear more weight than that."

"Have they found anything?"

"Nothing my dad's told me about. But he probably wouldn't, anyway." Knox rubs his bruised jaw absently. "He doesn't really share work stuff with me. He's not like Eli."

I hop onto the stool next to him and sip my drink. "Do you like working with Eli?"

"Love it," Knox says, instantly brightening. "He's great. Especially when you consider the amount of crap he has to put up with on a daily basis."

"Like what?"

"Well, with the kind of law he practices, he's just constantly hounded. By other lawyers, cops, the media. Plus people who either want him to take their case, or are mad because he took someone else's." Knox takes a long gulp of ginger ale. "He even gets death threats."

"Seriously?" I ask. My voice shakes a little on the word. Eli is always treated like a hero in the media, which I thought was a *good* thing. It never occurred to me that that kind of visibility could be dangerous.

"Yeah. Another one came in yesterday. Seems like it's from the same person, so they're taking it a little more seriously.

Sandeep—that's one of the lawyers who works there—says they're usually one-offs."

I put my glass down with a clatter. "That's horrible! Does Ashton know?"

Knox shrugs. "I mean, she must, right?"

"I guess." A shiver inches up my spine, and I give way to a full-body shudder to get rid of it. "Ugh, I'd be so scared. I get creeped out by random Instagram messages."

Knox's brow knits. "Are you still getting those? From, um . . ." He glances toward my closed bedroom door and lowers his voice. "Derek, or whoever?"

"Not lately. Here's hoping he's given up."

Our lock jangles noisily, for so long that I get off my seat and cross to the door. "Owen, despite the fact that he recently rewired a toaster, still hasn't fully mastered the art of the key," I explain, flipping the deadbolt and pulling open the door so my brother can enter.

"I heard that," Owen says, dropping his overloaded backpack onto the floor. "Who are you—oh, hi." He blinks at Knox like he's never seen him before. "Wow, your face is . . . ouch."

"It looks worse than it feels," Knox says.

"Knox is here to play *Bounty Wars* with you, Owen!" I say cheerfully. "Doesn't that sound fun?" Knox furrows his brow at me, like he can't figure out why I'm speaking to my preteen brother like a toddler. I can't, either, so I stop talking.

"Really?" Owen's face lights up with a shy grin when Knox nods. "Okay, cool."

"You want to show me your setup?" Knox asks.

The two of them disappear into Owen's room, and I feel

a strange mix of appreciation and regret as I watch them go. I have a sudden image of myself ten years from now, running into Knox on the street when he's gotten cute and has an amazing job and an awesome girlfriend, and kicking myself for not having been able to see him as anything but a friend in Bayview.

I finish my ginger ale and rinse my glass. My hair hangs heavy around my shoulders, begging for a ponytail. I start gathering my curls back and head for the hallway, cracking open our bedroom door. "Emma? I'm just getting an elastic."

Emma is sitting on her bed, sipping from a giant Bayview Wildcats tumbler cup. I walk to my dresser, stepping over a pile of clothes on the floor, and root around in the top drawer until I find a sparkly pink elastic. "I think I've had this since third grade," I say, holding it up to Emma. Then I notice the tears slipping down her cheeks.

I close my drawer and cross to her bed, shooting her a nervous look as I perch lightly on the corner edge. Even though we've been getting along better lately, I'm still never one hundred percent sure she won't tell me to get lost. "What's the matter?" I ask.

"Nothing." She swipes at her face, upsetting her balance enough that liquid from the cup sloshes over her hand. "Oopsie," she mutters, lifting the tail of her shirt to dab at the spill. There's something familiar and yet not familiar about the fumbling motion. Familiar, because I've done it dozens of times. Not familiar, because she hasn't.

I stretch my hair elastic between two fingers. "What are you drinking?"

"Huh? Nothing. Water."

Emma doesn't drink alcohol—not at parties, because she doesn't go to them, and definitely not at three o'clock in the afternoon in our bedroom. But she slurs the last word so badly that there can't be any other explanation. "Why are you drinking and crying?" I ask. "Are you feeling sad about Brandon?"

"I didn't even know Brandon," she mutters into her cup, her eyes filling again.

"I know, but—it's still sad, right?"

"Could you go?" Emma asks quietly. I don't move right away, and her voice gets even lower. "Please?"

Emma hasn't said *please* to me in a while, so I do what she asks. But it feels wrong to click our bedroom door shut behind me—like even though I'm giving her what she wants, it's not what she actually needs.

The rest of the afternoon passes quietly, and I have to pry Knox away from Owen at five o'clock. My little brother has a serious man crush. "Will you come back?" he asks plaintively.

"Sure," Knox says, putting his controller down. "I have to learn some new moves first, though, so I can keep up with you."

"I'll drive you," I say. I peeked in on Emma once since I left her, and she looked sound asleep. I keep wondering if I misunderstood the whole scene—maybe she really *was* drinking water? And just being extra clumsy?—but chances are good she shouldn't be behind a wheel. Either way, I hope she wakes up as her usual self by the time Mom gets home.

Knox winces, probably remembering all my near-accidents

the last time I drove him, but doesn't protest as I lead him to the elevator. "Thanks for being such a good sport," I tell him when the doors close. "That was a lot of *Bounty Wars* time."

"It's fine," Knox says. He puts his hands in his pockets and leans against the back of the elevator as it descends. "Owen is a great player. He has this whole strategy mapped out that's really—" He shakes his head. "Let's just say I was outmatched." We stop, and when the doors open I step out first to lead us to the car. "The weird thing is, though . . . the game reminded me of something."

I reach the Corolla and unlock the driver's side. "What do you mean?"

Knox doesn't answer until he's settled in the passenger seat beside me. "Like, you know it's a bounty hunter game, right?" I nod. "So, there's different ways you can kill people. You can shoot them or stab them, obviously."

"Obviously."

"Or you can be more creative. I had my target on top of a building and I was about to throw him over, like you do, and it reminded me of being at the construction site the day Brandon died. Then I got hit with this . . ." He blinks as we exit the dark garage into still-bright sunshine, and lowers the visor in front of him. "This—memory, I think."

"A memory?" I repeat, glancing over at him. "Of Brandon?" My skin prickles at the thought. I'm not sure I'm ready to hear anything new about what happened to Brandon that day.

"No," Knox says slowly. "Of Sean. It's just a flash, but . . . all of a sudden, in my mind's eye, I saw him standing at the edge of the construction site with his phone held up in front of him. Like he was taking a picture, or a video. And then he yelled, 'What the fuck are you doing here, Myers?'"

"Wait, really?" I turn, staring at him.

Knox braces himself against the dashboard as a horn blares. "That was a stop sign," he says.

"Oh. Shit. Sorry." I slow down and raise an apologetic hand toward whoever might be giving me the finger from another car. "But are you serious? I mean, it definitely *sounds* like Sean, but . . . why would he say that?"

Knox makes a frustrated noise as he rubs his temple. "Beats me. That's all I remember. I don't even know if it's real."

I chew the inside of my cheek, considering, as we make the short drive to Knox's house. Sean's whole *punching Knox to save him* story has never made much sense, but Monica and Jules were there too, and they've never contradicted him. Of course, Sean and Jules are joined at the hip now, so . . . there's that.

"Maybe you should play some more *Bounty Wars* with Owen and keep jogging your memory," I tell Knox as I pull into his driveway.

He grins at me and unclips his seat belt. "I have a feeling that's gonna happen anyway. Your brother might be small, but he's persistent."

CHAPTER SEVENTEEN

Knox
Tuesday, March 17

Prom is two months away, Knox!
   Who are you going with?
   You can't leave this till the last minute.
   Christ, my sisters. I'm tempted to close ChatApp without answering and finish my homework in peace, but they'll just track me down via text. *I'll probably take a friend,* I finally reply.
   Kiersten jumps in, lightning-quick. *Who? Maeve?*
   Yeah, right. Kiersten has no clue. I'm closer to her than any of my other sisters, but I didn't tell her about me and Maeve when it happened, and I sure as hell didn't let her know that I'd been Bayview High's favorite erectile dysfunction joke for a while. My thoughts have been in a tug-of-war since yesterday; part of me wants to let Sean's story stand so that mine doesn't

flare up again, and the other part wants to know what the hell he's up to.

Probably not Maeve, I respond to Kiersten. I wonder, fleetingly, if Phoebe might go with me. As friends, obviously, because she's so far out of my league that I'd have to be delusional to expect anything else. But I think we'd have fun.

Maeve and I still aren't great, or even good. Everything that happened with Brandon was the perfect excuse not to talk about this crap, so we haven't. And the longer we don't, the harder it is to start. Maybe that's okay, though. Maybe staying friends with the ex I failed at losing my virginity with has been a problem all along.

I stretch to look at the digital alarm clock on my bedside table from my seat at my desk. Almost eight. I'm usually in for the night at this point, but I'm restless. I could use a short trip somewhere, and maybe a snack. I think about the alfajores at Café Contigo, and my mouth starts watering. Phoebe is working tonight, and Maeve's been avoiding that place like the plague for some reason. It's as good a destination as any, so I head for the stairs.

I'm halfway down when I hear my father's voice. "It looks like there may have been structural support issues, but it's hard to be sure given how long the site was untouched." My parents are in our kitchen; I can hear the faint clatter of ceramic against wood as they empty the dishwasher. "The fact remains, though, that the kids were trespassing. Including ours. So if Lance Weber does decide to sue, he might wind up with a counter lawsuit on his hands."

I freeze where I am, one hand on the banister. Shit. Am I getting *sued*?

"Lance has some nerve." Mom's voice is tight. "I hope this is just the grief talking. I feel for him, of course, because—my God. To lose your son. It's a nightmare. But for Lance to bring up the possibility of a lawsuit after the strings he pulled to keep Brandon out of trouble—it's beyond hypocritical."

I inch closer, straining my ears. What is she talking about?

"That was a mistake from the start," Dad says grimly. "The case never should have been settled that way. Not for something like *that*. All it did was show Brandon that actions don't have to have consequences, which is a terrible lesson. Especially for a kid like him."

Mom breathes out a heavy sigh. "I know. I still regret not pushing harder. I think about it all the time. But it was my first year at Jenson and Howard, and I was trying not to make waves. If that came across my desk now, I'd treat it differently."

I wait for my father's response, but all I hear is a throaty growl and the sound of dog nails clicking across linoleum. Fritz enters the living room, snuffling loudly until he spots me. His tail starts wagging, and his snuffles turn into an excited whine. "Shh," I hiss. "Sit." Instead, he keeps whining and pokes his nose through the staircase railing.

A chair scrapes across the kitchen floor. "Knox?" my mother calls. "Is that you?"

I thud the rest of the way downstairs, Fritz tailing me into the kitchen. My mother is leaning beside the sink, and my father is sitting at the table. "Hey," I say. "What were you guys talking about?"

Dad gets that closed-off, irritated look he's had ever since I was released from the hospital. "Nothing that concerns you."

Mom gives me her best good-cop smile. "Do you need something, sweetie?"

"I'm going out for a while." Does she look relieved? I think she does. "But I heard you guys talking about Brandon. Was he in some kind of trouble?"

"Oh, sweetie, that's not important. Just your dad and me talking business."

"Okay, but . . ." I'm not sure why I'm not letting this go. Usually one steely glare from my father is enough to shut me up, and he's already given me two. "Your firm did a case with him? You never told me that. What was it?"

Mom stops smiling. "Knox, my work is confidential and you know that. I wasn't aware you were listening or I wouldn't have spoken. I'll ask you not to repeat anything you heard here, please. So." She clears her throat, and I can practically see her stuff the entire subject into a Do Not Revisit box. "Where are you going?"

I'm not getting anything out of her, obviously. And my dad's a lost cause. "Café Contigo. Can I take your car?"

"Sure," she says, too quickly. "Have fun but be home before eleven, please."

"I will." I pull her keys off the rack on our kitchen wall with the uncomfortable certainty that I'm missing something important. But I don't know what.

"What's up, my man?"

Crap. I came here to see Phoebe, not my new best friend, Sean. But she's not here and he is, holding up one meaty paw for a high five.

I give in reluctantly. "Hey, Sean."

"What are you up to?" Sean asks. He's leaning against the counter, waiting for his order, totally chill. Shooting the shit like he didn't watch his best friend die less than two weeks ago. Christ, I hate him.

Ever since that maybe-memory popped into my head, I can't stop thinking about it: Sean standing at the edge of the construction site with his phone trained on something. And then everything goes blank, like a TV shutting off, and I hear his voice: *What the fuck are you doing here, Myers?*

Did that actually happen? Or am I imagining things?

I wish I could be sure.

Sean is still talking. "I'm picking up dinner for my girl. Food here sucks, but she likes it. What can you do, right?"

"Yeah, right." I pull out a chair in a corner table near the register and set my backpack down but don't sit. Sean's phone is dangling from his hand while he waits. He's not the type of guy who deletes incriminating pictures or videos, I don't think. He doesn't have that much common sense. I clear my throat and lean against the table as Luis comes out of the kitchen with a brown paper bag. "So, hey, Sean," I say. "Can I ask a favor, man?"

Oh hell. That sounded ridiculous. I don't know how to talk to guys like Sean. He cocks his head, looking amused, and I keep plowing ahead. "Do you think I could borrow your phone? I have to look something up and I left mine at home."

Sean pulls his wallet out of his back pocket. "Knox, my man," he says, extracting a twenty. "You did not. Your phone's in the side pocket of your backpack."

I drop into my chair, defeated. I'm beyond pathetic. "Oh yeah. So it is. Thanks."

"How's it going?" Sean says to Luis, and they do a complicated fist bump. Sean plays baseball too, well enough that he was on varsity when Cooper and Luis were seniors. "We miss you on the team, man. You going to Fullerton Thursday for Coop's game?"

"Of course," Luis says, handing Sean his change.

"Me too, brother."

"See you there."

"Sweet." Sean turns from the register. "Catch you tomorrow, my man," he says as he passes my table, holding out his hand for yet another high five. I slap his palm, mostly so he'll get the hell out of here. He's useless to me now that my sad attempt at espionage fizzled.

I could've used Maeve's skills tonight.

When the door closes behind Sean, Luis grabs a glass and a pitcher of water from the bar and brings them over to my table. He sets both down and fills the glass. "Why'd you want his phone?" he asks.

"I, what?" I fumble. "I didn't."

"Come on." Luis drops into the chair across from me with a shrewd look. "You looked like somebody kicked your puppy when he pointed yours out."

"Um." We regard each other for a few seconds in silence. I don't really know Luis, other than the fact that he stuck by Cooper when almost nobody else did. Plus Phoebe thinks he's great, and his dad is basically the nicest guy on the planet. I could have worse allies, I guess. "He took a video I want to see. But I don't think he'd give it to me if I asked directly. Actually, I know he wouldn't."

"What kind of video?"

I hesitate. I don't even know if it's really there. The whole thing could be a product of my scrambled brain. But maybe it's not. "Of the construction site the day Brandon died."

"Huh." Luis is quiet for a moment, scanning the room to see if anybody else needs his attention. They don't, and he turns it back to me. "Why do you want it?"

Good question. "I can't remember much about that day, because of the concussion," I say. "Some of the things that people tell me happened don't make sense. I guess I'd like to see it with my own eyes."

"Luis!" Manny pops his head out of the kitchen. He's like a fun-house mirror image of Luis: bigger, broader, and a lot more confused-looking. "Do we make guac with garlic or without?"

Luis looks pained. "Jesus, Manny. You ask that every day."

"So . . . with?"

"I gotta go," Luis sighs, getting to his feet. "You want anything?"

"Alfajores," I say. "But no rush."

He leaves, and I gaze around me. Now what? I'd been relying on Phoebe to keep me company, and I don't really know what to do with myself alone in a restaurant. What did Maeve used to do for all those hours? I pull out my phone but immediately put it back when I see I have thirty-seven ChatApp notifications. Maybe later.

The door opens, and a guy my age walks in. I squint until I place him—it's Intense Guy from a few weeks ago. The one who came looking for Phoebe until Manny and Luis scared him off. I glance at the counter, but nobody's there. This time, the guy doesn't stride forward but drops into a corner table and slouches low in the seat. Ahmed, one of the servers, heads over to bring him water. They speak briefly, but nothing about the conversation seems to raise red flags for Ahmed, who leaves the table with his usual pleasant but preoccupied expression.

Intense Guy puts his head down when Manny makes a brief appearance at the counter, but otherwise he scans the room like he's watching a movie. Ahmed brings him a cup of coffee, and the guy just keeps sitting and staring without drinking it. I'm glad now that Phoebe's not working, because I have the feeling he's looking for her again.

Why? Who the hell is this guy? Emma's ex Derek, maybe? I've already forgotten his last name. I grab my phone and pull up Instagram, but it's pointless—there are millions of Dereks.

After about fifteen minutes of me watching Intense-Guy-slash-Maybe-Derek watch the room—which is just as riveting as it sounds—the guy tosses a bill on the table and takes off without ever having touched his coffee. I'm left with the same vague, uneasy feeling I had in my parents' kitchen earlier.

I'm missing something.

CHAPTER EIGHTEEN

Maeve
Thursday, March 19

Cooper tenses, winds up, and hurls a blistering fastball across home plate. The opposing batter looks like he's swatting at a fly when he misses, and the entire stadium erupts into cheers. The batter, down on strikes, hurls his bat toward the dugout in frustration and stalks away.

"Poor sport," Kris murmurs beside me, putting out an arm so Cooper's grandmother, seated on his other side, can lean against him while she gets to her feet for a standing ovation. She does it every time Cooper strikes somebody out, which has been a lot this game. It's the cutest thing I've ever seen.

We're at Goodwin Field at Cal State Fullerton on Thursday night, part of a capacity crowd watching Cooper pitch against UCLA. The stadium seating is like a horseshoe around the field, and we're almost directly behind home plate in a section that's full of Bayview High students, past and present. I got a ride here with Addy, who corralled Nate as soon as he showed up and is forcing him to be social. I think I caught a glimpse of Luis sitting with a bunch of Cooper's ex-teammates, but I looked away before I could be sure. After two weeks of total silence, I don't even know what I'd say if I ran into him tonight.

My phone buzzes in my hand. I expect a text from Bronwyn, who's been checking in on Cooper throughout the game, but it's just my mom asking what time I'll be home. I still can't get used to how quiet my phone is ever since I disabled the PingMe alerts. I'm glad I listened to Phoebe about that, especially since the Truth or Dare game ended on its own. I'd like to think whoever did it stopped out of respect for the fact that Bayview High is mourning Brandon, but it's more likely they just realized they'd lost everyone's attention.

Every once in a while I still wonder who was behind it all, and whether they had a personal grudge against Phoebe, Knox, and me. But I guess that doesn't matter. My real problem is that I haven't figured out how to make things up to Knox. Now that I've managed to alienate both him and Luis, my social circle has shrunk once again to Bronwyn's friends.

Well, and Phoebe. At least she's still speaking to me.

Cooper throws one of his infamous sliders, and the UCLA batter just stands there looking confused while it's called a strike. "You might as well sit down right now, young man," Cooper's grandmother calls. "You're already out."

My mood lifts a little as I lean toward Kris. "Nonny heckling batters might be my favorite thing ever."

He smiles. "Same. Never gets old."

"Do you think Cooper will go to the majors next year?" I ask.

"Not sure." Kris looks extra-cute in a green polo that brings out his eyes, his dark hair full of golden glints from sitting in so many baseball stadiums. "He's really torn. He loves being at school, and the team has been great. Not just about baseball, but—everything." Kris gestures wryly to himself. "The majors, on the other hand, still aren't particularly welcoming to gay players. It'd be a tough transition, especially with all the added pressure. But the reality is, his game won't advance the way it needs to if he stays at the college level much longer."

I watch Cooper on the mound, disconcerted by how impossible it is to recognize him from this distance. With his hat pulled low over his face, he could be anyone. "How do you make that choice?" I ask, almost to myself. "Between what you need and what you want?" I feel like my sister's going through her own version of that.

Kris's eyes are on Cooper, too. "You hope they become the same thing, I guess."

"What if they don't?"

"I have no idea." Kris sucks in a breath as the batter makes contact with Cooper's next pitch, but it's a harmless grounder that the shortstop fields easily. "The Padres keep checking in," he adds. "They really want him, and they have a high draft position this year."

"Would it be an easier decision if he could stay local? He'd still have to travel a ton, obviously, but at least he'd be close to home."

I don't mean Bayview, exactly, and I think Kris knows that. He allows himself a small smile. "It might."

I smile back through a tangle of conflicting emotions. On one hand, it feels strange to be here with dozens of other Bayview High students in such a cheerful atmosphere, two weeks after Brandon died. On the other, it's a relief to be focused on something positive for a change. I'm happy for Kris and Cooper, because they deserve every good thing, and I'm excited about their future.

Not so much about mine, though.

I push up the sleeve of my long-sleeved T-shirt to trace the outline of another bruise. I feel like a peach left too long on a windowsill, right before it collapses on itself. Deceptively smooth on the outside, but slowly rotting at the core.

And then I feel it: moisture trickling through my nose again. *Oh no. Not here.*

I grab a tissue from my bag and press it against my face, rising to my feet at the same time. "Bathroom," I say to Kris, stepping over him and Nonny with a murmured apology on my way to the aisle. The steps are clear, with nearly everyone in their seats and focused on Cooper, so I'm able to make my way to the women's room quickly. I don't look at the tissue until I'm in a stall with the door locked behind me.

Bright red.

I collapse onto the toilet seat and the tears come, silently but so hard that my shoulders shake. Despite my best efforts at pretending none of this is happening, it is, and I don't know what to do. I feel isolated, hopeless, terrified, and just plain exhausted. Tears mix with blood as I swipe tissue after tissue over my face, until I finally rip at least three feet of toilet paper out of the dispenser and bury my head in the entire thing.

Both the tears and the nosebleed stop around the same time. I stay where I am for at least another inning, letting my breathing even out and my heart rate slow. Then I stand, flush my mass of tissues and toilet paper, and leave the stall. I splash water on my face at the sink, staring at my reflection in the hazy mirror. Could be worse. My eyes aren't all that red, and I'm not wearing any makeup to smudge. I run a brush through my tangled hair, wash my hands, and step outside onto the concourse.

The restrooms are around the corner from the concession stand, and the first thing I see is a small knot of familiar faces: Sean, Jules, Monica, and Luis. Jules is wrapped so tightly around Sean that she's in danger of spilling the tray of snacks he's holding. Monica keeps touching Luis's arm, batting her eyelashes at him. They're all laughing and joking like they're on the greatest double date of their lives and don't have a care in the world.

For a second, I hate them all.

"All right, man, thanks," Luis says, handing something to Sean. "I gotta go."

Monica gives a flirty little pout. "You're not *leaving*, are you?" she asks. "After we bought all these snacks? Somebody has to share the popcorn with me."

"No way. I wouldn't miss Coop. I'll see you guys back in the seats, okay?" The other three turn away, still laughing, and

Luis heads in my direction. I should duck into the women's room again, but my legs refuse to cooperate.

He stops a few feet away when he spots me. "Maeve, hey." His brow furrows as he looks more closely. "Everything okay?"

Maybe my eyes aren't quite as normal as I'd hoped. "Fine," I say. I cross my arms and push away the memory of my crying spell in the bathroom. "He's an asshole, you know."

"What?" Luis turns around, like he thinks I'm talking about someone behind him. "Who?"

"Sean. He's been horrible to Knox and Phoebe and . . . other people."

"Oh. Yeah, well, we played ball together, so." He shrugs like that's the only explanation needed. My temper spikes and I'm glad for the distraction.

"So you're *bros*," I say sarcastically. "Awesome."

Luis goes still, his eyes narrowing. "What does that mean?"

"It means you all stick together, don't you? Dudebros unite, and who cares about anyone else." My skin prickles with residual fear, misplaced anger, and something else I can't put a name to. "I guess he can do whatever he wants as long as he throws a ball far enough."

"Dudebro," Luis says flatly. "That's what you think of me?"

"That's what you are." I don't even know what I'm saying anymore. All I know is that it feels good to unleash some of the frustration that's been building inside me for weeks.

His jaw ticks. "I see. Is that why you dropped off the face of the earth?"

"I didn't—" I pause. Okay, maybe I did. But he didn't

223

knock himself out looking for me, either. My nose tingles, and dread rushes up my spine. Another nosebleed is going to start again soon, I can tell. "I have to go. Enjoy your *popcorn*."

Oh. So that's the other thing I'm feeling. Jealous.

"Hang on." Luis's voice is commanding enough that I pause. His shoulders are squared, his face tense. "I was hoping to run into you tonight. I wanted to get your number, finally." My heart does a stupid leap despite itself, then crashes back down when he adds, "Now that I know how you feel about *dudebros,* I won't bother you, but there's still something I want to send you. It's for Knox, actually, but you're the one here, so." He pulls his phone out of his pocket. "Can you tell me your number? Once you have these you can go ahead and delete me from your phone or your life or whatever."

I'm seized with regret, but also with the certainty that I'm about to start bleeding in front of him. I recite my number quickly, and Luis presses a few keys before putting his phone away. "Might take a while to come through. They're big files. Tell Knox I hope it helps."

He strides away just as a trickle of blood escapes my nose. It starts to fall faster, even dripping onto my shirt, but I don't move to wipe it away. I don't know what just happened, other than the fact that I was horrible to Luis for no good reason, and trampled whatever might've been going on between us straight into the ground.

Which sucks, but it's not even close to my biggest problem right now.

"Maeve. What the *fuck*."

I look up to see Nate carrying a full cup of soda in each

hand, his eyes flicking from my face to the blood on my shirt. I've never told him what nosebleeds mean for me, but from the look on his face, Bronwyn did. Something breaks inside me, and before I can get hold of myself, I start crying again.

Nate tosses both sodas into a nearby trash can without another word. He puts an arm around me and leads me out of the main concourse to a side area with a few scattered picnic tables. It's not private, exactly, but we're the only ones there. He sits us both down, his arm still wrapped around my shoulders. I collapse into him, sobbing against his chest for I don't know how long. Nate keeps pulling crumpled napkins out of his pocket until he runs out and I have to press them together in a damp, bloodstained mess. All I can think, while I clutch Nate's jacket and he keeps a steady hand on my arm, is that I'm finally not alone with this.

When I sit up at last, wiping my eyes, he says, "Bronwyn didn't tell me."

I dig a tissue out of my purse and blow my nose. "She doesn't know."

Nate's dark-blue eyes widen. "Your parents didn't tell her?"

"They don't know, either. Nobody does."

"Maeve. What the *fuck*," he says again. It doesn't seem like the sort of comment that needs a reply, so I don't. "But doesn't this . . . I mean, just to make sure I'm understanding things here. This is something that happens when you relapse, right?" I nod. "So you can't . . . You have to . . . Why? Why would you keep something like this to yourself?"

My voice is low and hoarse. "You don't know what it's like."

"What what's like?" Nate asks.

"Relapsing."

"Tell me."

"It's just—everything changes. Everyone is sad. Normal life stops and we all climb on this miserable treatment roller coaster that only goes down. It's horrible and it hurts in every way possible, and the worst thing is, it *doesn't work*." I'd start crying again if I weren't completely spent. I sag against Nate's shoulder instead, and his arm tightens around me. "It never works for long. Four years is the longest ever. I thought maybe I'd never have to do it again and I . . . I don't know if I can."

Nate is quiet for a few seconds. "Okay," he says finally. "I get that. But this is your *life*, Maeve. You have to try. Don't you think?"

I'm so unbelievably tired. If I closed my eyes now, I'd sleep for days. It's not a comforting thought. "I don't know."

"If you won't do it for yourself, then do it for your family, okay?" Nate's voice gets urgent. "Think about your mom and dad. And Bronwyn. How would they feel if you . . . If something happens, they'll drive themselves crazy wondering whether things could have been different if you'd trusted them enough to tell them."

I stiffen. "It's not about *trust*."

"But that's what they'll think." I don't reply, and he presses. "You know it's what Bronwyn will think. She'll blame herself for not being here, or not guessing. And it will eat at her for the rest of her life."

Damn him. He just poked my Achilles' heel, and he knows it. When I sit up, he already looks relieved. "Fine," I mutter. "I'll talk to my parents."

As soon as I say it, a wave of relief crashes over me, washing away some of the dread that's been building for weeks. It hits me, then, how badly I've wanted to tell them, but I'd let myself get frozen with fear and indecision. I needed a push.

Nate exhales a long breath. "Thank Christ."

"You need to do something for me in return, though," I warn. He raises his eyebrows, quizzical. "Get your head out of your ass when it comes to my sister."

Nate's surprised laugh breaks the tension enough that I smile, too. "Listen, Maeve. You don't have to worry about Bronwyn and me. We're endgame."

I wipe a stray tear from the corner of my eye. "What does that mean?"

"It means we'll wind up together eventually. It might take a year for us to sort everything out, or two, or ten. Whatever. But it'll happen."

"Maybe you should tell *her* that," I suggest.

He gives me that famous Nate Macauley grin that always turns my sister into a puddle. "She knows. She might not admit it yet, but she knows."

CHAPTER NINETEEN

Phoebe
Friday, March 20

"You guys need to see this," Maeve says, pulling out her phone.

She looks positively green, although it might just be the lighting in here. We're backstage in the Bayview High auditorium, sitting on the floor of some little side room that the drama club uses as an office. I didn't even know it existed. A desk and chair take up half the space, and floor-to-ceiling bookshelves against one wall hold props, books, and folded costumes. The walls are covered in faded Broadway posters, and everything is coated in a thin layer of dust.

"What is it?" I ask. I'm positioned between her and Knox, which is where I always end up when the three of us are together lately. Knox might not be the school joke anymore, but that doesn't mean things are okay between him and Maeve. He only came because she insisted, with surprising force.

"A video that Luis gave me," Maeve says. "I got it yesterday but—I had kind of an intense night with my parents. Some family stuff going on . . . Anyway, that's not really the point. The point is, I didn't watch it until a little while ago. Luis sent a bunch of videos, I think because he didn't know what was important, and he *clearly* didn't go through it all himself, because he would have said something if he had, because—"

"Maeve," I interrupt. "Maybe you should just play the video."

"Yes. Okay." She unlocks her screen and opens her photos. "But just to set it up a little more—this is from Sean Murdock's phone. It was taken the day Brandon died."

I gasp. Knox, who'd been slouching listlessly beside me, sits bolt upright. "Wait. *What?*" he asks. He scrambles around me until he's sitting next to Maeve and can stare directly at her phone. "How did Luis get it?"

"I think he borrowed Sean's phone last night at Cooper's game," Maeve says.

"Oh my God, Knox," I say, realizing what she has. "It's *the* video. You were right!"

Maeve's forehead creases as her eyes dart between us. "You guys already knew about this?" she asks. She sounds both confused and hurt.

"I don't know what's on it," Knox says. "I had a memory come back of Sean recording *something* at the construction site but I didn't know what it was." He's practically vibrating with tension as he grips Maeve's arm. "Play it."

She taps Play, and my pulse starts racing when an image of Brandon fills the screen, his hair tousled by the wind. He's standing right at the edge of the construction site, looking down, and tears spring to my eyes. I almost forgot how beautiful he was. I used to spend entire class periods dreaming about those lips. "This is fucking boring," he says, and his familiar voice sends chills down my spine. "Why couldn't I have gotten something like yours?" Brandon continues, twisting to look at someone behind him off camera. "Or even yours."

"What are you waiting for, pretty boy?" Sean's voice, in a high falsetto, comes at us loud and clear. "Not scared of a little jump, are you?"

"I'm disappointed," Brandon says, putting his hands on his hips. "There's no glory in this. I should do a backflip or something."

"That would be amazing," comes a girl's breathless voice, and my heart stutters. *Jules.*

"At least you get to play," comes another voice that I recognize as Monica's. "Who or what does a girl have to do to get a freaking Dare around here?"

"Holy shit—" Knox starts, but I shush him.

"Me," Brandon says, and Sean cackles.

"For a guy who's not scared, Branny, you sure are talking a lot," he taunts. "Come on. Let's capture you for posterity. Jump, motherfucker! Jump, jump, jump!"

Jules and Monica pick up the chant, and they're clapping, and oh my God, this is so horrible that I actually whimper. "Does he . . . do you see him . . ." I stammer. Then Brandon bends his legs in preparation to jump, and I *can't.* I squeeze my eyes shut and press my face tightly against Maeve's shoulder. I hear the crash anyway.

"Fucking hell!" Sean's voice comes out like a scream, high

and terrified. "Bran! What the fuck just happened!" I can hear Jules and Monica screaming, too, and I cautiously raise my head to look at Maeve's screen. The video is nothing but dirt and grass, the ground pitching below Sean as he moves. "Bran! Are you—holy shit."

"Where is he?" Jules asks tearfully.

"He fell through the *fucking roof*!" Sean yells. His phone is still aimed at the ground, recording. Monica says something I can't hear. Then there's a couple minutes of low, urgent conversation that's impossible to catch until Sean's voice comes through again, loud and clear: "What the fuck are you doing here, Myers?" And then the screen goes black.

"Jesus," Knox says weakly.

Maeve swallows hard. "You guys got the gist of that, right?" she asks. "The game didn't end with Knox and me, after all. Brandon was doing a Dare."

"Yeah. Got it." I blink back tears and press my hands to my stomach. If I'd eaten lunch before watching that, I'd have thrown it up. "Oh my God. That was horrible."

Maeve puts a gentle hand on my arm. "I'm sorry. I should've warned you better. I keep forgetting that you guys, um, hung out for a while." She turns to Knox. "I think you were right. It doesn't seem like Sean punched you to help you. But I'm still not sure why he did."

Knox's eyes remain glued to her dark phone. "Me either. I thought seeing that would jog my memory, but it didn't." We're all quiet for a few minutes, lost in our own thoughts, until Knox adds, "Maeve, you said Luis sent a bunch of videos. Are there any other—"

"No," she interrupts quickly. "There's nothing else about Brandon. The rest is just . . . personal stuff." She goes bright red when she says it. Even though I'm still numb with shock, my mouth twists into a grimace.

"Ew. Please don't tell me you accidentally watched a Sean sex tape."

Maeve looks like she just sucked on a lemon. "No, but there was a . . . shower selfie."

"Oh my God." I stare at her in horrified commiseration. "Was it . . ."

"Full frontal," she confirms, shuddering at the memory.

Knox snorts out a humorless laugh. "Imagine how much fun we could have with that if we were assholes like him." Then he frowns and massages his temple. "So, what should we do about the video? Should we tell someone?"

"Well," I say cautiously. "It doesn't change anything, does it? It's still a shitty accident, except now they'd all get in trouble for lying." I don't care about Sean or Monica, but there's Jules to consider. "And then . . . the Truth or Dare game would be out there. Teachers would know about it, so we'd lose our phones at school. And *parents* would know." I glance at Knox to see if that's sinking in, and sure enough, he looks appalled at the thought. I'm sure he doesn't want his parents learning his Truth any more than I want my mother to hear mine.

"Right," Knox says decisively. "It doesn't change anything."

I turn toward Maeve. She's usually the first to jump in with an opinion, but she's been quiet for a while. Now that my eyes have gotten used to the drama club office lighting, she doesn't look as green anymore—but she does look exhausted. Dark circles ring her eyes, and her usually shiny hair is pulled back into a dull, messy bun. "What do you think?" I ask.

Her amber eyes droop. "Whatever you guys want to do." She picks up her messenger bag and loops it around her shoulder. "I have to go. I have a doctor's appointment in half an hour."

I pluck at her sleeve. "Everything okay?"

"Sure. Fine. It's just . . ." Maeve glances between Knox and me and bites her lip, her face conflicted. Then she seems to make up her mind about something. "It's just that I might not be around as much, for a while. Depending on how things go today. I've been having . . . symptoms. The sort of things that used to happen before I relapsed. So I'm getting that checked out. We're starting with a blood test, and then we'll see what's next."

My mouth falls open, and I'm rooted to the spot as Maeve gets to her feet. But Knox isn't; he jumps up with her, knocking his knee hard against the desk. He doesn't seem to notice. "Maeve, what the hell? Why didn't you tell me?"

She gives him a wry half smile. "We haven't exactly been talking."

"Yeah, but that—that doesn't matter. Not compared to this." Knox runs a hand through his hair and snatches his backpack up from the ground. "I'm coming with you."

"You can't," Maeve protests. "You have class."

"I'll cut. Phoebe showed me how."

"It's true," I volunteer, but neither of them is paying attention to me.

Maeve twists her hands together. "My parents are taking

me. I don't think they'd want a committee in my oncologist's office."

"Then I'll wait in the lobby. Or the parking lot." Knox slips his backpack over his shoulders and grips the straps so tightly that his knuckles turn white. "God, Maeve, I'm sorry. I feel like shit that I didn't know about this."

"You don't have anything to apologize for," Maeve says. "I do."

"You tried. I wouldn't listen."

I get the feeling, suddenly, that I'm intruding on an over-due conversation. I stand and enfold Maeve in a quick, hard hug. "I better go," I say into her hair. "Good luck. I'm thinking all the good thoughts for you." She murmurs her thanks as I slip through the office door.

I part the velvet curtains onstage and descend the side stair-case onto the auditorium floor. My thoughts are in a whirl, pinballing between Maeve's news and the video I just saw. When I reach the back of the auditorium, I almost trip over a sneakered foot jutting into the aisle.

"Hey," Matthias Schroeder says. "I have a message for you."

He's sitting in the back row, a brown paper bag in his lap, clutching half a sandwich. I pause and take him in: light blue hoodie with some Star Wars character I don't know, skinny black jeans, and weirdly jaunty red sneakers. His wispy blond hair is too long, hanging in his eyes. "You have a *message* for me?" I ask, skeptical. Matthias and I have never spoken before. "And you, what? Had to trip me before you could tell me?"

"I waved at you the entire time you were walking up the

aisle," he says. "You didn't notice me. Anyway, I had English with Emma before lunch and she doesn't feel well so she took your car and went home. I guess she doesn't have a phone, or whatever."

"Oh. Okay." I look at him warily. "How did you know I'd be here?"

"I followed you," he says. His expression gets defensive when my eyes pop. "I'm not, like, creeping on you. I was gonna tell you in the caf but you came here instead. I eat lunch here sometimes anyway, so I waited for you."

He takes a bite of sandwich. It's made with thin white bread and some kind of pale pink lunchmeat, a wilted leaf of lettuce poking out of one side. It's the loneliest-looking vegetable I've ever seen. When he places the sandwich on his paper bag, I can see indents where his fingers were pressing. "Well, thanks for letting me know," I say.

I should go then, probably, but instead I hitch my backpack higher on my shoulder. "Did you have anything to do with the Truth or Dare texting game?" I ask abruptly.

Matthias looks startled. "What? No. Why would you think that?"

Everybody thinks that, I almost say. "You started Simon Says."

Matthias looks down at his sandwich. "That was different."

"How?"

"I just wanted to know what it was like." It's dim in the auditorium, but I can still see Matthias's cheeks flush. "To have people pay attention."

235

"They paid attention to the Truth or Dare game, too."

"I *said* that wasn't me." Matthias seems surprised at the sound of his own voice echoing through the empty room. He lowers it. "I wouldn't even know how to find out that stuff. The secrets. Nobody talks to me. Or haven't you noticed?"

"I'm talking to you."

"Yeah, well." Matthias tosses the rest of his sandwich into the paper bag and crumples the whole thing into a ball. "We both know that won't last." He unfolds his lanky frame to stand up and I feel—I don't know. Like I shouldn't let him be right.

"If you don't want to eat lunch here tomorrow, you could, um, eat with us," I tell him.

Matthias stares at his red sneakers, looking mildly alarmed. "I don't think so. Thanks, though." He darts away before I can respond, and it's probably just as well. I don't know what we'd talk about for more than a few minutes anyway.

It's hot for March—not the best day for me to get ditched by a sick Emma—so I'm grumpy and sweating by the time I trudge onto my block. My phone rings, and I curse at it under my breath. Hardly anyone calls me except my mother, so I don't even have to look at the screen before I answer. "Hey, Mom," I say, pulling out my keys as I approach the front door of our building.

Her voice is harried. "Hi, Phoebe. Is Emma with you? Can you put her on?"

I insert my key in the lock with one hand and twist it to

the right. It doesn't budge, and I grunt in annoyance as I pull it out to try again. Everything in this building looks great on the surface but works like actual crap. "She's not with me," I say distractedly.

Mom heaves a frustrated sigh. "I don't understand. This isn't like her!"

"Huh?" My mind is only half on her words as I wrestle with the key until the lock finally gives. "What isn't like her?" I ask, pulling the door open.

"To just not show up like this. She's supposed to be doing a walk-through for me at the restaurant where Ashton and Eli are having their rehearsal dinner. The manager could only be there this afternoon and I can't leave work, so I asked Emma to go in my place. We had a whole list of questions prepared, but she never showed up. And she still hasn't replaced her phone, so I can't even call her."

I'm in the lobby now and pause in front of one of the potted plants. Mom is right. That's not like Emma at all, even if she isn't feeling well. She's dragged herself to tutoring sessions when she had a fever. "She's sick," I say. "She left school early. Didn't she tell you?"

Mom exhales into my ear. "No, she didn't. Okay. What's wrong with her? Is it that stomach thing again, or—"

"I don't know," I interrupt. "I haven't seen her. She asked somebody at school to tell me she was leaving, and I just got home." I cross the lobby to the elevator and reach it right as the doors are starting to close. I stick my hand between them until they spring back open, and smile apologetically at the old woman standing off to one side. She lives on our floor, so the button is already pressed. "Do you want me to go to the restaurant instead?"

"Oh, that's sweet of you, Phoebe, but it's too late. The manager already left. I'll figure something else out. Could you please check on your sister and call me back?"

"Okay," I say. Mom thanks me and disconnects as the elevator chimes. I'm kind of anxious about Emma now, because how sick does she have to be to forget she was supposed to help Mom out? That's the kind of thing *I'd* do.

I open our apartment door and it's completely silent when I walk in. "Emma?" I call, pulling off my ankle boots. I leave them beside the door and drop my keys and bag on the kitchen island, then pad toward our bedroom. "How are you feeling?"

There's no response. The door is closed, and I push it open. Emma is lying on her bed in a messy tangle of blanket and sheets. For once, her bed looks exactly like mine. She's out cold, breathing steadily through her half-open mouth. As I move closer, she lets out a little snore. I stub my toe against something on the floor and step into a patch of wetness. Emma's Bayview Wildcats tumbler is lying beside her bed, and I pick it up and sniff inside. I wrinkle my nose and recoil. Gin, this time.

"Jesus, Emma." I don't know whether to be disgusted or worried, so I settle on both. "What the hell is going on with you?"

I grab some Kleenex from my dresser and bend down to mop up the spill, wincing when my knee connects with something sharp. It's the edge of Emma's phone charger, lying useless on the floor since she still hasn't replaced her phone. She keeps borrowing mine any time she wants to look something up and doesn't have the laptop handy, which is annoying because—

I pause, damp tissues dangling from one hand. Whenever Emma asks to borrow my phone, I hand it over without question. Half the time, I leave her alone in our room with it. What if she opened my Instagram and saw the messages from Derek? I never deleted them. Is that the kind of thing that might send her spiraling?

"Phoebe?" Emma's sleepy voice startles me so much that I almost fall over. Her eyes flutter open and lock on me. "What're you doing?"

"Cleaning up your mess," I say, sitting back on my haunches. "There's half a cup of gin on the floor. You're not actually sick, are you? You're *drunk*. Do you even remember that you were supposed to help Mom with Ashton and Eli's rehearsal dinner?"

Emma blinks slowly at me. "I need to ask you something."

My frustration rises. "Did you hear a word I just said?"

"Did you love him?" she asks hoarsely.

I swallow hard. Crap. She definitely saw the messages from Derek. "No. That was a huge mistake and it's over. I wish it had never happened."

She snorts out a humorless laugh. "I *know* it's over. I'm not an idiot. It's just that I never imagined . . . I didn't think . . ." Her eyes droop, or maybe close. I can't really tell from this angle.

"Didn't think what?" I ask.

She doesn't answer, and I get to my feet again, her Bayview

Wildcats tumbler in my hand. I'm about to leave when I hear a whisper from Emma's bed, so faint I almost miss it. "I didn't think he'd keep going."

"Keep going with what?" I ask. But the snores start up again, so I guess that's all I'm going to get out of her for now.

I bring the cup into the bathroom and rinse it thoroughly, adding a few drops of liquid soap until it smells like lemons instead of alcohol. My head is pounding like I'm the one who drank God only knows how much straight gin. When I'm finished, I dry the cup with a hand towel and place it on the back of the toilet. Then I lean against the sink, meeting my tired eyes in the mirror. I don't know what's going on with my sister, or what I should do about it. I don't want to worry Mom when she's been so much more cheerful lately. I could try talking to Emma's friend Gillian, maybe, but Gillian pretty much hates me after the whole Derek reveal. When she sees me at school, she looks right through me. There's nobody else I can turn to who knows Emma well enough to help.

It almost makes me consider messaging Derek back. Almost. But not quite.

CHAPTER TWENTY

Knox
Friday, March 20

Sandeep frowns at the envelope and holds it up to the light. "Yeah, I think it's the same person who sent the last couple of threats. The label has the exact same font."

Bethany is perched at the edge of the desk Sandeep and I are sharing. She squints and leans closer. "Font? That looks like handwriting."

"That's how it's designed," Sandeep says. He reaches into the desk drawer for a Ziploc and drops the envelope inside, squeezing out all the air in the bag and sealing it before he holds it up to Bethany. "But look at the kerning. It's too even."

"The what?" Bethany asks.

"Kerning. The spacing between the individual letter forms," Sandeep explains. "It's a typography term."

Bethany rolls her eyes as she gets up and heads back to her desk. "You're such a nerd."

"It's not nerdy to care about fonts!" Sandeep calls after her. "Typography is an art form."

Bethany sticks her tongue out at him and grabs her bag. "If you say so. I'm out, boys. Don't stay too late."

I swivel in my desk chair beside Sandeep. "Aren't you going to open it? Read what's inside?"

"Later. When I'm wearing gloves," he says. I frown, confused—why would he need gloves?—and he adds, "At this point, we've gotten enough threats from this particular individual that we need to hand it over to the police. I want to contaminate the envelope as little as possible before then."

I can't take my eyes off the envelope. The last note I read is still seared into my brain: *I'll enjoy watching you die.* "What do you think this person's so mad about?" I ask.

"The threats aren't specific, but if I had to guess, it's the D'Agostino case," Sandeep says, so promptly that I can tell he's thought about this a lot. He pushes the Ziploc bag into one corner of the desk. "People get very angry when police officers are accused of a crime, but that anger is often displaced toward the accuser or the victim. The conflict between obedience to authority and personal conscience is well documented."

"Right," I say, although I only got about half of that. When Sandeep launches into professor mode, he's a little hard to follow. Plus I'm distracted, checking my phone for updates. Maeve's oncology appointment ended four hours ago, and she told me when we left the office that they wouldn't have results for a while. "They're rushing it, but it still might take a few days," she'd said. "Lab hours are hard to predict." Still, I keep hoping that "rushing it" means "this afternoon." We're in the twenty-first century, after all.

This morning, I was still mad at Maeve. I was okay with the fact that holding a grudge might lose me a friend. But that was when the loss wasn't a tangible, permanent thing. Now, I can't stop thinking about how rare it is to have someone you can be completely real with, even when things get raw and uncomfortable and a little scary. *Especially* then.

All I want is for my friend to be okay.

"Anyway, try not to worry too much. We'll take care of it." I blink at Sandeep's voice, and the office comes back into focus. He slides a pile of folders toward me across the desk. "In the meantime, Eli needs somebody to give him the details about next week's court schedule and I, my friend, am *not it.*" He runs a hand over his already-smooth dark hair. "I have a date."

I sneak one last look at my phone. Nothing. Six thirty on a Friday probably isn't prime time for medical updates. "What about those child labor laws you're always going on about?" I ask.

"They cease to exist when I have a date," Sandeep says, jerking his head toward the smaller conference room. "Eli's in Winterfell. He just needs the basics on his calendar for now. Make another one of your magic spreadsheets. He loves those." Then he tugs at his collar, looking guilty. "Unless you need to get home. I mean, it *is* kind of late."

"It's fine," I say. I don't mind the long hours at Until Proven, because what the hell else would I be doing on a Friday night?

Besides, Eli and Sandeep and Bethany and everybody else act like my presence here matters—like things work better when I'm around. It's a good feeling.

Sandeep grins and gets to his feet, stuffing his laptop into his bag and slinging it over his shoulder. "Good man. I'll see you Monday."

"Hang on," I call, grabbing a black leather jacket off the back of his chair. "You forgot your coat."

Sandeep pauses midstep and turns with a quizzical expression. "What? I didn't bring a coat." He peers at the jacket I'm holding up, and his face clears. "Ah, I think that's Nate Macauley's. He stopped by around lunchtime to talk with Eli about a case study on Simon Kelleher. He might publish it in the *Harvard Law Review*."

"Nate might?" I ask, confused.

Sandeep laughs. "Sure. Harvard always takes submissions from teenagers with no legal training. No, *Eli* might. But only if all the kids are comfortable with it. Anyway, just give that to Eli—he'll get it back to Nate."

"I could drop it off," I say. "One less thing for Eli to worry about. It's on my way." I've never actually been inside the sprawling old house where Nate rents a room, but it's only a couple of streets away from mine. Maeve points it out every time we drive past.

"You sure?" Sandeep asks, and I nod. "You're the best," he says, cocking finger guns at me as he continues backing out the door. Then he's gone, and I head for the conference room.

Eli's on the phone when I enter Winterfell and he waves me into a chair. "I promise I won't," he says. "I'll shut my phone off." His tone is a lot warmer than it is when he's talking to a client or another lawyer, so I would've guessed this wasn't a business call even if he hadn't added, "I love you more, angel. I'll see you soon." He puts his phone down and gives me a distracted nod. "I need to fit everything into four days next week. Come Friday, I'm off the clock."

"Wow, yeah." I pull a set of folders from the top of the stack. "Can't believe you're getting married in a week. You ready?" I don't know why I'm asking him that, except it seems like the sort of thing guys ask each other.

Eli grins. "I've been ready for a year. I'm just glad she is."

"Ashton is awesome. You lucked out," I blurt, and then I feel like an idiot because shit, that was insulting, wasn't it? But Eli just nods.

"Luckiest guy on the planet," he says. He steeples his fingers under his chin and gives me a thoughtful look. "I can tell you one thing, though. High school me couldn't have imagined that someday I'd be building a life with somebody as fantastic as Ashton. Back then, the only time girls paid attention to me was when they wanted help with their homework. I didn't even have a date until I was nineteen."

"Really?"

"Oh yeah." Eli shrugs. "Takes a while for some of us. Good thing life is long and high school is short, although it doesn't feel like it at the time." He gestures at one of the folders in my hand. "Is that Carrero? Let's start with that."

"Yeah," I say, and hand it to him. That was a transparent attempt to make me feel better about the fact that I'm here every Friday night, and you know what? It kind of worked.

* * *

I hear Nate's house before I see it. It's barely nine o'clock, but the sounds of rap music and laughing voices greet me at the corner, and only get louder as I approach the run-down old Victorian. Their neighbors must *love* them.

I ring the bell, but it's a lost cause. Nobody's going to hear me, so I crack the door and step inside. The music is so loud that the scarred wooden floor is practically vibrating, and I'm immediately hit with the smell of popcorn and stale beer. I'm in a narrow hallway in front of a staircase with a curved banister, where a group of kids a little older than me are yelling at a girl perched at the top. "Do it!" they call, raising red cups in the air. The girl slides down the banister and crashes into the knot of people below, scattering them like bowling pins.

"Noooo!" moans a guy in a vintage concert T-shirt, stumbling into me as his drink sloshes onto the floor. "Party foul!" He grabs my arm to steady himself and adds, "Don't try that at home."

"Is Nate here?" I ask loudly. The guy cups his hand around his ear like he can't hear, so I raise my voice even more. "IS. NATE. HERE."

"Upstairs," the guy yells back.

I hesitate, looking for a coatrack or someplace else where I could leave Nate's jacket, but there's nothing. So I head up the staircase, pressing against the wall to avoid people going up and down. I'm almost at the top when the girl who slid down the banister grabs hold of my shirt and hands me a cup full of beer. "You look like you need to catch up," she shouts into my ear.

"Um, thanks." She's looking at me expectantly, so I take a sip. It's warm and sour. The narrow hallway is crowded with people, but I don't recognize any of them. "Do you happen to know where Nate is?"

The girl gestures to a closed door at the end of the hall. "Being antisocial, like always. Tell him to come out and play." She reaches over to ruffle my hair. "You're cute, Nate's friend, except for this. Grow it out. Makes you look like you're in high school."

"I *am* in—" I start, but she's already sliding down the banister again.

I reach the door she pointed me toward and hesitate. I don't know if Nate's going to hear me knock, but I can't just go in, right? What if he's with somebody? Maybe I should leave the jacket on the floor and get out of here.

While I'm debating, the concert T-shirt guy from downstairs suddenly appears beside me. He slams into Nate's door, pushing it open and leaning into the room. "Come to my fucking party, Macauley!" he yells. Then he spins around and runs back toward the stairs, cackling. I'm alone in the doorway when Nate, who's sitting at a desk in the corner of a small room, turns around.

"That wasn't me," I say, lifting my hand in greeting. I'm still holding the cup of beer.

Nate blinks at me like I'm a mirage. "What are you doing here?" he asks. At least, I think that's what he says. I can't really hear him, though, so I step into the room and close the door behind me.

"You left your jacket at Until Proven," I say, crossing toward the desk so I can hand it to him. "I told Eli I'd drop it off. Maeve told me where you live."

"Shit, I didn't even notice it was gone. Thanks." Nate takes the jacket from me and tosses it onto the foot of his unmade bed. Other than that his room is relatively neat, especially compared to the rest of the house. Japanese movie posters cover the walls, but there's not much else here besides the desk, the bed, a low dresser, and an open terrarium containing a large, yellow-brown reptile. I jump when it scratches one claw against the glass. "That's Stan," Nate says. "Don't worry about him. He barely moves."

"What is he?" I ask. He looks like a miniature dinosaur.

"Bearded dragon."

God damn it. Even Nate's pet is cooler than mine.

"So you made it through the obstacle course downstairs, huh?" Nate asks.

"Is your house always like this?"

Nate shrugs. "Only on weekends. They usually clear out by ten." He leans back in his chair. "Hey, you have any update on Maeve? She said you were going with her to the doctor today, but that's the last I heard from her."

"Nothing yet. She doesn't think she'll hear till Monday at the earliest." I shove my free hand into my pocket with a rush of guilt. Instead of feeling jealous of Nate like usual, I should thank him for being a better friend to Maeve than I was. "I'm glad you convinced her to tell her parents. I didn't even know. I feel like a jerk."

"Yeah, well, don't beat yourself up about it. Nobody knew," Nate says, tapping the pencil he's holding against the desktop in front of him. The desk is empty except for a battered laptop, a stack of books, and two pictures—one of a kid posing with two adults in front of what looks like a Joshua tree, and the other of Nate and Bronwyn. She's behind him, her arms around his neck while she kisses his cheek, and he looks happier in the picture than I've ever seen him look in person. Nate's eyes linger on the photo, and I start to feel like an intruder. I'm about to back away when I catch sight of his laptop screen. "Are you doing . . . construction homework?" I ask.

"What?" Nate looks down with a short laugh. "Oh. No. I've been helping your dad document cleanup work at the mall site where Brandon Weber died. We have to take pictures of everything for the investigation." He gestures to the screen. "These are bugging me, so I keep looking at them."

"Why?" I ask, curious. My father won't tell me anything about the site investigation. The pictures on Nate's computer don't look like much. Just piles of shattered wood on a rough cement floor.

"Because of what's not there, I guess. There's not all the debris you'd expect when a well-constructed landing crashes down. Some of the beams don't even have any joists so, like, how were they supposed to stay up in the first place?" Nate narrows his eyes at his computer. "But the beams have holes like joists *used* to be there, so . . . if you were totally paranoid, you'd almost think somebody messed with the landing."

"Messed with it? Are you serious?" I lean forward, intrigued, and drain half my beer before remembering I have to go home after this. I set the cup down at the corner of Nate's desk and look more closely at the photos. They still look like nothing to me.

Nate shrugs. "Your dad thinks it's weird, too, but the company working on this was crap at their job and left shitty records. So we can't be sure of anything." He taps his pencil again. "Your dad really knows his stuff. Guys at work are always talking about how other companies cut corners, but he never does."

My first instinct is to be petty and say *I wouldn't know.* But there's an almost wistful tone to Nate's voice, like he's imagining what it would've been like to grow up with a dad who runs a respected business instead of one who abandoned his kid for a whiskey bottle. And when you put it like that—yeah, my father issues pretty much pale in comparison. So I just say, "He really likes working with you. He tells me that all the time."

Nate half smiles as the door bursts open, startling us both. Concert T-shirt Guy leans against the frame, looking flushed and sweaty as he points toward Nate. "Dude," he slurs. "Hypothetically speaking. If a bunch of us decide to streak through the neighborhood, are you in?"

"No," Nate says, rubbing a hand across his face as he turns to me with a weary expression. "If I were you, I'd take that as my cue to leave. Trust me."

When I get home from Nate's, my dad is alone at our kitchen table. It's the same table we've had since I was a kid, a wooden monstrosity that could seat all seven of us comfortably. I used to be squished in the middle next to the wall—the worst, hardest-to-access spot for the youngest kid. I can sit anywhere I want now, since there are only three of us left in the house, but somehow I still find myself squeezing into that chair every night.

Dad is writing on a yellow legal pad, surrounded by a pile of what look like blueprints. He's wearing a Myers Construction T-shirt that used to be black but has been washed so many times that it's turned pale gray. "You're home late," he says without looking up. Fritz is snoring lightly at his feet, paws twitching like he's dreaming about taking a walk.

I go to the refrigerator and pull out a Sprite. I need to wash the taste of sour beer out of my mouth. "My internship is really busy," I say. "Since Eli's getting married next week."

"Right." Dad scratches out a note on his pad. "Good to see you stick with something, I guess."

I pop the top from my soda and take a gulp, watching him over the rim as something inside me deflates. *Your dad really knows his stuff,* Nate said tonight. It's true, but Dad never shares any of that with me. All I get are these pointed little comments. I usually ignore them, but tonight I'm not in the mood. "What's that supposed to mean?" I ask.

Dad keeps writing. "Your mother said you quit that play you're in."

"So?" I prod. "Why do you care? You haven't been to one of my plays in years."

He finally looks up, and I'm struck by how deeply etched the lines in his face are. I could swear they weren't so prominent yesterday. "I care because when you make a commitment to something, you should stick with it."

Yeah. You *should.* Unless you're the laughingstock of the entire school and being onstage is only going to make it a hundred times worse. I would've ruined that play for everyone in it, even though most of them don't see it that way. Lucy doesn't; she's still not talking to me.

And if I'm being totally honest, it wasn't that hard a decision to make. I stopped caring about acting a while ago, but neither of my parents noticed. Dad acts like he wants me to change, but he doesn't really. Any time I try something different, he dismisses it.

But I can't tell my father that. I can't tell him anything.

"I had too much else going on," I say. He lets out a small, dismissive snort and goes back to his paperwork. Resentment swirls through my gut, making me bolder than usual. Or maybe it's that half beer I had. "Did you say something?" I ask. "I couldn't hear you."

Dad looks up, eyebrows raised. He waits a beat, and when I don't look away, he says, "If you think you have *too much* going on, with the number of video games you play and the amount of time you spend on your phone doing God knows what, then I pity your future employer when you have a real job."

My stomach drops. Jesus. *Say what you really mean, Dad.* He basically just called me useless. "Until Proven *is* a real job. I work hard there. I work hard in general. You'd know that, if you'd ever given me a shot working with you."

He frowns. "You've never had any interest in working with me."

"You never asked!" I blurt out. "It's a family business, supposedly, but you treat Nate Macauley like he's more of a son than I am." My mother must not be at home, because my voice is rising and there's no sign of her. Usually, this is when she steps in to play peacemaker. I gesture at the blueprints, my head still full of what Nate said in his room. "You won't even tell me what's up with the mall site investigation, and I was there when Brandon died!"

Dad's face gets thunderous. Uh-oh. That was the wrong card to play. I want to sink into the floor as he leans forward and points his pencil at me.

"You. Were. *Trespassing,*" he says, stabbing the pencil forward with every word. "And about to take an incredibly dangerous shortcut that I had specifically told you not to take. *You* could have been the one who died. I thank God every day that you didn't, but I'm livid that you were in that position in the first place. You grew up around construction work, Knox, and you know better. But you have zero respect for what I say, or the work I do."

I open my mouth, but no words come out. Shame makes my face burn. He's right on all counts except the last one. Does he really think I don't respect his work?

When I don't answer, Dad waves the pencil at me again. "Don't you have homework to do? Or television to watch?"

Dismissed, like always. But this time, I can't blame him, and I don't know how to apologize or explain myself. Especially since he's turned back to his work like I'm already gone. So I head upstairs with my Sprite, even though Nate's words keep running through my mind, burrowing into the groove of foggy half memories from the day Brandon died.

If you were totally paranoid, you'd almost think somebody messed with the landing.

CHAPTER TWENTY-ONE

Maeve
Monday, March 23

Knox is already in the drama club office when Phoebe and I get there at lunch, seated on the floor with an oversized Tupperware container in front of him. Phoebe peers into it, her expression quizzical, as she settles beside him. "Are you eating empty hot dog rolls for lunch?" she asks.

"Of course not," Knox says. "They have peanut butter inside."

Phoebe wrinkles her nose. "That's weird."

"Why? It's just different-shaped bread," Knox mumbles around a large bite. He swallows, takes a gulp of water from the bottle in front of him, and turns to me. "Any news from your doctor?"

He must have texted me that question a dozen times since Friday. But I don't mind; I'm just glad we're getting back to normal. "No, but the lab is open regular hours today, so hopefully I'll hear something soon," I say. Phoebe rubs my arm encouragingly and pulls a bottled smoothie out of her bag, popping the top and taking a sip of the thick purple liquid inside. I didn't bring anything, but my stomach is knotted way too tightly to eat.

"So why did you want to have lunch here instead of the cafeteria?" I ask Knox.

Knox inhales the rest of his first sandwich and chases it down with another drink of water before responding. "I wanted to talk to you guys about something without people eavesdropping," he says, wiping the back of his hand across his mouth.

"And by people, you mean Lucy," I mutter. I'm still not over her giving me a hard time when I was looking for Knox at play rehearsal.

"Or Sean," Knox says. "Or Monica, or Jules." Phoebe raises her eyebrows, and he adds, "Or anybody, basically. Something's been bugging me all weekend, so I want to see if you think it's weird or if I'm overreacting."

"Well, now I'm intrigued," I say, but I'm only half listening as I pluck at the beaded bracelet on my wrist. Ita gave it to me for luck the last time I went into the hospital, more than four years ago. I haven't worn it since and it's a little tight, but— that ended up being a good day. So maybe today will be, too. "What's up?"

"Okay, well, here's the thing. I saw Nate Friday night— don't ask," he adds, when my eyebrows shoot up. "It's a long story, work-related, not important. Anyway. Nate was looking at all these pictures from the construction site where Brandon fell. You know how I told you my dad is helping investigate the accident?" We both nod, and Knox continues, "Well, Nate says he thinks someone could've messed with the landing Brandon jumped on."

"Messed with it?" I echo. Now he has my full attention. "Like how?"

Knox shrugs, his mouth tight. "Removed some supports, I guess? I don't really know. I wanted to ask my dad, but . . . he wasn't in a great frame of mind. And Nate said the whole thing's inconclusive, anyway. But all weekend, I kept thinking about what that could mean. Why would anybody deliberately screw with an abandoned construction site? And that's when I started wondering . . . do you think there's any possibility that somebody wanted Brandon to get hurt? Like, was actually targeting him by giving him that Dare?"

Phoebe chokes on her smoothie, and I pound her on the back. "Are you serious?" I ask while she coughs. Knox nods. "Like who?"

He spreads his hands wide. "Not sure. Sean, maybe? He was right there when it happened, and he gave me a concussion when I got too close. Maybe he wanted Brandon out of the picture so he could finally be top dog at Bayview, or something."

"Huh." I prop my chin in my hands and stare at a poster for *Wicked* on the wall, a bold graphic print of a green witch with a sly smile. I think about the conversation I had with Lucy Chen in the auditorium during the *Into the Woods* rehearsal, right after Knox quit the play. *Everyone knows how to win this game by now,* she'd said. *Just take the Dare.* And she was right. After seeing what happened to Phoebe and me versus what happened to Sean and Jules, nobody at Bayview High who'd gotten a prompt would have done anything except text back *Dare.* Especially someone as competitive and confident as Brandon.

Still—this is Sean Murdock we're talking about. "I don't know," I say slowly. "Sean has always struck me as more of an in-your-face bully. Not to mention a short-term thinker. I can't picture him setting up something this elaborate."

Phoebe looks doubtful, too. "Your dad might've just meant that the construction company didn't do their job properly. They went bankrupt, right? That's probably because they're bad at constructing things."

"Entirely possible," Knox says.

"They're not done investigating the site yet, are they?" Phoebe asks. Knox shakes his head. "So maybe let your dad finish, and see what the final report says? The video's not going anywhere. We can share it anytime."

It all sounds perfectly reasonable but there's a little voice in the back of my mind urging me to turn PingMe back on. Just to keep an eye on any ongoing chatter related to the Truth or Dare game. I take my phone out of my pocket and reactivate the alerts, then jump when it rings in my hand. When I look down at the screen my heart nearly stops. *Dr. Ramon Gutierrez.*

"Oh my God, you guys." My voice is low, strangled. "It's my oncologist."

"Do you want us to stay or go?" Phoebe asks.

"I don't—" I can't think.

Phoebe stands as my phone continues to ring, grabbing Knox's arm to haul him to his feet. "We'll give you some privacy but we'll be right outside." She circles me in a one-armed hug while simultaneously shoving Knox out the door. "It'll be okay."

My phone is still ringing. Oh God, it's not. It stopped. I missed it. I stare at the screen until my phone locks, then unlock it with shaking hands and call back.

"Ramon Gutierrez's office," says a cool female voice.

I can't talk. I should have asked Phoebe to stay.

"Hello?" comes the voice again.

"Um. Hi," I croak. My palms are sweating so badly, I don't know how I'm managing to hang on to my phone. "This . . . this is Maeve . . ." I lose my words again, but she catches enough.

"Oh, Maeve, of course. Hold on, I'll put you right through."

I slide my bracelet up and down my wrist, the smooth glass beads reassuringly cool beneath my clammy fingers. *It'll be okay,* Phoebe said. Everyone says that, and sometimes they're right. But I've lived years on the other side of okay. I've always expected that, sooner or later, I'd wind up there for good.

"Maeve Rojas!" I don't recognize the hearty tone as Dr. Gutierrez's at first. "I just got off the phone with your mother, and she gave me permission to reach out to you directly while she—well. She needed a moment."

Oh God. What does *that* mean? But before I can torture myself with possibilities, Dr. Gutierrez keeps going. "I'm calling with good news. Your blood work is one hundred percent normal. Your white cell count is fine. I'll speak to your parents about running further diagnostics if they want additional reassurance, but as you know, this particular test has not steered us wrong before. As far as I'm concerned, your remission is not compromised."

"It's not?" The words aren't sinking in. I need him to say it a different way. "My leukemia isn't back?"

"That's correct. There is no indication in your blood work that the leukemia is back."

I let out a deep, shuddering sigh as all the tension I've been storing up over the past month flows out of me, leaving me light-headed and boneless. My eyes fill and quickly spill over. "But the nosebleeds . . . and the bruises . . ."

"You do show signs of an iron deficiency, which is obviously not something we like to see in someone with your history. So we're going to nip that in the bud with a vitamin prescription and more frequent check-ins. Also, I'd suggest you start putting Vaseline inside your nose twice a day. Your membranes are inflamed, which is exacerbating the issue."

"Vitamins and Vaseline. That's it?" The words slip out of me flat and numb, with none of the buoyant relief that's fizzing through my veins. My mouth hasn't caught up with my heart yet.

"That's it," Dr. Gutierrez says gently. "I'll talk to your parents in greater detail about follow-up and monitoring. This was a frightening bump in the road, but in my opinion it truly is just that."

"All right," I manage, and then he says some other things

but I don't hear them because I've already dropped my phone into my lap and put my head in my hands so that I can full-on bawl my eyes out. Hinges squeak and I smell floral shampoo as Phoebe kneels on the ground and wraps her arms around me. Knox crashes into me from the other side.

"We eavesdropped. I'm sorry, but we're so, so happy," Phoebe chokes out.

I can't speak enough yet to tell her *Me too*.

I need a few minutes by myself after the news. As much as I appreciate Phoebe and Knox being there, I'm relieved when they leave and let me pull myself together. I want to talk to my parents but the lunch bell is about to ring, so I send quick texts with a promise to call later. I already know what their reactions must be: so happy I'm not dying that they won't even be mad at me for keeping them in the dark for weeks.

Which, I'm only starting to realize, is something I need to sort out if I'm ever going to truly move on from being the sick girl. For most of my life, I've gotten a free pass for the things I do wrong. Hardly anyone gives me a hard time or holds a grudge. Even Knox came around once leukemia reared its ugly head again.

It's not a crutch I ever asked for, but I've been leaning on it anyway.

I send one final text to a number that I saved to Contacts instead of deleting like he'd suggested:

Hi Luis, it's Maeve. I've been meaning to thank you for the video. It was helpful. Also, I'm sorry for what I said at Cooper's

game. I didn't mean it. Not that this is any excuse, but I was hav-
ing a bad day and took it out on you.

I really am sorry.

I'd like to talk more sometime, if you would too.

Then I drop my phone in my bag. It's not enough, but it's a start.

CHAPTER TWENTY-TWO

Phoebe
Thursday, March 26

The graffiti scrawled across the dividing wall next to the paper towel dispenser in the girls' first-floor bathroom is brand-new, written in wavering blue ink. *Phoebe Lawton is a total . . .* Except I can't read the last word, because somebody crossed it out with a black Sharpie. Thank you, unknown benefactor who is probably Maeve. Then again, no. She'd have covered the whole thing so I wouldn't see my name.

My hands don't even shake as I'm washing them. At this point, personalized graffiti in the bathroom is nothing. In the past few days I've gotten two more Instagram messages from Derek, cleaned up after my sister twice, and flunked a science test because I can't concentrate in this hellhole. Plus Maeve keeps texting me screenshots of that forum she's gotten obsessed with all over again, where somebody named Darkestmind constantly yells *WHERE ARE YOU BAYVIEW2020?* Like it's some kind of Missed Connections board for freaky loners.

Me? I'm just relieved that school is over for the day, and I can forget about Bayview High for a few hours.

I'm pulling a paper towel from the dispenser when the door opens, and a second later Jules appears. "Oh, hi," I say, flustered. I haven't talked to Jules since I watched the video Luis took from Sean's phone. I barely see her at school anymore, unless you count all the times I've skulked past her hallway makeout sessions with Sean.

"Heyyy," Jules says, her eyes flicking toward the graffiti. She doesn't look surprised. I'd love to think she's the one who halfheartedly crossed it out, because at least that would mean she still cares a little bit about me. But it's just as likely that she wrote it in the first place, considering how far up Sean's ass she is now. She'll even lie for him—something I'd never have believed possible if I hadn't seen the video with my own eyes.

I toss my wet paper towel in the wastebasket. "How's Sean?"

Her mouth purses as she pulls out a tube of lip gloss and unscrews the top. "Don't pretend you care."

Watching her outline a perfect pout makes me acutely aware of my own dry lips. I pull a tube of Burt's Bees lip balm from my bag, grimacing when I realize it's coconut flavored. My least favorite. I swipe it across my mouth anyway. "He must miss Brandon, though."

Jules's eyes go flat as they meet mine in the mirror. "What's that supposed to mean?"

I shrug. "Nothing. I just feel bad for him." Even to my own ears, the words sound fake. Sean hasn't been acting like

263

someone who lost his best friend. If anything, he's swaggering around Bayview High more than ever.

Do you think there's any possibility that somebody wanted Brandon to get hurt?

Knox asked that, and I brushed it off as too ridiculous to even consider. Still, Sean was standing right next to Brandon when he died, egging him on. Sean sounded shocked and terrified in that video, but let's face it—he's proved since then that he can play a part when he has to.

I gaze at my reflection in the mirror, and tug on my ponytail to tighten it. "Pretty scary to know it could have been any one of you, huh?" I ask.

"What?" Jules blinks at me, confused.

"Any one of you could have fallen through that landing. Since you were all going to take the same shortcut."

Jules's face is blank for a few seconds too long. She's not a particularly good liar once you know to look for it. "Oh yeah," she says finally.

"Just random chance that Brandon went first," I add. I don't know why I'm still talking, or what I'm hoping to get out of the conversation. Jules won't confide in me. She picked her side a while ago. But there's still part of me hoping to spot a crack in her armor, some sign that we could talk like we used to.

Hey, Jules, did you know that lying to the police could get you in trouble?

Don't you think Brandon's parents deserve to know what really happened?

Did you ever think your new boyfriend might be a sociopath?

"I don't really like to talk about it." Jules smacks her lips and drops the tube of gloss in her bag, then flips her hair over one shoulder and turns for the door. "I have to go. Sean and I have plans after school."

"Me too," I say. Her eyebrows shoot up. "I mean, I have plans too."

Sort of. I'm working. But I'm bringing friends, so it counts.

Jules looks at me appraisingly. She knows my social options are pretty limited right now. "You and Knox?" she guesses. The disdain in her voice is clear enough that I know exactly what she's implying.

I resist the urge to say *It's not a date*. "And Maeve."

Jules smirks and heads for the door, yanking it open. "Well, *that* sounds like a fun ménage à trois."

I stomp after her, trying to marshal some kind of comeback, but as soon as she hits the hallway she's engulfed in the octopus-like embrace of Sean Murdock. "Baby," he growls, suctioning himself to her face. I skirt around them, my jaw clenched, suddenly wishing I'd tried to make the Nate thing happen while I had the chance.

Café Contigo is quiet for a Thursday, and by four o'clock most of the people in the restaurant are staff. Mrs. Santos, who's making a rare appearance at the cash register, gestures me over when my only customer gets up to leave. Ahmed, the other waiter on duty, is leaning against the counter beside her, his eye on the table full of hip young Bayview moms sitting in his station with expensive strollers. They're all wearing cute yoga clothes, their hair in carefully messy ponytails. The babies have been quiet since they arrived, but one of them has started to fuss.

"Hush, hush," the baby's mother says in a singsong voice, moving the stroller back and forth. "You're okay, go back to sleep." Ahmed looks wary, and I don't blame him. I have five cousins under the age of three, and I know for a fact that as soon as one baby starts to cry the rest will join in solidarity.

"Why don't you go ahead and clock out, Phoebe," Mrs. Santos says. She's tall and slender, with expressive dark eyes and elegant cheekbones. Luis gets his good looks from her. "Addy will be in at five, and Ahmed can handle the room until then."

"Okay," I say, starting to untie my apron.

Ahmed, still hovering beside Mrs. Santos with his eyes on the yoga mom table, asks, "Did you give Phoebe that thing, Mrs. S?" We both blink at him, and he clarifies, "The note?"

Mrs. Santos makes a *tsk* sound and shakes her head. "I completely forgot! My apologies, Phoebe. Ahmed said someone dropped this off for you earlier." She roots under the counter and hands me a sealed envelope with my name scrawled across the front. "A young man. What did he say again, Ahmed?"

"That you were expecting it," Ahmed says. The blondest yoga mom waves her hand to catch his attention, and he starts across the room toward her.

"Expecting what?" I ask, but he doesn't hear me. I pull my apron off and stash it behind the counter, heading for the table where Knox, Maeve, and Luis are sitting. Luis is working, supposedly, but he's been sitting and talking for the past hour. I could swear that every time I look over, his chair is a little closer to Maeve's. She's been looking especially pretty since she got her test results back, and today she's wearing a fitted T-shirt with shimmery gold threading that brings out the honey color of her eyes. That unexpected clean bill of health has her practically glowing. Or maybe something else does.

I rip the envelope open as I walk, curious, and pull out a single sheet of paper. "Are you done for the day?" Maeve asks, but I only half hear her. My heart jumps into my throat as I read the words in front of me:

> *What's with the disappearing act?*
> *We need to talk.*
> *Meet me at the gazebo in Callahan Park at*
> *5:30 today.*
> *DO NOT ignore this like you've been ignoring*
> *everything else.*

What the hell? "Ahmed!" I call. He's striding toward the kitchen at a rapid clip but pauses at my urgent tone.

"What?"

I wave the note. "Who left this?"

"I told you. Some guy."

"But *who*?"

"He didn't give his name. Just—a guy. He's been here before."

"What's going on?" Maeve asks. I hand her the note. Her eyes scan the page and she inhales sharply. "Whoa. Who is this from?"

"I don't know," I say helplessly. The only person I've been ignoring lately is Derek, and I never imagined that *actual* stalking was his style. But then again, other than the most ill-advised ten minutes of my life in Jules's laundry room during her Christmas party, it's not like I've spent quality time with the guy.

I wave frantically at Ahmed, who's trying to escape into the kitchen again. "Ahmed, wait! Could you please come here for a second?"

Maeve reads the note out loud to Luis and Knox as Ahmed approaches. Suddenly we're all talking at once, tripping over one another. Finally Maeve raises her voice above everyone else's. "Hang on. The guy who left this, you said he's been here before?" She tilts her head questioningly at Ahmed, who nods. "What did he look like?"

"I don't know. Standard white dude." Ahmed shrugs. "Little older than you guys, maybe. Brown hair. Pale. Kinda tall."

That's Derek, Derek, and Derek. Which puts my mind slightly at ease. At least Derek is a known quantity, sort of.

Knox's eyes get wide. "That sounds like . . . was the guy intense-looking?" he asks.

Ahmed frowns. "I don't know what that means."

"You know—focused. Serious," Knox says. "Like he's got a one-track mind."

One of the babies at the mom table starts flat-out wailing, and Ahmed tugs at his shirt collar. "Look, I have to put in their order, okay? Be back in a minute."

He hurries away and I turn to Knox, confused. "Why are you asking that?"

"Because that description Ahmed just gave reminds me of someone I've seen here before." Knox turns to Maeve and taps her arm. "You remember that guy who came in a while back? The one who was a dick to Mr. Santos and kept asking about Phoebe? The one Luis and Manny chased off?"

"I'm sorry, *what?*" I burst out. "When did this happen?"

"I remember," Luis says. "It was a few weeks ago, wasn't it?" He leans back in his chair, arms folded, and Maeve sneaks a glance at him with color rising in her cheeks. She looks like she just completely lost track of the conversation. I'm tempted to snap my fingers in her face and remind her that she's supposed to be worrying about *me* right now, not staring at Luis's admittedly nice biceps. Priorities.

"Yeah. I didn't think much of it at the time," Knox says, looking apologetic. "I thought it was just some jerk, but he came back a couple nights ago. Here, I mean. Ordered a coffee, sat around, then left without drinking it. I started wondering if it was maybe Derek, trying to find you because you're ignoring his messages."

I glare at him, hands on my hips. "Why are you just telling me this now?"

"I haven't been thinking straight," Knox says defensively. "I have a concussion."

"You *had* a concussion. Two weeks ago."

"The effects can linger for years," Knox informs me. He drums his fingers on the table. "Besides, I wasn't sure it meant anything. But do you think it might be him? Is Derek a tall, pale, brown-haired guy?"

"Yeah, he is." I say. "I personally wouldn't describe him as intense-looking, but to each their own, I guess." Maeve hands the note back to me, and I stuff it into my pocket, my mind spinning. Would Derek really do this—show up at my job and leave a threatening note just because I've been ignoring his Instagram messages? He never acted aggressive or possessive around Emma. As far as I know, anyway.

"Who's Derek?" Luis asks.

All I can think is *thank God he's out of the gossip loop.* It gives me hope that there's life after Bayview High that doesn't include ongoing, detailed analysis of everybody's worst mistakes. "Long story," I say, "but he's someone I've been blowing off lately."

"Do you have a picture of him?" Luis asks. "We all saw the guy. We could tell you whether it's him or not."

"Great idea. Why didn't I think of that?" Maeve asks. Luis smiles, and she gives him another lingering look that, in my opinion, answers the question.

"No," I say. "I mean, I can look him up right now but he never posts pictures of himself . . ." I take out my phone, open Instagram, and pull up Derek's profile to see if he's updated it recently. His entire feed is still nothing but animals, food, and artsy pictures of tree branches. I show it to Knox, who makes a face.

"No selfies? What kind of weirdo is he?" Then he glances at the clock on the wall, which Mr. Santos finally fixed. "Callahan Park is in Eastland, right? We could make it there before five thirty if we leave now."

"I'm not meeting him!" I protest, but Knox holds up a placating hand.

"I don't mean that. But maybe we can, like, spy on him. See if it's Derek. Then you can report him for harassment or something." He pulls out his wallet and removes a few bills, putting them on top of the twenty that's already on the table. "We could go to my house first and grab my binoculars so we don't have to get close."

"Binoculars?" I'm almost distracted for a second. "What do you have those for?"

Knox looks mildly baffled. "Doesn't everybody have binoculars?"

"No," Maeve and I say at the same time.

Luis's brow furrows. "You think that's a good idea? This guy is practically stalking you, Phoebe. Maybe you should tell the police, let them handle it."

"But I don't know for sure if Derek wrote the note," I say. "His Instagram messages were a lot more polite." I turn to Maeve. "Can you drive us?"

She twists her dark hair over one shoulder and nods. "Yeah, of course."

"I'll come with you," Luis says instantly. "It's quiet here, I can leave."

"Okay," I say, trying not to sound as relieved as I feel. I love Knox and Maeve, but they're not exactly my first picks as backup if anything goes wrong. Whoever this guy is, Luis scared him off once, and I'm pretty sure he can do it again. "It's a plan, then. Let's do a little stalking of our own."

CHAPTER TWENTY-THREE

Maeve
Thursday, March 26

"This is pointless," Phoebe grumbles. "I can't see anything."

We were over half an hour late to Callahan Park, thanks to rush hour traffic, but as soon as we pulled into a metered spot in front of the fence we spotted a lone figure sitting on the gazebo steps. It's directly within our line of sight, but too far away to see anything clearly, even with Knox's binoculars at full strength. Phoebe's been fiddling with them for almost five minutes, but she still can't make out who it is.

I turn to face her in the backseat. "Do you want to leave?"

She shakes her head vehemently. "No way. We've come this far, and he's right there. I just need to get a little closer." She peers through the window. "Hmm. Check out the climbing structure on the playground. There's a little house on top that would be perfect. If I go in there, I could see a lot better."

Luis frowns. "We said you'd stay in the car."

"Look at the path to the playground, though. It has those tall bushes. He'll never see me coming," Phoebe insists. "Plus the play area is nice and crowded. I can get up there all stealthy-like." She pokes Knox in the arm. "Can I have your sweatshirt?"

"Um, okay." He removes it with a bemused expression and hands it over. Phoebe pulls the faded gray hoodie over her pink shirt and zips it up.

"This smells nice," she says. "Did you just wash it?"

"No." Knox looks guilty. "Not for a while, actually. Sorry."

"Oh." Phoebe shrugs. "Well, you smell nice, then." She lifts the hood over her head and stuffs her bright curls beneath it. "There. Incognito. And I'm short, so I can pass for a kid."

Luis is still frowning. "I'll go with you," he says, but Phoebe shakes her head.

"He's seen you before, and you stick out too much. I'll take Knox."

"Sure, why not," Knox mutters. "I am utterly unobtrusive, after all."

I bite my lip and glance at the gazebo. The boy is pacing now, circling the small structure. "I don't know, Phoebe. Whoever this guy is, he's starting to freak me out. Maybe we should just leave."

"Not without getting a look at him," she says doggedly. "I need to know if it's Derek." She pops the door open and tugs at Knox's sleeve. "Are you coming or what?"

"Obviously I am." Knox sighs and turns to me. "Text us if he makes a move, okay?"

"He won't. He'll never see us coming," Phoebe says

273

confidently. I think she's probably right, but my stomach still twists as she and Knox get out of the car. I lose sight of them almost immediately on the woodsy path, then catch a glimpse of them weaving through the playground.

"This is fucked up," Luis mutters in the passenger seat beside me. "Is this what it was like last year when you and Bronwyn were following Simon's trail?"

"Not really," I say. "I only ever did online stuff. Bronwyn staked out a guy once, but he was harmless. He ended up helping us out, actually." I jump at my phone vibrating with a text and look down at it. It's from Knox. *We're here.* "They made it," I report, and text back, *Is it Derek?*

She hasn't looked yet. A lens popped out of my binoculars so we're putting it back.

"They're having technical difficulties with the binoculars," I tell Luis.

He flashes a smile. "Equipment failure. Always happens at the worst possible time."

I nod and think about making a joke back, except I'm suddenly hyperaware of the fact that I'm alone with Luis for the first time since I yelled at him at Cooper's game. We've texted back and forth since then, and he accepted my apology. But I haven't said any of the things that I really want to say. Just like always.

"So," I blurt out, right as he says, "Listen," and then we both pause. "You first," we say at the same time. Luis laughs a little, and I smile awkwardly. Then I gather up my courage and say, "No, you know what? Me first. If that's okay." Because if he says something I don't want to hear, then I won't tell him *my* thing. And even though my heart is practically pounding out of my chest at the thought of being fully honest with him, I still want him to know.

His eyes lock on mine, his expression unreadable. "Okay."

Deep breath. "I wanted to talk about what I said at Cooper's game . . ." I trail off and swallow, trying to loosen my throat so I can get the rest of the words out. But I've already started wrong, because Luis shakes his head.

"I told you, forget about that." He brushes my arm with his hand, his fingers lightly tracing the edge of a fading bruise. "I get it. You were in a bad place."

"It's not that. I mean yes, I was, but that's not the only reason I was rude." His hand stills but stays where it is. The heat from his skin radiating into mine is making it hard to think, but I don't want to pull away. I just need to get a couple more sentences out. "I was, um, jealous." I can't look at him right now, so I stare straight ahead at my car's control panel. "I saw you with Monica, and I got jealous because it looked like you were on a date and I—I wanted that to be me. Because I like you, Luis. I have for a while."

There. I said it.

I inhale quickly, still not looking at him, and add in a rush, "It's totally fine if you don't feel the same way, because we can still be friends and I won't be weird about it—"

"Whoa, hold up," Luis interrupts. "Can I answer before you answer for me?"

"Oh." My face flames, and I stare so hard at the dash that I'm surprised the numbers on my odometer don't move. "Yes. Of course. Sorry."

Luis's hand moves down my arm until his fingers lace with mine, and he tugs lightly at my hand. "Look at me, okay?" he says quietly. I turn my head, and there's such a soft, open expression on his face that I feel a spark of hope. "I like you too, Maeve," he says, his dark eyes steady on mine. "I have for a while."

My heart skips and then soars. "Oh," I say again. I've forgotten all the other words.

His lips quirk. "So, should we do something about this? Or would you rather keep torturing me from a distance?"

My smile back feels big enough to take over my entire face. "We should," I manage. "Do something."

"Good," Luis says. He touches my face and leans in close. My eyes flutter shut and warmth floods my veins as I wait for his lips to meet mine—until my lap buzzes loudly. We both startle and pull back. "Damn it all to hell," I mutter in frustration, snatching up my phone. "I forgot we were on a stakeout."

Luis laughs. "Never a dull moment with you. What's up?"

I read Knox's text, blink a few times, and read it again. "Phoebe says it's not Derek."

"Really?" Luis sounds as surprised as I feel. "Then who is it?"

"She doesn't know. She says she's never seen him before."

Luis frowns. "That's weird."

My phone buzzes with another text from Knox. *He's leaving.*

"Oh!" I grab Luis's arm. The figure we'd been watching at the gazebo is suddenly a lot closer. "That's him." Intense Guy is cutting across the grass and through the edge of the playground, but he doesn't spare a glance for the climbing structure where Phoebe is. He pushes past a group of kids and heads for the park exit. At this distance, there's no mistaking the same person who confronted Mr. Santos a few weeks back. There are two paths he could take out of the park, and he chooses the one leading almost straight to my car.

"Shit. He's coming right this way," I say, looking down to shield my face. The guy barely flicked his eyes over me at Café Contigo, but better safe than sorry. "Duck, Luis." Instead, Luis does exactly what he shouldn't do, which is lean forward for a better view. "Stop!" I hiss. "Don't let him see you, he'll recognize you!"

"So?" Luis says. Honest to God, he might be the hottest guy I've ever seen, but he's useless in a stakeout situation. I try to push him back, but he's still craning his neck and Intense Guy is *right there,* about to cross in front of the car, so I have no choice except to grab hold of Luis's face and kiss him.

I mean, I probably have other choices. But this is the best one.

I'm twisted awkwardly, held back by my seat belt until Luis reaches around me and unbuckles it. I break our kiss to slide out from behind the wheel. He pulls me closer, lifting me into his lap, and I return my hands to either side of his face. His arms feel warm and solid around me, holding me in place as we stare into each other's eyes for a beat. "Beautiful," he breathes, and I melt. Then his lips crash against mine, and it's happening again—the heat, the dizziness, and the desperate need to be as close to him as possible. His thumbs sweep over my cheeks, my fingers are twisted in his hair, and the kiss goes on and on until I've completely forgotten where we are and what we're supposed to be doing.

Right up until the loud rap on the window.

Oh God. It all comes rushing back as I look up, expecting to see Intense Guy glowering down at us. Instead, Phoebe cocks her head and waves, smiling brightly. Knox is still a few yards behind her, head down as he stuffs his binoculars into their case. She turns and positions herself in front of the window, her back to us.

I have no memory of this happening, but at some point either Luis or I reclined the seat so that we're practically flat. "Um. So." I reach across Luis's lap for the button, and can't keep from laughing as the seat starts slowly rising while we're still tangled up together. "This is the recline function," I say, smoothing my hair.

"Good to know." Luis kisses my neck, his palm warm against my waist. "Thanks for the demonstration."

"No problem. I do this for everybody. It's important to know how a vehicle operates." Reluctantly, I slide off Luis's lap and behind the wheel. Then I squeeze his hand, feeling giddy that apparently I can do that now. "To be continued?"

He smiles and squeezes back. "Definitely."

"Well!" Phoebe opens the rear door and crawls across the seat. The hood of Knox's sweatshirt is still up, the laces pulled tight around her face. Knox follows and closes the door behind him. He seems preoccupied with his binoculars. I'm pretty sure Phoebe ran interference quickly enough that he didn't see anything with Luis and me. "I have officially never seen that guy before in my life. I have absolutely no idea who he is."

"So now what?" I ask. "Should we—"

"Shit, here he comes!" Knox pulls Phoebe toward him, pressing her into his shoulder as she lets out a strangled yelp.

I duck down automatically in my seat, but Luis—of course—stays where he is. He really is terrible at this. "Sorry," Knox says in a calmer voice as he releases Phoebe. "But he just drove past us. Don't worry, he didn't look our way."

Phoebe leans forward and peers between the front seats. "The blue car?" she asks. When Knox grunts in agreement, she taps my shoulder. "Follow him. Let's see what this weirdo does when he isn't stalking girls he's never met."

CHAPTER TWENTY-FOUR

Knox
Thursday, March 26

A couple of hours after we leave the park, we have a license plate number, an address, and a name. Sort of.

"The car is registered to David Jackson," Maeve reports, her eyes on her laptop screen. "So maybe David Jackson is Intense Guy?" We're sitting at my kitchen table after dropping off Luis and Phoebe. My parents are out to dinner with the neighbors, so we're eating buttered noodles and carrot sticks because that's the extent of my culinary repertoire. Luis, I am not. In more ways than one.

Yeah, I saw. I'm trying to be happy for them. It's not like I'm jealous. It's just—for once in my life, I'd like somebody to have that kind of reaction to me. Maybe that only happens to guys like Luis, though. "Great," I say, unlocking my phone to open

Instagram. "That's a super uncommon name. If I search it I get . . . too many to count."

Maeve frowns. "I'm Googling his name and the town and—hmm. Nothing interesting." We tailed the blue car to a tiny ranch home in a rundown section of Rolando Village, which the city's assessor database tells us belongs to a couple named Paul and Lisa Curtin. Maeve thinks it must be a rental. "There's a local dentist with the name David Jackson. He has terrible Yelp reviews."

"Well, Intense Guy does seem like he'd have a bad bedside manner. Or chairside, I guess," I say. "But he's a little young to have made it through dental school."

Maeve bites into a carrot stick and Fritz, who's sitting between us, snaps his head toward her with a hopeful look. "You wouldn't like carrots," she assures him, petting the graying patch of fur between his ears. Fritz looks unconvinced. I lean across him so I can see Maeve's screen better, and she angles it toward me. "This David Jackson is in his fifties," she says. "This one just retired from a gas company . . ." Maeve clicks to the second page of results, then sighs and leans back in her chair. "They're all old."

"Maybe David Jackson is Intense Guy's father," I say. "Dad owns the car, and his kid is driving it?"

"Could be. That doesn't help us much, though." Maeve catches her lower lip between her teeth, looking pensive. "I wish Phoebe would talk to her mom about what's going on."

On the ride home from Rolando Village, all of us tried to convince Phoebe to tell Mrs. Lawton about Intense Guy and the note. But Phoebe wouldn't go for it. "My mom has enough to worry about," she insisted. "Plus, this is obviously a case of mistaken identity. He's looking for a different Phoebe."

I can understand wanting to think that. And I hope it's true. Although I feel sorry for Different Phoebe if it is.

An alert flashes across Maeve's laptop screen. *The website you are monitoring has been updated.* God, she has PingMe synced to *everything.* I swallow a groan as Maeve opens a new browser tab and brings up the Vengeance Is Mine forum. I'd rather plug David Jackson's name into social media platforms for the next hour than wander down this weird rabbit hole again.

Then a string of messages pops up:

Fuck you, Phoebe, for not showing up.
Yeah I used your name.
WE HAD A DEAL—Darkestmind

My jaw drops as Maeve turns to me, eyes wide. "Oh my God," she says. Fritz whines softly at the tension in her voice. "This *cannot* be a coincidence. Do you realize what this means?"

I do, finally. I've made fun of Maeve the entire time she's stalked the Vengeance Is Mine forum, because I didn't believe there was any connection between the delusional ramblings on there and what's been going on in Bayview. Now these messages are smacking me in the face with how wrong I've been. I point at the user name on the screen in front of us. "It means Darkestmind and Intense Guy are the same person."

"Not *only* that," Maeve says urgently. Fritz drops his head on her knee, and she strokes one of his floppy ears without taking her eyes off the computer. "I've thought all along that Darkestmind is the person behind Truth or Dare. Remember? He kept talking about Bayview, and a game, and he even said *tick-tock,* just like Unknown always did. So if I'm right about that—Intense Guy is *also* Unknown. The three strands we've been following all lead to a single person."

"Shit." I've been staring at the messages from Darkestmind for so long that the words are starting to waver. "So you're saying we just followed the Truth or Dare texter?"

"I think we did," Maeve says. "And he officially does not go to Bayview High. I knew it wasn't Matthias," she adds, almost to herself. "You could tell that little taste of visibility he got from Simon Says terrified him."

"Okay, but . . ." I blink a few times to clear my vision. "What the hell is this guy even talking about? He says he and Phoebe had a deal. A deal for *what*? Ruining her life at school? It doesn't make any sense."

"I don't understand that part, either," Maeve mutters. Her face gets thoughtful. "Do you think it's possible there's something she's not telling us about all this?"

"Like what?"

She lifts one shoulder in a shrug. "Like maybe she really does know the guy, but it's a bad-breakup kind of thing and she doesn't want to talk about it." Then she grimaces. "*Really* bad. That guy looked like he was out for blood."

Out for blood. The words strike a chord in me, and I sit up straighter. "Hold up," I say. "I just had a thought. Let's assume we're right, and that Intense Guy equals Darkestmind equals Unknown. By the way, let's stick with one nickname, because this is getting confusing. I vote for Intense Guy. That's the most descriptive, and also, I came up with it. Anyway. Does Intense Guy have some kind of bone to pick with Brandon?" I gesture at Maeve's screen. "I mean, this is a revenge forum, right? Nate thinks someone might've messed with the construction site landing. Intense Guy led Brandon there with a Dare. So maybe that wild theory I tossed out the other day was actually right, and he hurt Brandon on purpose."

"But why?" Maeve asks. "Do you think he was jealous, maybe? Because Brandon was hooking up with Phoebe?" Her hand stills on Fritz's head. "The whole game kicked off with a rumor about Phoebe and Derek, didn't it? Maybe this guy can't stand the thought of her with anyone else."

"Maybe," I say slowly. "But you weren't with Phoebe in the playground. She genuinely seemed clueless about him. And I was thinking along different lines, more like—" Maeve's phone buzzes and I pause. "Is that Phoebe?"

Maeve picks up her phone. Her entire face changes, taking on a rosy glow like somebody just injected her with pink champagne. "No," she says, fighting a smile as she lets go of Fritz so she can text with both hands. "I'm just going to . . . answer this real quick."

"Tell Luis I said hi," I say, gazing around the kitchen. Fritz pokes his nose into Maeve's thigh a couple of times, then sighs and flops onto the floor when he can't get her attention back.

My eyes land on my mother's black laptop bag, sitting in the empty chair where she always leaves it when she gets home from work. Being an insurance adjuster isn't a nine-to-five job, and Mom usually hauls her laptop out at least once a night to work on a case. But right now, she and my dad should be gone for at least another hour.

When Maeve finally puts her phone aside, I say, "Maybe we've been asking the question from the wrong angle."

"Hmm?" She still looks a little fizzy. "What question?"

"You asked why Intense Guy, in particular, would hate Brandon," I remind her. "But maybe we should be asking this instead: what could Brandon have done that would make *anybody* hate him enough to want him gone?"

Maeve knits her brow. "I don't get it."

"I was just thinking about a conversation I overheard between my mom and dad. You and I weren't talking then, so I didn't mention it, but I've been wondering about it ever since. My parents were saying how ironic it would be if Mr. Weber sues the construction site, because of some lawsuit involving Brandon that Mom's company settled three years ago. And my dad said something like, 'The case shouldn't have gone that way. All it did was show a kid like Brandon that actions don't have consequences.' When I asked them about it, they clammed up and said it was confidential. But maybe if we knew what happened back then, we'd know why somebody would go through this much trouble to target Brandon."

"So are you going to ask your mom again?" Maeve says.

"No point. She wouldn't tell me."

"What if you told her about all *this*?" Maeve asks, gesturing at her computer. "I mean, your dad already thinks Brandon's accident was sketchy, right? But he doesn't know it was part of a game that deliberately led Brandon to the construction site. We're the only ones besides Sean, Jules, and Monica who know that, because we're the only ones who saw the video from Sean's phone."

I swallow hard. "We could, I guess. But the thing is . . . basically, my dad thinks I'm an idiot." Maeve starts to murmur a dissent that I wave off. "It's true. He does. And if I come at him with *this*, ranting about texting games and anonymous forum posts that disappear, and how I think some rando I followed to a park is behind it all? He'd never take me seriously."

"Okay," Maeve says cautiously. She looks like she wants to argue the point, but all she says is, "Then I guess we'll just have to wait and see if your parents connect any of the same dots. They're the experts, after all."

"I don't want to wait," I say. "I want to know what Brandon did three years ago that was bad enough to get him involved in some kind of hush-hush settlement." I lean over and grab my mother's laptop case by its handle, hauling it onto the table between Maeve and me. "This is my mom's work computer."

Maeve blinks, startled. "Are you suggesting we . . . hack it?"

"No," I say. "That's ridiculous. I'm suggesting *you* hack it. I don't know how."

I open the case, pull out a black, blocky PC that looks like it's from the early aughts, and push it toward her. She lays a hand on the cover and hesitates, her eyes wide and questioning. "Do you really want me to do this?"

I raise my eyebrows. "*Can* you?"

Maeve makes a dismissive *psssh* sound. "Challenge accepted."

She opens the cover and presses the power button. "If your mom is running an old version of Windows there are some login workarounds—although, before I try that, what year was

Kiersten born?" I tell her, and she murmurs, "Kiersten plus birth year equals . . . okay, no. What about Katie?" We repeat the process, and Maeve's brow furrows. "Wow, I get six more tries before the system locks me out. That's way too many. Kelsey is the year after Katie?"

"Yeah, but—" I pause when she grins widely, turning the screen to face me as it powers up to an old picture of a family hiking trip. "You're kidding me. That actually worked?"

"Parents are the single worst threat to any type of cyber security," Maeve says calmly, flipping the screen back toward her. "Okay, let's search all documents for Brandon Weber." She types, then leans back in her chair, squinting. "Nothing. Maybe just Weber." She presses a few more keys, then grimaces. "Ugh, that's a lot. We're cursed with common last names tonight. Emails, phone directories, a bunch of other stuff . . ." She keeps scrolling and muttering to herself while I load our empty dishes into the dishwasher and top off the glasses of Sprite we've been drinking. Then I sip mine while she works.

"I think I've figured out your mom's naming system," Maeve says after a few minutes. "Cases are all tagged a certain way. So if I put those keywords in and cross-search with Weber . . . that's a much smaller universe of files. And this was three years ago, you said?"

"Yeah. When my mom first started at Jenson and Howard."

Her fingers fly across the keyboard, and she cracks a small smile. "Okay, we're down to two documents. Let me try opening one." She double clicks and nods, as though she just got exactly the result she was expecting. "Password protected, but—"

Fritz suddenly sits bolt upright, barking madly, and takes

off running for the front door. Maeve and I both freeze except for our eyes, which snap toward one another in mirrored panic. The only time Fritz ever moves like that is when a car pulls into our driveway. "I thought you said your parents weren't coming home till later," Maeve hisses. She starts shutting down the computer as I scramble to my feet and follow Fritz. He's still going berserk, and I hold his collar as I open the door and peer outside. The headlights shining into my eyes are a lot smaller than I expected.

"Hang on," I call to Maeve from the doorway. Fritz keeps barking, his tail thumping against my leg. "Don't put the computer away. It's Kiersten."

Maeve pauses. "Would she be okay with what we're doing?"

"Oh hell no. But I can distract her for a few minutes. Email yourself the files, okay? Come out to the driveway when you're done."

I open the door just enough to push through without letting Fritz out, and jog down the front steps. My movement triggers our garage floodlight as Kiersten's headlights flicker off. Her car door opens, and she steps onto the driveway. "Hey!" she calls, waving both hands in greeting. "I was nearby for a work thing so I just wanted to—"

Before she has a chance to finish, I'm hugging her so hard that I almost knock her over. "It's so good to see you!" I yell, lifting her as far off the ground as I can manage.

"Um, okay. Wow." Kiersten pats my back gingerly. "Good to see you too." I lower her onto the driveway without releasing her, and her pats get a little harder. "You can let go now," she says. Her voice is muffled in my shirt. I keep clinging, and she practically punches me between the shoulder blades. "Seriously. Thank you for the enthusiastic welcome, though."

"Thank *you*," I say, hugging her tighter. "For gracing us with your presence."

"For what? What do—" Kiersten stiffens and pulls back, craning her neck so she can get a good look at my face. "Knox, are you *drunk*?" She sniffs me noisily, then uses three fingers to pull down the skin beneath my left eye. "Or high? Are you on something right now?"

What the hell is keeping Maeve? "I'm fine," I say, disentangling myself hastily. "I'm just happy to see you because I wanted . . ." I pause for a few beats, searching my brain for something that will hold Kiersten's interest enough to make her forget we're still standing in the driveway. She narrows her eyes and taps a foot, waiting.

I swallow a sigh and say, "Relationship advice."

Kiersten's entire face lights up as she claps her hands together. *"Finally."*

Maeve comes out the front door then, her laptop bag slung over one shoulder. Kiersten's eyes pop, and she turns to me with a hopeful expression. "Not that relationship," I mutter as Maeve waves. "Still friends."

"Too bad," Kiersten sighs, and holds out her arms for a hug from Maeve. As Maeve strides past me to greet her, she whispers, "Got them." Whatever she found better be good, because I'm about to give up at least an hour of my life for it.

CHAPTER TWENTY-FIVE

Phoebe
Thursday, March 26

When I get home my mother is out, at another Golden Rings wedding planner get-together. She's left a note for me on the kitchen island: *Emma's still not feeling well. Owen has eaten & there are leftovers in the fridge. Can you make sure he does his homework?*

I set the note down with a sigh. I'd told my friends I wasn't going to say anything to Mom about what just happened at Café Contigo and Callahan Park, and I meant it. But a not-small part of me is tired of feeling like my own parent. It's not my mom's fault, I know that. She's doing the best she can. But I ache when I think of how I used to crawl into her lap when I was little and spill all my problems. It felt so *good*, getting them out.

Those were kid-sized problems, though. Broken toys and bruised knees. I wouldn't even know where to start if I tried to explain the past six weeks of my life. Or Emma's. Whatever's going on with my sister, one thing is clear: she doesn't have anyone she feels like she can confide in, either.

It sucks we can't be that for each other.

The apartment is quiet, except the faint video game sounds coming from Owen's room and the hum of the dishwasher. The one and only thing about our apartment that's better than our old house is that the dishwasher actually works. We used to have to hand-wash everything before loading it into the dishwasher, which always struck my dad as funny. "It's the world's most expensive drying rack," he'd complain. Every once in a while he'd try to fix it, but all of his usual handiness deserted him when it came to that dishwasher. The last time he'd tried, water ended up pouring out of a pipe in our basement closet.

"We should just get a new dishwasher," I'd told him as I helped position plastic beach buckets on the closet floor to catch the water. I didn't think about what things cost, back then. A new dishwasher didn't mean much more to me than new sneakers.

"Never," Dad said bracingly. "This dishwasher and I are locked in a battle of wills. One day, I will prevail."

Now I realize that we couldn't afford it. After he died we could suddenly afford *everything*—Mom took us to Disneyland, even though we were too old except Owen. She marched us through rides during the day, and cried into her hotel room pillow at night. We had new clothes and phones, and she got a new car so Emma and I could have hers. Everything was perfect and shiny and we didn't want any of it, not really, so we didn't mind when it stopped.

I kick the base of our quiet, efficient dishwasher. I hate it.

I'm not hungry, so I open the cabinet beneath the sink and conduct my new ritual: checking Mom's alcohol supply. Last night, a lone bottle of tequila remained. Today it's gone. It's sort of shocking that Mom hasn't caught on to what's been happening with Emma, but then again, Emma has all of us well-trained to trust that she'll always do what she's supposed to. If I didn't share a room with her, I wouldn't know either. And I wouldn't have this sick, worried feeling in my stomach every time I walk into the apartment. I never know what I'm going to find, or how to make any of it better.

This has to be the end, though, now that Emma's gone through all of Mom's alcohol. My introverted, straitlaced sister can't possibly have connections for getting more. With a sigh, I shut the cabinet door and head for our room to check on her. Chances are, she's left a mess for me to clean up again.

When I crack our door, the first thing that hits me is the sound—a low, gurgling noise. "Emma?" I ask, pushing through. "You okay?"

She's lying on her bed, twitching. At first I think she's breathing in mucus, like she has a terrible cold, but then it hits me—she's *choking*. Her eyes are closed, her lips blue, and as I watch in horror her entire body starts to convulse. "Emma! Emma, *no!*"

The word sounds like it's being ripped out of me. I lunge forward to grab her shoulders, almost tripping over the tequila bottle on the floor, and haul her onto her side. She's still making the gurgling sound, but now it's mixed in with a wheezing noise. "Emma!" I shriek, hitting her back in a panic. Then her entire body contracts and a stream of vomit pours from her mouth, soaking both my shirt and her sheet.

"Phoebe?" Owen peers around the door. "What's happening?" His mouth falls open when he sees Emma. "What . . . what's wrong with her?"

Emma gags once, then flops motionless on the bed. I prop her up so her head is angled on the pillow and vomit can continue to trickle out of her slack mouth. "Get my phone. It's on the island. Call 911. Tell them our address and that someone here has alcohol poisoning. *Now,*" I add, when Owen doesn't move. He darts out of the room as I grab the edge of Emma's sheet and try to clean out her mouth. The sour stench of vomit finally hits me, and my stomach rolls as I feel wetness seeping through the front of my T-shirt.

"How could you do this?" I whisper.

Emma's chest is rising and falling, but slowly. Her lips are still tinged blue. I lift her hand and feel for her pulse beneath the clammy skin of her wrist. It hardly seems to move, especially in contrast to how fast mine is racing. "Owen! Don't hang up! Bring me the phone!" I yell.

Owen returns to the bedroom, clutching my phone to his ear. "This lady says someone's coming," he whimpers. "Why is she poisoned?" he adds, his voice quavering as he stares at Emma's limp figure. Her hair is hanging in her face, too close to her mouth, and I push it back. "Who poisoned her?"

"Nobody," I grit out. Not literally, anyway. I can't speak to whoever or whatever has been poisoning her mind these past few weeks, but I'm starting to think it's not Derek. If Emma managed to avoid falling apart after she found out he and I *slept together,* surely she wouldn't nearly kill herself over a few unanswered Instagram messages. There has to be something else going on here. I reach my hand out to my brother. "Give me the phone."

He does, and I hold it to my ear. "Hello, help, I don't know what to do next," I say shakily. "I got her on her side and she threw up so she's not choking anymore, but she's also not moving. She's hardly breathing and I can't, I don't know—"

"All right, honey. You did good. Now listen so I can help you." The voice on the other end is no-nonsense but soothing. "An ambulance is on the way. I'm gonna ask you a few questions, and then we'll know what to do until they get there. We're in this together, okay?"

"Okay," I say. Tears start slipping down my cheeks, and I take a deep breath to steady myself. I try to focus on the woman's voice, instead of fixating on the two questions that keep rattling around in my brain.

Mine: *How could you do this?*

And Owen's: *Who poisoned her?*

CHAPTER TWENTY-SIX

Maeve
Friday, March 27

My sister is crushing me, but in the nicest possible way.

It's Friday afternoon, and I've only been home from school for half an hour. Bronwyn, who just took a Lyft from the airport, has her arms wrapped around my shoulders while I press my phone to my ear in my bedroom, trying to make sense of what Phoebe is telling me. "Well, that's good, right?" I ask.

"I think so." Phoebe sounds exhausted. When she didn't show up at school today, I was worried something else might have happened with Intense Guy. Knox and I sent her a bunch of increasingly urgent check-in texts, and she finally answered one during lunch to let us know she was at the hospital with Emma. She'd been there most of last night, she said, until her mom insisted she go home and try to sleep. She went back first thing this morning.

"They're still giving her fluids, but they stopped the oxygen therapy," Phoebe says now. "They say there shouldn't be any long-term effects. But they're talking about addiction treatment when she leaves the hospital. Like rehab or something. I don't even know."

"Did Emma say why she's been drinking?" I ask.

"No. She hasn't been awake much, though." Phoebe sighs through the phone, long and weary. "It's just one thing after another in this family."

My throat tightens. Before I heard about Emma, I'd been itching to tell Phoebe everything we'd learned about Intense Guy last night, and press her to think harder about whether she might have come across him before. But I can't put that on her now. One crisis at a time. "Can I do anything to help?" I ask.

"Thanks, but I can't think of anything. I should go. I need to make my mom eat something. I just wanted to let you know Emma will survive." She says it lightly, like it was never in question, but I've been anxious ever since her text came through earlier today. All I could think was *Phoebe can't lose anybody else.*

"Text if you need me," I say, but Phoebe's already disconnected. I drop my phone so I can hug my sister back. Her familiar apple-green shampoo smell engulfs me, and I relax for the first time in days. "Welcome home," I say, my words muffled against her shoulder. "Sorry Bayview is a horrible mess again. I missed you."

When she finally lets go, we settle onto my window seat. Our usual spot, just like she never left. Both our parents are still at work, so the rest of the house is quiet. "I don't even know where to start with everything that's been happening around here," Bronwyn says, folding one leg beneath her. She's wearing black leggings and a fitted V-neck Yale T-shirt. Points to her for a cute, yet comfortable, airplane outfit. "Emma is all right, though?"

"Yeah. Phoebe says she will be."

"God." Bronwyn shakes her head, eyes wide. "This town is falling apart. And you . . ." She grabs one of my hands and gives it a shake. "I'm mad at you. I've been fighting with you in my head all week. How could you not tell me what you were going through?" Her face is an equal mix of affection and reproach. "I thought we told each other everything. But I didn't have a clue any of this was happening until it was already over."

"It turned out to be nothing," I say, but she only tugs harder on my hand.

"Spending weeks thinking you're deathly ill again isn't *nothing*. And what if you'd lost valuable treatment time? You can't *do* that, Maeve. It's not fair to anyone."

"You're right. I was . . ." I hesitate, looking at our intertwined hands as I try to come up with the right words. "The thing is, I don't think I've ever really believed I'd make it out of high school. So I tried not to get too attached to people, or let them get too attached to me. It's just easier for everyone that way. But I could never do that with you. You wouldn't let me. You've always been *right here*, getting in my face and making me feel things." Bronwyn makes a tearful, strangled sound and squeezes my hand harder. "I guess, while you were gone, I forgot how that's actually better."

Bronwyn is crying for real now, and I am, too. We cling to each other for a few minutes and let the tears flow, and it feels

297

like washing away months of regret for all the things I should have said and done differently. *You can't change the past,* Luis said the night he made me ajiaco in the Café Contigo kitchen. *All you can do is try harder next time.*

And I will. I'm not repaying love with fake indifference anymore. I'm not going to pretend I don't want my life, and the people in it, so badly that I'm willing to break all our hearts if the worst does happen.

Bronwyn finally pulls away, wiping her eyes. "Swear you'll never do anything like that again."

I trace my finger twice across my chest. "Cross my heart, hope not to die." It's our childhood promise, modified by Bronwyn during my first hospital stint ten years ago, when she was eight and I was seven.

She laughs shakily and glances at her Apple watch. "Damn it, almost four. We didn't even get to the good stuff about Luis, but I need to go to Addy's. We're handling prep for the rehearsal dinner tonight so Mrs. Lawton can be with Emma."

"Are you staying for the dinner?" I ask.

"No, that's just for the wedding party. I'll leave once Addy and I get everything squared away, then come back for the afterparty."

"Do you guys want help?" I ask, even as my eyes stray to my laptop. I'd been trying to open the files I pulled from Knox's mother's computer before Bronwyn got here, with no luck. Mrs. Myers is a lot more careful about protecting her files than her network access. But I think I'm getting close.

"No, two of us will be plenty. It's probably overkill, honestly, but I can't let Addy do this alone." Bronwyn grimaces.

"She means well, but she's not the most organized person around."

"Can you believe Ashton and Eli are getting married *tomorrow*?" I say. "I feel like they just got engaged."

"Same," Bronwyn says. "Life comes at you fast."

"Do you need a ride to Addy's?" I ask.

Bronwyn's mouth curves in a small smile. "I have one."

I follow her gaze down to our driveway just as a motorcycle pulls in, and I can't help the pleased laugh that escapes me. "Well, well, well. This feels like déjà vu." We'd been sitting in this exact spot the first time Nate ever came to our house. I pluck at Bronwyn's sleeve as she full-on beams out the window, watching Nate take off his helmet. "What's going on?"

"I called him after you told me what happened at Cooper's baseball game. Hearing how he'd been there for you. Everything he and I had been arguing about seemed so pointless after that. We've been talking every night since. And watching movies." Her gray eyes are bright as she stands up, smoothing down the front of her shirt. "It's almost like he's right there with me, even with the distance. I haven't felt that way since I left."

"Hmm, interesting." I tap a finger against my chin, trying to look thoughtful while fighting off a grin. "So basically, if I'm understanding you correctly, my fake leukemia brought the two of you together? You're welcome."

A brief frown interrupts Bronwyn's glow. "That's not the correct conclusion to draw from this."

I nudge her sneaker with mine. "Look who's been keeping secrets *now*, Bronwyn. And here I thought we were supposed to tell one another everything." My voice is teasing, though, because I couldn't possibly be less mad at her.

Color rises higher in her cheeks, and she doesn't meet my eyes. Mostly, I think, because she can't tear hers away from the window. Nate's still on his motorcycle, waiting patiently. He doesn't bother coming to the door; I'm sure he knows exactly where we are. "It's only been a few days," she says. "I guess I didn't want to jinx it."

"You know he's crazy about you, right?" I ask. "More than ever? I was practically dying in front of him and all he could think about was *you*."

Bronwyn rolls her eyes. "You were not dying."

"Well, *Nate* didn't know that, did he?"

"I really love him," she says quietly.

"News flash: *we know*. You haven't been fooling anyone." I give her hip a gentle shove. "Enjoy the ride. I'm assuming you and Nate have plans once dinner prep is over, so I'll see you guys at the afterparty."

She leaves, and I stay at my window seat until I see her emerge onto the driveway. Nate gets off his motorcycle just in time to catch Bronwyn as she goes flying toward him. Her arms wrap around his neck as he spins her around, and I turn away with a smile so they can have their reunion kiss in private. "Endgame," I say to the empty room.

CHAPTER TWENTY-SEVEN

Maeve
Friday, March 27

"Is there a word for stalking your friend's stalker?" Knox asks in a low, musing voice.

"Congenial pursuit," I say without looking up from my laptop.

"That's two words. And terrible."

It's almost eight thirty on Friday night, and we're settled into a window table at a coffee shop in Rolando Village. Bronwyn is with Nate, Luis is working, my parents are at a charity event, and I couldn't stand rattling around my house alone for two hours while I waited for the afterparty at Ashton and Eli's rehearsal dinner to start. So I called Knox. Neither of us could talk about anything except Intense Guy. Talking turned into driving, and here we are.

The coffee in this place is awful, but the view is ideal. We're almost directly across from the house we followed Intense Guy to from Callahan Park.

"There's something comforting about knowing he's at home," Knox says. The driveway was empty when we got here, but the blue car pulled up a few minutes later, and we watched Intense Guy enter the small ranch house alone. He hasn't left since.

"I know," I say absently, my eyes on my laptop screen. I brought it along so I could keep working on opening the documents I pulled from Knox's mother's computer. Knox has his computer too, and he's been using it to Google "David Jackson" with the usual useless results.

Knox sucks down half a Sprite with one noisy pull on his straw and asks, "What time do we have to leave to get to—where is Ashton and Eli's party, again?"

"Talia's Restaurant, on Charles Street," I say. "We can hang out here for another twenty minutes or so."

"Great," Knox says, glancing around the nondescript coffee shop. The walls are prison-gray, the tables and chairs are grade-school cafeteria style, and the baked goods displayed on the counter look like they've been there for a while. The barista yawns as he erases *hot chocolate* from the chalkboard menu behind him and tosses an empty Swiss Miss cardboard box into the trash. "Do you think Phoebe will be there?"

"I doubt it. She's pretty much living at the hospital right now." Suddenly the document in front of me springs open, and I give Knox a triumphant smile. "I'm in! Got the first one open. This is . . . hmm. Probably not relevant. It's something to do with a case settled for the Weber Reed Consulting Group in Florida." I scan the first few pages quickly, then close the document and pull up the second. "Let me try the other one."

"Nice work, Sherlock," Knox says. He looks pensive, though, and rubs a hand over his face as he gazes out the window. "I wish we had the same luck digging dirt up on this guy. We're right across the street from him, and we still don't know who he is. Has the revenge forum said anything interesting lately? Or worrying?"

I have Vengeance Is Mine open in another browser and I've gotten a couple of PingMe alerts since we've been here, but it's just ranting from names I don't recognize. "Nothing from Darkestmind," I say. "He's been quiet since that post about Phoebe."

Knox shifts restlessly in his seat. "What did the note he left at Café Contigo say again? He didn't sign it with an initial or anything, did he?"

"No," I say decisively, and then I pause. I read that note pretty quickly, after all, and I wasn't in the calmest state of mind. "I don't think so, but let's double-check." I tear my eyes away from my screen, where the headline SETTLEMENT ON BE-HALF OF EAGLE GRANITE MANUFACTURING CORPORATION, EAST-LAND CA has popped up, to dig my phone out of my bag. I open my photos and scroll until I find the right one. "I took a picture," I say, handing the phone to Knox. "See for yourself."

Knox squints, and then every bit of color drains from his face. His head snaps up, his expression tense. "What. The. *Hell*." Before I can question the quick-change demeanor, he adds, "Why didn't you show this to me before?"

I blink. Is he *mad* at me? "What are you talking about? I read it to you at Café Contigo."

"That's not the same thing!" he insists.

My scalp prickles at the decidedly un-Knox tone of his voice. "How is it not the same thing? You know what it says."

"But I didn't know how it *looks*."

"I don't—"

He thrusts my phone at me, cutting off my next bewildered question. "I'm talking about the font. *How* the note was written. You know, this type that looks like handwriting but isn't? I've seen it before. The latest batch of death threats at Until Proven used it."

"What?" I ask. When Knox doesn't answer right away, I repeat, *"What?"*

"Yeah . . . hang on," Knox says. He puts my phone down and turns to his laptop, fingers flying over his keyboard. "Sandeep thought the threats were related to the D'Agostino case, so I'm gonna . . . I have a bunch of stuff in my G drive." He angles the computer so I can see his screen. "This is a spreadsheet of everybody involved in the D'Agostino case. I'll check for David Jackson." He types the name into the search bar, and neither of us breathes until it comes up blank.

"Try just Jackson," I say.

This time we get a result right away: *Officer Ray Jackson, defendant. Accused of assisting Sergeant Carl D'Agostino in blackmailing and framing seventeen innocent people for drug possession. Age: 24. Status: In jail, awaiting trial.*

"Huh," I say. "Ray Jackson. Maybe he's related to David Jackson?"

"Maybe," Knox says. He's still tapping away, eyes glued to the screen. "Hang on, I indexed all the media coverage too.

Let's see if they mention family." He's silent for a couple of minutes, then angles his screen toward me. "This article includes *Jackson* and *brother* in it somewhere."

A news clip fills the screen, showing Sergeant D'Agostino with his arm around a clean-cut young guy holding a plaque. "I remember this article," Knox says. "I read it with Bethany. It's about D'Agostino giving some mentoring award." He points to the caption. *"The week before his arrest, Sergeant Carl D'Agostino commended San Diego State University students for excellence in community peer mentoring."*

"Okay, so that's D'Agostino," I say. "What does it say about Jackson?" Both our eyes race over the page, but mine are faster. I almost gasp when I see it. *"Ironically, one of the at-risk youths receiving peer mentoring was Ray Jackson's younger brother Jared, 19, on probation last year for petty theft,"* I read. *"Program officials said Jared Jackson excelled in the program and now works part-time for a local construction company."* I turn toward Knox. "Is there a picture of Ray Jackson anywhere?"

"Yeah, not in this article, but . . ." Knox pulls up another news story with thumbnail photos of each of the accused officers. He clicks on the one marked *Ray Jackson,* then enlarges it until it fills half the screen. At that size, even though it's a little blurry, there's no mistaking the similarity around the mouth and eyes between Ray Jackson and the guy we trailed to and from Callahan Park.

"Intense Guy is Jared Jackson," I breathe. "Ray Jackson's brother. He must be. The age is right, and the face is right. They're definitely related."

"Yeah," Knox says. "And the note he left for Phoebe is

identical to the ones we've been getting at Until Proven, so . . . Jared Jackson must *also* be the person who's been sending threats to Eli." His brow furrows. "Which makes a twisted kind of sense, I guess, since Eli put his brother in jail. But what's his problem with Phoebe?"

"I don't know, but we'd better tell Eli," I say. Knox reaches for his phone, but I've already pressed Eli's number on mine. Within seconds his voice fills my ear: *This is Eli Kleinfelter. I'm not checking voice mail until Monday, March thirtieth. If you need immediate assistance with a legal matter, please call Sandeep Ghai of Until Proven at 555-239-4758. Otherwise, leave a message.* "Straight to voice mail," I tell Knox.

"Oh right," Knox says. "He promised Ashton he'd shut his phone off all weekend. So they could get married in peace."

Unease nips at my stomach. "Guess we'll have to tell him in person, then. It's almost time to leave for the party, anyway."

"Hang on." Knox's fingers move across his laptop's track-pad. "I just plugged Jared Jackson into Google and there's a lot here." His eyes flick up and down the screen. "So, yeah, he was arrested for stealing from a convenience store right after he graduated high school. Got probation, did that mentoring program, started working for a construction company." Something tugs at my subconscious then, but Knox is still talking and the fragment disappears. "He doesn't seem to have had any run-ins with the law since. But there's a bunch of stuff here on the fallout from his brother's arrest . . ."

He goes silent for a minute as he reads. "It doesn't mention their dad by name but I'll bet that's David Jackson. He has lung cancer, and they lost their house after Jared's brother went

306

to jail. So, that sucks, obviously. Understatement. And their mom . . . oh shit." Knox sucks in a sharp breath, raising troubled eyes toward me. "The mom killed herself on Christmas Eve. Well, they think it was suicide. She overdosed on sleeping pills, but she didn't leave a note."

"Oh no." My heart drops as I stare at the Jacksons' house, dark except for the yellowish glow of a lamp silhouetted in a first-floor window. Everything about the house looks forlorn, from the crooked lampshade to the lopsided blinds. "That's horrible."

"Yeah, it is." Knox follows my gaze. "Okay, now I feel bad for Jared. He's had a shit time. Maybe this is all just some twisted way of blowing off steam."

"Maybe," I say, and then I jump as the lamp in the Jacksons' window suddenly goes off, plunging the house into darkness. The door opens, and a shadowy figure emerges. Knox pushes his laptop to one side and fumbles with the zipper on his backpack, rooting around in it until he pulls out his binoculars. "Seriously?" I ask as he brings them to his eyes. We're the only ones in the coffee shop except the barista, who's been ignoring us since we got our drinks, but still. This is not exactly a stealthy way to keep tabs on your nemesis. "You brought those?"

"Of course I did. They have night vision mode." Knox adjusts the outer lenses and leans forward, peering through the window as the figure steps onto a section of the driveway illuminated by a nearby streetlight. "It's Jared."

"I could tell that *without* binoculars."

"He has a backpack and he's getting into the car."

"Knox, I can see him perfectly fine—"

A PingMe alert flashes across my screen. *The website you are monitoring has been updated.* I minimize the document from Mrs. Myers's computer and navigate to the Vengeance Is Mine forum.

Tick-tock, time's up. Guess I'll just fucking do it myself.—Darkestmind.

My blood chills. I don't know what the words mean, but I know beyond a shadow of a doubt that they can't be good. I slam my laptop closed and stuff it into my bag. "Come on, we need to follow him," I say. "He's up to something."

CHAPTER TWENTY-EIGHT

Knox
Friday, March 27

Maeve shoved her bag at me before she got behind the wheel, and now I'm holding too much crap to put my seat belt on as she tears out of Jared Jackson's street. I drop my backpack by my feet but keep hold of Maeve's bag. "You need anything in here?" I ask.

"Could you take my phone out?" Maeve asks, eyes on the blue car in front of us. It turns a corner, and she follows. "Just in case. You can put it in the cup holder."

I do, and then I look down at the MacBook sticking out from her still-open bag. I almost forgot what she'd been doing until Jared Jackson drove every other thought from my head. "Hey, what was that second document you opened? The one from my mom's computer?" I ask. "Was there anything about Brandon in there?"

"I don't know. I didn't get a chance to look at it. Do you want to read it now? It's still open, I just minimized it."

"Might as well." I pull out Maeve's computer, stuff her bag next to my backpack on the floor, and position the MacBook on my lap. I open the cover and click on the document icon at the bottom of the screen. "Is this it? *Settlement on Behalf of Eagle Granite Manufacturing Corporation* . . . wait. Hang on a second." I frown. "Why does that sound familiar?"

"It's local, isn't it?" Maeve asks. "I think it had an Eastland address."

"Yeah." I skim over a bunch of stuff I don't understand until I reach the company name again and start to read. "*Worker's compensation settlement negotiated by Jenson and Howard on behalf of Eagle Granite Manufacturing Corporation, concerning the accidental death of* . . . Oh shit." I can feel my eyes getting wide as I take in the familiar name.

"What?" Maeve asks distractedly. Jared is kind of an erratic driver, and she's speeding a lot more than she normally would to keep up with him.

"*The accidental death of Andrew Lawton.* That's Phoebe's dad. I forgot my mom handled that case when it happened." I think back to Owen gratefully pocketing a twenty-dollar bill at Café Contigo, and to Phoebe's apartment, which is nice but a lot smaller than average for a family of four in Bayview. "Mom always said Mrs. Lawton didn't get nearly as much money as she should have," I say.

"That's awful," Maeve says. Jared exits the highway, and she follows. I look up from her screen and register a familiar sign for Costco flashing past us; we're not far from home. She grips the steering wheel more tightly and adds, "Did you search for Weber?"

"I'm looking." Reading while riding in a car makes my stomach roll, but I keep scanning paragraphs until my eyes finally catch on the name. *"Lance Weber, executive vice president in charge of manufacturing for Eagle Granite Manufacturing Corporation,"* I read. My skin starts to prickle. "Lance Weber. Isn't that Brandon's father's name?"

I hear Maeve's breath hiss between her teeth as she quickly changes lanes to stay behind Jared's car. "Yeah. My parents were just talking about him the other night. My dad's done business with Mr. Weber before, and he's definitely a big deal in manufacturing. He works for an aircraft supplier now, though."

"Well, I guess he didn't used to." I keep reading, until I come to a paragraph that makes every hair on my body stand on end. I reread it twice to make sure it really says what I think it does, and then I say, "Maeve. Holy hell."

"What?" she asks. I can tell she's only half listening because she's concentrating so hard on keeping up with Jared's NASCAR moves, so I tap her arm for emphasis.

"You need to pay attention. For real. *Mr. Lance Weber acknowledges that on October seventh, which was Take Your Child to Work Day at Eagle Granite Manufacturing Corporation, his thirteen-year-old son was present on the manufacturing floor. Despite repeated admonitions to stay away from equipment, Mr. Weber's minor son mounted a forklift and operated its controls for what one worker reported as a five-minute period. That same forklift jammed shortly thereafter while transporting the slab of concrete that ultimately crushed Andrew Lawton."*

I look up from the document at Maeve's pale, rigid face. Her eyes are still trained on Jared's car. "That was Brandon. It has to be," I say. "Messing around with a forklift that killed Phoebe's father. Shit. Brandon fucking Weber."

Now, the conversation I overheard between my parents makes perfect sense. *The case never should have been settled that way,* my dad had said. By "that way," I'm guessing he meant keeping Brandon's involvement out of any public documentation of the accident. *All it did was show Brandon that actions don't have to have consequences.* For a second, I'm so angry at the mental image of Brandon screwing around with a piece of heavy machinery—Brandon, as usual, doing whatever he wanted and not caring how it might affect somebody else— that I forget he's dead.

And then I remember. The thought settles on my chest, compressing my lungs so it's hard to breathe. "Well, I guess that answers my question, doesn't it?" I ask.

"What question?"

"About who has a reason for hating Brandon enough to want him gone." I stare at the red taillights in front of us until they go blurry. "It's Phoebe."

"Phoebe?" Maeve echoes in a small voice.

"We kept wondering if maybe she knew Intense Guy, right? Seeing as how he's been chasing her all over town, talking about some deal they made on a *revenge forum.*" My stomach churns as every disturbing, damning thing we've uncovered about Jared in the past few hours comes crashing up against the girl I've gotten to know. Sweet-faced, sharp-tongued, impulsive Phoebe Lawton. "Maeve. Do you think there's any way she could've . . ."

"No," Maeve says instantly.

"You didn't let me finish."

"Phoebe had no clue about this," she says urgently. "She *can't* have. She was hooking up with Brandon! She'd never do that if she knew he'd had anything to do with her father's accident. Plus, she wouldn't spread horrible gossip about *herself.*" Then she hesitates. I can almost see the gears in her mind sifting through memories of Simon Kelleher and Jake Riordan, and all the twisted things the two of them did to get revenge last year—on people whose wrongs were a hell of a lot tamer than Brandon Weber's. "I mean," she says with less certainty, "someone would have to be a stone-cold killer with an unbelievably good game face to pull that off. Right?"

"Right." I try to laugh like it's ridiculous, because it is. Except for the part where it makes as much sense as anything else that's happened over the past few weeks. If it weren't for Brandon's carelessness, Phoebe's father would still be alive, and her whole life would be different. What does knowing something like that do to a person?

I take a minute to register our surroundings, and it hits me with sickening certainty that we have an entirely different problem right now. And as horrible as the last train of thought was, this is even worse. "Maeve, do you realize where we are?"

"Huh?" she asks, tense and distracted. "No. I've been staring at Jared's license plate for the entire drive. I don't even—" She lets her eyes rove for a second, and her face gets as pale as mine feels. "Oh. Oh my God."

We're on Charles Street in Bayview, the sign for Talia's Restaurant glowing white to our left. Eli and Ashton's rehearsal dinner afterparty is happening right now, and we're supposed to be there. But we're late, because we've been busy tailing the guy who sent Eli death threats for weeks. And that guy just pulled into a parking spot across the street and, finally, cut his engine.

CHAPTER TWENTY-NINE

Knox
Friday, March 27

"Okay, no," Maeve says, her voice tight. "This has to be a co-incidence. He's not going to Ashton and Eli's rehearsal dinner. How would he even know where it is?"

"You're always saying there are no coincidences," I remind her. Pressure starts to build behind my eyes. "And people can find anything online. Haven't we just proven that?"

I sound calm, but I'm not, because shit, this is bad. I'm only just starting to grasp how bad this is. Maeve has pulled off to the side of the road, a few parking spots behind Jared in the metered spaces that line Charles Street. He's still in his car.

"Oh God, oh God," Maeve groans. "We have to try Eli again."

"He won't pick up," I remind her, desperation making me hoarse. Of all the times for Eli to go off the grid.

"Then I'll call Bronwyn. She should be there by now. Oh God," Maeve says again, covering her face with her hands. "Bronwyn is *there*."

Everyone is there, I think. Except Phoebe and her family, even though they were supposed to be until Emma wound up in the hospital yesterday. Christ, I can't even think about that right now. Maeve is shaking so badly that she's having trouble placing the call, and I take her phone from her. "I got it," I say. But Bronwyn's number goes straight to voice mail, too. "She's not answering."

"Try Addy," Maeve says.

I do, with the same results. "Why is no one picking up?" I yell in frustration, banging my fist on my knee. "We're Generation Z, for God's sake. Our phones are supposed to be permanently attached to our hands."

Maeve's only response is a gasp, and I look up from her phone to see Jared standing at the edge of the road, waiting for cars to pass. My heart starts jackhammering in my chest as I hand Maeve's phone back to her and pull out my own. Then I set it to Video, and train it on Jared as he starts to walk.

"We need to go, too." Maeve says. She grabs my arm when I lower my phone. "No, keep recording. But follow him, okay? I'm going to call the police and tell them . . . I don't even know. Something. I'll be right behind you after that."

A horn honks as I climb out of the car, shielding my eyes against oncoming headlights. I wait for another car to roar past, then I cross to the sidewalk as Jared rounds a fence in front of Talia's. The restaurant is sandwiched between an office building and a bank, both closed and dark at this time of night.

Small outdoor seating areas flank the front door on either side. I can hear murmured voices and laughter from somewhere at the back of the building. The night is windy and a little foggy, mist swirling around the streetlight closest to the restaurant. I expect Jared to head for the front door, but he goes around the side instead.

I hesitate as he disappears, and Maeve comes up behind me, breathless. "Where is he?"

"He went around back. Should we try to find Eli?"

"Let's see what he's doing first."

Voices get louder as we approach the rear of the restaurant. I pause when we reach the corner, poking my head out just enough to take in the scene in front of me. Talia's has a raised, open-air deck that's about eight feet off the ground, surrounded by a wooden railing. White lights are strung everywhere, music is playing, and people stand in clusters on the deck, talking and laughing. I'm at an awkward angle, but I think I see the back of Cooper's head.

Jared is on one knee and has the backpack in front of him. My phone is still recording, so I lift it again and aim it for him. He reaches inside, and for one heart-stopping second, I think he's about to pull out a gun. Options flash through my brain: tackle him? Yell? Both? But when he takes his hand out, it's empty. He zips up the backpack and tosses it beneath the deck. Then he rises in a low crouch. I yank Maeve's arm, backpedaling with her until we're at the front of the restaurant. "Stairs," I whisper, and we run for the entrance, flattening ourselves against the wall beside the door.

Jared emerges a few seconds later from the side of the

building. He strides quickly across the parking lot, looking straight ahead the entire time. We watch him until he disappears around the fence. "What's he up to?" Maeve breathes.

I pull up the video I just took and send it to Eli. "I don't know, but I think we'd better get that backpack." I shove my phone into my pocket and grab Maeve's hand. Her palm feels reassuringly cool and dry in mine. "Come on."

We retrace our steps to the back of the building. The space beneath the deck isn't open like I'd thought it would be when I watched Jared throw his backpack from around the corner. It's thick wooden lattice, except for a squat, narrow crawl space in the middle. I kneel and reach an arm in, sweeping it in every direction, but I can't feel anything other than dirt and rocks.

Maeve hands me her phone, lit with the flashlight app, and I shine it inside. The backpack is almost directly in front of me but at least six feet away. "It's there. I'm going in," I say, taking a deep breath. I don't dislike closed spaces as much as heights, but I'm not a fan either. As soon as my head is inside the crawl space, though, I can tell the rest of me won't fit. Nobody would ever call my shoulders *broad*, but they still won't make it through. I reverse course and sit on my haunches next to the opening.

"Maybe we should tell everybody to leave," I say, wiping my chin against my shoulder. My face is a gross combination of sticky and gritty from just a few seconds in the crawl space. "Something bad is in that backpack, or he wouldn't have put it there."

Maeve drops to her knees beside me. "Let me try." She ducks her head through the opening, twisting her body so her shoulders are at a right angle. She's a lot narrower than I am and manages to slide the rest of the way through. The backpack emerges soon after, shoved out of the crawl space by Maeve's dirt-streaked hands. She follows, forcing her shoulders through with a painful grimace as I lift the backpack by one strap. It's a faded tan color, ripped along one side and heavy. I tug at the zipper and shine Maeve's phone inside.

Maeve coughs and brushes a cobweb from her hair. She's covered in dirt, and her right arm is bleeding from a long, jagged scrape. "What's in there?"

"Something round and metal," I report. "It has a lot of wires and . . . switches, or something." Alarm starts coursing through my veins, making me sweat. God, I wish I'd paid more attention to my father when he used to explain how stuff works. "I can't be sure, but this looks a lot like somebody's idea of a homemade bomb." My voice cracks on the last word.

Maeve's eyes get wide and scared. "What do we do?"

I'm frozen, indecisive. I want this to be somebody else's problem. I want Eli to check his damn phone. He's up there somewhere, and if I yell loud enough I could probably get his attention. But I don't know how much time we have.

"We have to get rid of it," I say, scanning the area. We're in luck, sort of, because the space behind Talia's is nothing but grass until you get to a bike path a hundred yards away. Tall bushes line the back of the path, and if I have my geography right, the Bayview Arboretum is right behind them. Which closes at six, so it has to be deserted this time of night.

I sprint for the bike path, Maeve right behind me. That's not what I intended—I thought she'd stay by the deck, but there's no time to argue. I've never run so fast in my life, and it still feels like it takes me forever to reach the edge of the path. When I get there, I pause for a few seconds, panting. Is this far enough? I really hope so, because I'm afraid of hanging on to this thing much longer, especially with Maeve next to me.

I hold my arm out to one side, the backpack dangling from my hand like I'm getting ready for a discus throw. "I wish Cooper were here," I mutter. Then I take a deep breath, twist my body halfway with my arm fully extended, and hurl the backpack as hard as I can over the bushes lining the edge of the arboretum. I watch it sail into blackness and I grab Maeve's hand. "Okay, let's get out of here and get help."

We're about to turn and run when a faint, familiar voice floats out from behind the bushes, stopping us in our tracks. "The fuck was that?" someone says.

My heart thuds to a stop, then drops to my shoes. Maeve freezes, her eyes as round as saucers. "Nate?" she breathes, and then she lifts her voice in a piercing scream. "Nate, *run*! This is Maeve. That was a backpack with a bomb inside, from someone who's been threatening Eli. You have to run toward the restaurant, now!"

We hear a loud rustling sound, and I tug at Maeve's hand. "We have to run too. I don't know how much time—"

"Maeve?" comes a girl's voice.

Maeve gasps and screams again, loud and panicked. *"Bronwyn?"*

Jesus Christ. Nate and Bronwyn picked the worst time possible for a moonlight stroll in the garden.

Maeve lunges forward, and I wrap an arm around her waist

to stop her. "Other way, Maeve! I'm sorry, but we have to go the other way!" I start dragging her backward, yelling toward the arboretum as I do. "This isn't a joke, you guys! Run!"

Two people crash through the bushes hand in hand, and I catch the silhouette of a flowing skirt against the dim moonlight. I'm still pulling Maeve along the grass, not making nearly as much progress as I'd like. As the figures running toward us get closer I can see Nate doing the same with Bronwyn, trying to use his momentum to pull her forward. Somehow, despite Maeve's best efforts, I've managed to get her more than halfway across the grassy space between the restaurant and the bike path.

"Come on!" I grit out in frustration. "Nate's with her! This isn't helping!" Maeve finally stops fighting me, and we race the rest of the way across the lawn until we're a few feet from the restaurant. Voices rise as people start to gather at the railing, their confused faces lit by the twinkling white lights.

"Get inside!" I gesture with the hand that's not holding Maeve's arm. I still don't trust her to stay put. And then, because nobody's paying any attention, I pull out my trump card "There's a bomb in the arboretum! Everybody get inside!"

The words use the last bit of lung capacity I have left, and I pant painfully as shouts and gasps fill the air. Nate and Bronwyn are almost halfway across the grass now. Nothing's happened yet, so I let myself feel a small burst of relief. Somebody who knows what the hell they're doing can take over now. Maybe it's not even as bad as we think, maybe we have plenty of time, or maybe the backpack was something else entirely—

When an explosion rips through the air, the noise is

deafening. Maeve and I both throw ourselves onto the ground as an orange ball of fire erupts from behind the bushes. I reach up instinctively to cover my head, but before my vision is blocked I look across the grass to where Nate and Bronwyn were just seconds before. I see white smoke billowing high and fast into the air, fragments of God only knows what swirling within it, and nothing else.

CHAPTER THIRTY

Phoebe
Friday, March 27

"Careful, not so close. You'll burn yourself."

I'm eight years old, sitting between my father and my sister in front of a small bonfire on the beach. It's a special trip, just the three of us. Mom's staying home with Owen, who's too little to toast marshmallows. But I'm good at it, holding my stick the right distance from the flames, rotating my marshmallow carefully until every side is bubbling brown. I'm better than Emma, because she's too tentative and won't get her marshmallow close enough to toast.

It's kind of satisfying, that I'm better than Emma at something. That almost never happens.

"Mine is no good," Emma says fretfully. She sounds on the edge of tears.

"Let me help you," Dad says, putting his hand over hers and holding her stick in place. And then I feel upset that I have to toast

my marshmallow alone, so I shove my stick too far in the flames and let it catch fire.

"I need help too!" I say.

Dad lets out an exasperated chuckle and takes the stick from me, blowing out the flaming marshmallow. He pokes the stick down in the sand between us so it stands upright, and the charred marshmallow on top instantly starts to droop. "Phoebe, you were doing fine," he says. "Save the cries for help for when you really need it."

"I did need it," I say sulkily, and he puts an arm around me.

"Your sister needed it a little more," he whispers in my ear. "But I'm always here for both of you. You know that, right?"

I feel better nestled against the warmth of his side, and sorry I didn't let Emma enjoy her perfect marshmallow. "Yes," I say.

He kisses the top of my head. "And make sure you're there for each other too. All of you. The world can be a rough place, and you guys need to stick together. Okay?"

I close my eyes and let the flames dancing in front of me paint my lids orange. "Okay."

The beeping wakes me up. A machine in Emma's room whirs to life and I do too, sitting bolt upright in my corner chair. I shove my hair out of my face as my dream-memory fades and I remember why I'm here. "Emma," I croak. I'm half on my feet when a nurse enters the room.

"It's all right," she says, fiddling with a knob on the machine behind Emma. "We're going to give her a little more fluids, that's all." My sister remains motionless on her bed, asleep.

The room is dim, and I'm alone except for my sister and the nurse. I have no idea what time it is, and my throat is paper dry.

"Can I have some water?" I ask.

"Of course. Come to the nurses' station with me, hon. Stretch those legs." The nurse disappears into the hallway. Before I follow, I take another look at Emma, so silent and still that she might as well be dead. Then I pull my phone out of my pocket and finally send the text I've been avoiding for weeks.

Hi Derek, it's Phoebe. Call me.

I leave the room, still feeling groggy, and find Emma's nurse waiting for me in the hallway. "Where's my mom?" I ask.

"Took your brother home to bed. There's a sitter coming, and she'll be back once he's settled," the nurse says.

A clock in the hallway reads ten fifteen, and the floor is quiet except for the muted conversation of three nurses clustered around the central desk. "Someone needs to clear those kids out of the waiting room," one of them says.

"I think they're all in shock," says another.

The woman who gave me the water makes a clucking noise as she leans her forearms on the counter surrounding the desk. "This town is going to hell in a handbasket. Kids dying, bombs going off—"

"What?" I almost choke on my water. "A *bomb*? What are you talking about?"

"Tonight," the nurse says. "At a wedding rehearsal dinner, of all things. There was a homemade explosive device planted by some disturbed young man."

"Aren't they all," another nurse says coldly.

My skin prickles, nerves jumping. "Wedding rehearsal?

325

In Bayview? Was it—" I grab my phone out of my pocket to check for new texts, but before I can, one of the nurses says, "Talia's Restaurant."

I drop my cup with a loud clatter, sending water splashing across the floor. I start shaking from head to toe, practically vibrating, and the nurse closest to me takes hold of my shoulders, speaking quickly. "I'm so sorry, we should have realized you might know people there. It's all right, someone got the bomb off the premises before it could do significant damage. Only one boy had more than superficial injuries—"

"Are they here?" I look wildly around me, as though my friends might be right around the corner and I just hadn't noticed them yet.

The nurse lets go of my shoulders and picks up my discarded cup. "There's a group in the waiting room closest to the ER downstairs."

I take off for the stairs before she can say anything else, my sneakers pounding against the linoleum. I know exactly where to go; I sat in that waiting room last night after the EMTs brought Emma in. It's one floor down, and when I push through the stairwell door into the hallway I'm immediately hit with a buzzing noise, much louder than upstairs. Several scrub-clad people are standing with their arms folded in front of Liz Rosen from Channel Seven, who looks camera-ready in a sharp red suit and perfect makeup. "No media beyond this point," a man says as I slip behind them.

The waiting room is packed, standing room only. My heart squeezes at the sight of so many people I know, looking more devastated than I've ever seen them. Bronwyn, her face stained with tears and her pretty red dress torn, is sitting between her mother and a middle-aged woman I don't recognize. Cooper and Kris are holding hands next to Addy, who's hunched forward and gnawing on her cuticles. Luis is on Addy's other side with Maeve on his lap, and he's holding her while she slumps motionless against his shoulder, eyes closed. Her right arm is wrapped in a white gauze bandage. I don't see Ashton, or Eli, or Knox anywhere.

Only one boy had more than superficial injuries . . .

I pick my way toward Maeve first, my throat tight with worry. "Is she okay?" I whisper.

"Fine," Luis says. "Sleeping. She crashed ten minutes ago." His arms tighten around her. "Long night."

"A nurse upstairs told me about the bomb." Saying the word out loud doesn't make it any less surreal. "What happened?"

Addy runs a hand over her face. "How much time do you have?"

Kris gets to his feet and gestures to his chair. "Here, have a seat. I need the restroom. Anybody want a drink or anything else while I'm up?"

"I'd kill for a Diet Coke," Addy says wearily. Kris circles the room taking additional requests as I drop into his chair.

"Is Knox okay?" I ask anxiously. "Why isn't he here?"

"He's fine," Addy says, and I exhale with relief. "The hero of the night, in fact, along with this one." She reaches over to lightly stroke Maeve's arm. "He, Ash, and Eli are talking to the police. Maeve was supposed to go too, but she conked out and they said to let her rest. Knox can give them the whole story, I guess. They were together all night."

I file that away. "Who's hurt? The nurse said someone was hurt," I say, glancing around the room and trying to catalog who's missing. "Is it—"

My eyes catch sight of Bronwyn's distraught face again right before Addy says, "Nate." I gasp and she quickly adds, "He's going to be all right, they say. It's just—he and Bronwyn were closest to the bomb when it exploded. He was basically a human shield over her, so he took the brunt of it." She reaches up a hand to twist one of her small gold earrings. "It was . . . do you remember the Boston Marathon bombing? How it was this pressure cooker thing with nails and stuff inside?" I manage to nod, even though I can't believe we're actually having a conversation in the middle of the Bayview Memorial Hospital waiting room about bomb techniques. "Same type of thing. They were pretty far away, thank God, but Nate's arm is kind of torn up, so they have to remove . . ."

She hesitates, and my breath catches in my throat. "His *arm?*"

"No! No, no," Addy says quickly. She tugs harder at her earring. "God, sorry. I was trying to remember the word for, like . . . flying bits from a bomb."

"Shrapnel," Luis says. I go limp with relief as Addy nods. "But he'll be okay?"

"That's what they say. I don't know how bad his arm is injured, though." Addy lowers her voice, flicking her eyes toward the middle-aged woman sitting next to Bronwyn. "It'll be terrible if he can't work. Nate needs that money so he can stay in his apartment. His mom's living with his dad, even though they don't really have a marriage anymore, because his dad's still in and out of rehab and somebody has to take care of him. It's so *tense* in that house. That can't be Nate's life again. It just can't."

There's too much information coming at me all at once, but still so much I don't understand. "Why would anybody do something like this?" I ask. "You said Knox and Maeve are heroes. What did they do?"

Addy exhales. "It's still sort of jumbled up. We haven't had much of a chance to talk to either of them, so we don't have the full picture, but . . . there was this guy Jared Jackson, I guess? His brother is one of the police officers in the news for framing people on fake drug charges. He'd been sending threatening letters to Eli, and he decided to follow through on them tonight. Knox and Maeve were tailing him—I'm not clear how they knew to do that, to be honest—and followed him straight to Talia's." She shudders and hunches down in her chair again. "We'd probably all be dead if they hadn't. The bomb was literally right below the deck we were standing on."

"At least police arrested the guy pretty fast," Luis says grimly.

"Thanks to Maeve and Knox," Addy says. "Knox caught the whole thing on video. The worst thing is, police were *there*, at the restaurant. Eli took precautions because of the threats. But they were inside. Nobody planned for *this*." Her lips form a tight line. "Like, is this my sister's life now? She has to deal with terrorists and death threats? I love Eli with my whole heart, I really do, but this is horrible."

Maeve stirs but doesn't wake, and Luis presses a light kiss on the top of her head. "Is the wedding still on for tomorrow?" he asks.

Addy sighs. "I don't even know."

My phone starts ringing in my pocket. I pull it out and stifle a groan when I see that it's Derek, calling me back already. His timing sucks, but I don't want to play phone tag with him. Might as well get it over with. Maybe by the time I'm done, Knox will be back to explain more of what happened tonight. "I have to take this," I murmur to Addy.

I stand and pick through the crowded waiting area until I'm in the corridor. "Hello," I say, plugging my free ear with my index finger.

"Phoebe, it's Derek. I'm really glad you got in touch." His voice sounds far away, and if I didn't already know who it was, I'd never have recognized it. *I have no idea who this person really is,* I think as I lean against the wall.

"Why," I say flatly.

Derek clears his throat. "Well, to be honest, the thing is . . . ever since that party at your friend's house, I can't stop thinking about you. I feel like we could have something special if—"

"Are you fucking kidding me?" I don't realize I'm yelling until a passing nurse gives me the evil eye. I lower my voice. "Do you realize Emma is in the hospital?"

"She's what?" Derek sounds bewildered. "No. How would

I know that? I haven't talked to Emma in months. What happened?"

"She's falling apart! And I think it has something to do with what happened between you and me—which, by the way, was not *special*. It was stupid. But anyway. Emma found out about us last month, and now she's suddenly drinking herself to death. So who did you blab to? Did you stop to think for one second that running your mouth might get back to Emma?"

"I . . ." Derek falls silent, the sound of his breathing the only sign that he hasn't disconnected. I'm feeling a surge of righteous satisfaction that my words must have hit their mark when he adds, "Phoebe, *I* told Emma. The day after it happened."

I plug my ear harder against the noise of the corridor. I can't have heard him right. "Excuse me? What did you say?"

"I told Emma about you and me. I felt like shit and I figured you were gonna tell her, so I just . . . wanted to get it off my chest, I guess."

"You told Emma," I repeat. I pull the phone away from my ear and stare at it, like that'll help me make sense of his words, and a series of texts from my mom flashes across the screen:

Phoebe, are you still here?

The nurses said you went downstairs.

I need you back in Emma's room.

Right now.

Oh shit. That doesn't sound good. I bring the phone back to my ear just long enough to tell Derek "I have to go" before I disconnect and retrace my steps upstairs.

* * *

I was steeling myself for lots of things when I reached Emma's room, but a police officer wasn't one of them.

"Um. Hi," I say nervously, clutching my phone as I step inside. Mom is sitting beside Emma's bed and the police officer is standing at its foot. The gray-haired nurse is writing something down on Emma's chart. Emma herself is still asleep. I gaze at her peaceful face, wishing I could see directly into her brain. Emma knew about Derek and me. She *knew.* Even when she confronted me in Café Contigo, red-faced and almost crying, waving her phone like it was the first time she'd ever heard the news.

Unless Derek is lying. But why would he? My head aches, my brain working overtime trying to connect the dots on all the new information that's hit me tonight.

Mom's strained voice pierces my tangled thoughts. "Phoebe, this is Detective Mendoza with the Bayview Police. He has some questions for you."

"For me?" I tear my eyes away from Emma as the nurse straightens.

"You can stay here, if you like," she says, crossing to the door. "We can close this for a few minutes and give you privacy. Just press the call button if the patient needs me."

I hover next to the door after it closes, and Detective Mendoza clears his throat. "Phoebe, I've already explained this to your mother, but you are not being accused of anything related to this evening's events. Your presence for the entirety of tonight is accounted for. However, we'd like your cooperation

332

as we build the case against Jared Jackson, and to do that effectively we need to understand your relationship with him."

"My . . . what?" I wish I had my cup of water back. My throat is suddenly so dry that it hurts. "I don't have a *relationship* with him. I only just learned his name downstairs."

"We've spent the past hour interviewing Mr. Jackson about his motivations for tonight's events at Talia's Restaurant. We also seized his phone, which he claims has months' worth of correspondence with you. He says he met you in an online forum called Vengeance Is Mine in late December, that the two of you bonded over family tragedies, and eventually agreed to, as he put it, *take out* one another's enemies. Mr. Jackson says he fulfilled his end of the bargain when he executed a texting-based Truth or Dare game at Bayview High that led to Brandon Weber's death earlier this month."

My legs suddenly go weak, and I barely make it into the corner chair. "I don't understand. Brandon . . . what about Brandon?" I dart my eyes toward Mom, who stirs beside Emma's bed like a sleepwalker trying to wake up.

"Wait. Brandon Weber?" she asks thickly. "You didn't mention him before."

Detective Mendoza looks down at a notepad in his hand. "According to Mr. Jackson, he used gossip about Bayview High students—yourself and your sister included—to kick the game off." He glances up at me briefly, then back at his notes. "The actions that led to Brandon Weber's death were the result of a Dare issued to him. Mr. Jackson made use of his background in construction work to remove supports from beneath that landing, causing Brandon to fall to his death. In return, you were

333

supposed to help Mr. Jackson get revenge on Eli Kleinfelter, for putting Mr. Jackson's brother in jail. However, Mr. Jackson says you fell out of touch after Brandon Weber's death, and became unresponsive to his attempts to contact you. Thus tonight's attack. He decided to take matters into his own hands, and conclude the deal without you."

Unresponsive to his attempts to contact you. We need to talk. That's what the note I got at Café Contigo yesterday said. If I'm understanding Detective Mendoza correctly, Jared Jackson must have sent that. And set up the entire Truth or Dare game . . . for me. Which makes no sense whatsoever. Even putting aside the insane idea that I'd agree to hurt Eli—how could a person I've never met believe I made a deal with him? And that I wanted Brandon *dead*?

I'm going to be sick. "No. That's not . . . I wouldn't in a million years do anything like that," I say. An image flashes through my brain of Brandon in my apartment, assaulting me and hurling insults. In that instant, I hated him. Did I tell the wrong person? Who did I tell? How could Jared Jackson even know about it, or about me? "Why would I? Brandon and I aren't . . . we didn't get along all the time, but he wasn't my *enemy*."

Detective Mendoza's tone doesn't change: calm and unemotional, like his notes are a textbook he's using to teach a class. "Mr. Jackson says you told him how Brandon Weber contributed to your father's death by causing a forklift to malfunction during a critical point in its operation."

Everything inside me stills. I forget how to breathe. The

tears that had been gathering behind my eyes freeze. My heart, which was just pounding loudly in my ears, is suddenly so silent that I wonder, briefly, if I'm dead.

"What." I push the word through numb lips, cold and flat. It doesn't seem like enough. There have to be more words. I search my brain for them. "Did. You say."

A strangled cry bursts out of Mom. "I never wanted you kids to know, Phoebe. What was the point of knowing something like that? I'm so sorry I didn't prepare you for it. But you could have *talked* to me. Why didn't you talk to me?"

Brandon. *Dad.* This is a nightmare. I'm asleep and having the worst dream of my entire life. I pinch my arm, as hard as I can. I don't even feel it, but I don't wake up, either.

"I didn't," I finally say. "Know any of that."

"According to Mr. Jackson, the two of you discussed this in great detail," Detective Mendoza says. "When you first told him about the accident, he looked you up online and saw media coverage of your mother's wedding planning business. That's why he proposed the revenge pact—he knew you could provide access to Mr. Kleinfelter." For the first time, Detective Mendoza's voice gets the tiniest bit gentle. "You were still processing a traumatic revelation when you met him. The law understands that, especially when we have your full cooperation. Can we count on that?"

"*No.*" My voice gains strength, finally, because the hell with this. The only thing I know for sure right now is that I had no clue who Jared Jackson was before tonight. "Jared Jackson is wrong, or lying. I never met him online or in person. I didn't know Brandon had anything to do with what happened to my dad until *right this second*." Everything's coming unglued now: tears fall, my heart accelerates, and my voice shakes. "I didn't do any of this."

"Then how would Jared know that Brandon was involved in your father's accident, Phoebe?" Detective Mendoza asks. Not like he's mad. More like he's genuinely curious.

I open my mouth. Close it.

"I told him."

I blink, utterly confused. Did I just say that?

Detective Mendoza's head swivels from me to Emma's bed. My eyes follow. She's sitting up, pale but alert. Her hand is folded in my mother's. "I told him," she repeats in a low voice. "And I told him I was Phoebe."

Mom's face goes rigid with shock as Detective Mendoza moves closer to the foot of the bed. "Are you saying you executed this revenge pact with Jared Jackson, Emma?" he asks.

"I . . . no," Emma says haltingly. "Not like you said. I met him online, and I pretended to be my sister because I was mad at her for . . . other stuff." She flicks a glance at me, and I flush. "And I told him what happened to my dad and he—he said we could help one another." Emma's voice trembles as she pulls her hand from Mom's and starts fumbling with the edge of her hospital blanket. "But he never mentioned Eli. I had no idea they even knew one another. And as soon as the Truth or Dare game started, I *hated* it. I regretted everything. I told Jared to shut it down, and he said he would."

Her voice shakes harder, and her eyes fill. "But the game kept going. I didn't understand why, but I was afraid to get in touch with Jared again. I kept hoping he'd get bored and stop. And Brandon . . ." Emma lets out a choked cry as tears spill down her cheeks. "Brandon wasn't supposed to die."

I hear my own sharp intake of breath as Detective Mendoza asks, "What was supposed to happen to Brandon?" The gentler tone from before is entirely gone.

Emma hesitates, and my mother speaks before she can. "That might be enough for now," Mom says, the shell-shocked look on her face slipping away. Her shoulders straighten, like something's finally clicking into place, as she adds, "I think we should hold off on any further conversation until we have a lawyer present."

CHAPTER THIRTY-ONE

Maeve
Saturday, March 28

"Ladies and gentlemen, here they are. Being introduced for the first time as husband and wife, please welcome Eli Kleinfelter and Ashton Prentiss!"

The crowd in the hotel ballroom gets to its feet for a standing ovation as Eli leads Ashton onto the dance floor. Everyone is clapping so loudly that we nearly drown out the music. Last night, Ashton and Eli told everyone that they still planned to get married today but understood completely if people didn't want to come.

We all did, down to the last guest. Except the Lawtons. The wedding is basically uncoordinated at this point, because Mrs. Lawton has her hands full elsewhere.

Nobody knows what really happened between Emma Lawton and Jared Jackson. Eli was only able to get bits and pieces of information last night and this morning. From what he can tell, Emma stumbled across paperwork for her father's worker's comp settlement shortly after Christmas. She was angry enough to look for Simon's old revenge forum, where she met Jared Jackson and told him what Brandon had done. Jared raised the idea of a revenge pact, and Emma didn't immediately shut him down. But after that, it gets murky.

According to Eli, Emma says she stopped talking to Jared right after the Truth or Dare game launched. She insists she didn't know Brandon was going to die, or that Eli was a target. And Jared insists that she did.

The rest of us are just waiting for the truth to come out.

I don't know how Eli managed to worry about Knox and me in the middle of all this, but he made sure we knew that Phoebe's only involvement was Emma using her name. "Phoebe is no longer a person of interest to the police," he told us.

Phoebe herself texted Knox and me right before we left for the wedding:

I love you both.
Thanks for what you did
I'm so glad you're ok.
I can't say anything else right now so please don't ask.
I'm sorry.

I wish things were different, and that she could have been part of today. Ashton and Eli's wedding ceremony turned out to be the perfect antidote to yesterday's trauma. Watching them exchange their vows reminded everybody that love and hope and beauty still exist, even when things seem impossibly dark. My mood has been lifting steadily all day, and now that

Ashton and Eli are moving across the dance floor—unsteadily, because Eli *cannot* dance, but beaming at one another—I almost feel normal.

Addy, who was in tears for most of last night, stands smiling at the edge of the dance floor in a beautiful, ice-blue maid of honor's dress. She's holding a bouquet of white roses in one hand, and the arm of cute groomsman-slash-molecular-biologist Daniel with the other. He bends toward her ear and says something that makes her laugh so hard that she almost drops her flowers.

"Ashton looks gorgeous," Bronwyn says. She's standing beside me at our reception table, her hand firmly in Nate's. I don't think she's let go of him since he was discharged from the hospital this morning. Nate's the least formally dressed of us all, since he couldn't manage to get anything except a T-shirt over his sling. Surgeons removed five chunks of metal from his left arm last night, and he's bandaged up to his shoulder. He'll have scars for life, probably, but he's incredibly lucky that he doesn't have nerve damage.

And that he works for Mr. Myers. Knox's dad came to the hospital last night to let Mrs. Macauley know that the company's disability policy will cover Nate's salary while he recuperates.

"For how long?" Mrs. Macauley asked nervously.

"As long as it takes," he replied.

Now, Nate grins at Bronwyn and me. "Eli looks like he's about to keel over."

"I'm pretty sure this is his first time on a dance floor," I say.

Nate nods. "I believe it."

Bronwyn gazes around the crowded ballroom. "Where's your date?" she asks me.

"Talking to Mom and Dad," I say, pointing a few tables over to where Mom is smiling brightly at Luis and Dad just clapped him on the shoulder.

My sister scowls as she watches them. "Oh, this is so not fair. Luis has been your boyfriend for five minutes and they're already falling all over him. It took a year before Mom and Dad even *started* to warm up to . . ." She glances toward Nate, who's still on her other side, and catches herself. "Anyone else."

Nate slips his good arm around her waist and pulls her close, nuzzling her neck. "What are you talking about?" he teases. "Your parents love me. Always have."

The DJ picks up his microphone again as the music changes to a pulsing beat. "Everyone, please join the happy couple on the dance floor!"

Kris grabs hold of Cooper's hand and starts to pull. "Come on. You'd better get ready, because I am a dancing machine at weddings. We're not stopping until the music does."

Cooper blinks as he follows. "There's still so much I don't know about you, isn't there?"

"Let's dance," Bronwyn says to Nate.

"Can't." He holds up his bandaged arm. "I'm injured."

She puts her hands on her hips. "Your *legs* aren't."

Nate grimaces and raises a hand to his forehead. "I feel dizzy all of a sudden," he says, sinking into the chair behind him. "I think I might pass out." When Bronwyn leans over him with a worried expression, he grabs her around the waist and pulls her onto his lap. "I probably need CPR. You're certified, right?"

"You're the worst," Bronwyn complains, but she's already started kissing him before she finishes the sentence.

I look over at my parents' table, where Luis is still making polite conversation. Another check mark in his pro column: Good with Parents. I'd suggest he give Nate lessons, but I think the whole *sacrificing himself to save Bronwyn* deal might've finally won them over. When Mom looks our way, she doesn't even glare at the makeout session happening to my right.

Luis and I spot one another at the same time, and I can't help but smile when he heads toward me. That boy in a suit—wow.

We meet up on the edge of the dance floor, and he holds out his hand. "Shall we?"

"We shall," I say. He spins me deftly so my skirt twirls in a glittering circle before he pulls me close. I put my head on his chest, breathing in his clean, soapy smell, and he brings his lips to my ear.

"How are you?"

It's a hard question to answer. I tilt my head so I can meet his eyes. "Right this second, really good. Today was beautiful. In general, though . . ." A shiver goes through me, raising goose bumps all over my body. "Things aren't great, are they? I'm scared for Ashton and Eli and everybody he works with. Nobody knows what's going on with Emma. And Brandon is still gone." My voice breaks a little. "If we'd figured out who Jared was sooner . . ."

Luis's arms tighten around me. "There's no possible way you could have seen into that guy's head any earlier than you did. Don't even go there. You did great, Maeve. You saved lives, you know. You and Knox."

That part doesn't seem real yet. My brain won't let me imagine an alternate scenario where we don't get Jared's backpack away from the restaurant. "I guess." I want to feel something good, something happy, so I wind my arms around Luis's neck and rise up on my toes to steal a soft kiss from his lips.

"One of these days," he says when I pull away, "I'm going to put the moves on you first."

A smile tugs at the corners of my mouth. It worked; my mood is lifting again. "Looking forward to it."

"Maybe when I take you on a real date."

I look around. "Is that not what this is?"

"Nah, there's too many other people. Plus we've been stuck inside all day. You know how I feel about inside."

"You're unnaturally prejudiced against it, yes. Where would you go instead? If, for example, we decided to do something tomorrow?"

"La Jolla Cove," he says instantly. "I'd take you kayaking."

I gulp. Oh God, not the beach. And the *ocean*. But then again, maybe all that would be different with Luis. A lot of things are. Still, I narrow my eyes at him. "Kayaking? Sounds like work."

"I'll do it all," he promises.

"Is this what dating you is going to be like? You'll just cart me around various scenic areas in greater San Diego?" It doesn't sound bad, actually.

He grins. "I'll teach you how to kayak, if you want. It's fun, I swear. My family goes all the time in the summer. They'd love for you to come."

I like the direction of this conversation, but . . . "I might not be here then," I say. His eyebrows rise. "I think I'm going to apply to be a counselor at this school in Peru with Addy. If I get accepted, I'd be there all of July and August."

I'd been thinking about the possibility ever since I saw that brochure at Addy's apartment, and even more after getting a clean bill of health from Dr. Gutierrez. Last night, when I couldn't sleep, I tried to count up the positive things that have come out of this horrible experience. Luis, definitely. Becoming friends with Phoebe. Learning that Knox and I will always be able to count on one another. And believing enough in my future to make plans for it.

"Two whole months? Damn." Here comes Luis's disappointed face again, until he shakes it off with a regretful smile. "I mean, that sounds great. Obviously. Just make sure you come back."

"I will. I promise." Out of the corner of my eye I catch sight of a familiar figure alone at an empty table. I've been keeping tabs on Knox, because every once in a while his cheerful façade cracks, and he starts drooping under the weight of last night. Now looks like one of those times. I pull away from Luis and squeeze his arm. "I'm just going to check on Knox, okay? He looks like he could use some company."

"Sure," Luis says. I turn to go, but he tugs me back and cups my cheek, bending down to plant a slow, lingering kiss on my lips. My breath catches in my throat, and when he pulls away he's smiling. "That's one."

"Yeah, well. You still have some catching up to do." I blow him a kiss over my shoulder and head for Knox.

When I reach him he's standing, a folded napkin in one hand. "Hey," he says. "I think I'm gonna head out."

"What? No! The reception just got started."

"I know, but—I'm wiped." Knox loosens the knot on his tie and tugs it downward. His hair is messy, his eyes shadowed with dark circles. "It's been a long day. Plus I thought I'd see how Phoebe's doing, and bring her some cake." He lifts the napkin in his hand, and now I notice the pearly white frosting poking through.

"They cut the cake already?" I ask. "How did I miss that?"

"They didn't," Knox says. "But one of the servers told me there's extra in the kitchen in case anyone wants to take some home. She gave me a slice to give to Phoebe."

"That's really nice of you." Impulsively, I step forward and squeeze his free hand. "You're a good friend, you know that?"

At some point, probably soon, our weird romantic history is going to leak outside of the Bayview gossip circles. The Jared Jackson story is huge, and reporters are already sniffing around for details. Mikhail Powers's crew has been calling my house nonstop. Mikhail himself even sent a giant bouquet of colorful, exotic flowers with a note: *My deepest admiration and respect, always, to the strong young women of the Rojas family.*

"Don't be swayed by his charm," Bronwyn lectured when I told her. Mikhail Powers has coaxed my sister into interviews more than once. They never go badly, but she always tells herself afterward that she's not going to do it again. Until she does. "If you do talk to him, though, tell him I said hi."

I don't plan on it. But I've lived through a media circus before, when Simon died. People won't rest until every Truth and Dare of the texting game has been exposed and analyzed—including what happened between Knox and me. I've made my peace with it, though, and I hope he doesn't care any more than I do. Neither of us has anything to explain, or be embarrassed about. We're lucky, that's all. Beyond lucky to have each other.

He squeezes my hand back with a crooked grin. "So are you."

CHAPTER THIRTY-TWO

Knox
Saturday, March 28

Mrs. Lawton greets me at the door, looking like she hasn't slept in a week. She does her best to rally, though, giving me a wan smile. "Hi, Knox. Don't you look handsome."

She doesn't ask me how the wedding went, and I don't offer. There are some conversations it's better not to have when things are this raw. "Thanks." I can make out the muted sounds of a video game somewhere in the apartment, and I hope Owen doesn't appear. I can't pretend to care about *Bounty Wars* right now. "Is Phoebe around?" I ask.

Mrs. Lawton hesitates. "I'm so sorry, Knox, but Phoebe probably shouldn't be talking with other witnesses in the Jackson case right now. It's a delicate time."

"No, I totally get that. Phoebe already said. I promise I won't ask. But I thought she could use a friend. Also . . ." I dig into my pocket and pull out a folded piece of paper. "I wanted to give you this. From Eli. It's a list of lawyers you could call, if you're looking for referrals or anything like that. He says they're good."

Eli emailed me the list before he left his apartment for the ceremony. *Until Proven can't touch the case, obviously, given our involvement,* he wrote. *But Emma should get representation as soon as possible. There's growing precedent for courts coming down hard on kids who are seen as inciting others, both in person and online. Even when they pull back, like Emma did.*

If she did. I want to believe Emma, but it's hard to imagine that Jared would see the Truth or Dare game all the way through without her being involved. Plus, there's the fact that she must've fed this guy gossip not only about Phoebe and Derek—which is seriously messed up—but me and Maeve. Even though neither of us has ever done a thing to her. I actually thought she liked me. So who even knows what Emma is capable of.

You sure she's telling the truth? I wrote to Eli.

He responded instantly. *Whether she is or not, she needs good representation.*

One of these days, I hope to be the type of person who worries about a girl who was allegedly part of a revenge-swapping plot to destroy me. I'm not there yet, though. I'm glad the hospital is keeping Emma for observation another day so there's no chance I'll run into her now.

"How incredibly kind." Mrs. Lawton's eyes get filmy when she takes the paper. "Please give him my thanks." She rubs her temple and offers a weak smile. "I suppose a few minutes with Phoebe couldn't hurt. You're right—she could use a friend. It would cheer her up immensely to see you, I'm sure. She's on the roof deck."

"Thanks so—" I was about to step inside, but I pause on the threshold. "Sorry. The what?"

"There's a new roof deck on the building. They just finished putting the railing up last week. Phoebe's there. You can take the elevator to the top floor, and there's a stairwell right next to it that leads to the roof."

"Oh." My fear of heights has gotten ten times worse since Brandon died, and a roof is the last place I want to be right now. It's okay, though. I'll just stay in the middle, where you can't see over the edge. Then it's more like a floor. A floor without walls or a ceiling. Crap. "Okay. So. I'm just going to go on the . . . roof." I try to give her a confident wave when I head down the hallway, but I don't think I pull it off.

The elevator has mirrored doors, which I could do without on the ride to the top floor. My untucked shirt is a wrinkled mess and my half-mast tie is askew. My hair looks like I combed it with a Weedwacker. At least it's finally growing out, I guess. When the doors open, I find the stairwell and climb two short sets of stairs to a heavy metal door. I push against it, and I'm immediately hit in the face with a gust of wind.

Right. Of course. Because the only thing worse than being on a roof is being on one so windy that you could blow right off.

I tamp down the thought and take a few tentative steps

forward, until I spot Phoebe leaning against what looks to be a very flimsy railing. "Hey," I call, and she turns. "I brought you some cake."

Phoebe lifts her hand in an anemic wave, but stays where she is, so I guess I'm going over there. I owe her, probably, after thinking for even a nanosecond in Maeve's car last night that she could've been involved in this mess.

"You brought me what?" Phoebe asks when we're close enough to talk. Her hair is pulled up in a messy bun on the top of her head, tendrils flying everywhere in the wind. She's wearing what look like pajama bottoms and a tank top. I'd think she'd be freezing, but she doesn't seem to notice the chill in the air.

"Cake," I gulp, holding it out when I'm a foot away. That's the absolute closest I can get to that deathtrap of a railing. "Wedding cake. From the . . . wedding." For a second she looks like she's going to cry, and regret seizes my chest. Was this a dumb thing to do? Then she smiles and takes it from me.

"Thanks. That's really nice of you." She breaks off a piece and eats it, then holds out the napkin. "Want some?" she asks through her mouthful.

"Nah, I'm good." I stuff my hands into my pockets and try to figure out where to look. Cold sweat has started to coat my face. There's nothing but open sky around us, which is making me dizzy, so I focus on Phoebe's face. Even when it's covered in crumbs, that's hardly a chore. "How are you?"

Phoebe's stuffing cake into her mouth like she hasn't eaten in days. Which is possible, I guess. She says something I can't understand, and I wait for her to swallow. "Shitty," she says when she does, taking another huge bite of cake.

"I guess, yeah. Sorry."

She swallows again and brushes crumbs from the corners of her mouth. "But you! I didn't get a chance to thank you. For figuring things out, first of all, and for saving everybody. Things would be so much worse if . . ." Her voice wavers. "If anybody besides Brandon . . . oh God." She folds the empty napkin in half so the clean side is facing outward and presses it against her eyes. "I'm sorry. Every time I think I'm done crying I start again." Her shoulders shake as she slumps against the railing, choking out noisy sobs. "I can't stop. I don't know when it's going to stop."

I'm frozen for a few seconds, torn between her total misery and the terrifying void behind her. Then I step forward, ignoring the way my head spins and my stomach dips when I'm right at the edge, and pull her into an awkward embrace. "Hey. It's okay." I pat her back as she cries against my shoulder. "It's going to be okay."

"How?" she wails. "Everything is horrible. My dad is dead because of Brandon, and Brandon's dead because of us!"

"Not you," I say, but she only sobs harder. I hold her for I don't know how long, until she's finally cried out and starts taking deep, uneven breaths. One of her palms is flat against my chest, and she looks up at me through swimming eyes.

"Knox, your heart is beating out of your chest."

"Yeah." I blink, trying to get rid of the spots dancing in my line of vision. "The thing is—I'm scared of heights, and this

351

railing is . . . it does not look safe. Or tall. It's not really tall enough for my liking."

"Oh my God." She lets out a tearful laugh and, to my indescribable relief, pulls me away from the edge until we're nearly at the center of the roof. "Why didn't you say something? I could've bawled on your shoulder here just as easily."

"Well, you know." My dizziness recedes to a manageable level. "I try not to make a big deal out of what a coward I am."

"Coward?" She stares at me, wiping her cheeks. "Are you kidding me? You're the bravest person I've ever met." I drop my eyes, embarrassed, and she laughs softly. "Do you know what I thought, back there? I thought your heart was beating so fast because of me."

"What?" I'm so startled that I practically yelp, and Phoebe makes a face.

"You don't have to look so horrified."

"I'm not horrified. At all," I say quickly. "It's just—that's not a thing I would consider, even, because . . ." I trail off and rub the back of my neck with one hand. "I would have no shot, obviously. You're way too hot for me. Not that I spend a weird or inappropriate amount of time analyzing how hot you are, but—"

And then I can't talk anymore, because Phoebe is kissing me.

Her mouth is soft and hard at the same time, colliding with mine, and every nerve ending I didn't know I had catches fire. She tastes like sugar, and she's all curves and warm skin. She lifts my shirt, trailing her fingers across my stomach and down toward the waistband of my pants, and my brain almost short-circuits. Not entirely, though, because when I lift my hands to cup her face, I feel the wetness of fresh tears.

"Phoebe." I pull back reluctantly, already missing the feel of her. She's breathing as heavily as I am and her eyes are glazed. I swipe a thumb across the tear tracks on her face. "That was amazing, but . . . I think you're really sad right now. And worried, and just—probably not in a good place to be doing this."

She lets out a sound that's halfway between a whimper and a moan. "God, I'm such a disaster. You must hate me."

"What? No! Are you kidding? Believe me, I would like nothing more than for you to try that again in, say, a week. Or whenever you're feeling better. If you want to. But if you don't, that's okay, too."

She exhales a shuddering breath. "Do you have any idea how great you are?"

"Not really, no." I adjust the front of my pants, which is kind of uncomfortable thanks to the bulge Phoebe's groping brought on. She catches the motion and smirks a little through her tears. "Let the record show, though, that all systems were go," I add. "In case there was any doubt, after . . . you know."

She starts giggling so hard that I'd be embarrassed if I weren't relieved to see her mood lift. "Oh my God, you actually made me laugh. I wasn't sure that was still possible." She swipes at her eyes with the back of her hand. "Thank you. I needed this. All of it."

"Good. I'm glad." I take her hand and pull her toward the stairwell. "Could we please leave this roof now?"

* * *

It's late when I get home.. I've been walking everywhere to-night: from the reception to Phoebe's apartment, and then from Phoebe's apartment back to my house. It's been hard to breathe since yesterday, and the cool air helps a little.

My lips are still tingling from Phoebe's kiss as I open our front door. I've relived that moment a few hundred times on the walk home. It was a one-time thing, probably, and that's okay. It doesn't have to be awkward. If Maeve and I could make it through the entire school knowing about our not–first time, one sad kiss on the roof is nothing.

And who knows, maybe Phoebe meant it. Wouldn't that be something?

The kitchen and living room lights are on, and I can hear the sound of some sort of ball game on television when I get inside. It's past my mother's bedtime so it's probably just my dad watching, and he doesn't like to be interrupted in the middle of a game. I drop my house keys on the table and head for the staircase.

"Knox?" Dad's voice stops me. Footsteps follow until he's framed in the kitchen doorway, a bottle of Bud Light in one hand. The faint yellowish glow of our light fixture deepens every crease in his face. "How was the wedding?"

"Oh." I'm blank for a minute. The wedding already feels like it was months ago. "It was . . . good, I guess. You know. As good as it could be, under the circumstances."

He nods heavily. "Yeah. Sure."

"Nate was there," I add. "He looked good. He was joking around, didn't seem like he was in too much pain or anything." I clear my throat. "It's really great, what you're doing for him.

You know, the disability stuff. Everybody kept saying . . . how great it was. Is. Will be."

Jesus. You can stop babbling anytime, Knox.

"Company policy," Dad says stiffly.

"I know, but, like . . . you make the policy," I point out.

To my surprise, his face breaks into a smile. "I guess I do."

It's as good a time as any to say what I've been meaning to tell him for a while. "Dad, I'm really sorry about cutting through the mall site. I shouldn't have done that. It's not that I don't listen to you, or respect your work. I do, a lot. I was just being thoughtless."

The lines of his face soften. "Well. You're seventeen. That's gonna happen sometimes, I guess." He takes a gulp of beer and looks at the floor. "I owe you an apology, too. I shouldn't have said you're not a hard worker. I know you are." His voice gets gruff. "And another thing. You were smart last night, and brave, and even though I wish you'd kept yourself a little safer in that situation, I'm so proud of what you did. I'm proud of you, period. Always."

Oh hell. I made it through the past twenty-four hours without crying and now my *dad*, of all people, is going to make me do it. Then he'll probably take everything he just said back because I'm such a wimp. Before I lose it, though, Dad sets his beer down on an accent table, lets out a choked sob of his own, and yanks me into a bone-crushing hug. Which hurts a little, but—all things considered?

Worth it.

CHAPTER THIRTY-THREE

Phoebe
Wednesday, April 1

I take my time getting out of the car in the school parking lot Wednesday morning. I've been gone since Sunday, staying with Owen and my aunt a few towns over. Mom thought we needed a break, and she was probably right. Owen is still there, because he's a genius and is months ahead on his schoolwork. But I can't stay away forever.

I'm scared to be here. Scared of what people will think, and say, now that the truth is starting to come out. I'm afraid they'll hate Emma—and me. I can't blame them, because most of the time I hate us, too. Emma for starting this mess, and me for giving her a push off the deep end by hooking up with Derek at the worst possible time.

And I hate Brandon for what he did three years ago, but not enough that I'm not sick with regret about what happened to him. I know the thoughtless mistake of a spoiled thirteen-year-old doesn't deserve *this*.

Everything hurts, basically. All the time.

My phone chimes in my bag, and I pull it out to a text from Knox. *Don't be nervous. We have your back.*

I send a thumbs-up emoji in return, my stomach fluttering. I keep replaying our time on the roof in my head—not just the kiss, which warmed my whole body from the inside out, but the way Knox held me at the railing for so long, even though he was scared out of his mind. And the way he made me laugh when I thought I'd forgotten how. Plus, he looked surprisingly hot with his wrinkled shirt and his messy hair, his face all lean and haunted from the night before.

Maybe I just have a thing for wounded heroes. Or maybe Future Phoebe, who could appreciate someone like Knox, isn't as far away as I thought.

My phone dings again. Maeve this time. *Come inside. Bell's about to ring.*

Argh. Can't avoid it forever, I guess. I get out of my car, lock the door, and trudge toward the back entrance. My eyes are on the ground, so when I reach the stairs I almost bump into the couple kissing passionately against the railing. "Sorry, my bad," I mutter, then freeze when they pull apart.

My stomach drops. It's Sean and Jules. Literally the last two people I wanted to see. I can't even imagine what Sean is going to say to me—no, I don't need to imagine it, because he's opening his big stupid mouth right now and why can't I move, this is going to be horrible.

"Hey, Phoebe," he says.

It's so different from what I expected that I'm struck mute.

Jules disentangles herself and shoves lightly at Sean's arm. "Go inside," she tells him. "I'll meet you at my locker." To my shock, he does as she says, lumbering up the stairs and disappearing through the door without another word.

"You trained him," I say. Then I want to sink through the ground because *God*, that was rude, and neither of them deserves it at this particular moment in time.

But Jules smiles. "Sean has some seriously toxic male role models in his life, but he's trying. He's not as bad as you think, Phoebe."

I guess she's right. Especially since I thought at one point that he might've started the whole texting game in order to kill his best friend. Joke's on me, I guess, that it was actually my sister who did that. Allegedly.

But there's still one thing I need to know. Maybe it's been in the media coverage already, but I've been avoiding that like the plague. I lean against the railing, shifting my weight from one foot to the other. "Why did you guys lie, Jules? About why Brandon jumped?"

A pink tinge washes across her cheeks. "It's just—Sean thought we'd get in trouble, you know? He said it would be better if people thought it was just a shortcut and then we wouldn't have to explain . . . everything." She tucks a strand of hair behind her ear. "Including what the game said about you and Emma."

"Sean didn't care about that," I say. That might be rude, too, but I know it's true.

"No," she admits. "I did, though." I believe her. "And Sean didn't mean to hit Knox that hard, honestly. He panicked."

"So he never thought Knox was running after Brandon," I say. Just to be sure.

Jules's mouth twists. "No. He was freaking out, and Knox was . . . there."

"Are you going to get into trouble?" I ask. "For lying, I mean?"

She sighs. "The police aren't happy with us, but we're *so* not the main issue right now. They told us that as long as we cooperate going forward, we'll be okay." She licks her lips and lowers her eyes. "Is Emma—"

I don't let her finish. "I can't really talk about Emma."

Jules nods quickly, almost like she's relieved. "I understand."

She probably doesn't, though. It's not only because I'm not allowed to say anything that hasn't been approved by Emma's new lawyer—who I'm supposed to meet for the first time later today—but because I don't know anything the rest of the world hasn't already heard. I've barely seen or spoken to Emma since I left her hospital room Friday night.

I know what she told Detective Mendoza. And I know she spoke up when she could have left me hanging out to dry. But that's it.

The bell rings. Jules and I both stay put, shifting our backpacks and shuffling our feet. "I wish I'd tried harder to talk to you about all this," I finally say.

"I wish I had, too," Jules says. "I'm sorry I wasn't there for you. I just got so caught up with Sean."

"I'm glad you're happy." It's a lie, because I can't imagine any sort of happiness with Sean Murdock that doesn't end with deep regret and possibly an STD, but I'm going to keep my mouth shut about that for once. There are worse things, I guess, than having an oaf for a boyfriend.

Jules links her arm in mine and pulls me toward the stairs. "Come on, Phoebe Jeebies. Let's get you back on track."

"I need you to be one hundred percent honest with me, Emma," Martin McCoy says, leaning his forearms on our kitchen table. They're lean and covered with freckles. My sister's new lawyer has bright orange hair, just like my dad's, and for some reason that makes me trust him. "Jared Jackson's actions are caught on video, and there's no question about his culpability in the Talia's Restaurant bombing. Furthermore, he admitted to causing Brandon Weber's death, despite there being no suspicion of his involvement at the time." Martin rubs his temple, like Jared's unsolicited confession hurts his lawyerly brain. "As far as I can tell, he did that purely to implicate *you*. To bring you down with him. And his lawyer has a mountain of chat transcripts"—he gestures to a thick manila folder on his right—"that he alleges were with you, agreeing to a revenge pact and planning the Truth or Dare game."

Emma looks nervously at the folder. "Have you read them?" she asks.

She showered before Martin got here, so she's looking more like her usual self. Her dark red hair is still damp, pulled back with a headband, and she's wearing one of her favorite oxford shirts. She missed the top button, but still. Progress.

"Not yet," Martin says. "They arrived in my office just before I left to come here. But I'd like to hear your version first, anyway."

I'm sitting next to Emma, wondering if I'm going to get kicked out of the conversation at some point. I've already told Martin everything I know about Jared. Now Mom keeps looking at me uneasily, like she's wishing I'd stayed at my aunt's house with Owen. I kind of feel the same way. But if I have to be in this apartment, I'd rather know what's going on than be stuck in my room alone. So I stay quiet, and stay put.

Emma bites her lip. "I mean. Mom told you, right? I did talk to him a lot. At first."

Mom shifts in her seat, but before she can answer, Martin says, "Explain to me exactly how you met Jared, what the two of you talked about, and how things ended. Don't sugarcoat or leave anything out. I can't help you unless I know the full story."

My sister takes a deep breath, and I do too. *Here we go.*

Emma's voice takes on a mechanical quality, like she's gearing up for a long speech. "It's true, what Jared said about how we met online. I was going through a bad time. I'd just found out that Phoebe and my ex-boyfriend hooked up, and I was really upset." I stare at the faux wood grain of our kitchen table, studiously avoiding Mom's eyes, because *that* was a shitty conversation I never want to repeat.

"That was bad enough," Emma continues. "But then I was

looking through Mom's files, trying to figure out how much money we have set aside for college, and I found the settlement paperwork from Dad's accident. I was . . . so angry." Her eyes are nothing but pupil. "When I read about what Brandon did, I hated him so much that I couldn't think straight. I wanted—I don't even know. I wanted to *do* something. I remembered Simon Kelleher's old revenge forum, and I went looking for it. It had moved, but I found it eventually. I made up a name and signed on. I met Jared there, and we started talking. We sort of—bonded, I guess. He suggested we talk offline with Chat-App. We used real names then. Well, I used Phoebe's name."

She darts a guilty look at me, and I try to keep my expression neutral. It stings that Emma did that, but it's like Jules said earlier: *so* not the main issue right now.

"I unloaded about everything to him," Emma says. "He was a good listener." She makes a face, as though it pains her to admit that. "Jared said Brandon sounded like the kind of person who'd never had to face a consequence in his life. And that he could help me figure out a way to get even, if I'd help him do the same."

"But he didn't tell you his story?" Martin asks. "You weren't aware of his connection to Eli Kleinfelter?"

"No," Emma says emphatically. "I didn't know anything about that until Detective Mendoza told me. He said Jared figured out Mom was Eli's wedding coordinator and decided to . . . use me." She swallows hard. "All Jared told me was that someone had ruined his brother's life, and his mom killed herself because of it. I felt horrible for him." Emma flushes and looks down at the table. "Jared said we could start with me. He thought we should do something to . . . hurt Brandon. So he wouldn't be able to play football anymore, and then he'd know what it's like to lose something important."

"Did you agree to that?" Martin asks evenly.

Emma licks her lips. "Yes," she says quietly, briefly closing her eyes at the shocked noise my mother can't hold back. "At the time it seemed . . . fair."

My heart is in my throat, threatening to choke me, but Martin's calm tone doesn't change. "And who came up with the Truth or Dare game?"

"Jared," Emma says. "He liked the idea of using Simon's . . . *legacy*, he called it, to create a gossip-based game that Bayview High students wouldn't be able to resist. The idea was to build the game slowly, until it got to the point that Brandon would take a Dare without question."

Emma tenses, and I hear her foot start tapping rhythmically on the floor. "Jared said people are easy to figure out. If you've ever played Truth or Dare, you know most people will take the Dare. Because they want to seem . . . daring, I guess. Plus nobody wants to deal with the truth. But first, we had to make sure people paid attention. We needed to launch the game with a real piece of gossip that nobody knew, something juicy and true and ugly. After that, Jared said, we just had to target people who would play along, and the game would be off and running."

"Okay," Martin says. "So you needed somebody to not engage in order to kick things off, and you needed a big secret about them. Did you provide that to Jared?"

Emma stills her tapping foot, and the only sound in our

kitchen is the faint ticking of the clock above my head. Then she takes a deep breath and says, "Yes." Mom swallows another strangled sound as Emma continues, "I was pretending to be Phoebe so I said, 'Well, I slept with my sister's ex, is that an ugly enough secret for you?'" I flinch as though she slapped me as Emma continues. "And Jared was like, 'You seriously want to use that?' And I said . . ." Emma's voice gets so low that I have to strain my ears to hear her. "I said, 'Sure, why not? It's not like I care about my sister. If I did, I wouldn't've done it in the first place.'"

I'm going to cry. Or throw up. Probably both. I want Emma to stop talking, but unfortunately Martin doesn't feel the same way. "Okay," he says. "And did you provide other names to Jared? People you thought would play along and take Dares?"

Emma nods. "Yes. I tutor Sean and I used to drive Jules to school, so I was pretty sure they'd love the attention."

"What about Maeve Rojas?" Martin asks.

"That was Jared's idea," Emma says. "He wanted Maeve involved, because she was part of everything that happened with Simon. That was a thing with Jared—he thought about Simon a *lot*. He wanted to be smarter than him, and fool somebody who Simon couldn't." Her cheeks redden as she looks down. "Maeve was supposed to take the Dare, like everybody else, but she didn't play along. And I have no idea how Jared found out about her and Knox. I wouldn't—I would never have told him that, even if I knew. I like them both."

It hurts more than I would've thought at this point, when I should be getting numb, to hear Emma say that after admitting she'd tossed me under the Jared bus.

"And what happened when the game launched?" Martin asks.

"It was horrible." Emma's voice breaks on the word. "People were so awful. All I could think about was this quote—I can't remember where I read it, but it goes something like *Holding on to resentment is like drinking poison and waiting for the other person to die.* That's exactly how I felt. I didn't want revenge anymore. I just wanted it to stop." She shoots me an imploring look. "I'm sorry, Phoebe. For all of it."

I curl my hands into fists on my lap so I won't say the first thing that springs into my mind, which is: *You can shove your apology right up your ass, Emma.* Because I know what it's like when your sister refuses to forgive your worst mistake. "I . . . it's okay," I grit out.

"In your statement to the police, you said you'd asked Jared to end the game and he agreed," Martin says. "Is that accurate?"

Emma nods. "Yes. He was mad, and we argued. But eventually he said he'd drop it, because it wouldn't work if I wasn't all in. I deleted ChatApp from my phone, and I thought that would be that."

Her voice breaks again. "But the game kept going. Then Brandon died and . . ." Tears start falling fast, streaming down her face and onto her dry, cracked lips. "I didn't know what to say or do. I was so scared all the time. I started drinking to try to calm down, and then I couldn't stop. I broke my phone and threw it away because I thought it might get me in trouble. And I'm *sorry*, I'm sorry for everything, I'm so sorry." She crumples against Mom, who holds her gingerly, like she's not sure how Emma is supposed to fit against her anymore.

I squeeze my eyes shut so I won't cry, too. It's all beyond horrible. All I can think is *This never would have happened if Emma and I were still close. Emma and I would still be close if Dad hadn't died. Dad wouldn't have died if it weren't for Brandon.* It's the worst kind of vicious circle, and I'm starting to see how it could take over your mind.

Martin lets Emma cry for a few minutes, sifting through his folder until her sobs turn to sniffles. When she finally detaches from Mom and wipes her eyes, he says, "I know that was difficult. Are you all right to continue?" She nods. "Can you tell me exactly when you stopped corresponding with Jared? The date and, ideally, the time?"

Emma takes a shaky breath. "I mean—it was pretty much right after the text about Phoebe went out. I spent the night at my friend Gillian's house, but I couldn't sleep. I started messaging Jared, and we argued until he agreed to stop the game. I logged off and went to bed, right before midnight, I think. That's the last I ever spoke to him."

Martin's looking at the papers in front of him. "That would be February nineteenth, then. Is this the conversation you're referring to?" He hands Emma a sheet of paper, and she nervously licks her lips as she takes it.

"Are these printouts?" she asks. "Of our ChatApp conversations?"

"Yes," Martin says. "Pulled from the burner phone Jared used. Just skimming them, it looks like they're consistent with what you told me, right up through February nineteenth. As you stated, you asked him to stop the game and, after some initial dissent, he agreed." For the first time since I met him, the lines around Martin's mouth get grim. My skin starts to prickle even before he says, "But after that, we have a problem."

"What do you mean?" Emma licks her lips again as Martin holds up another sheet of paper.

"This is a transcript from the morning of February twentieth," he says. "When the conversation between 'Phoebe' and Jared started right up again."

CHAPTER THIRTY-FOUR

Phoebe
Wednesday, April 1

My stomach drops as Mom says, *"Emma,"* in a low, warning tone. Emma turns to her, wide-eyed, and Mom adds, "You need to tell Martin everything."

"But I did," Emma insists, looking shocked. "That's not possible. Let me see."

Martin hands her the paper, and I edge closer so I can read it, too.

> **Phoebe:** Sorry about what I said earlier. I didn't mean it.
> **Jared:** Didn't mean what? That I'm "too extreme" and you're out?
> **Phoebe:** Yeah. I freaked for a sec but I'm on board now.
> **Phoebe:** Let's do this.

"No, no, *no!*" Emma drops the paper like it's on fire, staring at it with what seems like genuine confusion. "That's not me. I never communicated with Jared again after the night at Gillian's." She looks beseechingly between Mom and Martin, like she can get them to believe her through sheer force of will. "I swear to God. I swear on Dad's *grave.* Can't you . . . I don't know, check the IP address or something?"

Martin looks grim again. "I'll see how trackable the technology is, but messaging apps are tricky. Now, if we had your phone, we could possibly work with that. Is your device entirely unsalvageable?"

Emma flushes and drops her eyes. "Yeah. I smashed it with a hammer and threw it into a dumpster. I don't even know where it is anymore."

"I see." Martin's tone is calm, but he can't be happy about that.

Mom leans forward, her voice tense. "Isn't it possible this young man wrote all those chat messages to *himself* once Emma stopped talking to him?" she asks. "He's obviously disturbed."

"It's possible," Martin says. "Jared was certainly under an enormous amount of mental strain from his brother's arrest, his father's illness, and his mother's suicide. That may be a theory worth advancing, particularly if the later correspondence shows a marked difference in speech patterns."

Emma stretches out her hand like a drowning person who just spotted a life preserver. "Can I see more of them?"

"Of course." Martin hands her a sheaf of papers and a pencil. "Here's the rest of the February twentieth conversation. If you see anything that strikes you as dissonant, make a note."

Emma starts reading, and I do the same. After "Phoebe" returns and promises to keep the game going, Jared spends a good half page patting himself on the back for his brilliance. "Phoebe" agrees—and as I read those responses, a tiny spark of hope takes hold of me. This truly doesn't seem like Emma's messaging style. "Phoebe" is using way too many *lol*s and question marks, for one thing. And the flattery toward Jared seems excessive. Could Mom's Hail Mary theory actually be right?

Then I read to the bottom of the page.

> **Jared:** This game is genius. You can make people do whatever you want.
> **Jared:** Doesn't matter how strange it is, people will do it.
> **Phoebe:** The more bazaar the better right? lol

I swallow my gasp just in time. My heart starts pounding, so hard that it's physically painful, as I read the last sentence again. Not bizarre. *Bazaar.* I glance at Emma, whose face has gone red and splotchy. When her eyes meet mine, I know she's seen it too.

I'm frozen in my chair. I have absolutely no idea what to say or do. I just keep thinking about all the little things that meant nothing until now:

My sneaky brother always listening at our doors.

My tech-savvy brother networking all our devices.

My lonely brother hanging out at Café Contigo, where Maeve told Bronwyn what happened between her and Knox.

My scared brother watching Brandon insult me.

My sad brother saying *Our family is ruined* after Emma and I fought about Brandon.

And, oh yeah. My spelling bee champion brother making a rare yet memorable error. The reunion between "Phoebe" and Jared happened before I'd had the chance to correct him.

I'm starting to feel light-headed and take a deep, steadying breath as I mentally slot my brother into the events of the past few weeks. He fits. Owen could have been monitoring Emma's conversations with Jared all along—everything from our father's accident, to plans for the Truth or Dare game, to Emma's decision to pull out. And when she did, he could've easily stepped in. He probably would have been a lot more careful about covering his tracks than Emma was, too. The whole thing must have seemed like a video game to him: the ultimate *Bounty Wars* challenge, planning one move after the other.

Right up until Brandon died.

Emma lays the sheet of paper on the table so carefully that you'd have to be watching closely to see her hand tremble. "Can I see the last page, please?" she asks. "The very end of the transcripts?"

Martin thumbs through the sheaf he's holding and hands it to her. "Correspondence stops the day Brandon Weber died," he says.

I force myself not to look at Emma as we both start to read:

Phoebe: That wasn't supposed to happen.
Jared: Sure it was. It's what you wanted.
Phoebe: I . . . don't think I did.

Jared: He deserved it. It's done. You're welcome.

Jared: But we're only half finished. Now it's my turn.

Jared: Hello?????

Jared: Say something.

Jared: Don't you dare fucking ghost me.

Then it ends. I don't move except to shift my gaze toward Emma, waiting for her reaction. She meets my eyes again, and for the first time in years, we have a conversation with no words. Just like we used to when we were kids, reading the thoughts written across one another's faces. Invisible to anyone else, but perfectly clear to us.

Emma glances down, notices the undone button on her oxford shirt, and neatly fastens it. Then she looks up, pale now but composed, and pushes the transcript toward Martin. "I think my mother is right," she says. "Jared is delusional. This is nothing more than him talking to himself once I stopped speaking to him. And nobody can prove differently, can they?"

ACKNOWLEDGMENTS

One of us is lucky, and by that, I mean me. In my third book, I not only got the chance to revisit characters and a setting that I love, but I did it with the same phenomenal publishing team that has supported me from the start.

Endless thanks to Rosemary Stimola and Allison Remcheck for seeing the spark of possibility in that early query for *One of Us Is Lying* and for guiding this sequel (along with my career) with such insight and care. There's no one I'd rather have in my corner.

Krista Marino, sometimes I try to imagine what my books would look like without your editorial brilliance, but that's too terrifying a thought for this thriller writer to contemplate for very long. Thank you for helping me find the beating heart of "the Maeve book" and build a story that could both follow its older sibling and stand on its own.

Delacorte Press—where do I start? I'm so thankful to Barbara Marcus, Beverly Horowitz, and Judith Haut for giving my books, and me, such a wise and welcoming home. I'm constantly in awe of all the talented, dedicated professionals I have the pleasure of working with on a daily basis, including Monica Jean, Kathy Dunn, Dominique Cimina, Kate Keating, Elizabeth Ward, Kelly McGauley, Adrienne Weintraub, Felicia Frazier, Becky Green, Enid Chaban, Kimberly Langus, Kerry Milliron, Colleen Fellingham, Heather Lockwood Hughes, Alison Impey, Kenneth Crossland, Martha Rago, Tracy Heydweiller, Linda Palladino, and Denise DeGennaro.

Thank you to the incredible staff of Penguin UK, especially Holly Harris, Francesca Dow, Ruth Knowles, Amanda Punter, Harriet Venn, Simon Armstrong, Gemma Rostill, and Kat Baker, for being my literary home away from home. I hope we publish many more books together, and not only because that will mean more personalized cupcakes.

Thanks also to Jason Dravis, my amazing film agent, and to the agents who helped this book find homes around the world: Clementine Gaisman and Alice Natali of Intercontinental Literary Agency, Bastian Schlueck at Thomas Schlueck Agency, and Charlotte Bodman at Rights People. Thank you also to John Saachi and Matt Groesch of 5 More Minutes Productions and Pete Ryan and Erica Rand Silverman at Stimola Literary Studio. Huge shout-out to my amazing critique partners Erin Hahn, Meredith Ireland, and Kit Frick for helping me make sense of early drafts, and for being generally awesome people and friends.

Special thanks to my brother-in-law Luis Fernando for your help with translation, and thanks to the rest of my family for all your support: Mom, Dad, Lynne, Jay, April, and Julie. Lots of love to the next generation, who continually impress me with the young adults you're becoming: Kelsey, Drew, Ian, Zachary, Aiden, Shalyn, Gabriela, Carolina, Erik—and my son, Jack, who is funny, loyal, kind, and officially taller than me.

Finally, thank you to all the readers who keep coming along on this journey with me, because none of this happens without you.

ABOUT THE AUTHOR

Karen M. McManus earned her BA in English from the College of the Holy Cross and her MA in journalism from Northeastern University. She is the *New York Times* bestselling author of *One of Us Is Lying, Two Can Keep a Secret,* and *One of Us Is Next.* Her work has been published in more than forty countries.

karenmcmanus.com